FIERY PASSIONS

"Well, Jesse Kendrik, you've a good hand with a knife." He stepped out of the darkness into the amber circle of firelight. Jesse knew she had two choices—run or fight. She chose the latter.

"I could have shot you," she said.

"With this?" Jesse's mouth fell open in horror as she recognized her pistol dangling between Cale Cody's fingers like a tiny toy.

Wild with anger, she swung a heavy branch of mesquite wood at him with all her might. He clutched her waist, and she spun around to face him in a fury of blazing copper hair.

"What did you expect?" she spat, returning his appreciative regard coldly. "A warm reception?" Her words were silenced by the burning touch of his lips against hers. In that instant, even the flame of hatred that had driven her since her father had been murdered seemed like a mere ember next to the blaze that he had ignited within her.

"Yes, Jesse Kendrik, you certainly are a wild one," he whispered just before brushing another kiss across her lips . . .

Tender Texas Touch

April Ashmore

ZEBRA BOOKS
KENSINGTON PUBLISHING CORP.

To my mother and to Sam
Who read, proofed, and edited
encouraged, pushed, and cracked the whip
And who never lost the faith

ZEBRA BOOKS

are published by

Kensington Publishing Corp.
475 Park Avenue South
New York, NY 10016

First printing: December, 1990

Printed in the United States of America

Chapter One

"And I'm telling you, Lieutenant, she is the only one who can track those bastards." From where he stood, Shot Evans squinted up into the sun at the still-mounted young officer and then motioned to the young woman who knelt not far away. When he received a frown of disbelief from the lieutenant, Shot rubbed the back of his dirty hand across his mouth, leaving streaks across the bristly white beard that hid his leathery face. He cursed the stupidity of Texas Rangers under his breath before he spoke again. "Mister, I don't know how to put it any other way. She can track like an Indian and shoot twice as straight. She knows this country like the back of her hand. She's as good as her father was, and if you intend to catch the men you're looking for, you'd better take her with you."

From where he sat astride his tall bay gelding, Brett Anderson eyed the dust-covered trapper with a mixture of impatience and disbelief. He didn't like being told how to run his outfit, and he liked it even less coming from a hermit who smelled so bad that even the horses didn't want to get close to him.

"Mr. Evans." He started to lean closer to the man in hopes of keeping their conversation private, but then thought better of it. "Might I remind you that that is a woman?" He waved a neatly gloved hand in the direction of the girl who still knelt with her back to them. She was either ignoring them or couldn't hear them—he couldn't tell which. "She would only slow us down."

At that, Shot guffawed so loudly that the lieutenant's horse skitted a few steps away and regarded him questioningly.

"More like the other way around," he remarked when he had caught his breath. "I've said it every way I can . . ."

From where she knelt not far away, Jessalyn Kendrik heard the argument continue, but she did not look up. She cared little what the outcome might be. As she extended a hand and touched the neat pile of stones that covered her father's grave, she knew she had no choice. Whether the Texas Rangers decided to go or not, she would hunt down the men who had taken her father's life—and see them pay.

Slowly, she looked from the sun-bleached stones that had swallowed her father away to the silent rim of mountains that squatted like a faded colossus on the southern horizon. Tears blurred her eyes as she thought of all of the times she and her father had crossed those faraway peaks to trap, to trade, and just to see what lay beyond. Those days were gone now. In one bitter, crazy, senseless afternoon, the life she had known and loved was gone . . . and she didn't even know why. She hadn't been with her fa-

6

ther when he had been attacked. He had left her at their camp early that morning and ridden out to a meeting with someone, but he wouldn't tell her whom. She had begged him to take her along, but he had insisted that she stay behind. All day she had been haunted by a black specter of dread that wound its way around her like a silent serpent until it choked every ounce of hope from within her. She had expected the worst when she had gone out in search of her father—and now she was sitting by his grave suddenly realizing that he was really gone.

"Excuse me, ma'am?" The sound of a voice startled Jessalyn from her thoughts and she looked up in surprise to meet the deep blue eyes of Lieutenant Anderson.

Brett Anderson wasn't a man to be taken by surprise, but when the young beauty before him caught his gaze it held him speechless. Her long, brown hair danced in glittering waves on the desert breeze, sparkling copper and gold, like a sea of lost treasure, where the sun caught it. Her skin was deep olive and flawless, tanned to a rich velvet color that begged to be touched . . . But the most incredible thing was her eyes. They held him spellbound, motionless, powerless. They were the most unusual color of green, like new leaves bloomed too early in the spring and touched with glittering flecks of white frost. Tearing himself away, Brett looked toward the distant mountains and then back to the grave before he spoke again.

"I realize that this is a poor time to trouble you," he began tentatively, still wondering how he was going to reconcile himself to having a woman as a

7

scout and, worse yet, how he was going to explain it to his sergeant. He could picture the crusty old ranger now, laughing himself right off his horse at the whole affair. "Mr. Evans suggested . . ." He paused, absently trailing a finger in the dust as he searched for the right words—if there were any. "That is, I need to ask you if . . ." He paused again, removed his hat and rubbed his dark brow as if to rearrange the jumbled thoughts there. Letting out a sigh, he looked up at the girl to find her still watching him intently with those wide emerald eyes.

"I know what you're here to ask," Jessalyn said finally, more out of impatience than with the thought of sparing him further torment. "Shot is right, Lieutenant. I am the only one here who can track the men you're looking for. My father would certainly have expected me to see the men responsible brought to justice." The latter part was a lie, and Jessalyn winced inwardly when she said it, but kept a steady gaze on the ranger. Her father would have expected her to see the men responsible dead, not brought to justice, and she intended to do exactly what her father would have expected. "So you see, Lieutenant," she continued in a steady voice that was a strange contrast to the tempest that raged within her, "there really is no choice to be made on either of our parts." Without giving him a chance to protest, she stood up and looked around the small box canyon that had been the only witness to her father's murder. If only rocks and sand could speak, she thought as she surveyed the sight. But in a way, the canyon did tell a story to a person who knew how to read the words—and this story had Comanchero written all over it.

It seemed odd that Lane Kendrik would meet his end at the hands of the Comanchero when all his life he had been a friend to both the Comanche and the Comanchero. In fact, he had been planning a trip to Washington to try to convince the president and Congress to guarantee the Comanche that their territories would remain intact if Texas became a state. Here was the gratitude he received—a bullet in the back shot by some coward hiding on the canyon wall. At least his death had been quick, she thought. If people thought that the Indians were the most brutal killers on the plains, they hadn't met the Comanchero.

Her eyes caught for a moment on something brightly colored caught in brush not far away. She took a few steps toward it before she stopped, her breath catching in her throat like it had suddenly become solid. What had drawn her attention was a Navaho blanket woven in brightly colored blue, black, and white flying like a heavy flag in the afternoon breeze. The blanket itself was not particularly interesting, but the symbol that was woven into it made the skin crawl on the back of her neck. Her eyes narrowed to icy slivers of jade as she fought the terror that sent her heart pounding like a caged bird against her chest. It was the sign of El Halcon, The Hawk, that fluttered in the breeze before her, and everyone on the Texas plains knew his mark. Everyone who knew the mark knew that no one had ever gone up against El Halcon and lived.

* * *

9

"Now, Jesse girl, you've got to eat," Shot pleaded from behind a tin plate of stew. "It's just a small plate." Shot pushed it a little closer to her. "Now come on, tell me you'll eat it."

Jessalyn grimaced noticeably, her full lips drawing to a tight line as she glanced at the plate. From where she sat, it looked like a huge plate of stew, and her stomach turned rebelliously at the smell of it.

"I can't," she replied, leaning back a bit to escape the nauseating odor of food. "I'm just not hungry." With that, she leveled a look of determination at him that would have turned back a herd of stampeding buffalo.

Shot's grey eyes locked with hers for a moment, and he stood steadfastly with the look of a mother hen bent on correcting an errant chick. But after a moment his resolve began to fade in the face of nineteen years of pure female determination, and he withdrew from the fireside, taking the rejected meal with him. In the next instant he had disappeared into the darkness, and Jessalyn looked after him with a mixture of amusement and irritation.

It was odd that Shot Evans had suddenly taken such a fatherly interest in her, very odd. She had known him for most of her life, but he had never been one of her father's closest friends. In fact, his association with her father had been little more than that of casual acquaintance, and he had never shown much interest in her. She wasn't sure that she could ever remember him calling her by name in the past. Now suddenly he was using the nickname that her father had called her by, and somehow it twisted within her like a knife. The wounds that this ill-fated

10

day had left on her were still too fresh to allow reminders of what she'd lost. Right now it seemed like they always would be.

Looking around the small rim of light spread by the crackling campfire that Shot had built, Jessalyn was grateful that the old man had gone away, at least for a while. No doubt, he was entertaining himself at one of the rangers' campfires which dotted the prairie all around her, throwing off odd washes of light on unfamiliar faces. It had been against her wishes that her camp had been placed safely within the perimeter of theirs, but the lieutenant had insisted. Now here she was, hemmed in by their dimly lit faces, pressed by the murmur of their conversations, and no doubt visible to every Comanche for fifty miles.

She gave the Comanche little more than a passing thought, though, as she knew most of their leaders. Her father had always been well loved among them. Unfortunately, the country on which the rangers were camped tonight wasn't really Comanche territory. It was a sort of borderland, and a popular summer area for the Cheyenne and Arapaho. The Arapaho were probably not a problem, but the Cheyenne worried her somewhat. She knew their language fairly well, but she and her father had had very few dealings with them, and now probably wasn't a good time to start.

Her father had always said that the Painted Arrow People, the Cheyenne, were an honorable sort, and not nearly so hot-blooded as the Comanche. Her father—he had known so much, and it seemed now that she had had so little time to learn all of those

11

things. It was as if half of her world had been suddenly stolen from her, and now she was left trying to balance herself on the half that was left. Before each move she made, she looked back as if to suddenly find his guiding presence once again behind her. She had leaned so much on his knowledge and his strength for as long as she could remember. Now she was like a crippled person trying to walk for the first time without a crutch, trying to find strength of her own, and trying to lead fifty men across the Texas plains. Each step felt uncertain, each move only half right, but she couldn't falter—couldn't let anyone know.

With a deep sigh, she drew her long legs up under the full buckskin skirt that she wore and wrapped her arms around them. Resting her chin on her knees, she watched the flames dance into the dark air and the sparks tear away to float up into oblivion like tiny shooting stars headed back to heaven. Her bright eyes glittered with sadness in the dim light, but no tears escaped them. Instead, her tears were burned away by a growing flame of hatred and a smoldering need for revenge.

Jessalyn didn't need to look at the half-buried tracks to tell where they were leading. Still, she sat astride her mount patiently waiting for Lieutenant Anderson's scout to clean the tracks out with a small brush and analyze them in detail. Beneath her, Diablo, the Appaloosa stallion that had always been her father's favorite mount, pawed the ground, nervously stirring a cloud of dust into the mid-afternoon

12

breeze. When the scout cast a perturbed glance in Diablo's direction, Jessalyn rode him a short distance away and surveyed the path southward. It wasn't until Brett Anderson spoke that she noticed he was beside her.

"Johnson says that the tracks are about a day old," he said, nodding over his shoulder toward the scout who still squatted in the dust behind them. "Looks like the men we're after are riding pretty hard. No doubt they know they're being followed."

Jessalyn frowned and cast a narrow gaze from the plains to the sun that already had crept to half-mast in the cloudless sky. After a time, she looked back at Brett, her eyes sparkling like a mirage of color against the amber and brown of the summer-dry plains.

"I doubt they know that we're behind them," she replied. "If they did they would be heading east, toward the mountains, but they're not." An odd look came into the lieutenant's cool blue eyes, and for a moment, Jessalyn felt herself doubt her own words. In defense, she looked away quickly and hooded her eyes beneath a thick brush of dusky lashes. "They're headed for Bent's Fort. No doubt they need supplies and trade goods. From there, they might head southwest to Taos or Santa Fe, but it's more likely that they'll head straight for the pass country near the Paso Del Norte border." Gathering her courage, she met his gaze again, and this time noted with pleasure that his usual stoic mask had been replaced by an unfamiliar look of surprise.

Still watching her from the corner of his eye, he removed his hat and wiped the sweat from his tanned

13

brow with the back of his sleeve. Replacing the hat loosely on the back of his head, he rested both hands on the front of his saddle and sat watching her squarely with the look of a horse that was finally ready to give in to the bridle.

"Well, it appears that you're way ahead of us once again," he said after a moment, a slight grin softening the stern lines of his handsome face.

A smile curved on Jessalyn's full lips in response, and she cast him a wry glance of emerald. In the past, she would have sweetened the air with the music of good-natured laughter, as the situation was, indeed, humorous, but somehow now it seemed wrong. In the two days since she had found her father dead, any small bit of happiness that had come to her had brought guilt in its wake. Somewhere within, she heard her father's voice reminding her that she owed him her loyalty and that loyalty overrode all else.

"If we ride straight toward Bent's, we can get to the fort by midday tomorrow," she urged, hoping that he would take her suggestion. "We might have a chance of catching the men we're after while they are still at the fort." She faltered from his gaze when she spoke these last words. She knew that there was little chance of catching El Halcon or his men at Bent's Fort—they would never be so stupid as to wait around to be caught. No doubt they would be at Bent's only long enough to purchase supplies, and then they would melt back into the desert to the south, disappearing like a noonday mirage. It mattered little; she could pick up their trail again after they left the fort. Right now, she just wanted to see the familiar adobe walls of the trading post that had been her second home for so many years. There was someone there she needed to see, someone who could help her.

Jessalyn looked up at the old sergeant with an obvious air of surprise on her delicate young face. She considered his question silently for a moment before she spoke.

"Yes, I suppose that my father was an Indian lover," she replied after a moment, wondering silently at the other's ability to make loving a race of one's fellow man sound like a sin. She had been riding next to the gristly old sergeant for nearly a half an hour, and in that time he had managed to make her father's friendship with the Comanche sound like a pact with the devil. In fact, that was how the old man had categorized the Comanche—"Devils every one," he had said, "devils every one."

Sergeant Mike shook his head and cast her a narrow squint at her reply. It seemed a shame for so beautiful a young girl to have such dangerous ideas. Innocence—that's what it was—just pure innocence. If Jessalyn Kendrik had ever seen the way a Comanche could kill a person, could torture a person until death seemed like a blessing, she wouldn't be so fond of them. If she knew what those Comanche devils would do to her if they caught her, she'd hightail it back to civilization where she belonged and forget tracking down the Comancheros that had killed her father. She might have been safe on the plains before, when she'd had her father to protect her, but she wasn't safe any more. He'd spent the last half hour trying to convince her of that fact, but it was like trying to convince a stone wall to grow legs and walk. Still, he had to try. She was a sweet thing, and scared to the bone, though she tried not to show it. Something bad was in store for her on this trip—he could feel it in that bum knee of his. It always warned him of danger, and right now it was tingling like a hot poker had been stuck into it. Something was waiting around the corner for young Jessalyn Kendrik, and it seemed like a damn shame to just let it happen.

"Well, I can say one thing," he said, squinting up into the blazing sun and wishing for a patch of shade and a bottle of whiskey. "I'll be glad to see Texas again. It makes me nervous being here."

Jessalyn smiled a bit at his remark, her soft eyes twinkling in a mist of memory.

"My father used to say that every time we headed for Texas territory." Her voice was soft as she remembered, like the lilting sound of leaves on the wind. "He loved Texas. I suppose that's why he wanted to see that there would be a place for everyone there after statehood—everyone, including the Comanches. My father was a good man." She bowed her head, and looked down at the dust that swirled beneath Diablo's feet. Her shoulders quivered perceptibly for a moment before she squared them again and lifted her chin, biting back the tears that had crept into her eyes.

The sergeant shifted uncomfortably in his saddle and looked away, feeling her tears tug his heart as if she had it on a string. There was something about

16

Jessalyn that made a man want to take care of her. Maybe it was because she was so sure she didn't need it. Maybe it was because she was the most beautiful thing he'd ever seen—he wasn't too old to realize that.

"I wish we'd of gotten there to meet your father a day sooner," he said lamely, still avoiding her liquid gaze. "We could of stopped what happened."

"You couldn't have known," she said, but she silently wished the rangers had gotten there a day sooner also. If they had, she and her father would have left with the company as they had planned. They would all be on their way to Austin now for a meeting with members of the government of the Republic of Texas. After that, they would have gone to Washington to negotiate for the Comanches' land rights in the new statehood agreement, but the Comancheros had put a stop to that. For whatever reason, or perhaps for no reason at all, El Halcon had destroyed the only hope the Comanche had of getting a fair deal in the statehood agreement. It was certain that no one else in Texas would have the guts to take the side of the Comanche—it wasn't exactly a popular view. In fact, it had turned out to be a lethal one.

For a time, they rode on without speaking, and the silence grew until the air between them was stretched tight as a fiddle string. Finally, the sergeant made his excuses and rode back to check his men. Before he reached them, he stopped and turned back to watch Jessalyn lope her tall Appaloosa stallion away across the uneven landscape. The stallion's black coat glistened in the sun and the white patches that covered his flanks flashed like the beacon of a bolting deer. In another moment, he had faded into the shimmering heat waves that rose from the simmering earth, and only the coppery flash of Jessalyn's billowing hair marked their presence.

Finally, the sand hills swallowed them away completely, and Sergeant Mike watched the spot where they had disappeared, cataloging the vision of her astride the powerful stallion among the most beautiful things he had seen in his sixty-one years of life. In his younger days, he might not have recognized the beauty of the moment for what it was, but to an old man with a bum leg and a touch of rheumitiz, it was all too evident what had made him stop and watch. It was freedom that made Jessalyn so special, and freedom was something that was harder and harder to find in this world. In that moment, he learned to respect her.

Normally, Jessalyn wouldn't have left the rangers so far behind, but the sand hills that they were crossing now were as familiar to her as the folds of her favorite childhood blanket, and felt just as safe. She couldn't count the times that she had crossed them, and it had always felt like coming home. Bent's Fort was less than a mile away, and she couldn't bear to wait for the slow-moving company of rangers. They'd have to find the way on their own — she was bound for home, and Diablo knew it. With a snort, he pinned his ears and stretched his long legs over the sand, gracefully dodging small groves of mesquite and greasewood. In a few silent moments, he had melted away the mile as if it were inches and Jessalyn stopped him as the fort came into view.

Diablo pranced nervously as Jessalyn guided him along the well-worn trail that led down the valley to the gate that was the only passage through the high adobe wall which surrounded the trading post. Beside the fort near the shores of the shallow Arrowhead river squatted a small group of Kiowa lodges. Dwarfed by the towering shadow of the eighteen-foot fort wall, they looked like toys in a child's doll set placed in a haphazard fashion up and down the river bank. Drawing nearer to them, Jessalyn recognized the markings on some of the largest lodges. They were the lodges of Sounds on the Wind, a Kiowa chief who had always been a close friend to her father. In fact, she and her father had wintered with Sounds on the Wind and his band just the previous year. She had spent hours with the young chief debating philosophy and talking about the Way of Things.

Sounds on the Wind stood up from where he had been sitting in front of his lodge when he saw Lane Kendrik's Appaloosa stallion approaching. It didn't take long for him to discern that something was terribly wrong. The normally breathtaking smile was gone from Jessalyn's face, and as she came closer, he could not help but see that the light was gone from her spring green eyes. There was a new somberness about her that made her unlike the playful girl that he had seen just the previous spring, the butterfly that so many of the men in his camp had wanted to tame, but who was too free to submit to any of them. She had stopped before him and sat astride her mount, her eyes like a window to what had happened, and he knew the answer to his question before he spoke it.

"Where is your father, Jea-seh?" he questioned, his grey eyes regarding her with a fondness and understanding that seemed to draw the pain from within her, breaking the hasty barrier that she had built to keep it away. In defense, she hooded her eyes from his and braced herself with a deep breath before she spoke again.

"He is dead," she replied in Sounds on the Wind's tongue. "He was ambushed from high in the rocks one day north of here. I was not with him when it happened."

Sounds on the Wind nodded gravely and reached up to put a strong hand over her smaller ones.

"Who has done this?" he asked, knowing well that by asking the question, he was committing himself to avenging the death of the white man who had been his spirit brother.

"I don't know." Jessalyn winced inwardly at the lie, and her jade eyes caught his guiltily before she looked down again. The last thing she needed was for Sounds on the Wind to know what she was planning or who she was after. He would never let her go through with tracking down El Halcon. He would tell her what she already was well aware of—that El Halcon was like a spirit who could disappear on the desert wind and then appear again to kill his enemies, that his blade was as swift as the strike of a viper, and that no one who had ever gone up against him had lived.

The Kiowa's eyes narrowed suspiciously, and he bent slightly to catch her gaze. It was obvious that there was more to the story than she was telling, and he meant to know the truth.

"You know you are welcome to stay with us," he offered. "Come into the lodge and we can talk about it."

Jessalyn forced a slight smile as she met his gaze with the determination that spoke of the uncommon will that had led the Kendrik family from war-torn Ireland to the untamed wilderness west of the American states.

"I need to go see Mamacita," she replied, and then righted her seat and drew up her reins as Sounds on the Wind stepped back from Diablo's side.

"You will come back later?" he pressed with a tone that made the words more a command than a question.

Jessalyn nodded in return and spun Diablo away from the lodge, sending him in an easy lope toward the main gate of the fort. To the northeast, she could see the rangers approaching, but she gave them little more than a glance. As she had several times over the past two days, she considered leaving the fort without the rangers and setting out after El Halcon on her own. She quickly realized the insanity of the thought, though, and resigned herself to continuing on with them. Their slow, structured way of traveling frustrated her until she thought at times that she would go mad. Still, they amounted, at the very least, to fifty guns—and fifty guns could be the difference between life and death if El Halcon decided to turn around and attack.

"Ay, querida!" Rosa exclaimed, looking up from

the gorditas she had been rolling with wide-eyed disbelief. Wiping the flour from her chubby hands, she marched resolutely across the room to stand before the young woman whom she had raised like one of her own daughters. "Haf you loosed jour mind?" She flailed her hands in the air and then motioned to her head to indicate that she didn't believe what she had just heard. *Que es eso?* She continued with her heated commentary, pacing first to the wall and then back to Jessalyn, who sat beside the dinner table with her head bowed as if to protect herself from a blow. *Que? Que?* Rosa repeated, her round face red with anger and effort. "Wha do you tink your goin to do against El Halcon? Jou, jus as girl. Jour going to kill the man who owns the desert, the man no one can even get near?"

Jessalyn ran her shaking fingers through the thick mass of her coppery hair, combing it back from her face. Tilting her head back, she sighed and leaned against the back of the chair, her eyes fixed on the ceiling.

"I have no choice, Mamacita." Her voice was little more than a quivering whisper as a single tear found its way down the olive curve of her cheek. "I can feel my father, his spirit, his . . ." she paused, and then for lack of a better word continued, "anger, and it won't go away until things are made right." She sighed again and squinted up at dark wooden beams of the heavy ceiling. After a moment of silence had passed between them, she stood up and started toward the door. It would be best to let her mamacita cool off for a while. Eventually, she would have to see that there was no other choice for Jessalyn but to go. She paused at the door and turned back to give a slight smile of reassurance to the woman who had cared for her so many times when her father could not take her along on trapping and trading trips. "This is all that is left that I can do for him," she whispered, and then walked through the heavy adobe doorway into the dimming late afternoon sunlight.

Her eyes caught suddenly on two men who were standing not far away examining Diablo as if they owned him—or meant to steal him. She covered the short distance to the hitching post on long, graceful strides, and pointedly gave the men little notice as she reached to take the reins from the shorter man, who had obviously untied them from the hitching post.

"I believe the reins that you're holding are attached to my horse," she said flatly, standing to her full five-and-a-half-foot stature and almost meeting his gaze from an even height. It was obvious from his long dark hair and dark skin that he was part Indian, probably Comanche.

With a wry twist of a sideways smile, Sam Horn handed the reins to the beautiful young spitfire before him, and stood regarding her with the same look he would have given to a lion that was going to put up a good chase.

"Last time I saw this stallion, he was Lane Kendrik's horse," he remarked. "And he told me on more occasions than one that he'd never part with it."

A bitter ire rose in Jessalyn's throat at having to defend herself to this horse thief whom she'd never met and who was suddenly pretending to have been a

23

great friend of her father's.

"Lane Kendrik was my father," she returned hotly. "If you knew him as well as you say, you would know that." Her eyes glittered with bitterness as they turned to narrow slivers of emerald. "And you would probably also know that he won't have much need of a horse now. Someone shot him in the back."

At that, the taller man stepped forward, and Jessalyn noticed him for the first time, in the same instant wondering how she could have failed to notice him before. His height and muscular build were imposing, but it was something else about him that struck her. His hair was a tawny blond and fell in loose curls about the nape of his neck. His skin was dark from the sun, setting off the strong, square features of his face and the compelling hazel-gold eyes that now held her spellbound. Even from several feet away, there was a strange sense of authority about him that held her silent and motionless though every ounce of Kendrik blood within her rebelled against it.

"Is he all right?" She heard his question as if it had come through a long tunnel from somewhere far away, like an echo from the darkest reaches of some unseen cave. Suddenly, her heart was pounding like that of a scared rabbit, and she forced herself to look away from him to regain enough composure to speak.

"My father is dead," she replied dryly, her lost composure now replaced by anger at herself for having allowed this stranger to have so taken her aback. Tossing Diablo's reins over his head quickly, she vaulted aboard his bare back in a flourish of buckskin skirt and flaming hair. She guided Diablo quickly away without looking at the stranger again, yet still she felt his haunting eyes bore through her as if she were made of glass.

Chapter Two

It was almost noon the next day before Jessalyn awoke. The air was heavy and sweltering even within the cooling adobe walls of her mamacita's small room. Taking a deep breath and closing her eyes, she listened to the familiar clank of pans from the fort kitchen not far away. No doubt mamacita was bustling about cooking a hearty lunch for all of Charles and William Bent's hired hands. That had been Rosa's job for as long as Jessalyn could remember.

Rolling over onto her back, Jessalyn stretched her long, slender arms toward the dim ceiling and then let them drop. Lying very still in the warm room, she remembered her fourteenth birthday. The air had been hot that day also—particularly hot for April—and the pans had been making their heavy music in the kitchen just the way they were today. She had lain in the same bed on that faraway day, feeling safe in the care of her mamacita, and knowing that her father would return any moment from his trip to Santa Fe.

That year the trapping had been scarce in the

mountains and her father had gone to work for the Bents as a trader. The repeated trips to Santa Fe had soon come to bore Jessalyn, and she had chosen often to stay behind at Bent's Fort, opting for the company of those who lived at the fort and the occasional prospect of meeting someone her own age on a passing wagon train. What a strange mixture of child and woman she had been then! Thinking back, it was hard to imagine what she had thought and what she had believed during that strange year. Still, she could remember very well what she had pictured for her future: a husband, children, a stable life, and a home. How she had pursued those things—even at the expense of leaving her father to go on his travels alone. If only someone had told her then how short their time together would be, how much she would need him when he was gone. Something Sounds on the Wind had once said came to her mind now. "Life is never what we plan for it to be," he had said, with that oddly omniscient smile of his. "No matter what picture we paint, in the long run, the colors will turn out to be wrong."

This had proved much more true than she wanted to admit. In all the pictures that she had painted for herself, the color of blood was one that she had never used. Now blood haunted her like a great black bird, its talons twisting in her heart each time she found a moment's peace. She saw her father, dead in a pool of crimson-stained sand, and she saw El Halcon, whoever he was, dead by her hand. After that, she could see nothing, and it was likely that there would be little need to look further into the future. As many friends as El Halcon had, there probably wouldn't be any future for the one who killed him.

Wild hazel eyes crowded away her thoughts suddenly, their golden depths burning with a thousand tiny fires. She considered them absently for a moment, how they had seemed to look into her soul in the moment that her eyes had met his.

In the next instant, she pushed the heavy Navaho blankets aside impatiently, and swung her long legs over the side of the bed. Anger welled inside her as she drew on the pale blue cotton blouse and heavy royal blue riding skirt that her mamacita had given to her only the night before. Sitting lightly on the edge of the bed, she reached for the knee-high Blackfoot-style moccasins that she had unpacked the previous night. Though she had several pairs of fine leather riding boots, she preferred the moccasins for the comfort and freedom they allowed. This pair, in particular, was special. They had been given to her by Many Summers, an ancient Blackfoot medicine woman who was a friend of her father's. The old woman's love and wonderful spirit showed in every stitch of the delicate blue and white beadwork. Normally, Jessalyn would have reserved them only for special occasions, but today she would lead fifty men back into the desert and she needed every ounce of pride and confidence she could muster. Besides, if she really was never to come back to Bent's Fort, she wanted to be remembered in a way that would have done justice to the proud Kendrik name.

Taking a small hairbrush from the heavy wooden bedside table, she leaned close to the small mirror that her mamacita treasured as if it were made of diamond dust. Absently, she pulled the thick copper-colored tresses forward over her shoulder, and combed them into a shining mass of dancing curls before tossing them back. Had she not been so determined to believe the contrary, she might have wondered if her sudden concern for her appearance this morning had something to do with a certain stranger's presence at Bent's Fort. Though she had tried not to think of their strange meeting, she had found her thoughts dwelling on it. She had even spent several hours the night before asking discreet questions as to the man's identity. No one seemed to know much, though. Even William Bent, who generally kept abreast of the identities and habits of nearby red and white men alike, seemed to know little about the tall stranger and his compadre. Sounds on the Wind claimed that he thought he recognized the man, but he couldn't remember from where.

Jessalyn sighed, staring into the mirror at the strange green eyes that bespoke a mixture of sadness and confusion. Sounds on the Wind was going to be a problem, she thought heavily. He knew she was planning something, and he had probed her incessantly when she had gone to visit him the night before. He had even asked Shot Evans to his lodge to help try to batter information from her. The two of them had driven her nearly mad before the evening was out, but in a way her suffering had served a purpose. She had feared before that Shot knew she was tracking El Halcon. It was hard to believe that he could have missed the sign of the hawk that had been left in the small box canyon where her father had been murdered, but now it seemed he must have.

If he hadn't, Shot would no doubt have told Sounds on the Wind, and then there would have been trouble.

A beckoning in her stomach drove her thoughts away like grains of dust before an insistent wind, and she put the mirror away carefully before opening the heavy wooden door. The tantalizing aroma of food danced to her in full force when she stepped into the hallway, and she quickened her step to the kitchen. She had rounded the corner into the room and opened her mouth to inquire about lunch before she realized that there was a stranger sitting on the sturdy bench beside the small breakfast table. Even before he stood to his full height and turned around, she realized who the intruder was. Had she not spent most of her life in the company of mountain men and Indians, she would have been embarrassed by the fact that he was naked above the waist save for a short necklace of bone beads and bear claws.

Her eyes caught for a moment on the strong, lean muscles that rippled beneath his tanned skin like graceful dancers. She was certain she'd never seen a man so powerfully built, or so handsome. His eyes stole her breath in the next instant, and she stood watching him oddly for a heartbeat before her defenses rallied about her. Tearing her gaze away, she looked to her mamacita, who had sat in a shadow by the doorway watching the strange interchange with interest.

"*Querida.*" Her soft, dark eyes found Jessalyn's, and she smiled fondly. It was easy to see that sparks had flown between her adopted daughter and their handsome guest. "This is Cale Cody." She cast an encouraging eye and a wink up at Cale. "He is an old friend." With a self-satisfied smile, she bent back over the buckskin shirt she had been mending for Cale. Now it was time to let things run their course. Cale Cody had obviously come here looking for an introduction to her beautiful daughter, and she was more than happy to oblige.

Jessalyn's spine stiffened as if an arrow had been driven lengthwise through it as she stepped forward to take the man's outstretched hand. If there was one thing her father had taught her, it was to give a man the benefit of the doubt. Well, in Cale Cody's case, that was one hell of a gift, but somehow she'd manage it.

"Well, any friend of Mama's . . . ," she paused, realizing the words had come out of habit, and wishing she hadn't said them. She didn't want Cale Cody for a friend. There was something about him that she didn't trust, and this was hardly the basis for a friendship. Still, she forced a dazzling hint of smile, and finished her statement, " . . . Is a friend of mine." She withdrew her hand with all of the poise that she could muster, and forced herself to stand her ground against his intimidating height. "I'm Jesse Kendrik."

Cale's whiskey-colored eyes glittered warmly, and he smiled a smile that would have charmed a charging buffalo as he took a step backward and leaned comfortably against the breakfast table.

"Well, Jesse Kendrik." His words, easy and genuine, flowed through the air like a length of invisible silk. "I've been waiting to meet you ever since our encounter yesterday, but you're a hard person to track down." He paused, as if waiting for her to reply.

Jessalyn searched silently for a response, but was rescued suddenly when Brett Anderson appeared in the doorway.

"It looks like I'll remain that way," she remarked, turning to follow the lieutenant out onto the porch. Casting a coy sideways glance in Cale's direction, she smiled slightly, her jade eyes flashing like gems. "If you'll excuse me, Mr. Cody." It was obviously a statement, not a request. She hardly intended to beg his permission to leave. "It was good to meet you."

Cale only gave her another charming smile, seemingly unabashed by her dismissal, and crossed his arms over his sleek chest.

"I'm sure we'll be seeing each other again," he returned, and cast her a knowing wink before turning back to Rosa to inquire after his shirt.

Seizing her chance for escape, Jessalyn hurried through the doorway and out onto the porch where Lieutenant Anderson now stood beside a dustier-than-usual Sergeant Mike. Smiling inwardly, Jessalyn noted the difference between the trail-worn sergeant and his crisp young commander. She had noticed on their journey to the fort that the two made a good pair. It was as if their differences balanced out to give the ranger company the benefit of the best of both. Of course, their compromises didn't come without arguments and complaints, but somehow things seemed to work out. Today, however, looked to be an exception. Both men looked sour and irritable. The sergeant looked like he had been run over by a herd of cattle, and Brett Anderson looked like he was at the end of his rope. Still, Jessalyn ventured a question into the stony silence.

"When will we be able to leave?" It was obviously the wrong question. Both men shot angry glances around like bullets, first at each other and then at Jessalyn. Without speaking, Sergeant Mike shook his head, stepped down from the porch, and stalked off across the yard in his usual bowlegged fashion.

"I'm afraid we're going to be delayed," Brett replied, his deep blue eyes boiling like water in an capped caldron. Jessalyn stood back a little, waiting for the lid to blow.

"The longer we wait, the colder the trail will be," she ventured. Had she not been so intent on hunting down her father's murderers, she wouldn't have pushed the matter. Still, her desperation made her reckless, and, when he did not reply, she pressed harder. "We have to leave now to be certain of finding their trail." She took a step toward her horse, who stood in a corral nearby, but was stopped by the firm grip of a hand on her arm. Shocked, she spun back to him, her eyes flashing with white shards of anger.

A sudden familiarity came into his eyes, replacing the cool aloofness that usually reigned there. For a moment, he stood looking down into her eyes silently before he spoke.

"I know what's at stake for you, Jesse," he said quietly, with a gentleness that she had not known he possessed. "But I have forty horses that have somehow managed to get scattered loose on the desert, and it's going to take a while to round them all up." There was a flash of anger against the deep blue of his eyes as he thought of the fiasco that he had awakened to that morning. Forty horses somehow let loose on the desert! He'd have the hide of the man responsible—if he ever figured out who it was that had turned them loose. "I don't have time to watch you too," he continued, a bit more sternly. He didn't like the way she just came and went around Bent's Fort. It wasn't safe, and, even if he succeeded in nothing else, he intended to see Jessalyn Kendrik safely through this manhunt. "Just promise me you'll stay here in the fort so that we can find you when we're ready to pull out."

Jessalyn bristled at his suggestion that she was incapable of deciding for herself where she should go around the fort. Angrily, she pulled her arm away and opened her mouth to retort, but then bit back the words. Arguing with him would only slow things down, and that was the last thing she wanted.

"Just let me know when you're ready to leave," she muttered dryly before turning about on her heels and stalking away, her blue cotton skirt billowing about her slim legs like a loose piece of evening sky. In her anger, she failed to sense the two sets of appreciative eyes that followed her departure across the yard.

The day came and went slowly and brought little progress in the horse hunt. In the later afternoon, an exhausted Sergeant Mike limped into the fort, muttering under his breath that it was as if the devil himself had led the horses out onto the desert and swallowed them alive. He was careful to add, of course, that this was cursed country anyway, and that he'd be glad to see Texas again.

By the time Jessalyn had listened to his repertoire of complaints twice over, she had had enough, and she politely excused herself from his presence. She went to her room quickly and packed a few essentials into her saddlebags. On her way out, she stopped by the kitchen and wrapped a small chunk of bread and some jerked meat in a towel, then tucked them in with the rest of her things before slinging the burgeoning bags over her shoulder and heading for the stable. She skirted the main courtyard, and instead hurried along the back alleyway that was used to drive stock to the sheltered corrals within the fort wall. As she had hoped, she avoided running into her mamacita or Lieutenant Anderson, both of whom would have put up a strong fight about her spending the night alone on the prairie. Still, she didn't seem to have much choice. She had to pick up the trail of the men they were after before any more time passed. In the desert, even a stiff wind could erase all signs of a horse and rider passing, and she couldn't take that chance. She had to know if she had been right in her guess about where the men were heading. If they were going to the Paso Del Norte country on the border, it would be easy to tell—they would be headed nearly straight south. If they were going to Santa Fe or Taos, they would head west or southwest, depending on the trail they took. Either way, once she knew where they were headed, she could circle back and retrieve the ranger company. There was even a remote chance that by then they would all be mounted again.

When she reached the corral where Diablo stood waiting, she breathed a sigh of relief. She hadn't been in the mood for a fight, and she couldn't see the point of arguing the matter anyway. She was more than aware of the dangers that waited on the desert for a rider alone, man or woman. Her father had certainly taught her of these if nothing else, and she had a catalog of all of the signs of danger in her mind—everything from rattlesnakes to alkali water. She knew how to spot most of them at a distance, and besides, she had Diablo. He was a better guard than fifty Texas Rangers.

She bridled and saddled the Appaloosa quickly and then quietly slid the split-rail bars of the corral out of the way and led him out. She had replaced the rails and turned to lead Diablo out through the back alley before she noticed Sam Horn watching her from the cool shade of the eight-foot-thick adobe fort wall. Even from far away, his large, luminous, dark eyes seemed somehow compelling, and Jessalyn stopped for a moment to return his strange regard. It was Sam who smiled first—a sweet, infectious, mischievous smile that was almost childlike.

"Going somewhere?" he questioned with the good nature and warmth that he always afforded to friends and strangers alike. Oddly, Jessalyn found herself returning his smile, her bright spring green eyes twinkling with some of the brilliance that had been absent since her father's death.

"I suppose I am," she returned, feeling the need to keep her secret guarded even though Sam had, in some strange way, wormed his way into her heart. "But don't tell anyone." She smiled again and climbed quickly onto Diablo's broad back. "It will be our secret."

Sam Horn stood back and shook his head, laughing to himself as he watched her ride away astride the magnificent spotted horse. He hadn't ever met a woman quite like Jessalyn Kendrik, but he had to admire her. It was easy to see why Cale had taken such a sudden interest in her, but he had to admit that, if his compadre was after this woman, he'd have his work cut out for him. In fact, if he were a gambling man, he might have bet on the filly in this race. All in all, he was glad to be a spectator in this one. Jesse was the kind of woman who could ruin a man for life.

Jesse rounded the bend out the gate of the fort, and then urged Diablo into a ground-eating run. Together they streaked across the low sandhills like a silent shadow, parting the warm wind, and then letting it flow back into place behind them as if they had never passed. Finally Diablo tired, and Jessalyn slowed him to a walk as they continued along the trail that had been left by El Halcon and his men. Fortunately, the winds had been fairly mild since the Comancheros had passed, and the tracks were still easy to follow, even from horseback.

She continued on along the trail until evening began to paint the western sky with brilliant shades of crimson and amber. Before the evening light became too dim, she guided Diablo to the crest of a small mountain and gazed out over the desert to the south. As she had suspected, the fading line of tracks continued southward until they disappeared completely into the distance. El Halcon and his men were headed straight for their home country, near Paso Del Norte on the Mexican border.

Most of the territory to the northeast of the pass belonged to El Halcon, and no one ever challenged his right to the maze of sharp rock mountains that he claimed for his own. It was said that he had eyes watching every inch of those mountains, and that he knew if someone was coming before they came within fifty miles of his main fort.

Jessalyn could not be sure how much of what she had heard was true. She had never been to El Halcon's camp, or even seen him; few people had. He did most of his trading away from his main fort at smaller outposts near the edge of his territory, and he rarely traded in person — particularly with the white men. Some said he was a Comanche half-breed, but others said he was a white man who had turned Comanche. It was true that he had some strange attachment with the Comanche, but she had never quite figured out what it was. She knew that her father had been to parley and trade with El Halcon on several occasions, but he had always insisted that she stay behind at Bent's Fort. She had questioned him each time he had returned, but he would tell her little other than that El Halcon would be important in securing the Comanche land rights in the Texas statehood agreement.

Jessalyn sighed, and reached down to stroke Diablo's glistening black neck absently. Somewhere deep in her memory, she could hear something her father had told her several years before when she had been struggling to understand the tide of hatred that had swept the white man against the Indian. "All men should have a place in this world," he had said then. "We each have things to learn from those who are different from ourselves, but some men are frightened by those things. White men are a greedy bunch.

They want it all for themselves." He had swept his hand to the brilliant sunset that had lit the sky over the mountains on that long-ago evening. "The red men are in that sunset too, Jess," he had said. "Remember that. Every man has a right to his piece of the world, and no man is born better than the next. The world would be a better place if everyone remembered that."

Shaking her head, Jesse guided her stallion down from the mountain through the lengthening shadows of a maze of crazily strewn boulders. At the base was a small canyon cut by a spring stream that dripped strangely from a crack in the bottom of the sheer rock on the east side of the mountain. At the end of the canyon it flowed into a clear pool between two slabs of overturned rock. In all, it was an oasis in the desert, and a good spot to make camp for the night.

Jessalyn unsaddled Diablo quickly and laid her saddle and packs in a sheltered hollow beneath an overhang of rock. Giving the stallion an affectionate pat on the neck, she pulled the bridle from his head and turned him loose. Impatiently, he nudged her for an expected serving of oats, and she pushed him away, laughing.

"You're on your own tonight, Diablo," she informed the impatient stallion, who now stood watching her indignantly. With a snort, he pawed up a storm of dust, like a child pitching a tantrum, and then stopped to watch her again, waiting for results.

"Go on," she giggled. "You're not going to starve." With that, she swished the loose bridle reins at him. Frustrated, he trotted a few steps away and began to pick the ripe beans from a bush of prickly mesquite.

She stood watching him for a moment, admiring him as she had many times in the past. It would have been hard to say who had loved the stallion more, she or her father. Together, they had chosen him from a herd of fine spotted Nez Percé horses near the Palouse river country. Together, they had broken and trained him, and the stallion had returned their love with undying loyalty. Some had said that he was a dangerous mount, as the bold white spots over his flanks made him an easy target for a hostile gun. Even her father had agreed with that, and for that reason, he had usually been the one to ride Diablo. Now, the magnificent stallion was hers alone, but the price paid for him had been too dear.

Running her fingers through her tangled hair, Jessalyn forced away the memories of her father. She could not bear them yet — they left a bitter taste on her tongue and fanned the flames of hatred within her until she thought she would be driven mad. Like oil to a flame, those memories. They made her reckless, and she couldn't risk that.

Her eyes drifted longingly to the small spring pool that twinkled enticingly between the two jagged slabs of rock at the end of the canyon. In the next moment, a sweltering wind blew over her, seeming to beckon her toward the cool water with unseen fingers. It was all the encouragement she needed after a long day on the desert. Taking her pistol from the holster that held it on her saddle, she trotted quickly to the pool, and sat down on a flat rock to remove her moccasins. She unlaced the knee-highs carefully and laid them beside her pistol on a rock where both would be easily in reach if she should need them.

Standing up, she slipped out of her skirt and blouse, shaking the dust from them before setting them beside her other things. Without embarrassment, she slipped out of her soft cream-colored camisole and pantaloons, baring her firm young body to the dusky amber rays of evening sunlight. Standing like a statue beside the water, she reveled in the kiss of the air over her gently upturned breasts and molded hips. She had bathed under the vast desert sky for as long as she could remember, and she had always relished the feeling of freedom that came from the gentle breezes against her skin. It was almost as if she were part of that wind—as if she could spread her arms, and fly like one of the desert eagles into the clouds.

Taking one last look at the canyon around her and finding no sign of intruders, she trotted to the shore like a frisky fawn and dove in. The cool spring water stole her breath for a moment, and she came to the surface with a screech. From where he stood not far away, Diablo nickered his concern, then looked away again.

Jessalyn floated contentedly on the surface of the pool until the lowering sun forced her to think of gathering wood for a fire before darkness made it impossible. Before leaving the pool, she plucked the blossoms from a small yucca plant by the shore. Grinding the blossoms between her palms, she made a soapy substance, and washed her hair hurriedly before climbing ashore. Having brought nothing to dry herself with, she used her undergarments, and then slipped back into her skirt and blouse without them.

41

Her mamacita would have called it shameless, but it hardly seemed so when there was no one to watch.

She gathered wood for a fire in the last bits of evening light, and easily set the dry greasewood and mesquite to flame. Propping two sticks in the ground beside the fire, she hung her sodden underthings to dry. Finally, she reached for her packs to take out the food that she had brought, but stopped when a sound caught her ears. Her heart leapt into her throat as a small chunk of rock fell from the overhang of rock above her and fell near her feet. Seemingly in slow motion, it slowly clattered away.

Frantically, she thought about her pistol. Where had she left it? At the spring pool? Angrily, she cursed her carelessness. If she left the shelter of the overhang to find it, she would be open to attack from whatever, or whoever, waited in the rocks overhead.

A thousand possibilities spun wildly in her mind like opposing winds buffeting her from one course of action to another. Silently, she slid her knife from its scabbard, and stood up, her eyes searching the darkness for movement. The moments crept by slowly, stealing her courage like skilled thieves. Finally, she saw something unmistakable — a movement — and she drew back her knife to strike.

42

Chapter Three

With deadly purpose, Jessalyn let the knife fly, but her quarry ducked out of the path of the spinning blade at the last minute. The blade flashed in the dim light of the half moon as it flew by the shadowed figure, and then whined away, disappearing into the darkness. As the knife clattered to a stop against the unseen stones somewhere, the hopelessness of the situation struck her with startling reality. Frantically, she felt the bare rock beneath her for a weapon—a branch, a stone . . . anything—but her fingers came up as empty as a summer sky.

"Well, Jesse Kendrik, you're quite a good hand with a knife." The voice from the shadowed figure touched her ears strangely at first, and she struggled to recognize it. Before she could put her spinning thoughts to rights, her guest saved her the trouble and stepped into the amber circle of firelight. For a moment, she crouched there, staring at him, tottering precariously between fear and relief. Standing up, she swallowed the lump in her throat like a giant chunk of ice, and struggled to find her voice.

"I didn't mean to give you quite that much of a scare," Cale apologized, his whiskey-colored eyes as bright as the flames themselves. As casually as if he'd been invited, he stepped to the fireside, and crouched down beside the dancing flames. With a strange air of belonging there, he took a stick and stoked the fire before adding some wood to the coals. The flames devoured the new deadwood hungrily, populating Jesse's small camp with an unearthly company of lights and shadows. Running a hand through his tousled honey brown hair, Cale looked up at Jessalyn, who still stood watching him with mute mistrust and shock glittering in her emerald eyes.

"Hello?" he ventured, his brow wrinkling with slight amusement as he waved his hand in her direction.

Like a wild colt spurred from what a cowboy would have called a "sull," Jesse had two choices—run or fight. She chose the latter.

"I could have shot you." She feigned concern for his safety, but within herself, she was still wishing she had a gun in her hand. Cale Cody wouldn't be sitting casually beside her fire then!

From where he sat, Cale gave her a sideways glance and a crooked smile as he reached behind himself and drew something from the belt he wore over his buckskin shirt.

"With this?" He produced a pistol, and held the trigger guard loosely between two fingers.

Jessalyn's mouth fell open in horror as she recognized the pistol—her pistol—dangling between Cale

44

Cody's fingers like a tiny toy. The implications of his having her pistol hit her like a broadside slap, and her eyes brightened to two bits of green flame. If he had her pistol, then he had to have been watching her for some time from up in the rocks — long enough . . . to have seen her at the pond? Before she could stop it, the realization found its way to her lips.

"You were watching me." Her voice was barely more than a whisper, and her eyes were wild with anger.

Cale bowed his head a bit and looked back at the flames to conceal the mischievous smile that found its way to his lips. He'd been watching, all right — Lord, who wouldn't have? He hadn't started out to invade her bath that way, but he had been tracking her all day, and he'd just happened to catch up about the time she was taking a dip . . . Couldn't have planned it better if he'd tried.

"Well, I suppose you could put it like that." He cast a quick glance in her direction, sizing up her anger, and then looked down again to hide another smile. "But just be glad it was me and not some scoundrel." He checked the hammer of the gun and then laid it down on the ground beside him. He would have thrown it back to her, but it was obvious that he couldn't trust her not to shoot him with it. "You ought to be more careful where you leave your gun."

Jessalyn had been at the boiling point ever since he had produced her gun, but his last comment finally pushed her over. Wild with anger, she swept a heavy branch of mesquite wood from the ground at her feet and swung it at him with all of her might. When he leapt back, and her weapon missed its mark, she took a few quick steps in his direction and swung again. When her second attack brought no satisfaction, she let the branch fly in his direction, and then dove for the pistol. The clutch of a strong arm around her waist brought her up short, and she spun about to face him in a fury of blazing copper hair.

White-hot anger flashed in her eyes like wild summer lightning as he pinned her like a rag doll against his chest with one strong arm. With the other hand, he caught her free arm as she raised it to land a blow.

"Jesse, Jesse," he admonished, shaking his head as if she were an errant child. He fell silent as his amber gaze met the wild emerald seas that were her eyes and he realized that he was looking at the most beautiful thing he'd ever seen. "You are a wild one."

"What did you expect?" she spat, returning his appreciative regard coldly. "A warm reception?"

"It would be nice," he remarked, again with the casual nature that made it seem as if he were an old friend.

"When pigs fly!" she returned, not to be soothed by the outpouring of his warm nature.

Tossing his tawny head back, Cale laughed heartily. He wasn't sure if he'd ever met a woman with so much fire, and he knew that he'd never met one so beautiful.

"A truce then." He gave her that easy, charming smile for which there was no defense.

Reluctantly, she nodded, and then met his gaze

with determination. He'd bested her once, but, by God, she intended to let him know that it wouldn't happen again. She also intended to find out what Cale Cody was doing trailing her out onto the desert. Third, she intended to kill Sam Horn when she saw him next for telling Cale about her leaving in the first place.

"All right, but just don't . . ." Her words were silenced by the burning touch of his lips against hers, and her thoughts spun away from her like mutineers from a fight. Unwillingly, she clung to him, her mind surrendering to the insane whirlwind that swept away her strength, her lips surrendering to his. In that instant, even the flame of hatred that had driven her since her father had been murdered seemed like a mere ember next to the blaze that he had ignited within her. Gently, he raised his head and reached up to cup her small chin in his hand. His hazel eyes glittered with a thousand tiny flecks of gold as he gazed down into hers.

"Yes, Jesse Kendrik, you certainly are a wild one," he whispered just before brushing another kiss across her lips. Like the touch of a midsummer breeze, it was sweet and then it was gone. Releasing her, he turned away and walked back to the fire as if nothing had happened.

Fighting to quell the mass of conflicting impulses that boiled like an enraged sea within her, Jesse stood where he had left her, watching the hard line of his shoulders with disbelief, and then with pain. Who was this man who could stir her so and then walk away as if she were of no more consequence than a fly on his shirt? How could she have allowed

47

him to gain such power? When had she given it up? Suddenly, she felt like a victim. It was a role she'd never been reduced to before, and she hated him for it.

Cale could feel her watching him, but he didn't turn around—and, though he hated to admit it, he knew why. They were alone, twenty miles from the nearest human soul, and he was afraid if he took one more look at those deep emerald eyes, he'd lose every bit of sense he had. As if she were still there in the pool, he could see her slender young body, bare and perfect, and as wild as the desert wind. And then when he'd seen those magnificent eyes, glittering up at him with the reflection of a thousand summer stars—well, it was just a good thing he'd quit when he did. If she'd been any other woman . . . but she wasn't. She was Lane Kendrik's daughter, and whether she knew it or not, she was setting herself up for a lot of trouble.

"Come on, Jesse." He beckoned her toward the fire with one hand. "Sit back down by the fire." Without another word, he stepped out of the circle of firelight and disappeared into the darkness.

Jessalyn listened as his footsteps went a short distance away and then stopped. With a shudder, she went back to the fireside and snatched her underthings from their drying racks before sitting down beside the fire. Having no time to redress herself, she tucked the petticoats into her packs and then drew her long legs up under her full skirt. Staring blankly into the flames, she wished fervently that the desert would swallow Cale Cody alive and he would never return. At the same time, part of her marveled at the

48

ecstasy of his kiss, his touch, and wished that he had never left. It was silly for her to waste her time thinking of him, she reminded herself. He was probably six or eight years older than she, and no doubt he had left more broken hearts behind on the trail than he could count. She didn't intend to join the ranks, that was for sure, and besides, she had no time for love. She had a job to do, and it could very well be her last.

"Well, it's a good thing I happened by these on the way." Cale held out a pair of skinned rabbits as he stepped back into the circle of firelight. "It doesn't look like you planned much for dinner."

Jessalyn cast him a sarcastic smile from where she sat, and intentionally made no move to help him as he skewered the carcasses and braced them on a y-shaped stick over the fire.

"I wasn't expecting company." She watched him as he took a seat across the fire from her, then after a moment, spoke again. "What are you doing here, anyway?"

Cale threw up his hands in feigned innocence, and waved nonchalantly toward the desert around them.

"Just happened to be passing by?" he offered, looking her way with upturned brows. When she responded to his humor with an unamused frown, he sighed and put on a more serious mask. His face was strangely handsome with its stern lines framed in the firelight. "Two reasons," he returned. "Sam told me he saw you leaving the fort, and Rosa told me what you were planning to do." At the outrage that lit in the beautiful young face across from him, he tried to explain the fears that Rosa had expressed for young

Jessalyn's safety. "She is worried about you, Jesse."

"That isn't your concern!" Jessalyn felt rage drive her blood like a wild river through her veins. How dare her mamacita discuss her with this . . . stranger! What gave him the right to follow her onto the desert and question her judgment as if he had some claim to her! "Mamacita had no business telling you that, and what right do you have to question me?"

Cale watched her steadily, unabashed by her anger. He had expected it, but he had to talk her out of going on with her crusade if he could. A lot of things depended on it.

"None," he returned. "But Rosa and I are old friends, and I knew your father." That was a little less than the truth—he had known her father much better than this implied. "He wouldn't have wanted this."

"You know what my father would have wanted better than I?" she questioned hotly, her anger raised even higher by the fact that, deep within herself, she was afraid he was right. If her father were alive, he wouldn't have allowed this, and she knew it.

With a sigh, Cale turned his attention to their dinner. From where he sat, this looked like a stalemate. He'd had the same feeling one time when he'd been packing a mule through the mountains and it had sat down beside a stream and refused to move. Jesse may not have looked anything like that mule, but she was definitely made of the same stuff. He wasn't a man used to taking no for an answer, but he knew enough to stop and let the fire of youth cool a bit before he pushed the point.

* * *

Jessalyn looked up at the dark sky and frowned, confused by the strangeness of it. Clouds must have drifted in while she was asleep, because she couldn't see the stars now, and the night had become still and close, as if it were closing in around her. There was something else strange about it—something haunting—but she couldn't quite put her finger on it.

There was something strange within her, too, something that seemed to mirror that odd, featureless sky. A chilling fear crept namelessly about her soul, hiding first in one dark corner and then the next as she tried to seek it out.

The high-pitched sound of a horse's scream split through her like a bolt of lightning, and she spun about to see Diablo crossing the desert in a fury of whipping mane and stinging tail. Cupping her hands to her mouth, she called for him, but he did not turn to come to her. As he drew to the top of the mountain above her, she saw why. On his back was a rider—her father.

Frantically, Jessalyn scrambled up the loose, slippery rocks of the slope toward him. Halfway up, she stopped, and her blood chilled to ice within her as the figure on the horse looked in her direction. It was her father, but as she had seen him in death, his eyes hollow and his scalp nothing but a bloody red patch where his hair had been. With an eerie smile, he extended a hand to motion her closer, but she could not bring herself to move toward him. In horror, she screamed as the wind swirled up from behind him, blowing her toward his outstretched bloody hand.

The sound of a scream shot Cale from his bedroll as if he'd been fired from a cannon. Before he realized what was happening, he was on his feet with his pistol in his hand. Another scream lit the night like an invisible flame, and Cale spun about, his thoughts now on Jessalyn, and his finger ready on the trigger. The gun nearly fell from his hand at what he saw, and he took a step backward to right himself. Near her bedroll stood Jessalyn, her eyes white-rimmed like those of a horrified animal, and trained on the peak of the mountain above them. Her copper hair glistened in the light of the bright moon, and billowed around her as if it had life of its own. Covering her face with her hands, she screamed again, and Cale dropped the pistol, running to her side and sweeping her trembling body into his arms.

Tottering between sleep and awareness, she laid her head against his strong chest and looked up at him. Gently, he sat back down beside the fire, and cradled her in his lap like a frightened child. Brushing a few stray strands of hair back from her face, he kissed her softly on her forehead and then sat stroking her silken hair as she relaxed in his arms.

"What was that about?" he whispered in the same soothing voice that he used when breaking colts. He didn't expect an answer. It was obvious that she was not in her senses by the way that she was curled so willingly against him. So there was a softer side to her after all, he thought, leaning back against the cool stone of the cliff and closing his eyes. He'd begun to wonder, having spent the evening trying to bend her iron will. But Jesse Kendrik wasn't the woman of steel that she pretended to be; he realized that now. Part of her, at least, was just a child — and a frightened one at that.

He held her close to him as the night deepened around them, the blackness growing silent and soulful as if even the wind had drifted away to leave them in a private world. Resting his chin on the top of her glossy head, he drank in the sweet scent of her hair, and painted the fragrance, the feel of her with soft colors in his mind. Stroking the curls that fell over her shoulder, he remembered again the pure, wild beauty of her in the spring pool. He'd never seen a woman as beautiful as her, but that wasn't all that drew him to her. There was something else that he couldn't quite put his finger on that made her compelling, and he wasn't the only one who saw it. There were quite a few others who were obviously bewitched by young Jessalyn — Brett Anderson, for one, and that was a problem. Anderson's desire to be near her seemed to have warped his judgement about the wisdom of parading fifty rangers into a Comanchero lair. Either the man was smitten, or he was an idiot to begin with — Cale wasn't sure which.

Laying his head back against the cool rock again, Cale let the thoughts slip from his mind. He needed to get some sleep. Tomorrow was another day with Jessalyn, and it was bound to be a long one. In fact, the minute she woke up and found herself in his arms, the day was likely to start with a screech.

Jessalyn awoke as the first rays of dawn crept across the jagged floor of the small box canyon where she had made her camp. As the warm light touched her face, she sighed contentedly, and then opened her heavy eyes. As she felt someone stir beneath her, her eyes flew open like shutters, and her gaze darted around. Before ten seconds had ticked away, she realized where she was and her heart rammed like an angry bull against her chest. Forcing herself to remain still so as not to wake her captor, she assessed the situation and made a plan for escape. As carefully as if she were laying a sleeping child down to rest, she lifted his heavy arm from around her and laid it on the ground beside him. Watching to make sure that she had not disturbed him, she slid away from him and then backed onto her haunches.

She sat watching him for a moment, her eyes narrow and catlike, intent on every movement of the muscles of his handsome face. Without the threat of his compelling amber eyes, she could examine him objectively, and, lingering a moment, she took advantage of the opportunity. It was hard to say what she found so threatening about him. She wasn't normally one to be preoccupied with a man—even a handsome one—though she had to admit she'd never seen one quite like Cale Cody. There was something mysterious about him, something that didn't quite fit, like a piece of a puzzle that didn't seem to go anywhere. No one around Bent's Fort seemed to know anything about him, other than that he was a trapper and a shootist who claimed to have come from somewhere up north near Dakota territory. Her mamacita definitely knew him well, but she wasn't forthcoming with any information about Cale, other than that she had once known his family. And then there was a strange air of . . . authority about him, like that of a commander, and not like that of a drifter who traveled with only one compadre.

Jessalyn rose to her feet finally, determined to leave Cale, in body and in thought, behind in the canyon. If she was lucky, he'd sleep long enough for her to be well on her way back to the fort before he knew she was gone. If there was one thing she didn't need, it was any more of his lectures on the idiocy of tracking down El Halcon. He spoke to her as if she were a child, and she didn't like it. Worse yet, he acted as if he had some right to direct her actions. She hoped she'd made it quite clear to him last night that she wouldn't be thrown off of El Halcon's trail by him or anyone else.

Moving silently, she grabbed her packs and saddle and stole away from his camp, her moccasins landing so lightly on the canyon floor that they barely turned a stone. Diablo stood waiting not far away and tied to a bush beside him was a handsome buckskin stallion that must have belonged to Cale. For a moment, Jessalyn considered untying the horse's reins and chasing him off when she rode out, but then she decided against it. Even Cale didn't deserve that. Being out on the desert without a horse was certain death, and she had to admit she didn't want him dead—just out of her way.

A memory crept into her mind as she threw the saddle onto Diablo's back and he wrapped his head around lazily, touching her arm with his velvety muzzle. She could feel another touch there, one that sent shivers through her like ripples through a pool of still water. Closing her eyes and leaning against Diablo's warm shoulder, she remembered the fire of the moment that he had kissed her. She had never known that a man could make her feel . . . so . . . alive. In the past, a man's arms had always made her feel trapped, but Cale's made her feel as if she had sprouted wings. A dimmer memory crept into her mind — one of a horrifying dream and a gentle savior who had held her until the demon disappeared.

"Well, Sam has always said, 'If you bed down with a wildcat, you're likely to wake up with your arm chewed off.' " A voice came from behind her, and she breathed a sigh of defeat. "But he never said anything about waking up to find your horse stolen."

Jessalyn rolled her wide emerald eyes and turned slowly around to face him.

"I wasn't going to take your horse," she informed him flatly, and then added in a more heated tone, "and we didn't 'bed down' together. If you tell anyone we did, I'll skin you for a liar."

Cale threw his hands high above his head in mock surrender, his amber eyes smiling despite the feigned horror on his face.

"As you wish, my dear," he replied, breaking out into a self-satisfied grin as if he were enjoying the game of words between them. "How about a little swim before breakfast?" He nodded toward the spring pool, and raised his eyebrows hopefully.

An unwelcome flush rose in Jessalyn's cheeks, and her eyes narrowed to two angry slivers of ice. If looks could have killed, Cale Cody would have been a dead man within seconds.

"Ooooohhh!" she growled, clenching her fists and stomping a moccasin against the ground to keep from letting fists fly against him. She'd learned last night that that was no use—she'd just end up his prisoner again. "Cale Cody, you make me so angry! If I had a gun, I'd shoot you and leave you for the crows!" In one swift movement, she spun about, grabbed the saddle horn, and swung herself onto Diablo's back. Before he could stop her, she spun the stallion about and put her heels to him, leaving Cale behind in a shower of dust.

Irritated, he brushed himself off and stalked back to the camp to get his things. Hurriedly, he saddled his stallion and put his packs in place before climbing aboard. He gave one last look to the remains of their campsite before sending the stallion off after the trail of dust that Jessalyn had stirred into the air. It had been one hell of a night, he thought, one hell of a night. Still, he wouldn't have traded it for anything.

It was only a matter of time before Cale's big buckskin ran down Jessalyn's Appaloosa. The buckskin stood at least a hand taller, and covered the ground with the easy strides of a thoroughbred. By the time he caught up, Jessalyn had already slowed Diablo to a walk, her anger washed away by the cooling feel of the morning wind against her skin.

"You're just like a bad weed," she remarked as Cale's horse moved alongside of hers and fell into stride. "So tell me," she said without looking over at him. "Why is it that I, of all people, have been cursed with you?"

"Don't know," Cale replied, but it wasn't the truth.

"Maybe because you need someone to keep you from killing yourself." He squinted thoughtfully toward the faraway horizon which was still hazy and purple, almost mystical, in the early morning light. "Tell me something, Jesse." His voice had suddenly become serious, and his eyes were trained on her from beneath the shadow of his tawny brows.

"I might," she replied, looking up at him, and feeling herself drawn by the sudden honesty in his eyes. "That depends on what it is."

"Why aren't you married?" He asked the question without breaking stride, as if his curiosity were completely natural.

Jessalyn raised a questioning brow in his direction at the question, but considered an answer for a moment before she spoke.

"I don't know." That much was honest. "I used to think that was what I wanted, but I guess I've just changed my mind." Looking out at the distant mountains, she knew the reason, and added, more to herself than to him, "I guess I realized that it would mean being tied to one place, and I don't want that."

Her words struck Cale oddly, and held him silent for a moment. He'd said the same thing more times than he could count, and now it felt sort of strange being on the other side of the coin.

"Not all men are farmers, Jesse," he returned finally, and then remembered a time when a woman had tried to tell him that getting married didn't mean giving up his freedom. He hadn't believed it then, so he wasn't surprised when Jessalyn shrugged off his words as if they were unwelcome clouds in the clear picture of life that she had painted.

"I suppose not." The words were obviously more a courtesy than a concession — the hard glint in her jade eyes told him that she was far from agreeing with his point of view. With a frown, she grew thoughtful, and then after a moment, cast a sly sideways glance in his direction.

"And why haven't you married, Cale?" she questioned wryly. "Since you seem to be so much in favor of the institution."

Cale chuckled a bit and gave her a one-sided smile as payment for her cleverness.

"Touché," he conceded the point to her in their battle of words. Beaten or not, he was enjoying their civil exchange — it was the first he could remember having with her. "Still, you should listen to me. I'm older than you . . . and wiser."

With a smile, Jessalyn tossed back her coppery hair and giggled, her laughter floating away like an airy dancer on the cool morning breeze.

"Older, maybe," she granted playfully and then swished the ends of her reins in his direction, causing his horse to startle and dance away sideways. "But hardly wiser. If you were that, you'd know better than to bother tracking me all the way out here to try and talk me out of . . ." she stopped, realizing too late that she was opening up the issue that they had spent the majority of the night arguing about.

"And that's another matter." He slid easily into the crack that she had unwittingly opened. "I don't know how much you know about Halcon's mountains, but I've been there, and you don't have a prayer of taking fifty rangers in there. He'll see you coming and cut you down before you get within fifty miles."

"And who said I planned to take the rangers into the mountains at all?" she replied carelessly, and then gave herself a mental kick for having opened her mouth. The last thing she needed for him to know was that she intended to slip into Halcon's main camp alone. With the fancy footwork of a skilled dancer, she changed the subject. "So how is it that, while you seem to know so much about everyone, no one seems to know much about you?"

Put under scrutiny, he shrugged noncommittally.

"That's the way I like it." The handsome lines of his face grew suddenly serious. It was obvious that she'd been asking some questions about him, and he didn't like the feeling. "My business is mine. I like to keep it that way."

"I feel the same way myself," she said pointedly, and then catching sight of Bent's Fort glittering like a great white mirage on the horizon, she kicked Diablo into a run and headed for home. "What's the matter?" she called back, glancing back over her shoulder through a sea of glittering curls. "Can't that old bag of bones keep up?"

Cale spurred his buckskin after her, and he reached the fort just in time to see her clatter down the back alley to the corral. When he reached the stables, he found her in a fury and Sam Horn cornered against the stable wall. With her shimmering hair askew and her hands braced squarely on her hips, she looked like a lioness ready for a kill, and Cale was glad he wasn't in Sam's place at the moment. Laughing to himself, he unsaddled his mount and then stood leaning against the stone fence of the corral, waiting for the storm between Jessalyn and Sam to play itself out.

After a while, Sam saw an opening and ducked away from Jessalyn's onslaught. Skimming across the yard like a egg-faced dog from a woman's broom, he leapt the fence behind Cale and stood catching his breath.

"Jesus, Cale, look at the trouble you got me into," he complained as Jessalyn crossed the yard toward them with quick, purposeful strides. "I take it the lady didn't enjoy your company."

Cale laughed at his compadre's humor, and then cast a commanding look in Jessalyn's direction. Surprisingly, it held her silent.

"Have the rangers left yet?" he asked, turning back to Sam with a curious tilt of brows that spoke of some unsaid secret between the two.

"Nope," Sam replied, trying to suppress a smile. "They seem to be having a problem finding their horses." Looking down at the ground, he drew a line in the sand with the toe of his moccasins and then raised his shoulders in mock innocence. "They seem to think someone might have hid them somewhere," he added, looking sideways up at Cale, who stood nearly half a head taller. "Now Cale, can you imagine that?"

"That's enough, Sam," Cale said, taking on that unexplainable air of command. Almost instantly, Sam grew silent, and a brooding look clouded in his dark eyes.

Jessalyn's brows drew together mistrustfully and she looked from one man to the other, at a loss to explain the exchange, which had clearly shown one as the commander. One other thing was obvious by the way both men had suddenly turned to stone—she'd seen all that she was going to see until one of them slipped again.

Chapter Four

It was morning again and this time Jessalyn was packing her things for good. She folded the new cotton skirts and blouses that her mamacita had made for her as carefully as if they were made of crystal and placed them in her packs. They were precious, not only because good cloth was a hard commodity to come by, but also because her mamacita had made them. The careful stitches were like a signature, and they always made Jessalyn feel close to the only mother she had ever known, the same way that the Blackfoot moccasins made by Many Summers reminded her of the time that she and her father had spent with the Blackfoot.

Holding one of the new blouses loosely in her hands, she looked down at it and ran a thoughtful finger lightly over the perfect seams. A hot rush of tears threatened her eyes, and she took a deep breath to hold them back. Sitting down on the edge of the bed, she hugged the rose-colored cloth to her and looked around the room seeing each detail, each small line and crack in the uneven adobe. They were small things that had been there, but she had seen them so many times that she had ceased to even notice them. Now she realized that she might never see those things again, and suddenly she knew how much they meant to her. She felt the same way about her mamacita.

Thinking back, she couldn't remember a time when Rosa hadn't been her playmate, her protector, her confessor. Jessalyn had stopped asking about her real mother years ago—at some point it had no longer seemed to matter. She had accepted Rosa as her mamacita, and she needed no other.

She looked up as the door opened, and Rosa's dark face appeared from the early morning shadows of the hallway. Still clutching the blouse, Jessalyn managed a trembling smile, her green eyes glittering with the mist of tears.

"It's time for me to go, Mamacita." Her voice sounded strange and hoarse, as if it were coming from somewhere outside of her.

Rosa nodded grimly. It was obvious that there was no hope of keeping Jessalyn from leaving. Now she could only pray to the saints for the child's safe return.

"Have you packed everything you will need?" she queried. It was the question she asked Jessalyn each time she left, whether for a week or a year.

"Yes, Mama, of course," Jessalyn replied. It was the answer she always gave. Somehow the passing of the usual routine between them seemed to mute the possible finality of this parting; it was as if they were actors playing roles that they had portrayed many times before, and as if saying the lines in the right way would ensure that the drama ended in the same happy reunion as it always had.

"You be careful." Rosa reached out to smooth Jessalyn's willful hair away from her face. This also was part of the ritual of parting.

Reaching out, Jessalyn hugged the older woman quickly and then took her packs up off the bed.

"I'll see you soon," she whispered, and moved to the doorway without looking back. As she hurried down the hall, her thoughts narrowed as if traveling down a long tunnel of darkness to a tiny point of light. Finally, she thought only of putting one foot down and then the next. If she thought of anything else, she knew, she'd turn back in an instant.

Diablo was waiting outside where she had tied him after riding out at dawn to check the progress of the horse hunt. Almost as if by miracle, the rangers' horses had suddenly started wandering back into the fort area after having disappeared like ghosts for two days. Some believed that the animals had wandered far afield and then come back to the fort in search of water, but Sergeant Mike was certain that the Kiowa who were camped near the fort had been responsible. Jessalyn knew better than that. Sounds on the Wind was a good friend and he would never have thwarted her search for her father's killers by stealing the rangers' horses. Still, she could not explain what had happened.

If there had been time, she could have followed the trails of the animals' disappearance, but time was one luxury that was again scarce. El Halcon and his men had a three-day head start now, and she knew she'd have to push hard to have a prayer of keeping on their trail. One good storm would wipe away all signs, she knew. If that happened, the hunt would not be over, but it would become infinitely more dangerous. She knew where to find The Hawk's lair, and she could lead the rangers there easily enough, but without a trail to follow, she could not guarantee that El Halcon was still in front of them. She'd learned the dangers of following an enemy blindly many times in the past. Following without a trail gave the enemy the chance to double back and attack from behind.

She tied her saddlebags on the back of her saddle and then threw her packs back over her shoulder. Leading Diablo behind her, she went to the corrals and haltered the small coyote dun mare that had been her mount before her father had died and left her Diablo. She crafted a makeshift harness out of two lengths of rope and then tied her packs to the mare before tying the dun's halter rope to the horn of her saddle. Making one last check of her gear, she mounted up and trotted Diablo down the back alley and out the gate.

As she rounded the corner of the three-foot-thick mud wall, the wind caught her like a playful dance partner, lifting her hair with its exuberant fingers. She took a deep breath of the fresh, sweet air, noting as strange the moist scent that rose up from the glistening waters of the shallow Arrowhead river. Water would be another thing she would have to worry about, she thought gravely. Alone, she knew the places to find enough water for herself and her mount — but with fifty rangers and a small remuda of spare horses? It would make tracking El Halcon all that much harder. She knew the country ahead well enough to know that there were many places where she would have to detour the company at least a half day to get to sufficient water. No doubt, The Hawk wouldn't have that problem. With only three men along and one spare horse, he could take the dryest route home without any problems.

Still calculating the problem in her mind, Jessalyn rode on to where the ranger company had finally broken camp and was now assembling to move out. Near the head of the commotion sat Brett Anderson astride his tall bay, and leaning over to shake his hand from the buckskin horse next to him was Cale Cody.

Jessalyn's blood boiled within her instantly at the sight of him, and she rode up to the two with her eyes narrowed suspiciously on Cale. When Brett Anderson started to speak, she dismounted and turned to face him, forcing the mask of anger from her face until it chilled only in the depths of her willow green eyes. For a moment, Brett stood speechless. It had been a few days since he'd looked in those bewitching green eyes, and he hadn't been prepared for their hypnotic effect. Giving himself a mental shove, he remembered he was in the presence of a lady, and pulled his hat off of his head. Surprisingly, or perhaps not so much so, his dark hair was neat and perfect underneath.

"Jesse," he addressed her, and paused, wondering if he should have used "Miss Kendrik" instead, then deciding that "Jesse" had sounded natural enough. "This is Cale Cody." He motioned to Cale, and for a moment thought he saw something strange in the taller man's eyes. He pushed the thought aside. It would be impossible for him to know what was strange to Cale Cody, since he'd only met the man a day ago. "He has agreed to sign on with us for this trip as a hunter and shootist."

Jessalyn fought to swallow the protest that shot like an arrow to her lips. She'd sooner have bitten her tongue out than let anyone know exactly how well she was acquainted with Cale.

"I thought Shot Evans was going to do your hunting." This seemed the only protest that she could concoct.

Brett shook his head and tried to act regretful. In reality, he wasn't one ounce sorry to have found out that Shot wouldn't be coming along. The old coot was a miserable bastard who stirred the men up with tales of Indian tortures. Besides, he openly disagreed with every command decision that was made, and that didn't do much for morale.

"He has decided not to come along," Brett told her, and then wondered why he felt the need to explain the changes in the company to her as if she were commanding and not he. Hearing Sergeant Mike call for formation, he placed his hat back on his head crisply, and then tipped the brim in Jessalyn's direction. "If you will excuse me."

She nodded, but barely realized that he was leaving. Her thoughts were already spinning ahead of her to the implications of having Cale along on their quest. Any way she looked at it, the result was disastrous.

"I don't know what you think you're doing here," she turned her frosty gaze in his direction, and tried to look calm, though her stomach churned like it was being buffeted about on some unseen sea. "But I'm warning you, stay out of my way."

Cale grinned, unabashed by her anger, and silently reached out to lift her chin with a folded index finger.

"Don't worry," he whispered, his gold-sprinkled eyes looking laughingly into the cool depths of hers. "I don't want to become the target of that wicked knife arm of yours." Shaking his head as she shrugged her chin from his grasp, he added, "Or that wicked temper."

Remarkably, she forced the rage within her to cool and stood watching him impassively, her eyes unearthly green, like those of a cat sizing up a fence before jumping it. Anger wasn't going to get her anywhere, that was obvious. Not only was he immune to it, but he seemed to draw some sort of infuriating pleasure from watching her steam. She'd just have to let things go as they would for now. Cale Cody was just another problem she'd have to solve—like the lack of water or the possibility of a storm wiping away the trail.

"And what about your compadre?" she questioned, hoping fiercely that Sam would be coming along on their journey. At least then, there would be a fairly good possibility of the two of them losing interest and leaving to set off on their own at some point. She wasn't sure about Cale, but Sam definitely didn't seem the type to spend very long poking along in the company of fifty Texas Rangers.

Cale shrugged noncommittally and nodded back toward the fort. Outwardly, he was impassive, but inwardly, he wondered what she was thinking and why her mood had swung so quickly about.

"I think Sam will be riding by himself for a while," he replied as if Sam's whereabouts were no concern of his. In reality, he and his were rarely separated, but Cale wasn't worried. It was all part of the plan. "I think he might be staying with your Kiowa friends for a while. He seems to have found a girl there he fancies." He looked back toward the Kiowa camp and could almost see Sam curled up with the pretty little thing that he'd been chasing after the past few days. It was a good thing that Sam wouldn't really be staying around long enough to get her cornered — the girl was the wife of a warrior who was big enough to break Sam like a twig. His mind started to run through the orders that he'd given to Sam again, but he pushed the thoughts away and turned his attention back to Jessalyn. "He's more red than white himself, you know — Comanche though, but the Kiowa are their friends."

She rolled her eyes a bit at him and cast him a sarcastic frown. As if she didn't know that the Kiowa and Comanche were allies, she thought to herself, and as if she couldn't have told by Sam Horn's features and style of clothing that he was Comanche. Just how ignorant did Cale think she was?

"It's a shame he won't be coming along," she remarked flatly, letting his lesson on Indian affairs drop. "I like Sam." Without another word, she swung herself into her saddle and rode off toward the head of the company where Brett already sat astride his anxious bay.

Watching her ride away, Cale frowned and wondered to himself what exactly was between her and Sam that she suddenly had such a fondness for him. Running his hand through his tawny curls, he shook his head and reached for the reins of his buckskin.

"Well, Smoke." He patted the horse affectionately as he climbed half-heartedly into the saddle. "This is going to be one hell of an interesting trip." The stallion bowed his head and snorted as if in response, anxious to be off, and showing more enthusiasm than his rider. Cale loosened the reins and clucked to the horse to set him into an easy canter. The next month on the trail with the rangers was bound to be no less than an exercise in self-torture, but he could see no other way to take care of the problem that Jessalyn's determination had caused.

Watching the company pull out behind Jessalyn and Brett Anderson, he pulled his mount up to ride beside the company a short distance behind her. Sitting comfortably back in his saddle, he watched the easy sway of her strong young body as she mirrored the movements of her horse. Her shimmering copper hair swung in unison with its movements, giving her and the horse the appearance of a piece of bright silk floating along on a benevolent wind.

Squinting, he looked up at the already scorching sun and then back down to Jessalyn, wondering which was brighter. Perhaps the trip would have its good points after all, he decided. Deep inside he knew that despite the heat, and the varmints, and the slow pace of the company, he'd rather be riding out into miles of yawning desert with her than staying behind and watching her ride away. She was like an elusive prize—the golden fleece—and he meant to

71

have her, at least for a time. Those who knew Cale Cody well enough to know him at all acknowledged that he always got exactly what he set out for.

From where she rode at the head of the company, Jessalyn could feel Cale's eyes. With grim determination, she forced herself not to turn around and jeer at him. Briefly, she considered scouting ahead of the company, but they were riding the part of the trail that she had already followed on her excursion alone. Cale would know that she had left solely to avoid him, and that in itself would be a sort of surrender. She couldn't let him know how much he disturbed her, how he set her heart to pounding and her emotions into turmoil. She had to stay strong, to remain steady and wait until his interest in her, and his determination to make her fail at her quest, faded.

Jessalyn drove the ranger company hard most of the day, her mind slowly, contemplatively turning over one plan and then another. By midafternoon, the sun was high, and the last traces of the cooling breeze had melted away like morning mists running from the scorching sun. The men's horses sweated and stumbled under the heavy loads of a rider and packs. Even Diablo, with only Jessalyn's slight weight and a small set of saddlebags, had finally grown weary and hung his raven head low. Mile after mile, the vast expanse of desert plodded away, looking from one hour to the next unmercifully unchanged, as if the company had never moved at all. Finally, Brett whipped his tired horse forward and fell in line beside Jessalyn, who rode at the head of the company, oblivious to the men, the tired horses, the heat or the desert — to everything but her own thoughts.

"We're going to have to stop soon." He tried to make it sound more like a request than an order. The truth was, if she pushed his men much further, he was going to haul her off that horse himself and make her give them all a rest. He would have ordered them to halt several hours before, but he knew that she would have ridden on ahead, and he hated the idea of her being alone in this godforsaken country. It didn't matter that she obviously knew her way around the territory like a mouse knows the tunnels of its own burrow. He kept seeing her lying on the desert somewhere dead, and he couldn't stand the picture. When she didn't answer, and failed to turn her blank stare from the trail in front of her, he repeated his words a bit louder.

"Jesse, we're going to have to stop soon."

The sound of her name startled her thoughts away like frightened starlings, and she turned to look at him as if noticing his presence for the first time.

"I'm sorry, what did you say?" she asked, trying to loose her mind from the thoughts that had chained it since they had started out that morning.

"I said we're going to have to stop soon," he repeated himself for the third time, and wondered why he was bothering. After all, the last time he checked *he* was the commander of both the company and special commissions, one of which was she.

Glancing up at the sun, Jessalyn realized how much time had droned by. It gave her the odd feeling of suddenly waking up to find herself in a place other than where she expected to be. Luckily, some measure of sanity must have remained within her, for they were still soundly on the trail of Halcon and his men. Looking back at the bedraggled line of soldiers and mounts behind her, she felt a pang of guilt, and wished she had come to her senses earlier.

"Of course." She looked back to Brett, her jade eyes still looking numb, as if covered by a shroud of cool fog. "Stop here for now. I'll go on ahead and scout for a watering hole and a campsite. I think I know a place not far from here."

Pulling his hat off and wiping the sweat from his forehead with the back of his dusty sleeve, Brett sighed. He couldn't win. No matter what he did, she always found a way to ride off on her own—which was what scouts were supposed to do, he reminded himself. But he wasn't accustomed to having a beautiful, fragile young woman as a scout. In fact, he was beginning to wonder if he'd ever get used to it. "I'll bring up some men to accompany you." He turned to wave up two of the exhausted men behind him.

Gathering up her reins, Jessalyn dismissed him with a shrug and a slight smile of reassurance.

"I don't need them," she informed him casually. "Let them stay here and rest." Putting her heels to Diablo, she urged him into a reluctant lope and left the company behind without giving the lieutenant a chance to protest.

Stopping his bay where she'd left him, Brett watched her go and waved the dismount signal to his men. His eyes were still following the flow of the girl and her ebony mount as Sergeant Mike rode up beside him.

"She's made of steel, that one," the old sergeant remarked in his usual gruff voice, his eyes following the lieutenant's gaze.

Remembering the almost inhuman look that had been in Jessalyn's eyes in the first instant that she had turned to look at him, Brett shook his head. That look wasn't one of steel, it was one of rage. If Jessalyn Kendrik was made of anything right now, she was sculpted from a driving need for revenge and little more. As she disappeared into the maze of sandhills and greasewood, he wondered how long she could contain the pressure of that hatred before it shattered her into a million tiny pieces.

"Tell the men to dismount and loosen their cinches, Sergeant," he ordered, once again claiming the command that he seemed to lose when Jessalyn was present. "And tell our hunter to get busy at his work. That's what we're paying him for. These men could use fresh meat for dinner."

Jessalyn followed the trail left by El Halcon and his men for a short distance, growing hopeful when it led in the direction of a small backwash that most people called Boggy Hole. It would be a good place to water and camp for the night, and hopefully traveling to it wouldn't take them off of the trail left by The Hawk. Unfortunately, her quarry turned out to be more clever than she had thought, and the trail turned south nearly two miles before the watering hole. Disappointed, she left the trail and rode on to check the water hole.

It was exactly where she had remembered it, but somewhat smaller than the last time she and her father had camped there. It had been spring then, and the now-dry creekbed beside the backwash hole had thundered with water from some thaw far to the north. The water had been pure, and sweet, and amazingly cool then, but now the hole had shrunk to a thick, muddy pool. In another month, it would be gone altogether and waiting hungrily with all of the other desert creatures for autumn to come with its rains and feed them again. Still, even in its present condition, it was a welcome oasis in the hostile dryness.

Climbing stiffly down from her horse, Jessalyn bent over the water and brought a small handful to her mouth to test it. Often, watering holes that had been good for years suddenly turned sour with alkali, and one poison hole could quickly be the death of an entire party. She had seen the results of it more times than she cared to think about—miles of empty wagons and dead livestock, horses, mules, oxen, stretched out and rotting into the prairie dust. That, her father had carefully pointed out, was the result of people who were unprepared pitting themselves against the desert. "She claims those she can," he had said once as they had looked down over the remnants of a lost wagon train. "And those of us who are left are just living here by her good graces. She's like a horse that could turn loose and really buck—she might decide to shake us off any moment."

Mounting her horse, Jessalyn allowed him to wade into the pool up to his stomach, and he pawed the water with delight, sending a chaotic shower of tiny droplets into the air around them. Laughing, Jessalyn dropped the reins and extended her hands to catch the sudden shower. When they were thoroughly soaked, she wiped the dust from her face with a cloth from her packs and then reached up to smooth back her damp copper hair.

"That's mighty unkind of you sitting there cooling off when you left all of those men back there sweltering in the sand hills." The sound of Cale's voice caused her to stiffen, and she reluctantly rolled her head around to stare at him through narrow eyes.

"I notice that you also managed to find your way to the water without bringing along those poor, thirsty men," she observed flatly, watching him cut the carcasses of several long-eared desert hares and a relatively large antelope down from his packhorse.

"Oh, well begging your pardon, miss, but it's only my job to feed them." He gave her that irresistibly roguish smile. "Seeing them to water, now that's your job. Why, if it were up to me to find water for your lieutenant friend and his men, they'd probably all die of thirst out there on the desert." The strange tone of his voice and the evil twinkle of gold in his eyes indicated that his words were more true than she might have liked to think—but not because he would have been incapable of scouting water for the company.

Turning Diablo around, she guided him back to the bank and slid down to face Cale where he stood. Her jade eyes were narrow and suspicious as they met with his.

"It's plain that you have no fondness for them, and you don't agree with what I intend to do, so why are you here?" She fired the question as straight as an arrow—with no curves and no cushion, as was her nature. She'd had a belly full of fencing words with him, and now she meant to get an honest answer—if that was possible.

Surveying her straight, proud posture appreciatively, and noticing the steady aim of her clear eyes and the determined line of her small chin, Cale gave her credit for courage. She knew how to hold her own with a man, and how to put out a question without mincing words—that in itself set her apart from most of the women he'd known. Looking into those wide, wild green eyes, he found himself wishing that he could give her an honest answer, but he looked away, and shook the feeling off like an unwanted coat.

"To look after you," he replied finally. That, at least, was part of the truth.

"Why?" she questioned, bridling at the suggestion that she needed someone to take care of her as if she were a child—or a greenhorn. She wasn't sure which was worse.

"Because I knew your father," he returned, his explanations still coming easily, as they were partly true. "He was a good man, and a friend."

Anger flashed like streaks of wild summer lightning in the crystal depths of her eyes and she reached up to slap him, but he caught her wrist and held it tightly where he had stopped it. Unable to attack him physically, she resorted to words.

"You liar!" she screamed, her words firing at him like red-hot daggers. "You were no friend of his. If you had been, you would be the first one behind me avenging his death!" Her temper having now driven away her reason, she swung at him with the other arm, but he caught it and held it also. Her burning eyes locked with his, she continued her assault, her mind now pushed beyond the harness of sanity. "You're a miserable little coward, Cale Cody! A coward and a filthy liar!" She started to aim a sharp kick at his knee to free herself, but froze when her eyes met the angry amber flames that were his. His eyes narrowed to icy slits and the muscles in his jaw twitched with rage as he pulled her close and leaned toward her until each glared into the other's eyes from only a few inches away. For a moment, her heart leapt into her throat, and she thought that he would scalp her on the spot.

"Let me tell you something about yourself, Jesse Kendrik," he growled from between clenched teeth, obviously straining to keep the reins to his temper. Without warning, his scowl rose to a grin and he said simply, "You're beautiful when you're angry." Before she could protest, those mocking lips descended on hers, at first with frightening anger, and then with a gentle hunger as he parted her lips and tasted the inner sweetness of her mouth. She pushed against his chest to free herself as his arms moved like deceptive serpents around her. Slowly, his hands found the small hollow of her back, and she arched against him, her slender form melting willingly against the hard muscles of his chest. Somewhere deep within she heard a small cry of protest call out, but it was lost in the swirling caldron of passion that had stolen her senses.

She gasped as his lips left hers and trailed slowly, artfully down the soft curve of her neck, sending a

79

wave of fire through her that was like nothing she had ever known. In the bright light that consumed her, she pictured his eyes, and they were brighter. She heard his name whispered—or her own rebellious lips had whispered it—but the sound seemed to come from somewhere far away.

Slowly, carefully, his lips tasted the tiny hollow at the base of her neck as his hand moved slowly over the rough burgundy cotton of her shirt to cup a firm, full breast. Guided by a strange mix of instinct and desire, she arched backward as his fingers coaxed her erect nipple, sending her spinning backward as if she were caught in a silent whirlwind. Helplessly, she clung to him, whispering his name again and pressing her hips against the wonderful firmness of his thighs.

The vision of her as she had stood by the spring pool danced in Cale's mind like a beckoning siren as he moved to taste her lips again, and his fingers moved to the buttons that held back the ripeness of her straining breasts. Dimly, he realized that he hadn't meant for this to happen, and he also realized that he wasn't going to be able to stop himself. He had only one hope, he realized as he lifted her into his arms. They hit the water of the spring pool with a splash.

Shocked by the sudden dousing and the relative coolness of the water, Jesse came up sputtering and still bound in his arms, her eyes wide with some unreadable emotion. She'd been in enough gold camps and Indian villages to know what had been about to happen. Captured again by the pull of his eyes, she wondered about the fact that she now felt empty and disappointed rather than grateful that her chastity had been saved.

Laughing, Cale smoothed back her sodden hair and pulled her into the warmth of his chest, kissing her lightly on the forehead.

"Thank God for the water," he muttered, out loud but to himself, and then, bending to catch her eyes again, he added, "Jesse, I think you're going to see to it that I end up either dead or crazy."

"I think I prefer dead," she replied, her willow green eyes now filled with wicked sparks. Pulling away from him, she stalked out of the water and then stopped on the shore to ring the water out of her hair and dress. Sitting knee-deep in water, Cale raised his arms up as if to dive in.

"I'll drown myself right here," he offered with a winning smile. When she showed no appreciation for his cleverness, he added, "Come on, Jesse, don't you like me even a little bit?"

From the shore, Jesse gave him an evil grin, and then reached for the reins of her horse.

"No, Cale," she said, but the corners of her mouth turned up into a hint of an irrepressible smile that contradicted her words. "I don't like you . . . even a little bit." With that, she mounted her horse and spurred him away, leaving Cale in the murky hole with the memory of the twinkle that had been in her eye. So she was melting, he thought. She wasn't completely made of ice, and she didn't care that he knew it.

Chapter Five

Five days had trickled slowly by, each one a miserable mirror of the last. Jessalyn rode relentlessly each day until the lieutenant would insist that they stop, and then she would ride ahead to scout water. As she had feared, the need to water seventy horses and fifty men forced them farther and farther off El Halcon's trail as they moved further south. Each day they rode away from the trail as far as need be to water, then rode back in the morning. And each day it grew more apparent that their quarry was easily outdistancing them. The trail grew colder and colder.

When, on the afternoon of the fifth day, a chill wind howled up onto their heels like some great invisible hound, Jessalyn knew it was only a matter of time before the trail was lost. By nightfall, the whipping breeze had begun to carry the scent of water and the clouds over the horizon had turned deadly black, whipped forward by great, jagged slashes of lightning.

As the rangers struggled to fasten the flapping,

dirty canvas of their tents, Jessalyn tied Diablo and her packhorse securely beside the sheltered wall of the canyon she had selected for their campsite. Had it been spring, she would not have decided to camp there at all, as the sandy floor of the canyon was gutted with the channels of runoff from desert floods. There was little chance of that in midsummer, she knew, and the canyon walls offered the shelter of several small caves for those who were smart enough to use them. Shaking her head at the rangers as they struggled to stay their tents against the wind, she took her saddle and packs and climbed up the loose gravel beside the wall to the dark, yawning mouth of a cave. Safe inside, she looked down at the men again and sighed. She didn't know where Brett Anderson was from—probably up north somewhere, where the country was more kind—but the man was a fool. The problem wasn't that he didn't care about his men, but that he was a stickler for propriety, even to the absence of common sense. Jessalyn had tried for half an hour to convince him to let his men camp in the caves for the night, but he had insisted on proceeding, in his words, "as is proper." She hoped that it was "proper" to spend the night cold and wet, because she could almost guarantee that they were marching headlong in that direction.

Looking into the darkness of the cave, Jessalyn shuddered a bit, setting her packs down. She noticed the pile of gnarled mesquite wood not far back, and for the first time was grateful that Cale had begun to make a habit of setting up her camp when he had finished hunting each evening. She had struggled to avoid him since the evening that they had met at the backwash. She had even begun to take her meals in the company of Sergeant Mike and some of the men to avoid the possibility of being alone with Cale. Not tonight, she decided. She'd rather face the blazing eyes of Cale Cody than the raging torrents of a desert rainstorm.

Piling some of the wood a short distance from the entrance, she lit it easily and watched the twisted branches crackle to life. Unrolling her bedroll beside the dancing flames, she sank wearily to the ground and hugged her knees to her chest. Resting her head atop them, she looked into the waving yellow and white depths of the fire and allowed her thoughts to slip from the prison that caged them each day. Carrying the fates of fifty men on her shoulders took away the wonderful freedom that she had always treasured above all else. She now felt harnessed, chained by her duty to the dead and her responsibility to the living, and she was slowly becoming aware that there would soon be a decision to make. Her fondness for some of the men now weighed heavily against her need to avenge her father, and whichever way the scales might tip, she was frightened. One thing was for certain, if she survived the battle against El Halcon, she would never again let herself be responsible for someone else. She'd ride up north into the mountains alone, and free as the spring wind . . . and she'd never come down.

She thought again of the Kiowa and Sounds on the Wind. Looking deep into the flames, she could almost feel the warmth of his lodge, and hear the cold winter winds howling outside. His voice was deep—almost like thunder, only it made her feel warm—and his counsel was wise. How she wished for that counsel now. The memory of the cool, snowy breeze chilled in her lungs as she thought of the two of them standing in the center of a frozen lake and watching the silent world glitter around them. She tried to imagine what he might say, what his words might be if he were with her now, but she could not. Regardless of where she looked for help, one conclusion stood before her like an immovable stone wall: the decision was hers, and she had only her own knowledge and wisdom on which to rely.

She swept the thoughts away finally, like a clutter of cobwebs, knowing they would build themselves again in the corners of her mind. Her life had become so complicated and so bitter in the past weeks; inwardly she shrunk at the driven person that she had become. And there was another thought that pressed against the doorways of her mind so relentlessly that she spent every inward moment struggling to drive it away. Still, it burned like a flame within her, but she was at a loss to understand it. "It" was Cale Cody, though she rarely allowed herself to speak his name, even in her mind.

She could not understand the desire that haunted her. She had never before felt her spirit and body so possessed by a man—particularly one she didn't even like. Cale Cody was arrogant and a scoundrel. He was handsome, she was well enough aware of that fact—but, obviously, so was he. He was also aware that he had managed to ignite some willful strain of desire within her, and that maddened her further. It was plain that the hold was one-sided, and that he considered her little more than a toy, no doubt like countless other women he had used for his amusement. Well, he had another thing coming if he thought she was fool enough for that. She had been raised in a man's world, and she knew most of their tricks. He wasn't the first to desire her, but she'd not sell herself like some cheap saloon girl, and that was obviously all he wanted.

The sound of footsteps echoing into the cave stole her musings away, and she looked up to find Cale in the entrance. As if by some magic power, the promises that she had made to herself skittered away like mice suddenly come face to face with a lion. She searched her mind for a civil word, but could find none, and finally turned her gaze back to the fire.

"I brought you some food," Cale said, laying down a skin filled with charred meat before crossing his long legs and sitting down beside the fire opposite her.

"Thank you," she returned, feeling foolish, like a tongue-tied child, and blaming him for it. "How are our friends doing out there?"

Scoffing merrily, Cale pantomimed the raging winds and flapping tents, and then shook his tawny head, still grinning.

"Looks like a Founders' Day parade out there," he joked. "Those tents are flying from their stakes like flags. All except the tent of your friend Anderson, that is. He's got four men sitting out there holding the corners down."

Jessalyn looked up in shock for a moment at his

statement, but on spotting the twinkle of jest in his eye, realized that he was only joking.

"I am sure they know what they're doing," she remarked dryly, somehow bristling inwardly at his criticism of the rangers even though she had just been thinking nearly the same thing herself.

He cocked a questioning brow in her direction as if he couldn't believe that she had made the statement, and then looked slowly toward the doorway of the cave thoughtfully.

"Like fish in the desert," he muttered, more to himself than to her. "Yes ma'am, those boys are right at home." His sarcasm again held the slight edge that made her uncomfortable, but she didn't know exactly why. "After all," he continued wryly, "why would anyone want to spend the night in this warm dry cave when he could be bunking in a soggy fallen-down tent?"

"Well, I hope you don't think *you're* staying here for the night," she retorted, refusing to allow his remarks to gall her. In response, he gave her a sly sideways grin and a knowing wink.

"You might need me to protect you," he suggested.

"From what?" she scoffed disbelievingly.

At that, he rolled his eyes backward and squinted a brow thoughtfully.

"Uh . . . from the storm, of course." He leaned forward, waiting to see how she would swallow his suggestion, and looking for all the world like a sly boy trying to trick his mother into giving him a taste of pie.

Unable to resist his boyish charm, Jessalyn rolled

87

her own sparkling green eyes and awarded him a dazzling smile for his efforts.

"You are impossible." She reached for the meat, and picking up a small piece, took a delicate bite, pretending to be only mildly interested in his presence.

"I know." He winked again, looking satisfied, as if he knew that he had been the victor in yet another battle of wills between them. "And that's one of my better features," he added wryly. Taking a piece of meat for himself, he bit off a chunk and ate it heartily as the two of them lapsed into a strange silence. Watching her as she pointedly avoided watching him, Cale felt himself captured again by her beauty, and wondered at the feeling. Privately, he wondered what he wanted from her. He needed to earn her trust, even her friendship, if his plan was going to work, but something inside told him that he wanted something more. Each time he looked into those wild, determined green eyes, that voice grew louder, but he still could not quite understand the message. Wasn't his purpose to save her skin, to keep her from unwittingly putting herself into the middle of things she didn't understand, and then to return to his business?

After a time, he stood up in an effort to shake off the disturbing question, and walked to the mouth of the cave. Looking down at the chaos below, he forgot his concerns and broke into a wide grin. Leaning casually against the side of the entrance, he folded his strong arms across his chest.

"You really should come and take a look at your friends," he remarked good-naturedly, without turning back to look at her.

"No thank you," she retorted with a deliberate air of disapproval. "And if you weren't such a worthless sot, you would be down there helping instead of watching." She looked back into the fire, striving to appear pointedly disinterested.

"Your problem," he complained, his handsome face framed with serious lines as he walked back to the fire and squatted down beside her. Placing a finger beneath her chin and forcing her to meet his eyes, he continued, "Your problem is that you take everything too seriously. My father used to say that the world is full of laughter, but you have to let yourself look for it."

"I have no time for that," she replied, her eyes cooling to two green shards of stone. Pulling her chin away, she looked down, suddenly realizing how much she had changed since the death of her father. In the past, she had always been the first to see the humor in things, or to echo another's laughter.

"Why?" he questioned.

"Because I have to . . ." she paused cautiously, and then finished her statement lamely, "I have to see that my father's murderers are brought to justice."

Again, he countered her with the same sword, his amber eyes growing soft and liquid with a look of compassion and wisdom. "Why?" he repeated as if her first answer had been incomplete.

"I owe it to my father," she insisted, trying desperately to cling to the convictions that had brought her so far already. Lifting her chin, she met his eyes defensively, desperately fighting the urge to escape him and run to some safe place where he could not find her.

"Do you really think this is what he would have wanted?" he pressed. "Will the loss of your life bring him back?"

"I don't care about that." She looked away with the feeling that he could see through her as easily as if she were made of glass. If he couldn't, he was getting dangerously close.

"About dying?" he interpreted.

"Yes." Her words came in a strange whisper that hung in the air above them like a great black specter. Without warning, the feelings that she had been so carefully guarding found words and spilled to her quivering lips. "I would rather die." She paused, and bowed her head further, hooding her shimmering eyes from him with a shield of dark lashes. "It's as if I'm on fire inside." Wringing her hands in her lap, she fought the need to put words to the hatred that consumed her, the rage that had been gnawing slowly at her soul, sculpting her into someone that she didn't recognize. "If I give up now, it will be with me forever, and I'd rather die than live with this . . ." The wall that she had built behind her eyes crashed to a million tiny fragments, and she looked back to him for help, her eyes wild, desperate, confused. For the first time, he saw the extent of the pain and hatred that was within her, but he also saw the innocent child that she had been such a short time ago. He wondered how long both entities could struggle within the same soul before each would destroy the other.

Taking a seat beside her on the ground, he pulled

her into his arms gently and cradled her against him. With tenderness that belied his size, he stroked the stray tendrils of copper away from her damp cheeks. Resting his chin on the top of her glossy head, he sighed.

"Jesse, Jesse," he whispered, at a loss for better words. He had been prepared for a flare of that deadly temper of hers, but instead he was faced with tears. From what he could guess, they were the first she had cried for her father. "You can't turn yourself against the whole world because of the actions of a few men," he continued, and, like a reflection in a pool, he saw his grandfather telling him the same thing after the death of his own father. There had been another piece of advice also— one that he had seen the wisdom of too late. "Sometimes it is best to forget," he said, partly to her and partly to himself.

Her tears having grown to uncontrollable sobs that stole her voice away, she shook her head and clung more tightly to the strength of his arms. A renewed rush of hot tears deepened the stains in her cheeks and drew quicksilver trails against her olive skin.

"I can't forget," she choked with effort, recalling clearly the haunting vision of her father as she had seen him in her dream—scalped, bloodied, and with vengeance flaming in his eyes. "I won't forget. I won't forget," she vowed, speaking now to the vision rather than to Cale.

Unable to combat her hysteria, Cale held her tenderly, stroking her silken hair as if soothing a frightened child. He felt her shudder against the hollow of his chest and thought of the night that he had held her in the spring canyon.

It seemed hard to fathom that the small, frightened thing in his arms was the same woman who rode bravely at the head of the company each day. She was as solid and cool as stone then—it was quite an act, he thought ruefully. Watching the smoke curl up from the fire and fly over them like an angry ghost, he wondered at the demons that haunted her. Was it possible that her only purpose in driving herself after El Halcon was to fulfill her duty to her father, or was there something more? Almost against his will, he found himself wishing that he could chase those evil spirits away, that they could be dispelled as easily as the visions from a child's nightmare. Whether he liked it or not, she had found a spot in his heart, with her wild beauty and flashing green eyes, and watching her cry was like watching a butterfly struggle to fly with a broken wing.

For a time after she quieted he sat, still soothing her, enjoying the chance to be, at least for a while, within the wall that she had built around herself. It was like coming into a sacred garden and holding a beautiful, wild thing that he could never have touched in the world outside. Finally, she pushed away from him, and he regretfully let her go.

"I'm sorry," she said simply, her eyes weighted away from him by the shame that she felt. Surely he would think her a weak and simpering fool now.

Reaching out, he dried the last tear from her eye with the back of his fingers, his handsome face lifting into a warm smile.

"There is nothing to be ashamed of," he said quietly, the warmth of his amber eyes drawing away her fears. Unwilling to be comforted, she stole her eyes away again and fastened them to the dark wall of the cave in front of her.

"What do you want of me?" She changed the subject, voicing the question that had plagued her ever since her first meeting with him.

Cale sat back against the wall and regarded her silently for a moment as he considered the question. It was a difficult one, and he wasn't sure he knew the answer himself. He was certain of one thing, though—he wanted to convince her to give up this insane quest for vengeance before it was too late. Beyond that, he wasn't sure.

"I want you to give up and go home." He knew that would fly over like lead, but it was the most he dared to say. He couldn't tell her why it was so important that she give up, and he didn't want to debate the personal aspects of the situation—he wouldn't make promises to her that he couldn't keep. After all, there was no place for her in his life.

In the next heartbeat, he looked deep into her bewitching green eyes, and forgot all about promises. Leaning close, he kissed her hungrily and pulled her close to him, laying her gently back against the soft, red blanket that she had laid out beside the fire. Slowly, he stroked the soft curve of her hips until she arched her body to meet him, her fingers exploring the firm curves of his body.

His lips moved artfully, almost rhythmically over hers as he gently parted her lips and tasted the sweet wetness within. His hands moved possessively upward to the ripening swell of her soft breasts, and he felt the excited fluttering of her heart drive through his fingertips and send fire through his veins. Driven now to caress, to taste, every inch of her lithe young body, he freed the buttons of her blouse and camisole hungrily.

Jessalyn gasped as his fingers drew trails of fire over her breasts, taunting their flushed peaks until she pressed harder against him — seeking, needing satisfaction for the hunger that had exploded within her. Waves of exquisite sensations tickled through her, and she lay her head helplessly against the blanket, moaning encouragement as his lips followed the trail of his hands. Feeling lost, she clung to him as the warm, wet caress of his lips conquered her creamy skin and his hands moved lower to lift her skirt and feel the softness of her thighs. She wanted him to keep touching her this way forever . . .

A crash of thunder rang through the cave like the Lord's own voice, and each of them sat up, like dreamers suddenly startled away from a perfect dream. Their eyes locked for an instant, each of them understanding the bond that was between them, and each knowing in that instant that the other realized it also. It was Jessalyn who spoke first, her eyes still misty, like leaves wet with morning dew.

"My God," she whispered, and then looked away. "What have I done?" Without another word, she stood up and walked purposefully from the cave, righting her clothes on the way. Where she had left him, Cale sat watching her and realizing that the same words had come to his lips, though he had refrained from saying them. There wasn't any way it could work, he tried to remind himself. If she knew what he really was, she'd be aiming at him with a gun rather than words. He probably would have preferred it that way. Watching the empty doorway, he tried the speech again—there wasn't any way it could work, if she knew what he really was . . . but it was useless. Pounding an angry fist against the rock wall, he stood up and paced crazily from one end of the cave to the other. There was no excuse for it. He was acting like a cow-eyed pup, not a leader that thousands of people were depending on.

Muttering to himself, he continued to wear a trail in the floor, trying out one line of reasoning and then another, but none seemed to work. Finally, he sat stoically beside the fire. His amber eyes blazing as bright as the flames themselves, he cursed the day that Lane Kendrik had died and left him with this problem in the first place.

Sliding down the slippery gravel slope beneath the mouth of the cave, Jessalyn willed her tired feet to move faster, running as if the hounds of hell nipped at her heels. Above her, the storm was breaking into full fury, but she neither saw nor felt the torrents of water that rushed like a river spit from the sky. The horses danced nervously to the end of their pickets when she burst into their sheltered rock hollow, but she ignored them, grabbing Diablo's line and working crazily to unbind the sodden rope knot. When it would not relent, she pulled the halter over his head and swung herself onto his bare back with only the pressure of her legs to guide him.

His hooves flashed ominous sparks against the canyon bedrock as she spurred him into a mad run and guided him out onto the barren desert. Pushed beyond reason, she rode him like a wild animal desperately trying for escape, as if she could somehow run so far or so fast that she would never have to return. Around them, the lightning split the great black dome of the sky and drove to the earth, leaving great charred holes in the sand. Whipped to a frenzy by the exploding sky, her stallion crashed blindly through tight thickets of mesquite and greasewood, his eyes growing demonic and white-rimmed as the long thorns tore through the flesh of his sleek shoulders.

Herself unable to feel the ripping of the cruel thorns, Jessalyn clung more tightly to him to keep from being torn off by the sharp fingers that grabbed at her from all sides. Before them, the deepest reaches of the storm stretched like a howling giant above the blackened desert, pitching lightning bolts forward to drive the horse and rider into its depths. Unable to turn back, Jessalyn drove her frightened mount forward, knowing that whatever lay ahead could not match the danger that waited behind her.

"Father!" she cried, squinting upward into the downpour, her tears running with the rainwater to the ground. A bolt of lightning struck just before them, and Diablo reared into the air to avoid being drawn into the crackling hole. Unprepared, Jessalyn fell backward from his slippery back and landed among the tiny waterways that had formed in the sand. Clutching the wet sand into her hands as if it were holy water, she sobbed bitterly, her head bowed against the falling rain. "Father," she said again, this time in a whisper that was drowned out by the angry winds. "How could you have left me? I'm not ready." She watched the sand escape between her clutched fingers, and felt her treasured childhood escaping with it. "I'm not ready. I'm not ready." She whispered the words again and again, as if saying them could somehow force the world to spin backward to a more familiar place in time.

Finally, the storm ebbed and was gone almost as quickly as it had come, leaving in its wake a grey sky streaked with what the Comanche called the wolf road, and what the white men called the milky way. It was supposed to be a good omen, she knew, but it seemed to her like the glittering bars to a prison a cage that would not let her return to the life, she longed to live again.

She sat and absently watched the water flow away from her to settle into creekbeds and backwashes in the valleys, thinking of special moments, like still pictures, of her childhood. One by one, they flowed away from her on the tiny rivers until she was left with nothing but the uncertain future, the weight of revenge, and a consuming desire for a man with whom she could have no future.

Once again, she wondered how her mutinous heart had slipped away from her and tried to isolate in her mind the hour, the second, that a piece of her had become his. His? It made her sound like a possession, exactly the thing that she had fought against being her whole life. She had been determined to belong only to herself and not to be bound to any man. Why, then, had she sold herself for so little? A few stolen kisses, smiles, kind words—that was all that had been offered, yet she had wagered her heart against them, as if both were of the same value.

Slowly, the last of the clouds floated from the sky above her and the stars twinkled to life, a million tiny points of light against a carpet of blue-black velvet. Finally, the moon rose to challenge their brightness, and lit the silent desert with an un-earthly glow of silver. Looking around, Jessalyn could almost feel the thunder spirits walking the glittering earth in the wake of the storm. Almost out of reflex, she shuddered at the thought, and re-membered a time when Spirit Eyes, an old Chey-enne whom she could barely remember, had told the story of the great bird Thunder who brought the storm, and the mischievous spirits, the Mistai, who roamed the earth on quiet nights in Thunder's wake. She could almost feel them crowding around her now, choking her breath away with their icy fin-gers, and whispering terrible words of foreboding in her ears.

Unable to bear the eerie silence any longer, she called to Diablo, who stood not far away, almost hidden by the mist. He trotted through the cloud to her, seeming eager as she to leave the haunting soli-tude. When she stood up, Jessalyn winced and nearly fell back to the ground at the pain that burned from her legs upward. Confused, she felt the deep cuts that had now swollen and begun to burn with the poison of the thorns. She could not remember how she had gotten the wounds, but it was obvious what had caused them. Tears welled in her eyes again as she felt the long scratches that lashed across Diablo's chest and shoulders, and she wrapped her arms around his thick neck, hugging him tightly.

"I'm sorry, Diab," she whispered, patting his nose apologetically before swinging herself aboard. Unsure of how far they had come, or of which direction she should return, she let her stallion have his head. He moved slowly, stiffly, but with certainty as to the direction of companionship, oats, and much-needed rest.

The moon had topped the endless dome of the pitch sky before they found their way back to the camp and crept silently back through the wreckage of tents to the canyon wall. Tying Diablo beside the coyote dun mare, Jessalyn crept back to the ranger's horse picket, noting with disgust that if she were a Comanche she could have easily stolen all of their horses without their noticing. As it was, she helped herself to a can of salve and some oats from the horses' provisions and then left on the skilled feet of an experienced thief.

Wearily, she removed the imbedded thorns from Diablo's wounds and swabbed them with salve. When she had finished, she considered curling up on the rocks beside him for the night, but the chill in the damp air caused her to think better of it. Reluctantly, she climbed the slope to the cave, hoping Cale would be gone, or at least asleep. She lacked the strength to face him, at least tonight, and given her choice, she'd wake in the morning to find him gone like a bad dream.

When she reached the mouth of the cave, she stood for a moment outside, noticing the bright light from the fire, and knowing he was, no doubt, still inside. Taking a deep breath, she summoned the last ounces of determination within her and stepped through the opening feeling as if she were stepping through the portal to hell, and into Satan's arms.

She found Cale much as she had left him, and for a long moment, he seemed oblivious to her presence. His amber eyes were fixed steadfastly on some minute point of light in the embers of the dancing fire, and the square lines of his jaw were tight and closed. His honey-colored hair stood out from his head in wild curls, as if he had nearly pulled it from the roots over the past hours. His eyes finally rose to hers, and Jessalyn stopped a few paces from the fire, watching him uncertainly.

Chapter Six

As he looked up from the flames into Jessalyn's wide green eyes, Cale's first response was anger. It shot through him like a thousand tiny shards of glass and drew hard lines on his handsome face. His mind rang with angry words, but, for some unexplainable reason, he held them back. He wanted to grab her and crush that ridiculous pride from her with all of his strength, to force her to answer the questions that clawed at his brain. Why had she run into the storm, leaving him behind to go mad with worry? Why had she run from him as if he were some sort of villain? Why couldn't she give up her useless quest for revenge and go back to Bent's Fort where she belonged? Why, why, why—the storm raged a million questions within him in the split second that his iron gaze held her shackled.

Through it all, there was one question that raged above all others, though he fought to bury it in the clamor. Why did he care anyway? He could easily solve the whole problem by seeing to it that she disappeared during one of her scouting trips and was held somewhere safe until it was too late for her to do any damage. Somehow, he couldn't make himself do it, though. She was like a high-spirited filly that needed to be won over with kindness, not with force. Again, he reminded himself of what a dangerous enemy she would be, and vowed to renew his efforts to send her back to Bent's Fort. He might even have rekindled the campaign then, but his eyes caught on the festering wounds that trickled blood down her smooth thighs and onto the torn, muddied, colorless fabric of her skirt. His anger fell away from him like a crumbling stone wall, and his eyes softened to the deep, warm color of Tennessee whiskey.

"What have you done to yourself?" He stood up, moving quickly to support her, as she looked like she might fall from exhaustion or loss of blood—or both. When he reached for her, she flinched away, watching him with the uncomprehending fear of a wounded doe, unable to recognize the hands of one who might help her. Scooping her stiff body into his arms forcefully, he brought her to the fire and laid her on the pallet before grabbing a bucket and going outside to get some water from a hollow in the rocks.

When the cool night air hit the bare skin of his chest, he realized that another danger threatened the tortured girl inside—pneumonia. He'd seen it happen more than once in the desert summer, when the days turned cloudy and cool for a short time and the body was unprepared for the shock. Sam used to say that it happened because the blood was too thin in the summer to keep out the chill, but

Cale tended to doubt his half-white, half-Comanche medical science. One thing was for sure, he thought, mentally bracing himself for a fight. Whether Jessalyn liked it or not, she was going to have to come out of those wet clothes. Actually, he didn't find the idea unpleasant at all, and if he could have figured a way to accomplish it without getting his eyes clawed out, he would have been looking forward to it.

Finding a good pool of water trapped in a small basin of the rock ledge from which the cave opened, Cale scooped up a bucketful and went back inside. Setting the bucket back down beside the fire, he turned to Jessalyn but found her asleep, her muddied face flushed but peaceful against the tangled swirl of her brassy hair. With a sigh, he began the complicated process of removing her clothes while she protested lamely through her exhaustion and swung at him with ill-aimed fists.

One by one, he removed the torn, wet garments, tearing them away from the crusted blood on her skin as carefully as he could. He worked almost mechanically to wash the streaks of mud from her, determined to ignore the lure of her slender young body. Still, he found himself admiring her tawny perfection as he moved the soft cloth over her skin. She was almost like a statue, lying there so still, like something an artist could dream of, but never quite create.

When he had finished bathing her, he sat back on his heels to survey the angry wounds that slashed across her legs and arms. Reluctantly, he covered her with a blanket and then climbed down to the valley floor to collect whatever healing plants he could find by the dim moonlight. It was an imperfect process at best, but he finally managed to collect a satisfactory armful of plants which he carried back to the cave for closer examination.

When he entered, he found Jessalyn beside the fire as he had left her, but curled protectively into herself like a child asleep. He watched her from the corner of his eye as he sorted through the plants, taking out the fragrant yucca blossoms and a pungent scarlet-stemmed plant the Comanche called "red root." With the skilled hands of one who knew the task well, he made a soapy paste from the yucca blossoms and a separate salve from the red root. When he was satisfied with the results, he scooped the ingredients into two small piles on a flat slab of rock and carried it over to her.

Pulling the blanket from her, he turned his attention to dressing the wounds and began rubbing the stinging soap into the worst of them. As it sank deeper into her torn skin, she winced, and her eyes fluttered open. Sitting up as if propelled by a bolt of lightning, she regarded him with a wide-eyed stare that began in confusion, melted to mistrust, and ended in horror. Springing back on her haunches, she clutched the blanket to her to cover her nakedness.

"Leave me be!" she snarled, her eyes hurling invisible daggers at him.

Standing with the platter of potions still in his hands, Cale watched her with the calm regard of a mother addressing an errant child.

"Those wounds have to be dressed," he persisted

flatly, nodding at the angry welts that glared like serpents from the edges of the blanket, trickling a mixture of blood and poison down the smooth skin of her thighs.

Following Cale's gaze, she looked down and then back up in shock, as if noticing the damage for the first time.

"I . . . ," she struggled to maintain her indignance in light of the fact that he had obviously been trying to help her. Again, she felt foolish. "I can do it myself." She raised her chin proudly, struggling to regain some of her lost dignity.

"You'll be lucky if you manage to stay conscious while it's done." Cale was right and he knew it. He could feel his patience being rapidly spent by her fit of temper.

With hard-won humility, she swallowed her pride like a lump of bitterroot, and wrapped the blanket around herself so that only her arms and legs were revealed.

"All right." She almost choked on the words, but sat obediently on the blanket beside the fire, stretching her long legs in front of her. She bit her lip and turned away as he began dressing the wounds, and a wave of star-filled blackness swung before her eyes like an iridescent veil. When she was almost certain that she could stand no more, Cale finally pulled the blanket back over her aching legs and stood up.

"Get some sleep," he said stiffly. "No doubt tomorrow is going to be a long day."

Wrapping herself up like a caterpillar about to go into cocoon, she lay back against the blanket and closed her eyes, trying to ignore the sound of him moving about the cave. In spite of herself, she found her mind wandering back to the moment that his lips had possessed hers. She could see his eyes as they had looked down at her, honest and full, like the gold-rimmed clouds of a summer sunrise. Struggling to suppress the memory, she tossed toward the fire and then back away, seeing him on his pallet on the other side. How would she ever forget him when this was over? She tried to picture herself watching him ride away for the last time, but she couldn't. Suddenly, death at the hands of El Halcon's men didn't seem to be such a bad alternative.

Pushing her head harder into the folded blanket that served her as a pillow, she tried again to erase the thoughts from her mind, to find sleep, but it eluded her like a playful dancer, coming close and then sliding away again. One long minute after she searched for absolution, for some form of respite from the tauntings of her treacherous heart. With painful sloth, the moments crept into hours, and the night was half spent before she rolled again toward the fire and looked at him through the flames.

Slowly, contemplatively, he rolled his head sideways and looked over the crackling coals into her eyes.

"Why did you run away?" he posed the question that had tossed from one side of his mind to the other all night.

Exhausted, Jessalyn propped herself up on one elbow and supported her head with her palm. She was to tired to manage to respond with anything

106

but the truth.

"I don't know." That was the truth. She didn't know why she'd run away like some sort of addled schoolgirl.

"Do you still intend to go on with this hunt?" Cale pressed. He had to know. It was plain that he'd have no rest until he did. He'd thought and thought about it—what if she continued to press on, what then?

Jessalyn nodded, hooding her sea green eyes beneath a shield of dusky lashes. The long night had worn away the armor that might normally have guarded her heart.

"Yes." Her voice came in a whisper that hung in the damp air of the cave like a bad omen. "I have to." Gathering her strength, she faced the intensity of his gaze again, and added, "I don't expect you to understand."

Cale watched her for a moment longer, his eyes dark and unreadable, then lay back against the blanket, folding his arms behind his head. A long, labored sigh escaped him as he considered her response. It wasn't the one that he'd hoped for—at least, he'd thought it wasn't. Now a strange feeling of desire spread over him like warm water as he considered the bright-eyed girl who sat watching him intently, and the prospect of spending a little more time with her didn't seem so bad. After a moment, he sat up, his long legs crossed in front of him, and his eyes again trained thoughtfully on her.

"Come over here, Jesse." His voice was warm and thick, like the comforting caress of a summer breeze, but still it chilled Jessalyn to the bone.

Slowly, she wrapped the blanket around herself and forced her shaking knees to support her as she stood up. With the reluctant legs of a child being led to a whipping, she walked around the fire to him, her proud chin lowered, unable to meet his eyes. Now he'd scold her as if she were an idiot child, she thought grimly. It was obvious that he didn't agree with her, and he'd feel bound to tell her so. There would probably also be some well-planned words about what her father would have wanted, and how she couldn't hope to succeed. Oh God, how could she bear it? How could she sit there and look into his eyes while he told her those things?

Slowly, stiffly, she forced herself to sit beside him, but safely out of reach. The last thing she wanted was for him to touch her—it would only make things worse. Her eyes were dry, but the full red curve of her lips trembled slightly at the corners when she looked up at him. Her ears rang with the silence, or with the words that she knew were coming, she didn't know which. She was barely aware of it when he spoke again, and she only recognized the words when she replayed them in her mind. "Well then, I guess I'll have to go along?" Was that what he'd said?

"Wha . . . ?" she stammered dumbly, mistrusting her ears. Perhaps she had only imagined what she had wanted to hear.

"I said we'll do it your way," he repeated, struggling for words, and frustrated by the fact. He wasn't accustomed to being reduced to a stuttering idiot, but this was hard. He hated lying to her, but

108

he couldn't see any other way to buy her trust. By the look on her face, she still hadn't understood him, and he was going to have to repeat it again. Damn, he'd killed men easier than this! Leaning forward, he brushed a kiss across her lips and then sat back on his heels, smiling, his composure regained.

"Damn, woman!" He wished she'd snap out of it. "You sure make it hard for a man to let you have your way." He cut his speech off there. Laughing, he swept her into his arms and twirled her to the other side of the fire. Laying her gently down on the blanket, he fell beside her, propping himself up on one elbow. "Jesse Kendrik." He kissed the end of her small nose playfully and then leaned back again. "You're one tough customer."

Her eyes brightened to the soft green of willow leaves, and she smiled up into his handsome face. She didn't speak. She couldn't. She only lay there watching him, smiling, and feeling her heart take wings and fly.

Jessalyn passed the next days as if in a dream. There was little tracking to do, since all sign of their quarry had been washed away by the storm. Suddenly, it was as if they had never existed at all. With no more tracks to follow, Jessalyn turned the party east, hoping to continue to the edge of the long chain of mountains that ran from Santa Fe to El Paso. At the rim, they would turn south again, and continue in the shadow of the great mountains, where water and grazing were more plentiful, until they drew near the Paso Del Norte country. When they did, she wasn't sure what would come next. One thing at a time, she reminded herself. They had to get there first.

As the days passed and the mountains turned from a faint shadow on the far horizon to a staggering colossus of jagged rock above them, Jessalyn felt her heart soar with the rising peaks. She spent much of her time with Cale, helping him hunt and prepare the meat each day. Then, together, they would set up camp a short distance from the ranger company and talk together until late into the night.

As her days fell into the steady, comfortable pattern, Jessalyn felt the thoughts of avenging her father's death wander farther and farther from her, until they had almost drifted so far as to disappear. The hate that had frozen her heart now melted in the face of the warm friendship that had developed between her and Cale, but still there was something that gnawed at the back of her mind. It was there each morning, just before her thoughts awakened to the realization of a new day. She felt it each night when he kissed her as if she were a child and then left her alone in her camp. She longed for him to caress her, to kiss her as he had before, but he did not, and she was too proud and too shy to ask him why. It was as if there were a wall between them suddenly. He would come close, but part of him was always hidden away.

Some nights, she would wake to the muffled sounds of hoofbeats, and hear him riding away from the camp into the darkness. Many times, she had wanted to ask him where he went when he left, but it seemed as if she hardly had the right to intrude on his wanderings. After all, they weren't . . . and that was another problem — what were they, exactly? At the very least, they were friends, but were they something more? Did she want them to be? She was not certain what she felt for him. In fact, she was certain of little other than the fact that her heart raced each time she caught sight of him, and her soul leapt away and raced into his arms each time their eyes met.

Finally, when she could stand no more of this teetering existence, she steeled herself to broach the subject as they rode away from the party in search of water one evening.

"Cale," she began, struggling to form the turmoil of thoughts that spun in her mind into the question that had haunted her.

"Ummm?" he replied absently as he squinted out into the desert in search of game.

"I need to know something," she stammered, unaccustomed to the growing feeling of uncertainty within her that bade her to hold her tongue. What if he thought her question prying?

"What?" he prodded after a few seconds of silence had passed between them. Turning to her, he suddenly realized that they weren't making idle conversation. She had something on her mind, and he could tell by the stubborn set of her chin that she meant to have an answer for it. Silently, he watched her, and waited for her to continue.

Inwardly, she hastily bolstered her sagging courage, and spit out the question that had been festering within her like a lump of poison.

"What will happen to us when this is over?" The words were slightly minced, lacking the strength she'd wanted them to have. For a moment she wondered if he had understood the true question that cowered beneath the one she had asked.

With a sigh, Cale regarded her with a narrow eye, his handsome face constricted into lines that almost made him look as if he were in pain.

"You have a talent for asking the wrong questions." He sidestepped the subject with the skill of an experienced dancer. It wasn't the first time a woman had tried to pin him down—only this time, things were different. He almost wanted to make the promise that she wanted to hear, but there was one big problem looming between the two of them that she couldn't see. He couldn't tell her of it, either. Even though he sensed that she had come to care about him, still he knew that this wouldn't be enough to overcome her wrath if she found out the truth about him. Somehow, he was going to have to arrange things so that she never did find out, and the only way he could see of doing that was to convince her to give up her bloodlust for El Halcon.

Irritated with his answer, Jessalyn turned a wicked glance at him, her green eyes bright with a thousand glittering shards of glass.

"I have a right to know," she insisted, her indignance and ire now rising. "What have you to hide? Are you really my friend at all, Cale, or is this all a plan to stop me from finding El Halcon?" There, she'd said it, and now the words hung like a giant weight in the air above them. She waited breathlessly for him to cut the thread and send it crashing

112

down upon her.

The muscles of Cale's jaw began to twitch angrily, and his whiskey-colored eyes bored threateningly into hers. He wasn't sure what he was getting his fur up about, though—she'd just about hit the nail right on the head.

"I wouldn't lie to you that way, Jesse." He said it as easily as if it were true. Then, feeling the tug of the strings that she held to his heart, he added softly, "There are some things that you don't know about me . . . but now isn't the time." He looked away from her into the mass of fluffy clouds that floated like patches of cotton in the sky above the mountains. "When this is over, we'll talk about them, and then you can decide for yourself. If you want to leave then, I won't stop you." He wasn't sure if the last statement was true, but he let it stand, knowing it was a poor substitute for the commitment that she wanted.

Winding her hands into Diablo's thick ebony mane to quell the wave of insecurity that swept over her, Jessalyn sat watching him, replaying his last words in her mind. What was it that she didn't know? Was he only making excuses so that he could leave her gracefully when this was over? Tears welled like dewdrops against her willow green eyes, and she swallowed hard to drive them away. "I need you." The words sounded strange, almost as if she'd spoken them in a language other than her own. "But if you're only using me, I want to know. I have to know, Cale. . . . Please." Reaching out, she placed her small hand over the rippling muscles of his arm, as if to draw the truth from him by some

113

form of sorcery. When he looked back into her shimmering eyes, he could have sworn that she *had* cast some form of spell over him. He longed to tell her the truth—all of it—but the thought of the lives that hung in the balance forced him to remain mute. Nothing could outweigh his duty to the people he had committed himself to save—nothing.

"No, I'm not. It isn't that," he answered her question simply, feeling like a man leaving a wounded fawn to suffer for want of a fatal blow.

"Then what?" she insisted, relieved, and mortified, and angry all in the same moment.

"It's as I said," he replied in a voice as cool as stone. "I can't tell you—not until after this is over."

"And if I said that it was over now?" The words raced from her mouth like reckless warriors ready to sacrifice themselves to save their queen. The moment she heard them, she shrunk inwardly from what she had become. Had she lost all honor, all courage, that she would sell her father's memory so cheaply?

"If you said it, would it be true?" Cale knew the answer before he asked the question. The beautiful young girl beside him was many things, but she was certainly not a quitter.

Gathering every ounce of the fire of her Kendrik blood, Jesse raised her proud chin and flashed a defiant glance of frosty green in his direction.

"No, I suppose it would be just one more lie between us," she replied, and then to twist the knife a bit further into his deceptive heart, she added, "I guess time will tell, won't it?" He nodded grimly, his mouth set into a hard line, and his gold-flecked

114

eyes narrowed to icy slivers. She wondered if he ached inside as she did, but rather than weaken, she mirrored his proud, cold posture, and promised herself one thing. There would be no more secrets between them. The next time Cale left her in the night, she'd follow him, and she had a feeling that would give her the key to open the doors that he had so carefully kept locked.

Several days passed, and Cale left only in the evenings to hunt. Lying on her pallet at night, Jessalyn waited with her ears strained and her nerves stretched like fiddle strings, but his horse remained securely tied through the long night hours. As several days passed, and they drew near the Paso Del Norte country, she found herself wondering if he had ever left in the night at all, or if she had only imagined it. Still, there was the nagging reality of his coolness toward her, and it flaunted its icy presence each time the hours found them alone together. In fact, as the Guadalupe mountains grew larger against the southern horizon, he grew further and further distant from her, until he afforded her little more attention than that he gave to Brett Anderson or any of the other men. In response, Jessalyn stopped her evening rides with him and drew back into the obscurity of the ranger company to escape the chill that had crept between them.

Riding beside Brett Anderson, she watched as Cale rode away on his big buckskin to hunt one evening. Following her line of vision, the lieutenant frowned, and then looked back at her with a hard, narrow eye. It drove him crazy watching her waste herself on a worthless drifter like Cody, and more than once, he'd come within a breath of telling her what he thought, but it hardly seemed his place.

"I think you should start camping with the company. We're close to Halcon country, and outside the perimeter it's likely to be unsafe." It was a perfect excuse, and privately, he commended himself for thinking of it. He knew there was no way that Cody would camp inside the perimeter, so keeping Jessalyn within would solve the problem, at least for the time being. He halfway expected a fight from her, in fact he would have bet his best horse on it, but she only nodded and looked over at him with those wide, soulful eyes.

"Very well," she said quietly. She was exhausted from too many nights without sleep, and the last thing she wanted was a lecture from Brett. "But if El Halcon finds us, it won't matter much who is within the camp's borders and who isn't," she added matter-of-factly, neglecting to mention the fact that, at this very moment, El Halcon and his men could be right behind them—or a hundred miles away. With no trail to follow, there was no way to tell.

"While we're on the subject," Brett began as tactfully as possible to mention her carrying on with Cody. They weren't on the subject, but he had a feeling this might be about as close as they would get. "I wanted to talk to you about Cody." The instant he said it, he wished he'd left things alone. Beside him, Jessalyn's thin frame stiffened as if she were made of wood, and her jade eyes took aim on him like the barrels of a shotgun.

"I hardly think that is your business," she said haughtily, her delicate chin raised indignantly to cover the guilt that swelled within her. She'd been behaving like a harlot, and she knew it, but having Brett point out the fact only made it seem worse. Without the reproach of his commanding voice and the stern presence of his steely blue eyes, she'd almost been able to pretend that he and his men didn't exist, that she and Cale were alone somewhere, free from the constraints of propriety.

Brett bristled at the air of defiance in her voice. He wasn't used to being challenged — except occasionally by Sergeant Mike, and he'd learned to ignore that. Still, he was in command here, though obviously not in her eyes.

"Jesse, why are you wasting your time with Cody?" He decided to try the personal approach. "I wouldn't trust him as far as I could throw my horse. He's a drifter and a no-good and you know it." At least he hoped she knew it, otherwise he was in for a storm that would rival the one that had shredded their tents the week before.

She opened her mouth to answer him, but stopped when his scout rounded the tall mound of mesquite brush before them and slid his mount to a halt. His face was flushed crimson beneath his disorderly mop of boyish blond hair, and his hands were clutched white-knuckled to the reins.

"Sir," he panted, struggling to catch his breath, which the wind seemed to whip it away from him. His faint blue eyes bulging with near hysteria, he spilled a string of words that tumbled so quickly one after the other as to be unintelligible. When he

117

saw that he had failed to get his message across, he swallowed hard and tried again. "Indians, sir." He choked on the lump of air that he'd fought so hard to swallow. "Comanches—they like to have scalped me!"

Anderson nodded calmly, with not even a hint of change in his cool blue eyes, and wondered to himself how much good the young scout was going to be in an Indian fight.

"Fall in with the company, ranger." He saluted the younger man away and reminded himself not to send him out on scout again. A soldier who lost his head at a little Indian sign was liable to get himself killed—or worse yet, to lead the Indians back to the company. As he watched the young ranger make his way back to the company to fall in, it occurred to him to wonder how many Indians the scout had seen and whether they were camped or traveling. Had he not been fairly certain he couldn't trust the man's answer, he would have called him back to ask. From the corner of his eye, he saw Jessalyn gather up her reins, and he reached over just in time to catch the sweat-soaked leather.

"Where do you think you're going?" he questioned, his brows darkening to an ominous line like gathering storm clouds above the deep blue of his eyes.

Jessalyn's mouth dropped open with shock, and she faced him with a glare that was equally as threatening as his.

"You know where," she returned as naturally as if she were going to the henhouse to gather a basket of eggs. "I know who your scout's Indians are. This

118

time of year, they'll be camped at Dog Canyon, and there's a good chance they have been down to trade with El Halcon recently. They might have some information about where he's camped." She neglected to add that she also wanted to leave to escape the discussion that had been about to take place between them. "Take your men five miles east and then south again to the Salt Lakes. There will be water there this time of year for camp." Impatiently, she tugged at the imprisoned bridle rein and rolled her eyes in exasperation when he did not release it. "Lieutenant, please." The words were more an order than a plea. "I know these bands well. They're Kiowa—Apache, not Comanche, and they were friends of my father's. I'll be in no danger." With that, she tried the bridle rein again, and he released it without a word.

With a frown, Brett considered the fact that he was about to allow a woman to ride alone into an Indian camp. Lord, had he lost his mind? At the same time, he wondered how he would keep her from going. It was obvious by the hard glint of determination in her eyes that even if he ordered her to stay, she would be gone the minute he turned his back.

"You'll rendezvous with us at the Salt Lakes then?" He found himself picturing the ridiculous look he would get from Sergeant Mike when he heard about this. It didn't make things any easier.

Jessalyn nodded, tossing her molten hair back over her shoulder, and squinting up into the sun to gauge the hours left in the day. It would be easier for her to go to the Kiowa-Apache camp and then get to the Salt Lakes by morning.

"In the morning," she replied steadily, and then spun Diablo off to the side and put her heels to him. In a cloud of billowing dust, they exploded away like birds set free of a cage. Crouching low over his neck, she molded herself against his surging muscles, her long coppery hair dancing on the wind behind her like a swirling stream of sunfire. Looking up at the mountains as the distance swallowed the ranger company into the desert, she felt her spirit fill with the sheer magnificence of the jutting masses of rock that reached with violet fingers to touch the sky.

Chapter Seven

Jessalyn allowed her mount to continue his ground-eating pace for as long as the terrain would allow, enjoying the soft caress of freedom and the low singing of the wind in her ear. When the low hills finally climbed to steep slopes of sharp, loose rock, she forced him to slow, but still he worried anxiously at the bit. She didn't stop to wonder at his impatient posture—she felt much the same herself. It was good to be free of the confines of the ranger company. She wanted to run straight up the edge of those slopes, and leap off the edge into the sky. It was a strange thing, the wanderlust that danced within her. It was like a playful wind nagging at the feathers of a roosting bird, bidding it to fly away.

She had been reared too freely, she thought, for she doubted more and more that she could ever settle down to one home. Her time with the rangers had made her realize just how much a wanderer she truly was. For the thousandth time, she wondered what the future would bring for her, if she would have any at all, and if she wanted any. It wasn't much of a world for a woman who wouldn't be bound by the ties of any one spot of earth. For men, this was permitted, for women, unheard of.

Perhaps she would return to travel with Sounds on the Wind and his Kiowa, she mused — that is, if she returned at all. Even that hardly seemed to matter much now. The thought of not having to find a place in the world five years hence, or ten, or fifty, seemed almost a relief. Her father had always told her to spend each moment wisely and cherish each hour as if it were made of gold, but a wealth of time hardly seemed precious when it was empty, and uncertain, and nagging to be filled.

And then she thought of Cale. A week ago, she'd been certain at least of his friendship, but now that confidence seemed like a cruel delusion. His cool treatment of her had begun to etch a scar across her heart that she knew would someday become permanent. For now, she fanned a small flame of hope and rehearsed a thousand excuses for his aloof posture in her mind — a thousand excuses other than the one that she feared the most.

Tossing the thoughts back and forth in her mind, like weights balanced on a scale, she rode on through the narrow canyons of the Guadalupes. What great imposters those mountains were, she thought, and smiled to herself. From the outside, they looked as dry and barren as any part of the desert, a formidable enemy. In fact, she suspected that there were only a handful of white men alive who knew what the Apache knew about the mighty Guadalupes — that within their dusty folds were hidden valleys with clear running springs, trees, grass, and beauty to rival any place on earth.

Rounding the bend into the upper elbow of Dog Canyon, she let Diablo have his head to navigate the slippery slope of loose rock that descended to the river below. Looking down at the water, a new idea wandered into her mind dimly, then grew bright and drove her other thoughts away. Perhaps Cale was like those mountains — one thing on the outside and another within. She heard the thought if someone else had said it, and then looked around instinctively to see who had spoken, but no one was there.

The sounds of running feet and children's laughter caught her ears and chased her thoughts away. In a few more strides, she rounded the bend and a small camp, beside the ambling stream on the floor of the canyon, came into view. It was not, as she had hoped, a main camp, but a small hunting camp with perhaps three or four families. Crude brush shelters had been carelessly lashed between several of the trees, and in front of them stood racks laden with meat. Near the racks, two women and a young girl labored over the stretched skins of velvety brown mule deer.

Jessalyn gave little thought to riding into their camp with her rifle holstered. Though she did not recognize any of the women, she suspected that they would recognize her, and if they did not, they would know Diablo for certain. She and her father had always been welcomed in the camps of the Comanche and Kiowa, and even maintained a slightly strained rapport with the fickle Apache. None had ever considered Lane Kendrik an enemy, and most had counted him as a friend. When the oldest of the women looked up from her work, and then sat back on her heels with a toothless grin, Jessalyn knew that these were among the friends.

The women moved curiously to her as she slid down from her horse and waited by his side. It would have been rude to advance first, she knew, and equally rude to have remained horseback, so she stood and waited while they smiled and discussed her behind their hands. After a moment, the old woman said several words in Apache and then waited for an answer. Jessalyn was far from fluent in their language, but she recognized the last word "Ker-dik," a mottled variety of Kendrik that she heard often. In response, she nodded, and then dropped Diablo's reins so that she could speak to them in sign.

"Ker-dik." She spoke their version of her surname out loud, and then signed, "is my father." She neglected to mention the fact of her father's death. As she didn't know them, it was better that they believe she was still under his protection. "My name is," she signed, and then spoke slowly, "Jess-a-lyn."

The older woman nodded, and then made a concerted effort to imitate Jessalyn's pronunciation. Behind her, the younger woman and the girl laughed. Doubtless, her pronunciation meant something strange in Apache.

"Come and sit with us, daughter," the old woman signed, her soft, wide eyes kind and genuine as they peeked from beneath the band of cloth that wrapped her forehead. "You are welcome here, of course." With that, she and the others turned to return to the shade of the trees, motioning for Jessalyn to follow.

Behind them, Jessalyn listened to their chatter and

smiled to herself as she caught the words for "hair" and something about "strange eyes." It was a reaction that she received often from those among the tribes who did not know her. For many of them, she was one of the few white women they had seen, and they were consistently fascinated with the differences in her coloring as compared to their own.

When they came to the skins that they had been working so carefully, they passed them without thought and continued to the ample shade of a crooked elm tree. The older woman sat first and then the younger woman, and finally the girl, though the latter sat a little further back, as if unsure of the visitor. Tucking her long legs to the side of her, Jessalyn sat in a circle across from the girl, and closest to the old woman.

"You are hunting,'" she said in sign. It was always best to begin with small talk. "Is the hunt good?" The older woman nodded in response, and signed "good" much as Jessalyn had done. Jessalyn smiled in response, a little disappointed in the other's relative lack of response. She'd have to think of another way to start things up. Her green gaze had wandered to two small children, a girl of perhaps five and a boy of about two, who watched her curiously from behind the trunk of the tree. With the resourcefulness of a skilled trader, she seized the opportunity and signed to the old woman, "They are beautiful children," for good measure, adding, "You must be very proud." That was exactly what it took to loosen the ice and open the floodgates between them.

"They are my grandchildren," the old woman signed. "This is my daughter, their mother . . ." and then she said a word in Apache that Jessalyn neither recognized or felt apt to reproduce. She'd learned the hard way that if you couldn't say a word in another language exactly right, it best to keep your mouth shut. There was always the danger that you might be calling someone a horse's backside, or something. She smiled a bit at the thought, and nearly missed the old woman's further recital of the names of the two young children and the girl who sat in the circle with them.

"It is good to meet friends on the trail," she signed, thinking it best not to tell them she'd hunted them down. They might connect her with the ranger company, whose scout their husbands had "almost scalped"—at least according to the scout. She suspected that the Apache the man had run into were more interested in hunting than in chasing down one measly Texas Ranger.

The conversation continued much in the same vein for a time, covering the different facets of hunting, drying meat, and preparing skins, and whether the skins were better this year than last. After a time, the younger woman and even the girl joined in the silent conversation, and the two young children ventured from behind the tree to look at Jessalyn with wide, sable eyes. Finally, the little boy mustered his courage and tottered over to her to touch the shimmering copper locks of her hair and point a chubby finger at her eyes. That gave the license, and then everyone wanted to look and to touch, and Jessalyn waited patiently, having endured such treatment many times before. When the excitement died, she cast a calculating eye in the direction of the sinking sun and realized that she would have to turn the conversation to the real reason why she had come.

"My father, Ker-dik, is with The Hawk," she began, and she saw by the sudden look of fear in her companion's eyes that they recognized the name. In most villages, just speaking of him was like mentioning the name of a spirit, and that was what most of them believed him to be—half spirit and half man, half devil and half friend. "I must find him. Has The Hawk traveled this way?" When they didn't answer, she added. "Do you know where he is?"

The younger woman and the girl only watched her with eyes guarded beneath their cloth headbands, and the old woman leaned slightly back and eyed her speculatively over the brim of her hooked nose. It was obvious that she knew something, but was uncertain whether to reveal it to this strange young woman who had ridden alone out of the wilderness into their camp. Finally, she signed simply, "The Hair Face." It was another name for El Halcon, Jessalyn guessed, and she cataloged it with her other information about the man while the old woman continued, "has not been here, but we saw three of his men. They stopped at our camp two days past."

Jessalyn felt like she'd just been given a wonderful gift on Christmas morning, and she had to concentrate hard to suppress a smile. So she'd guessed right about the path El Halcon and his men would take. Even with no trail to follow, they were still right on target. To give her story an extra ounce of validity, she asked, "Was my father with them?" It hurt just to think the question, and saying it was like ramming a white-hot dart into her heart. *Strength, Jessalyn, strength,* she coached herself silently.

The old woman shook her head, apparently unaware of the crash of emotion that had leveled Jessalyn's spirits.

"We did not see your father," she signed simply, and then a strange silence fell over the four of them, as if no one knew quite how to continue the strange conversation. After a time, the younger woman rescued them, her black button eyes turning to the skins that were still staked in the lengthening shade. Leaning to the older woman, she whispered something in Apache, as if to keep a secret. The old woman nodded, and then signed to Jessalyn, "The skins are drying. We must finish working them. Will you stay with us tonight, daughter?"

With every fiber of her nineteen-year-old body, Jessalyn longed to say yes, but she knew better. As much as she would have welcomed the good company and safe camp of the group, she reminded herself that she didn't know them, nor could she trust them exactly. They weren't Comanche, and it was impossible to predict exactly where the Apaches' sentiments lay in most cases. It had been her experience that they cared only for their own kind, and with others they weren't above smiling one minute and slitting someone's throat the next. Anyway, she'd found out what she'd come for, and she had a long trip ahead of her to the Salt Lakes.

"I have to go on and find my father," she replied with an honest look of regret, and wished in some corner of her mind that they were Comanche, or Kiowa. It would have been good to spend a few hours in the company of people who made her feel safe. "I

128

wish I could stay longer and talk, but you have work to do." With that, she smiled slightly in parting, and strode off to Diablo, mounting without breaking stride. Once aboard, she looked back to where the women sat watching her with a mixture of awe and confusion, and signed, "Goodbye and be safe," before turning the stallion around and heading up the canyon the way she'd come. She didn't breathe easy until she'd left the jagged chasm of Dog Canyon behind.

She let Diablo wander slowly southward, picking his way up one long slope and then down the next. With a calculated eye turned inward, she replayed her conversation with the Apache women in her mind. It was a small, but invaluable bit of news that they'd given her, letting her know she was still on the right trail. They had called El Halcon "The Hair Face," she remembered again, meaning that the man she was looking for must have a beard. No doubt he was also part Mexican or Indian—most Comancheros were. In fact, though she had never met the man, she had formed a clear picture of him in her mind—all the way down to his tobacco-stained teeth and small, cold, greedy eyes. She saw them sometimes in her sleep at night, looming above her like the glittering gem eyes of a snake, and in them was a mirror of her own hatred. She'd see that man dead, she promised herself for the thousandth time. She'd see that man dead, and left for the buzzards to pick his devil's bones—she loved the picture of it, but, in truth, felt sorry for the buzzards.

The ride through the mountains was slow, but she preferred it that way, not having seen the Guadalupes for several years. Her mind drifted back to a time when her father had taken her there as a child. They had ridden all the way there from Santa Fe, spending weeks on the trail just so that he could show her the beautiful fossils of shells and coral that glittered in the pitted cliffs there, and take her into the big caves that dipped like doorways to hell from the mountainsides. That was pretty much the way their life had been—one whim after another, with a small measure of work thrown in. Through trapping and running trade routes, they had always made more money than they could ever have use of, and Lane Kendrik had rarely let work interfere with his enjoyment of life, or Jessalyn's.

Thinking about it, that was what Jessalyn missed most—just having him there to share the carefree hours with. He always saw the beauty in things. They had traveled to places and done things, if for no other reason, just for the sake of the experience. Without her father to protect her from the dangers of life, she knew she would never be that way again. She was like a butterfly flown from the shelter of a benevolent leaf and into an ill wind. She couldn't just drift where she wanted any longer—she'd go where life forced her.

Her thoughts were dashed away like specks of dust before the cruel broom of necessity, and she reached up with trembling fingers to wipe away a tear. It was getting dark, too dark to navigate the rocky slopes, she realized. For lack of better alternatives, she pulled Diablo up on the leeward side of a small mountain, where it curved like a saddleback, and slid down off his back. She pulled his saddle and bridle off quickly, setting them carefully on the rocky ground. If there was one thing her father had taught her, it was to take good care of her tack.

Taking her pistol from the saddle holster, she took a few steps up the slope to a small knoll that afforded a good view of the area. Kicking the loose stones away to check for varmints, she settled herself beside a massive boulder, which she used as a backrest, and drew her tired legs up underneath the fringes of her creamy doeskin skirt. Hugging her knees to her chest, she watched the sky, calculating how long it would be before the moon came up. It had been full the night before, and would be again, and thus would provide enough light for her to travel.

Her stomach fretted annoyingly for food, and she hugged her knees tighter, trying to ignore it. She wished she'd had the foresight to take her pack mare from the string and bring her along. At least then she would have had some supplies, and a little jerky to eat. Apparently, Diablo was of the same mind, because he reached down to butt her demandingly for his dinner. In an unusually poor humor, she shoved his nose away and gave him a cool stare that dared him to come back.

Resting her china-doll chin on her knees, she let her silky hair fall around her like a warm blanket, and closed her wide seawater eyes. Shortly after, the dusky brush of her lashes twitched in sleep against the soft skin of her cheek, and she didn't think of food, or tracking, or death, or hatred anymore.

* * *

The moon was well up before Jessalyn awoke again, and she wouldn't have opened her eyes then except for the persistent, soulful call of a coyote that rent the still night air. It wandered into her cloudy consciousness slowly at first, like a mole poking blindly around in the darkness there, and then finally prodded her drowsy mind awake. Startled at first, she stood up in a flourish of brassy hair that glowed like pale fire in the moonlight. How much time had she wasted?

Batting the dust from her skirt angrily, she called for Diablo, and then turned a critical eye to the moon as if to chastise it for hanging too high in the sky. She should have been on her way hours before to reach the Salt Lakes in time to steal a few hours sleep before the company would be ready to start out in the morning. As it was, she would be lucky to make it there in time to step off of her horse, stretch, and climb back on.

She bridled and saddled Diablo efficiently despite the sleep-laden feeling in her limbs, and then holstered her pistol again in the saddle leather. Raising one boot up with effort, she slipped it into the near stirrup and then grabbed the saddle horn to swing herself aboard. Her bones creaked like rusty hinges as she did, and she groaned to herself, feeling a million years old — or at least like she'd been in the saddle that long. Life had never pushed Jessalyn so hard for so long before, and she was beginning to wonder privately if she'd be able to bear up under the strain.

As Diablo headed on toward the next slope in the dim golden light, she began to take an inventory of her aches and pains, for lack of a better way to keep her mind from slipping into the sleep it hungered for. All right, feet—she started from the bottom—I can hardly feel my feet except to sense that they're wet and sticky like the inside of an old man's wallet. Come on, feet, hang in there. I promise to take those boots off before morning. Only moccasins tomorrow. Ankles, she wandered on to the next howling body part, you guys feel like someone's twisted a corkscrew through you. Well, once we're over the steep slopes, I'll take you out of the stirrups and stretch you out for a while. Knees? About the same as the ankles. Legs as a whole? Whew, cramped from sleeping, cramped from riding. Feel like they're made of rope and tied full of knots. Stomach? . . .

And so she went on until she had finished, successfully managing to pass the better part of an hour with the strange dialogue. In the end, she felt no better, and her exhausted muscles and screaming joints were hardly convinced to give up their protests. So they went on, one after another, each time she shifted in the saddle, and all at once when Diablo stumbled over a rock or catapulted himself up a steep slope. Jessalyn lost track of the hours and the slow trek of the moon across the great ebony orb of the night sky, concentrating only on her struggle to keep her sagging eyes open and to hold Diablo on course. A miser couldn't have been happier to see a pot of gold than Jessalyn was to see the sheer slope of El Capitan rise black against the southern sky, like Goliath squatting in wait for travelers. With its chapel-like crest of bare rock, it marked the southern edge of the Guadalupes. Below it were the Salt Lakes.

At the base of El Capitan, Jessalyn stopped to look down over the blackened desert below. Like tiny stars twinkling against the darkness, she could see the fires of the rangers' camp. Fires, she thought scornfully, visible to every Apache that might be wandering around the Guadalupes, and they had lit fires. With a shake of her head, she dismounted, unsaddled her horse, and settled herself into the protective lap of El Capitan. She had a feeling it would be safer, and smarter, to wait for morning where she was. Taking her bedroll from behind her saddle, she rolled it out, wrapped herself in it like a caterpillar going into cocoon, and laid her head on her saddle for a pillow. She'd made better speed than she had anticipated—she'd have time to catch a few hours' sleep after all.

She was up with the sun, and feeling better than she had the night before. Unwrapping herself from her blanket with a bit of difficulty, she stood up and stretched like a tawny cat in the warm sun. With a leftover yawn, she reached down to pick up her bedroll, but then froze as if she'd been struck by lightning, the blanket dangling limply from her hand. In the dim light below, she could see the foggy images of men and horses stirring to life, and of one horse and rider creeping unseen back into camp. Even from nearly a mile away, she couldn't mistake Cale Cody and his big buckskin horse.

With anger sizzling like hot bacon grease through her veins, she watched as he unsaddled, picketed his horse, rolled out his bedroll, and then lay down on it as if he'd been there all night. Though she knew it was impossible, she would have sworn she could see the arrogant smirk on his face as he pulled his hat low over his eyes and crossed his arms behind his head. A string of obscenities that shocked even herself shouted through her mind, and she regretted only the fact that he wasn't there to hear them. So he *had* been sneaking off before, she mused, and he had only stopped because he had somehow known that she was watching. Well that was fine. If he wanted a game of cat and mouse, he'd get it, but he was going to find out that he'd just stepped into the ring with a mountain lion.

The exercise of saddling and riding down the southern edge of the Guadalupes in the cool morning air was therapeutic, and she had successfully erased all traces of her anger before she reached the Salt Lakes. The rangers had camped on the edge of the vast white-sand plain that was the remains of the long-dead inland sea that had sculpted all of south Texas in a time before time. Another stupid move, Jessalyn noted a bit bitterly, and wondered how the rangers had survived this long. It was proof that God protected fools and children. Cale Cody, on the other hand was neither one, and he was definitely in for a shower of brimstone.

She guided Diablo around the edge of the huge salt pit toward their camp, knowing that in places the thin coating of frothy sand disguised deep pits and deep bogs. Looking out across the white-sand pit, she watched the dancing mirage of reflections that made it look for all the world like a vast, cool, blue lake. Had she not been to the Salt Lakes before, she might have been fooled, but experience told her, and strangely in her father's voice, that the lakes rarely ever had any water in them, and when they did it was tainted with alkali. There was fresh water not far off, though, in several small runoffs, and there was even a large spring-fed lake that stayed the year around. She wondered why the rangers hadn't camped by one of those, as even the most incompetent of their scouts couldn't have failed to find them, and decided that it had to have been for her benefit. By now she was well enough acquainted with Brett Anderson to know that if she said, "At the Salt Lakes," he'd be the type to camp right in the middle of them. No doubt, he had pictured her riding down out of the mountains and going into a squalling female panic at not finding them exactly at the lakes.

She hadn't even made the rangers' camp when she came face-to-face with Sergeant Mike's opinion of the camping arrangements. His leathery face was red with corked anger and he was puffing like a steam engine as he strode across the salty sand to her.

"Well, thank God and all the saints by name you're back!" He flailed his arms skyward as if receiving a blessing. "You could of told the man, 'Near the Salt Lakes,' or, 'One-half mile south of the Salt Lakes,' but, NO, 'At the Salt Lakes,' you said, and here we sit like a bunch of turkeys trussed up for Christmas dinner. Even lit fires last night so every damned redskin in the territory would know right where to come to get 'is gifts." Deflated like a squashed balloon, he stopped, sucked in a great gasp of air, and then went on, shaking his head all the while. "Damn! Next time you're going to ride out, take me with you. I'm a sight sure it'd be safer. It's a wonder you didn't come back to find us all sitting around drinking coffee without our scalps."

Sliding down from Diablo's back, Jessalyn hung for a minute from her saddle horn to let the blood tingle into her feet before standing down on them. Her laughter tinkled in the air like the sounds of good fortune bells as she turned back to him, her young face bright with mirth.

"I had no idea you had become so dependent on me," she chirped cheerfully. "But you shouldn't have worried. I was sitting right up there by El Capitan, watching over all of you like Saint Gabriel."

This time, he laughed with her, cherishing the sparkle in her emerald eyes and wondering what it was about her that made her laughter so infectious. It was worse than the pox.

"Yeah, well you'd of had to of been one hell of a shot to have done us much good from up there," he retorted, and then regretted his use of the obscenity. She seemed so much like part of the company that he sometimes forgot that she was a young lady.

She smiled again, wide, sweet, ear-to-ear smile that made her look like a schoolgirl.

"Yes, well," she imitated the scratchy tone of his aged voice with a fair amount of skill, "Sergeant, I am one . . . heck of a shot." She couldn't bring herself to say "hell." Her father would have come down out of heaven and slapped her full across the face for it, she was sure.

They turned to stroll back to camp, Jessalyn laughing, and the sergeant wondering what had put her into such a good humor. He wasn't sure exactly what she'd done on her trip, but, whatever it was, it must have turned out exceptionally well.

Beside him, Jessalyn was laughing and wondering much the same thing. She didn't have much of a reason to be so cheerful, but for some reason, she'd almost forgotten all about the anger that had burned within her at seeing Cale slip into camp earlier that morning. Perhaps it was Sergeant Mike's comical display that had made her so giggly. Perhaps it was the benefit of a clear day and the promise of a good breakfast, but more than likely it was the effect of exhaustion.

When they reached the camp, she left Sergeant Mike to go on about his business, which consisted of bellowing at one man and then the next. Tying Diablo next to her coyote dun mare on the picket, she noted with a bit of confusion that none of the horses were yet saddled. Looking around, she saw the reason in the form of a young ranger, Judd Smythe who was, in keeping with his name, busily resetting shoes on the lieutenant's big bay. Letting the gelding's foot down, he stood up and gave her a wink and a smile.

"Takin' advantage of the delay to set a few loose shoes." He talked in a long, slow, southern drawl that oozed like molasses through the warming air. "I did yer mare already, but I'd reckon yer stud horse could use it too."

Jessalyn opened her mouth to assure him that, while she hated the task, she was capable of shoeing a horse herself, but a strange sincerity in his brown eyes stopped her. She said, instead, "Yes, Mr. Smythe, he could." And she awarded a smile that was genuinely grateful. Though her father had taught her how to shoe as soon as she was big enough, she'd usually begged off of the backbreaking task. "But don't put yourself out, please." She couldn't help but feel that she was taking advantage, and she smiled again, a bit more guiltily. Before turning to head for camp, she added. "And thank you for shoeing my mare. It was awfully kind." She went away feeling nervous, awkward, and a bit embarrassed. For as long as she could remember, people had been going out of their way to be kind to her for a number of different reasons—because she was Lane Kendrik's daughter, because she had no mother of her own, or because her hair and eyes differed from their own. It had never embarrassed her before, but now she felt shy and strangely bewildered by it.

At nineteen, Jessalyn Kendrik was as arrestingly beautiful as a goddess, as modest as a school marm, as clever as a gambler, and totally bewildered as to why men seemed to bend over backward to accommodate her.

Chapter Eight

Jessalyn ate her breakfast like a grizzly bear coming out of hibernation, and, though it consisted only of stringy rabbit meat and tough beans left from the night before, to her it tasted like a feast. In fact, she would have gone for a second helping had she not become embarrassed and decided to take her horse to water instead. To her surprise, he had already been taken to water when she arrived, no doubt by the young Ranger Smythe, and stood in his newly set shoes looking dreamily about and dripping from nose to tail. Rolling her wide, gemlike eyes, she laughed, wondering how badly the young ranger had been surprised by her stallion's drinking habits. When Diablo went to water, he meant to have a swim of it, and no matter how hard they tried, a few hundred pounds of human resistance wasn't going to keep him away from it.

Still giggling to herself, she wished that she could have joined him, and absently considered it, but shook the thought away. It wouldn't have been much of a swim anyway with fifty rangers coming and going from the watering hole.

Scratching a toe in the dirt, she uncovered a small chunk of sandstone, and bent to pick it up. A smile twitched on her coral lips when she turned it over in her hands and realized that it was what her father had called a "rose rock," a small piece of glittering red sandstone inexplicably formed to look like a perfect rose, frozen in time at the moment that it had fully bloomed. Once when she was a child, she had collected a pocketful of them and made herself a tiny garden to see if they would grow. It had only been when her father had explained the difference between rose rocks and roses that she had finally given up the experiment.

It seemed a strange thing to remember now, she thought, as she'd never particularly recalled it before. In a dim reality, the answer to the sudden importance of that long-ago event came to her, and she clutched the stone tighter. That day in her rose garden had been the day that she had first understood what it meant for something to have life. Her stone roses had taught her the difference between life and lifelessness that day, and her vast universe had tightened a painful notch. Life had been a series of those sorts of discoveries, most of them painful, and each time the former vastness of the world had seemed just a little more constricting. She supposed it was that way for everyone. Life had only so many molds, and whatever shape a person was born to, he'd be pushed and stretched around until he fit into one of them.

With a sigh, she turned away, the stone rose still clutched in her fingers, and wandered back toward the camp. Gazing up at the clouds that rose over the Guadalupes like a set of fluffy, snow-capped peaks, she turned the rock over and over in her fingers absently and thought of the clouds. After a moment, she stopped to watch them billow above El Capitan into an imposing line and draw the morning sunlight as if they had suddenly become something solid. The stark chapel rock of Capitan which had ruled over the Guadalupes just a few moments before now looked like a dwarf squatting at the feet of the towering cloud-mountains, like a court jester who had only been pretending to the king's throne in his absence. What deceptive country, she thought, with lakes that weren't lakes, mountains that weren't mountains, and roses that weren't roses—a perfect place to be hunting a man who wasn't a man, or to be hunted by one.

She would have stumbled over Cale's outstretched boot if he hadn't seen her coming and pulled it lazily out of the way.

"You'd better watch where you're going." His voice was touched with honey and laughter, and the barest hint of a smile tugged at the corner of his mouth from beneath his lowered hat brim. "If I'd have been a rattler, you'd be in trouble."

Jessalyn watched him in shock for a moment, regaining her balance. Her thoughts had been so deep that she hadn't realized she'd started walking. Now, she'd clumsily brought herself face to face with exactly the man she'd been trying to avoid. It was a rotten way to spoil a good morning.

"If you'd have been a snake, you'd have made some noise to warn me off," she retorted coldly, recalling his stolen entrance into camp earlier, and her blood boiled once again at his acting as if nothing had happened. Her jade eyes glistening white-hot with veiled suspicion, she added, "But then, perhaps all snakes don't play by the same rules."

He nodded a point to her in the joust of words and pulled his hat back away from his eyes slightly to look up at her.

"Begging your pardon, ma'am." He spoke with exaggerated formality. "But we snakes have a code of ethics just like everyone else."

Not to be seduced by his honeyed manner, Jessalyn dropped the stone that a moment ago had been so important to her, and held an imaginary pad and pencil out as if she were going to write something.

"I'd like to know where to report an infraction of the rules, then." If it hadn't been for the firm set of her pretty chin, he might have considered it a joke. It mattered little, though, as she didn't remain to see his reaction, but spun on her heel and continued about her way with determined strides.

Watching her go, Cale shook his head and laughed to himself, his amber eyes turned soft and golden with humor. Reaching out, he took the stone from the dust where she had dropped it, and held it gently in his large hand. Blowing the dust from it, he kissed it softly as if it were a fragrant bloom, and then dropped it into his shirt pocket, saying, "Stone roses, roses of stone." It was a line of a poem he remembered from a life that seemed a million years away.

Jessalyn rode beside Brett at the head of the company, her eyes a deep seawater green in the shade of the tawny leather bolero that she had fixed over her glossy head. Her gaze was steady and fixed ahead of her, and her face was carved with the same cool, oblivious expression that she had worn for most of their trip. Beside her, Brett could tell it was going to be a long day. She'd set an impossible goal for them to reach—nearly forty miles yet—and she showed no sign of relenting. When he'd questioned the wisdom of trying to push that far, particularly in the grinding heat of August, she'd given him a chilly, narrow look from beneath half-closed lids and had informed him that they'd have to go that far to reach the next good source of water. He was in a poor position to disagree with her, as the only man he had who could track water was bone-afraid of Indians.

Feeling the pressure of Brett's steady blue gaze, Jessalyn looked off to the side and let her hair fall like a silk curtain between his probing gaze and her thoughts.

"Tonight, we'll be camping about ten miles out of El Paso," she said, after a while, in the overly casual tone that usually bespoke some insane plan. "I'm going to ride in tomorrow and try to gather some information about El Halcon's fortress."

If the lieutenant thought he'd heard everything before, he was certain of it now.

"Not alone," he returned steadily. This time, he wasn't about to give in. She'd warped his view of this command almost to the point where he couldn't recognize it, but not to the point where he'd let a beautiful young woman go alone into a hive like El Paso.

"Better alone than with fifty Texas Rangers," she

144

retorted, now turned to face him. "Everyone in that town is wanted somewhere for something. If fifty rangers ride in there, the whole town is likely to go into a fit." She almost laughed at a mental picture of the dusty border town turned topsy-turvy by the appearance of a troop of Texas Rangers riding down main street. It would be like a hill of ants suddenly dug up by a shovel—chaos—except these ants had shiny guns, itchy trigger fingers, and bad tempers.

"Just you and I will go, then," Brett suggested quickly, almost too quickly. In the back of his mind, he'd been afraid she would suggest that she make the trip with Cody. He hadn't missed the sudden rift between them, and, given his druthers, he'd prefer to widen it all he could.

She eyed him with a little surprise for a moment, and then nodded, her dusky lashes brushing her cheeks with each nod of her head. There was no reason to fight with him over it. She couldn't have him with her in El Paso, mainly because he'd stick out as a Texas Ranger anywhere, even without a badge. Given that fact, there was only one solution—she'd have to pretend to agree now, and then leave without his knowing it in the morning.

Jessalyn sat atop Diablo's weary back looking down into a shallow sinkhole canyon. In the bottom of the canyon, like water trapped in the neck of a funnel, sat a small pond which reflected the deep blue of the cloudless summer sky. She was tempted to rush headlong down the hill and dive right in, but she held back. Even from where she stood it was obvious that something was wrong. There were no tracks around the small pool—which meant, of course, that it was poisoned with alkali.

If she'd been fool enough to think that the world was ruled fairly, she would have complained to the man in charge. Poisoning the only source of water for ten miles seemed a pretty cruel trick to play on fifty thirsty men and a herd of exhausted horses. Turning around in her saddle she could see the company crawling like a lazy caterpillar over the far horizon. The tired horses hung their heads near the ground, and the men angled their hats awkwardly against the persistent late afternoon sun. Men and mounts alike were covered with a thin coat of silty dust, until all were nearly the same color. Slowly, they moved one step and then the next, carried only by the promise that the day's travels were almost over. It wasn't going pleasant telling them that they were going to have to ride ten more miles after all.

Mercifully, it didn't turn out to be quite as far as she had remembered to the next source of sweetwater, and they reached it just as the heavy waning moon was rising large on the eastern horizon. Slowly, stiffly, men dismounted and led their horses to the small backwash hole that hid in a dry creekbed near the base of a stark cliff. To anyone else, it might have looked like too small a watering hole for so many, but to them it looked like an ocean, and each patiently waited in line while the others watered three at a time.

It was nearly half an hour before the horses had all been watered and picketed, and the men went wearily about gathering dead mesquite wood for fires. In the process, they grumbled about the ride, the country, the command, and the absence of fresh meat for dinner, and asked what were they paying Cale Cody for, anyway, if he couldn't show up on time. To Jessalyn, who had been trying with singular determination to ignore the fact that Cale was strangely absent, the discussion finally became unbearable. Taking her horses and packs, she set up camp in a protected crook of the dry creekbed a slight distance outside their perimeter. As she led her horses away, she saw Brett, and then Sergeant Mike, frown at her action, but she ignored them, and neither came to challenge her openly.

Before she had had time to settle her horses and get her packs moved to her campsite, Ranger Smythe appeared with an armload of wood. Smiling almost shyly from beneath his mop of brown hair, he started a fire for her, and then inquired if he could do anything else on her behalf. When she replied in the negative, he bid her good night almost reluctantly, saying he'd be only a holler away if she should need him, and then walked slowly back to camp. Watching him go, she smiled to herself at the tendency of men to assume that a woman was helpless. She could scout water all day long, meet with Indians, ride into unknown territory, and lead a party of Texas Rangers for hundreds of miles, but everyone in camp—down to the last man—was certain that she was completely incapable of gathering wood for a fire.

She lingered on that thought for only a moment, then turned briefly to thoughts of dinner, but these faded in the face of the weariness that had begun to overtake her. Before long, she'd laid out her bedroll and thrown a good stack of wood onto the fire, and then she'd curled up beside it, and fallen deeply asleep.

She dreamed that night of the stone rose garden, only this time the sandstone buds were planted in neat rows that stretched as far as she could see. She, sitting in the middle, was a child again, and she could hear her father's voice from somewhere far away, but she could not see him. Lost, she called to him, running up one row and then down the next, like a child lost in a cornfield, but no matter which direction she went, his voice was still just as distant. She ran faster as his words began to fade, and she could hear the fragile stone roses crunching like dry grass beneath her feet. A few seconds later, her foggy mind awakened to the realization that the crunching sound of the footsteps was real. With a start, she sat up and reached for her pistol, but it was not on her bedroll where she had left it.

"Looking for this?" It was Cale's voice. When she looked up, he was sitting across the fire from her dangling the small gun upside down between his fingers in exactly the same manner as he had that night in the spring canyon. The corners of his mouth lifted into a smile as he set the gun down beside him and explained, "I didn't want you to shoot me before you knew who I was."

Even in a drowsy stupor, Jessalyn found a good answer for that, and her eyes crackled with white sparks as she spoke.

"How about after?" She extended her hand to request the return of her pistol. "If you'll give me my gun, I'll be glad to shoot you anyway."

Throwing back his tawny head, Cale let out a raucous laugh at her quip, and slid the pistol around behind himself. As he had once before, he had the strange feeling that she was only halfway kidding.

"You look angry, love," he remarked. That much was more than obvious. What he didn't know was what he'd done to deserve such wrath. Granted, he had sidestepped the issue of commitment with her, and he might have avoided her to keep the conversation from cropping up again, but that hardly seemed to warrant the anger that flashed like green fire in her eyes.

More than anything, Jessalyn would have loved to confront him about his sneaking into camp like a thief the morning before. She would have liked to demand that he explain where he'd been and why, but instead she pasted a mirthless smile on her pretty lips, and said, "You know what they say." Her voice was sharp with sarcasm. "Heaven hath no wrath like a woman—"

"Scorned?" he finished, before she had a chance to.

She nodded, a downward brush of sooty lashes against her cheek hiding the thoughts revealed in her clear green eyes.

"That's what they say." The pale reflections of the flames danced like fireflies against the measureless depths of her eyes as she looked up again. Thoughtfully, she repeated the statement, turning her eyes upward in mock contemplation. "Heaven hath no wrath like a woman scorned," she said, and then added, "Hmmm . . . It has a certain ring of truth to it, don't you think?"

The inviting smile on Cale's lips dipped to a frown at the razor's edge of ire in her voice. His eyes were hard as two pieces of cool brown stone before he spoke again.

"And why is it that you feel you've been scorned, my dear Jesse?" Then he answered the question himself. "Perhaps because I don't play this game the way that you would like?" This time, it was Cale who turned a thoughtful eye upward in a nearly perfect imitation of Jessalyn's former posture. "And why all of this anger when you claim to only want friendship? Perhaps because it is more than friendship that you want?"

Clenching her fists into the folds of her skirt to hide her anger, Jessalyn leveled a narrow gaze at him that could have spit hellfire.

"Not if you were the last man in the Republic!" she countered, her voice shaking with restrained anger. "I don't want anything from you, Cale Cody. Not your friendship, not your help, and least of all your . . ." A flush of embarrassment rose over the proud curve of her cheeks, and finally, she finished, "Anything else."

Meeting her eyes with indifference to her anger, Cale stood up.

"Methinks she doth protest too much," he quoted from a play he'd read in that long-ago lifetime he only half remembered. From where he stood, he looked down at her as if she were a wounded animal, as if he were deciding whether to save or shoot her. Shaking his head, he said, "You're a child in a man's world, Jesse, and a dangerously pretty one at that." With a quick step, he came around the fire to her

150

and bent over to catch her chin as she backed onto her haunches. With his eyes meeting hers levelly, he added, "You'd better watch more closely what kind of men you choose for friends, Jesse mine. More than a few of them might have your skirts in mind."

Her mouth dropping slack in shock, Jessalyn winced inwardly as the words struck some unnamed portion of her heart. In their wake came a hot sting of tears, and she scolded herself desperately to keep them away. *Oh, Lord, don't start blubbering like a child now, Jesse,* she thought bitterly. *This idiot will think he's been right all along.* Her bottom lip quivered ever so slightly as she struggled to find her quaking voice and mold it into something convincing.

"I'm not as stupid as you seem to think," she said, but evidence to the contrary glistened like crystal in the corners of her gemlike eyes. "I had you pegged right all along." Pulling loose of his grip, she rose to her feet, and bit her lip to keep the tears back as he stood up and towered sternly above her like a domineering father. "Don't concern yourself with me, Cale Cody." She couldn't force herself to meet his eyes, and instead stood watching the fire, like a youngster guilty of some misdoing. "I survived fine before you came along, and I wager I'll be fine after you're gone." With all the dignity that she could muster, she turned to walk away—to find some dark place to hide—but the gentle grip of his hand on her arm stopped her suddenly. Reluctantly, she let herself be turned around, and, as her eyes met the heat of his, her defenses came crashing down around her like towers built of ice.

151

In that moment, faced with her fragile young beauty and wide, desperate eyes, Cale melted as if he'd been made of salt, and all he could do was pull her close and stroke her coppery head. It took every ounce of strength within him to keep from telling her that every thing would be all right. Things weren't all right, he knew, and they weren't going to be. Despite everything he'd tried, she had stubbornly led fifty rangers right to the edge of Halcon country, and now things were going to have to come down to a fight. What gnawed at him the most was how he was going to keep her out of the middle of it. He'd considered every possible course of action, and none seemed to solve the problem.

"Let me go after Halcon for you," he said after a time. It was an idea he hadn't thought of before, and he was still formulating the plan in his head as he spoke. It was a stroke of genius—if only she would settle for it. "I promise you I'll see him brought to trial for your father's murder." He could feel the resistance gathering in her slender young body even before she stiffened and pulled away from him.

"No," she said simply, taking another step backward. "It has to be me that goes after him." Her face grew dark and unreadable, and her eyes chilled with the blind hatred that had driven her since the day of her father's death.

"Jesse," he scolded, his voice so sweet it could have dripped maple syrup. He reached out to take her hand in his, but she pulled away and watched him warily from a safe distance. "What difference does it make? Why do you want to drag fifty men in there and get them killed?"

"I'm not going to take them in there," Jessalyn blurted out before she'd had time to think. Her eyes widened in horror as the plan that she had so carefully kept secret painted itself like a picture in the air between them.

"You are going alone, then?" Cale said it, but he didn't believe it. Even mad with grief, she couldn't be that insane—or could she? "You can't possibly hope to bring him . . ." Cale paused as some small hint in the depths of her eyes confessed the rest of her plan. "You don't intend to bring him out, do you? You're going to sneak in there and try to gun him down." He realized he'd hit the nail right on the head as the blood poured out of her face, leaving her ghostly white against the dancing brass border of her hair. "Do you realize how much blood will be shed in the aftermath?" He waved a hand toward the lights of the ranger camp. "The blood of those men you claim to care for so much?"

Desperately, Jessalyn struggled to sort out the mass of conflicting emotions within her—and to maintain the belief that she could somehow bring about El Halcon's death without bringing his devil's wrath down upon the ranger company.

"There already has been bloodshed!" she defended herself valiantly, though even she was hard pressed to believe the twisted logic that had driven her after El Halcon. "My father is dead, and I won't see his spirit leave this world unavenged. I owe him that!"

They stood face to face, only a few feet apart, yet separated by a vast chasm that ran with a river of blood, and hatred, and sorrow. It was Cale who first realized that this was a stalemate, and it wasn't the first time he'd found himself on the business end of her unwavering determination. Still, every decent shred of him — albeit they were a minority — demanded that he do something to save her from herself. Silently, he vowed that if it came down to it, he'd carry her off kicking and screaming and lock her away some place where she couldn't hurt herself.

"I guess there's no point in arguing about this," he observed, an easy smile playing on his sensuous lips as he took a step closer to her. "You wouldn't have enough sense to come in out of the rain, child," he remarked fondly, catching her in his strong arms in the frozen moment before she would have retreated from him.

Far away, a clap of thunder roared as if on cue, and a jagged streak of lightning rent the horizon. Out of reflex, both of them looked at it, and Cale rested his chin on the top of her head, watching the storm. "It'll never make it over the mountains," Cale remarked absently, referring to the storm, and then looked deeply into her eyes to watch the tempest there. Gently, he bent and kissed the softness of her lips, and then smoothed a few stray strands of copper away from her cheek. Feeling an almost-familiar pang of desire, he forced himself not to linger in her charms, and instead stepped away. No matter how much he wanted her, it would have been too cruel to have acted on that desire. For all of her courage and skill on the frontier, she was little more than a child, and even he was repelled at the thought of spoiling a thing so beautiful and so fragile. In a few days, he would never see her again, and everything he did to make sure that they wouldn't remember each other would, in the long run, be for the best.

Jessalyn awoke in the early hours of the morning either because of a sound or because of some strange instinct, she didn't know which. It seemed as if every nerve in her body had been set afire at once, and she was sitting upright on her bedroll before she realized what was happening. Sitting very still, she strained her ears into the darkness. From somewhere very near, she heard the muffled sound of stones crunching beneath a horse's hooves, and she knew almost immediately that the horse was Cale's. A glance toward the picket where her own horses stood confirmed her suspicions, as the big buckskin was no longer beside Diablo.

Reaching for her moccasins, she thought of the strange meeting that she had with Cale only a few hours before—of being reduced to tears, of giving away her plan, of accepting comfort from him. All along something had whispered deep within her that she should not trust him, that he would stop at nothing to keep her from going after El Halcon, but she had driven those fears away. Now, they came rushing back to her with righteous vigor as she took her saddle and moved quickly to tack up her stallion. Part of her feared that he had left to go after El Halcon alone, and part of her feared something worse, but she could not put words to those feelings. They dwelt in some cloudy corner of her mind that was ruled by intuition, or instinct, and they were growing more powerful each moment.

Without a reservation, she checked to be sure that

her rifle was loaded, and then holstered it and her pistol on her saddle. Leaving her belongings and her packhorse behind, she mounted and set out after the lone rider who was already just an eerie moving shadow in the faraway moonlight. She was grateful for the light color of his mount, which made him easy to follow. To her advantage, the dark color of her mount made her almost impossible to see against the moonshadowed desert, and she rode easily out of earshot, but within sight of Cale.

For nearly an hour he picked a trail through the chaparral brush and sand hills, and she followed carefully behind him, occasionally losing sight of him for a time among the thickest tangles of mesquite and greasewood, but never long enough to lose him completely. As the misty fingers of dawn spread lazily from the sky behind them, she dropped back even further for fear of being spotted. The sun was just sitting like an overturned teacup on the horizon when his destination, a towering volcanic dome of glittering red rock, leapt up in the west with strange suddenness. She recognized it immediately, as she had been there before. Most called it El Hueco, or The Hollow. With its myriad caves and water-holding basin, it was a popular camping spot for Apaches, travelers, and outlaws. Now, as Cale disappeared around the edge of the huge, cup-like mass of rock, it looked like a perfect place for something terrible to happen, and Jessalyn approached it with a growing sense of dread. She had a feeling she was going to learn something that she didn't want to know — like the day that her father had told her about the stone roses. How strange that she should think of that again just now.

Stopping on one side of the dome, she watched Cale disappear into the inner hollow, and decided that it would be wise not to follow. Once inside, she would be trapped, and easy to spot. Looking up at the twisted mass of once-molten rock, she plotted a better alternative, and dismounted from her horse.

Taking her rifle, she slung it over her shoulder by the leather thong that was tied from the barrel to the pistol guard, and started up the tumble of massive rock. It was slow climbing, but not difficult, and her strong, agile legs quickly carried her to the top rim of the cup-shaped *hueco*. Moving on all fours, she crept to the edge of the rim, where she could see clearly into the basin below, and then laid her rifle down beside her to peer over the edge.

In the basin, she could see at least four men, mostly Mexican or Indian, and six horses, four for riding and two for packs. They were in the process of giving Cale a boisterous greeting as he dismounted from his buckskin, and Cale, in his unmistakable way, was returning their good-natured jabs. It was more than obvious that they all knew each other well, and that none of them suspected that they were being watched. Sitting together around a small fire, Cale and the others began to discuss something, but from where she hid, Jessalyn could hear only the sounds of voices, not the words. In the next heartbeat, she was glad she couldn't. Her eyes caught on something that came into view as one of the saddle horses swung around to look at the men. On the saddle pad, woven unmistakably in bright shades of red and blue was the sign of The Hawk, and Jessalyn knew all at once why she had dreaded coming to El Hueco. She'd learned something she didn't want to know, all right. She'd been carrying along a spy ever since they had left Bent's Fort. Cale Cody was one of El Halcon's men, and no doubt he'd told them every move the ranger company had made.

Laying her head down on the cool surface of the rock she clenched the butt of her rifle until the blood drained from her fingers and left them ghostly white. She thought of every time that Cale had touched her, of how she had allowed herself to need him, to trust him. Her stomach turned violently, and she thought for a moment that she would be sick, but swallowed the bile. Rolling onto her back, she slid away from the edge into the safety of a deep crevice between two boulders and wrapped her arms tightly around herself. Pulling her knees to her chest, she leaned against the rough, cool rock and sat staring blankly ahead, unable to face the turmoil of pain and confusion within her.

Chapter Nine

The minutes melted slowly away, disguised in robes of horror and betrayal, and finally Jessalyn closed her eyes tightly to the blossoming day around her, unable to bear the contrast between that and the shivering darkness within her. Memories of each moment she had spent with Cale flooded her like swallowed poison, and she put the heels of her hands to her ears to shut out the haunting faraway sounds of laughter — his laughter. Hatred began to kindle like a slow flame against the murky dampness in her soul, and one by one she drove each of her memories of his touch, his kiss, his laughing eye, behind a stone wall and locked them away.

Taking her gun from the ground beside her, she held the barrel tightly and leaned her forehead against the blackened metal. Breathing deeply, she fought the urge to climb back to the top and put a bullet through his treacherous heart. It would have been foolish, she knew, and the wilderness had not raised her to be a fool. She wanted to see him suffer for having betrayed her — and her father — but her original purpose still ran deeper than her hatred for Cale. She had vowed on her father's grave that she would see El Halcon dead, and she would.

Slowly, she began forming a new strategy in her mind. It would do her no good to lead the ranger company any further, as Cale would no doubt be telling his Comanchero friends every move they made. Her only alternative was to go on to El Halcon's mountain fortress on her own, but first she'd have to get her packhorse and provisions. Her moccasins lifted by the wings of her new purpose, she climbed out of the crevice and jumped skillfully from one shelf of rock to the next as she descended the dome. Diablo stood where she had left him, and she mounted quickly and gave him her heels. The ride that had taken an hour in the darkness wouldn't take long at full speed, and if she was lucky she could get back to camp and out again before the rangers were up and about.

Her hastily laid plan worked perfectly, as she made it to the camp before the bulk of the ranger company had stirred from their bedrolls. Packing her camp with resolute, but nonetheless shaking, fingers, she kicked her fire out and then tied one of the unburned pieces of brush to her pack mare's tail. Mounting up, she secured the mare's line to the back of her saddle, and headed into the cover of the sandhills and brush. Behind her, the branch trailed from the mare's tail and wiped from the sand all traces of her passing. Even the most skilled eye would have been hard pressed to trail her, and she was counting on that. Whatever happened, she didn't want the rangers to be able to follow her to

El Halcon. It was her fight, not theirs. They wouldn't have a chance against the Comancheros in this country, and she owed them what little protection she could give.

After she was safely away from the camp, Jessalyn stopped and untied what was left of the branch from her mare's tail before continuing on. Behind her, the safety of the ranger company faded into the distance, and ahead loomed the barren mountains that hid El Halcon's fortress. Like dusty sentinels, they rose from the level sandhills and stood shoulder to shoulder, blocking the horizon. Anyone who didn't know better would have sworn that the line of sheer cliffs was impenetrable, but Jessalyn knew otherwise. Several years before, she'd watched her father cross through a narrow pass into those mountains to trade with El Halcon. As usual, he had left her behind with the pack animals, but luckily he hadn't kept her from seeing the location of the pass.

A short distance from the cliffs, she dismounted in a shady thicket of tall mesquite and untied her coyote dun from Diablo's saddle. Stroking the mare's black-tipped muzzle affectionately, she unstrapped the packs and laid them on the ground. Then, she gave a jerk on the mare's halter rope and let it fall to the ground. She knew the well-trained mare wouldn't wander from the ground-tie unless thirst eventually forced her to break her training and seek water. It was the only safe way to leave an animal behind on the desert — particularly when the chances of returning were slight.

From the packs, she took a small amount of

jerked beef and a few other necessities and wrapped them in a bandana which she tied to her stallion's saddle. Signaling the ground-tie one last time to the mare by again jerking down on the rope, she mounted Diablo and headed back into the blazing afternoon sun. Ahead of her, the cliffs of El Halcon glinted in the sunlight, as if they had been carved from layers upon layers of gold and silver.

When she drew close enough to the cliffs, she began to study them with a calculating eye, trying to remember that long-ago day when she had been there with her father. Recognizing the pass that he had used was her only hope of getting in, she knew. With countless miles of unbroken cliff face, she could ride for days before happening on the hidden entrance, and by then, the ranger company would have found her. With jade eyes narrow and intense like those of a prowling cat, she studied each feature of the growing mountains—each outcropping, each crevice, each curve of rock layers or change of color—searching for something familiar. In the end, it was an insignificant buckle in the welded layers of rock that caught her attention. She knew immediately that she had found the pass, and she spurred her horse toward it.

When she had made it to the opening, she slowed Diablo as his hooves began to clatter on the hard bedrock of the mountains. A strange shudder shook her small shoulders and then ran the length of her body all the way to her toes as she passed through the narrow break in the cliffs. Her mind recalled a lithograph of sinners entering the gateway to hell that she had once seen in a book. She felt frighteningly like one of those lost souls as she looked up at the sheer towers of rock on either side of her. More than anything, she hoped the devil hadn't set a guard at his back gate that day.

The hawks were gliding in graceful hunting circles above when Jessalyn found El Halcon's fortress and climbed the steep slope to the south of it. Like a chameleon, she crept up the slope in the cover of the large long-dead volcanic rivers that cut like jagged scars through the mountainside. She had spent nearly an hour studying the fortress from the east slope, watching the men come and go, before she had decided that the south rim of the canyon would afford the best chance to get off a shot and then escape. She had positioned Diablo at the bottom, in the cover of a scrappy-looking thicket of greasewood, before starting the long climb up the slope.

Her mind raced over every detail of the fortress as she climbed. She pictured every inch of the adobe-walled fortress that she would have a clear shot of from the south wall, and estimated it to be only about thirty percent of the fortress. That had worried her at first, for she couldn't call down and ask El Halcon to present himself in the clear-shot area so that she could kill him—and then she had spotted the well. She had easily figured out that El Halcon was not in the fort; therefore, he must be out with some of his men—and where was the first place thirsty men went when they returned from the desert? To the well, of course. Given that, she figured that her chances were good—her chances of firing a shot that hit true, that is. Her chances of getting away were somewhat poorer, but that seemed only a small hitch in an otherwise brilliant plan.

There was another problem in the fact that she had never seen El Halcon in person. In truth, any of the dark-skinned Mexican and Indian men below could have been him, except that none of them fit the two things that she knew about the man she had hunted. The first she had learned from the Apache, who had called him "The Hair Face." The second she had heard her father telling another man. "You'll know him when you see him," Lane Kendrik had said then, with no idea of how important the statement would later be. "He always wears a red bandana with the sign of The Hawk embroidered on it in gold." It wasn't so much to go on, Jessalyn knew, but it was enough. Somehow, she felt that she would have known the man even without those two signs, felt as if she would have sensed his presence like that of some evil spirit, half born of her own hatred and half born of the devil.

Had she not been so preoccupied with the climb and her plot, she might have noticed the man who stood on the ledge above her before he cocked his rifle. As it was, she didn't look up until he spoke.

"Entonces, what haf we here?" His voice was thick with a Spanish accent, but she heard the words as if they were in perfect English. Wildly, she stumbled backward and reached for her pistol, but stopped and was forced to the side as he jumped down from the rocks above her and landed where she had just stood. "I wouldn' do thot, señorita."

164

The threat in his voice was as unmistakable as that in his hard, black eyes.

Taking another step backward, Jessalyn fought her rushing heart, and tried to think of some plan for escape. As she heard the steps of another man behind her, she knew there was no hope. In the next instant, she was dragged roughly backward by her hair and pinned up against a greasy, naked chest. She coughed involuntarily as the stench of filth and sweat filled her nostrils, and struggled wildly as her captor dragged her back down the hill, speaking in deep, rapid Spanish to his partner. It was the first time in her life she'd wished she didn't understand the language, and as the reality of their plans for her penetrated every fiber of her body, she set loose with claws and teeth and sharp feet to free herself.

She might have managed it, had there not been two of them, but when she had finally freed herself, the younger man took a step forward and swept a boot across her ankles, sending her sprawling backward. She landed hard against the rocky ground, and felt the air rush from her lungs, leaving her dazed for a moment.

"Ah, compadre, I thing she like you," said the huge man who had been her captor as he bent over to nurse a newly injured knee. "I let you haf her first, eh?"

Together, they laughed as the younger man set down his rifle and took a menacing step toward Jessalyn's crumpled form. Driven to action, but unable to force her limbs to move, she scrambled away, hardly aware of the sharp gravel that cut into her back and elbows like slivers of glass. Before she could struggle to her feet, he pushed her down again, and squatted over her, his hard eyes on fire from beneath dark brows. In another instance, she might have thought him handsome, but as he grabbed her chin and thrust his mouth toward hers, she felt her stomach retch, and a horrified scream was torn from her lips. Another would have followed, for her mind had nearly reached complete hysteria, but he clamped a hand down roughly over her mouth and leaned close to her ear.

"Ah, *querida,* do not bring others to our little nest," he threatened in a low voice, and then caught her tender earlobe in a bite which drew blood before he released it. "It would be so much more pleasant if it were only you and I." He laughed, and shrugged toward his partner. "And Oso, of course, but I doubt that he will be as gentle as I." Soft, wicked laughter caressed her cheek as he moved to her mouth, stopping only for a moment to whisper. "Don't fight. Perhaps you will enjoy it." His hand moved away from her trembling lips, and his lips came down hard in its place, wetting her mouth carelessly and smothering her screams. She felt his hand move greedily, hurriedly to the fabric of her shirt and tear it away, baring the creamy skin of her breasts. Grabbing roughly, he kneaded her tender skin in time with the rhythm that had started to move his thighs against her.

It was at that point that the horrified fog in Jessalyn's brain evaporated like magic, and instinct took over. Her mind ran to the knife that she always kept tucked inside her boot, and she moved her hand slowly downward until she felt the carved bone handle. With the speed of a skilled hunter, she had it against the man's throat, and was staring up into his eyes as he froze.

"Don't think I wouldn't," she warned in the most steady voice she could manage. Still, her words quaked pitifully, and she wondered if they would convince anyone. Without giving him time to assess her intentions, she added, "Now get up . . . very slowly."

"All right, children, that will be quite enough." A voice from behind them startled them both to their feet, and Jessalyn's captive took a step back to safety. Before she turned around, Jessalyn had already identified the source of the new voice with a name.

"Sam Horn," she said as she spun about to face him, and found herself staring into the barrel of a well-aimed shotgun. "I'm surprised to find you hanging around with this Comanchero filth."

Sam smiled, tossing his loose waist-length hair back of his shoulders like a dark cape, but not lowering the rifle.

"Oh really?" he questioned, his handsome face lit with the mirth of a good joke. "What sort of filth did you expect to find me with?" His eyes sparkled with a boyish charm that made him seem younger than his twenty-two years as he looked from Jessalyn's poised knife to the two men whom she had pinned against the rocks. "Now, Jesse," he said with an air of reproach. "I think it would be best if you'd put that knife down."

Jessalyn cast him a narrow-eyed sneer in response, and flipped the knife into the air, watching it turn over twice, and then catching it by the back of the blade. Wrapping her slim fingers around the cool metal, she made ready to throw.

"I'm sure you do," she replied sarcastically to Sam's suggestion. "But I think it would be better if I ran one of them through with it." She had no doubts that from this distance she could do it. Her father had been almost legendary with a knife, and in the past few years, she had become almost as skilled as he.

With a laugh, Sam gave the two captives an appraising glance.

"But which one?" he questioned, appearing as unconcerned as if he were merely an actor in a scene to which he already knew the ending. "Oso is a bigger target, but too fat to kill with one throw." Sam ignored the indignant look he received from the large man, and cocked his head to one side, closing one eye as he appraised the second man. "No . . . I think you'd better go for the mestizo if you want to kill someone. He's been asking for it anyway." For his decision, Sam received a wicked glare from the sentenced man.

"You're a lousy bastard," he complained, obviously failing to see the humor in the situation. "I'll come back from the grave and take you with me."

Sam shrugged off the other's lack of appreciation for what he considered to be a very good joke, and jumped down into the crevice with them, his blue-black hair flying like a dark cloud around him.

"I shouldn't bother to save you," he said over his shoulder as he turned his back to the men and took a step toward Jessalyn, extending his hand palm-up

168

for the knife. "Damned Mexican half-breed," he muttered absently, advancing a step closer to Jessalyn. "Never met a mestizo that wasn't as mean as the devil's elbow. Mexican and Indian blood is a bad mix." He continued advancing toward Jessalyn and talking at the same time, hoping to distract her from throwing the knife, which he was quite certain she could do well. "Now me on the other hand, well, you can see that white and Indian blood mixes well—creates a superior specimen. Nope, none of the mean Mexican blood here."

Worried as he came almost within reach of her, Jessalyn drew back the knife and took aim at the mestizo.

"Don't," she said, watching Sam from the corner of her eye, "come any closer." Catching what she thought was a wrinkle of apprehension in his smooth brow, she pressed her advantage. "Tell them to get out of my way. All I want is to leave."

Sam shook his head, drew up the rifle on her, and cocked back the hammer.

"I can't do that, my dear." He said it with a note of regret. Honestly, he wished he could have let her go, but now she knew how to get into their fortress, and who they were. According to Cale, she was determined to kill El Halcon no matter what she had to sacrifice to do it, which meant, of course, that he couldn't let her go no matter how much he wanted to. What bothered him most about the situation was the fact that he couldn't fathom an end to the problem. With what she knew, he couldn't see how they could ever set her free, yet they couldn't hold her prisoner forever. He tried not to think of it as he met her wild green eyes. She looked like an animal in a trap. "Now put that down, Jesse," he coaxed, lowering the aim of his rifle, "or I'm going to have to shoot you . . . in the foot to keep you from killing these men."

Jessalyn's cool emerald eyes searched his face for a moment, gauging the seriousness of his intentions. Despite the faint lines of a smile that still tugged at the corners of his mouth, he looked deadly serious. Finally, she could see no alternative but to surrender, and she flipped the knife into the palm of her hand, extending it to him as if on a platter. Her pretty lips bit a bitter scowl as he stepped aside and motioned for her to walk in front of him. With reluctant obedience, she moved around him, discreetly reassembling her blouse on the way. When one of the other men moved to come beside her, she spun around with the fury of a harpy.

"Keep your friends away from me." She shuddered visibly, remembering the horror that they had dealt her only a few minutes before. She'd rather be dead than be touched by either of those men again.

Indulgently, Sam waved the men away with a slight sideways nod.

"Go back to your posts," he ordered with a commanding ease that seemed to come naturally. "I'm sure I can get her to the fort from here." At the doubting glance he received from Oso, he laughed, and added, "Don't worry." He motioned for Jessalyn to move on and fell into step behind her, calling back, "If I have to, I'll shoot her in the foot."

Her face hidden from his view, Jessalyn seethed in silence at his betrayal of the short friendship that they had shared at Bent's Fort. With the instincts of a true survivor, she began planning again as they walked down a long valley to the entrance of El Halcon's fortress. When they rounded the corner, and started down the narrow passageway that was the only entrance to Halcon's canyon, she felt her hopes fall down to her toes. Looking up at the sheer cliffs that lined the canyon, she was seized by the realization that they looked ten times as formidable from the bottom as they had from the top. A hundred Texas Rangers and a thousand prayers wouldn't be able to rescue her from there. One thing was certain—she was now truly, and irrevocably, on her own.

Flinging herself down on the bed, Jessalyn stared up into the darkness that lent strange shapes to the beam and mud ceiling. There was nothing left to do. She had paced the room for hours, searching every inch, every crack and crevice of the bare chamber for a weapon or a tool with which she might chip away the mortar from the window bars. Even if she could have found something, it would have been a useless task, she knew. El Halcon had built his prison well, and even if she'd had the benefit of a hammer and chisel, it would have taken a hundred years to chip her way out. In defeat, she settled down to think of another way, but fear and doubt drove away each plan that began to take shape in her mind.

Resolutely, she began again to analyze all that she knew about the compound, about El Halcon, and about her own small cell. It added up to a pitifully small bowl of porridge, and she chafed at her own foolishness for having set out after a man she knew so little about. Even worse was the fact that she had let herself get captured. She couldn't help but imagine what her father would have said, how disappointed he would have been in her. And she had failed not only him but herself.

With a sigh, she swung her long legs over the side of the low bed, stretching her toes within her knee-high moccasins and wishing she could take them off. She would have if it hadn't been for the fact that at any moment someone could come to haul her away, and she wanted to be fully dressed if that happened. Running her slim fingers through her hair, she rested her elbows on her knees and sat cradling her head in her hands, thinking.

Her brightest and best hope, if it could be called that, lay with Sam Horn, who had hardly proven so far to be a knight in shining armor. Still, he was not the same kind of ruthless beast as the men who had almost . . . she couldn't bear to think of what the other men had almost done to her. Sam had even treated her with some remote form of kindness while bringing her to her cell. He had ordered the hordes of greedy-eyed Comancheros to keep back from her as they had crossed through the yard, and surprisingly, they had all kept silent. He had even given her one of his own shirts to wear in place of the one the mestizo had torn. What he had refused to do was to tell her what they intended to do with her—and this was what she needed to know the most.

The worst thing about the moments that ticked silently by her in the dark room was the uncertainty that they bore. If she had known for certain that they intended to kill her, the knowledge would almost have been a welcome gift. Then she could have made her peace with God, whom she seldom prayed to but always tried to follow, and waited for the time to come. In fact, if she had had a weapon, she would undoubtedly have saved them the trouble. She'd seen the way that Comancheros could kill a person, and she'd much rather have robbed them of the joy of it. Considering the grisly details, she recalled having once heard an old trapper say, "Always save one bullet for yourself," and now she realized the wisdom of it. Still, even if she'd had a bullet, she would lack a gun to fire with—Sam had made sure of that. He'd carefully, and humiliatingly, checked her for weapons in a manner that insinuated it was a fairly routine chore for him—only with men, not with women.

Sam was undoubtedly one of El Halcon's right-hand men, Jesse thought to herself almost as if speaking to another person in her mind. It was plain that he held a place of high rank in the Comanchero band, and he moved about in the fortress with the ease and certainty of a recognized commander. Privately, she struggled to reconcile this fact with the fact that he so often seemed little more than a carefree youth. No matter how hard she tried, she couldn't picture Sam Horn raping women, killing children, and scalping other men, but she knew Comancheros too well to think any differently. Comancheros were worse than the Comanches themselves for brutality—the Comanche, at least, were bound by a strict code of ethics and beliefs. The Comancheros were bound by none. They were a ruthless bunch of Mexican, Indian, and half-breed renegades who were little more than pirates and killers.

There were two questions that rapped away at the walls of her clear picture of Comancheros. The first was the question of where exactly Cale Cody fit into their band, and the second was the question of why her father had been involved with them to begin with. Her father might not have been an angel, but he had never condoned killing the innocent or stealing from other folk. He could not have approved of El Halcon and his men. Where, then, was the link?

The sound of the bolt moving in the door exploded her thoughts away, and sent her heart pounding into her throat. She'd found her feet and dashed to the far wall before her mind even caught up with her instincts. Out of fear, she searched the room again for a weapon, but it was obvious that the stark furnishings had been designed with prisoners in mind. She watched the door open slowly and saw a massive, bearded man who outsized even Oso lean in to check the room. She didn't miss the greedy leer in his dark eyes or the yellow-toothed smile he cast in her direction, and she pressed harder against the wall behind her. It probably would have been a good time for a display of courage, she thought miserably, but even this seemed to

174

have left her and she could only stand helplessly, watching him with wide, glittering eyes.

In another moment, the man stepped back, and Sam appeared in the doorway. When he saw her, the corners of his mouth tilted upward into an amused grin.

"Now that's hardly the girl I remember," he teased, as if they were two friends sitting in a parlor over tea, rather than captor and captive. When she made no move to respond, he nodded to the tray he carried in his hands. "Thought you might like something to eat and drink. Killing outlaws is thirsty work." He set the wooden tray down on the table beside the bed, his eyes never straying from the motionless girl. With a slight shrug of his shoulder, he slid the saddlebags that had rested there into his hand and set them on the bed, saying, "Thought I'd bring you your things before everyone had a chance to divvy them up. Had a hell of a time catching your stud horse, though—thought I might have to shoot him in the foot too." At the horror that washed her face white, he rolled his dark eyes, and gave her an incredulous look. "Now do you really think I'd do that? You're not much for jokes, are you?"

"Not at the moment," Jessalyn replied after taking a deep breath in an effort to gather her scattered wits. "Somehow this isn't so funny from my point of view."

Sam gave her a noncommittal shrug, and turned away slightly, as if to keep himself apart from her plight.

"It shouldn't be," he said honestly. "You're in a

lot of trouble." A serious expression tightened his handsome young face, and then with a toss of raven hair, he shrugged it away. "Have something to eat," he suggested. "I'll wager it's better than that trail food you've been eating."

At his request, Jessalyn took a step forward and cast the food a critical glance down her small nose. The last thing she wanted to think of was food—in fact, the very sight of it made her stomach flip unmercifully.

"My last meal?" The question was partly in jest, and partly a ploy to gather information about their intentions for her. Sam recognized the disguised attempt immediately, and turned a heartless stare in her direction.

"Could be," he said simply. "That depends on what . . . Halcon decides to do with you when he gets back." Lazily, he took a heavy chair from beside the window, where she had earlier been using it as a stepping stool, and brought it over to the bed. Turning it backward, he straddled it and crossed his arms over the back.

Jessalyn's eyes narrowed a bit as she replayed his last words in her mind. There had been something strange about them—something odd in the way he had called El Halcon's name, almost as if he were unaccustomed to it, if he hardly knew the man. With a forced look of interest, she moved to the bed and sat down, taking the tray of food in her lap. Indeed, the fresh, grilled chicken and gravied bread meal were a feast compared to the trail food that she had been eating, and she felt her appetite tug at her stomach. She took a small bite of the bread stuffing before looking at Sam with a deliberately nonchalant look.

"Have you ridden with El Halcon long?" She hoped the question didn't sound as planned as it was.

Realizing her words for what they were, Sam parried her thrust by saying, "Ummm, quite a while." Smiling white against his dark skin, he raised his hands into the air in a gesture of helplessness. "Quick riches, you know. How's a poor half-breed supposed to resist a deal like that? Women, money, excitement, horses, . . . women—oh, I already named that one, didn't I?" He laughed with boyish amusement at his own humor, and then gave her a petulant frown when she only eyed him narrowly. "I have to admit we've had livelier captives than you, Jesse," he complained. "You could at least cry and beg for mercy or something."

A sarcastic smile twitched her full lips, and she tossed her coppery hair back resolutely.

"When pigs fly," she said, hoping it sounded more defiant than it felt. The way her stomach was flipping around, she suspected that, in order for her to keep the oath, the sky would have to fill with winged swine very soon. Stubbornly, she fixed her eyes on the tray in her lap, and finished several more bites of the food before her throat constricted with a prickle of tears. Setting the tray aside, she took a swallow of water from the clay cup Sam had brought, and washed the tears into her stomach.

"That's the spirit," Sam complimented her, and then stood up, reaching for the tray. Before going out the door, he turned back and gave her another glance, his eyes meeting the wide expanse of hers. He could tell by looking that her hard-won courage had about deserted her, and the realization left him with a bad feeling. She'd need every ounce of guts she had when Halcon got back. She'd led an entire company of rangers down Halcon's throat, and he was mad. In fact, Sam had never seen him worse, and that bode ill for the cause of the problem— which was, unfortunately, Jesse Kendrik.

Chapter Ten

Three days passed slowly by the small, iron-barred window that was Jessalyn's only portal to the outside world. Save for Sam, who came several times daily with food and fresh water, she had seen no one. She was no closer to learning their plans for her than she had been when she first arrived, and it was the uncertainty of each passing moment that lashed the deepest welts in her spirit. She probed Sam when she could, but more and more often he came in a temper that could only have been called sulky, and he stood near the door watching the window and thinking. She desperately wondered what it was that had made him so unlike himself, but the deep, brooding cast in his raven eyes warned her to hold her tongue.

Each day, the food remained fresh and wondrous, a banquet compared to the meager trail rations she had been eating for a month, but finally her appetite dwindled under the weight of her burdened mind. Her appearance grew unkempt and careless, which she had never before allowed it to become, even on the worst of trail trips, and finally she felt so little like herself that even her unconquerable spirit fell to its knees.

As the third day grew dusky outside her window, she sat curled into the corner of the hard bed, her head resting on the cool wall. Her eyes, which were fixed on the last pale strips of sunlight left in the bleak room, didn't stray when the door bolt opened and Sam stepped in. Behind him came two large, dark-skinned men who bore in their hands an enormous copper tub. With a few odd looks and several rapidfire questions in Spanish, they set the tub in the center of the floor, and then walked slowly out of the room. In the doorway, they stopped to look at the tub, then at each other, then exchanged a helpless shrug and walked away speculating about the doubtful condition of Sam's faculties.

In the wake of the two Comancheros came two rather hefty Comanche women bearing wooden buckets, which they emptied efficiently into the tub before going for more. After several trips, they had filled it nearly three-quarters full, and then they left, exchanging gossip behind their hands and giggling, Sam followed them out with a quick word to the guard at the door. He reappeared shortly, carrying packs which Jessalyn recognized as her own; apparently they had found her mare and her belongings where she had left them. She watched with a mixture of curiosity and mistrust as he laid her packs on the bed, along with soap, a wash brush, and a clean piece of cotton yardage for a towel.

"What is that for?" she asked finally, unable to watch the strange goings-on in silence any longer. Perhaps, she thought, she was staying in their usual bath chamber, and they had now decided to make double use of the room.

With a flick of his silky hair, Sam stretched a hand toward the bath in ceremonious fashion, and gave her a smile that glistened like pearl against his cinnamon skin.

"You look like you could use a bath," he remarked, and for his reply received from her the same perplexed frown that he had been given by the two Comancheros who had brought the tub.

"You . . . you have to be kidding," she said after a moment. Suddenly, she felt like she'd been transformed from a prisoner to a queen. In the next instant, this brought her a bit of relief. After all, you didn't bother to bathe people you were about to kill — and that was a good sign. As Sam took a step in her direction, a touch of fear widened her wide kitten eyes, and she stood up, protesting, "Not . . . I can't with you here . . . you have to leave first."

Sam smiled at her modesty and cocked an obstinant sideways glance in her direction, folding his strong arms over his chest.

"What are you worried about?" he questioned. "I see this sort of thing every day. After all, we Comancheros pillage women for a living, you know."

"That's what I'm afraid of," she replied quickly, taking the posture of a reluctant goat determined not to be tugged to water. With a righteous fervor straightening every inch of her small form, she stood her ground, waving a nervous finger at the tub. "If you think I'm going to take a bath in that tub, while you stand there and watch," looking like a preacher on judgment day, she moved the accusing finger in Sam's direction, and finished, "you've gone completely out of your mind!"

Sam buckled forward in laughter, propping his palms on his knees to support himself. Several moments danced away to the chorus of his raucous laughter before he could again straighten up. With exaggerated pomp, he waved a hand over the tub, as if to present it to her.

"As you wish, milady." He stood back, folding one arm behind his back in a dapper fashion that conflicted hilariously with his rugged Comanchero-style clothing and uncut hair. As fair reward for his performance, he received from Jessalyn a reluctant smile, which lasted only for a second and then faded. Expectantly, she looked from him to the door before moving an inch toward the bath.

His steps light with laughter, Sam went to the door and knocked twice for the guard outside to slide back the bolt. Waiting, he cast a more serious eye at Jessalyn, who had moved to the bed to inspect her newly recovered belongings. Looking from her to the copper bath, he wondered about the wisdom of borrowing El Halcon's tub, but then shrugged the thought away. It had been worth the trouble and possible repercussions. The battle over the bath had done exactly what he had hoped it would—restored Jesse's spirits, and she was going to need every ounce of fire she had when Halcon rode in. Besides, he decided, in the condition she'd been in, it was likely that Halcon would have thrown her to the coyotes. After a bath and a change of clothing, Sam thought with a smirk, the man would have a hard time levying so cruel a judgment on her.

Jessalyn looked up as Sam disappeared through the doorway, leaving her alone, and breathed a sigh of relief. For a moment, she had feared that he'd been serious about watching her bathe, and she'd rather have stunk like Grandma's lard bucket than to have endured that. Now, the bath beckoned irresistibly, and, picking up the towel linen, the scrub brush, and the soap, she went to test the water. It was deliciously warm as she dipped her fingertips into it, and she closed her eyes, swirling her hand around and drinking in the scent of the sweet yucca soap.

The water hadn't cooled another degree before she had shed her soiled clothes and stood naked beside the bath. Wrapping her arms around herself, she glanced around shyly, half expecting to see a pair of greedy eyes leering at her from the window, or to hear the bolt slide open in the door. With a shiver that shook her inside and out, she stepped hurriedly into the warm water and sank down until the sweet-scented murky liquid enveloped her small waist and teased at the taunt peaks of her breasts. Her breath drew in involuntarily in a gasp as the warm water caressed them, and she closed her eyes for a long moment, vaguely remembering the strong touch that had once lingered there.

Her peace was short-lived, and soon she again felt the uncertainty that whispered in small voices from every corner of the room. Her mind again beset with the perilous nature of her own future, she forced herself to go about the business of washing her hair with the sweet-scented soap. Then, flipping her wet mane back over her shoulder, she sat up and carefully scrubbed every inch of her skin until it glowed soft, pink, and clean. Finally, she lay back against the curve of the oval-shaped tub and rested her head against its warmed copper rim. Her eyes drifted closed as she absently stirred patterns in the layer of fluffy soap bubbles that had formed on the top of the tub. She'd intended to rest for only a moment or two, but in that moment, sleep danced in on the shimmering bubbles and stole her away like a clever thief.

When Jessalyn awoke, it had grown dark outside, and even darker still within her small cell. Only the misty streams of moonlight that filtered through the bars gave any light for her to see by. The bathwater had grown cold, and her teeth chattered unmercifully as she stepped out and dried herself stiffly. Wrapping the damp yardage around herself, she trotted clumsily to the bedside table where her one small kerosene lantern sat, and lit it, holding her hand around the globe for warmth. In short order, it blazed yellow light into the room, and she moved to the bed to sort some clothing from her packs.

Strangely, when she started unpacking her things, she found most of her common clothing to be missing. Only the new outfits that her mamacita had made remained, and she chose a dark burgundy skirt and a soft rose blouse that had been embroidered to match. It felt strange to be dressing herself at what must have been close to midnight, and her softened skin protested the prickly cotton clothing. Still, she reminded herself of the necessity of being prepared should anything happen—and it could, at any time.

When she had finished dressing, she took her hairbrush, stopping for a moment to run a thoughtful finger over the carved doe on the handle. Her father had made it for her—how long ago had that been? It seemed like a million years ago. Suddenly, everything did.

Running the brush through the long, willful tangle of her coppery hair, she looked up at the barred window, which framed a host of glittering stars. She considered each day that had passed since her father's death one by one, as she brushed her silken tresses into curls around her finger and dropped the shimmering ribbons to her waist. At that moment it seemed that she had wasted too much precious time fanning the flames of her hatred for her father's murderers, yet at the same time she hated them still. Part of her vowed that somehow she would see that a life paid for a life, yet a gentler person within her regretted each moment that she had wasted in hatred, like pearls thrown to the wind.

She sat listening to the good and evil within herself battle like ghosts in the silent darkness around her. Finally, her eyes fell closed, and her hand fell slack in her lap, the brush dropping from her fingers and clattering away in the darkness onto the floor. The hollow sound it made startled her eyes open for a moment, and she pulled the rough wool cover back and slid into the warmth of the bed. The voices in her mind battled on for a time before they, too, became weary, and sleep ferried them all away to some peaceful isle of imagination.

Jessalyn awoke what seemed like only moments

later to the sound of the bolt in the door. Only the fact that the oil lamp had burned out told her that she had been asleep for hours rather than for only a few minutes. Her body tensing and turning to ice, she sat up and fumbled for the dial of the lamp to raise the wick. Her eyes shot back to the door, and her hand froze in midair as the heavy hinges creaked open, and the black outline of a figure appeared there.

She opened her mouth to speak, but her voice seemed strangled in her throat, and she could only sit mutely on the bed, frozen like a statue. Finally she reached again to fumble for the lamp, and this time succeeded in turning up the wick. She watched the black abyss of the doorway with piercing intensity until the lamp finally blazed up, filling the room with light. When the light reached her visitor, revealing his identity, she wished she had never turned the lamp up in the first place.

"Cale," she breathed, hovering between anger and relief. At least, it wasn't El Halcon come to kill her, or one of his men come to do worse. Still, as Cale came closer, there was a vague threat in the caramel depths of his eyes that she had never seen before. It was almost as if he were a different person than the one she had known. The laughter and mockery was gone from his features, leaving in its wake only hard, unrelenting lines that made him at once more handsome and more frightening.

For a moment, Jessalyn could not find her tongue, but when she did, it was wicked. As he stepped to the side of the bed where she sat, still pressed into the corner, she skitted to the other end

186

and jumped to her feet. Glaring at him with hatred blazing like an altar flame in the depths of her green eyes, she braced her hands on her hips to keep from flying at him with claws bared.

"You bastard." She spat the words as if they were poison, her voice low and quivering with the force of the wrath that had been simmering in her ever since she had seen him with the Comancheros at El Hueco. "You said you were my father's friend. You said you would help me." She pointed an accusing finger in his direction, her aim shaking wildly in the near-hysteria that had overtaken her. "You said you would help me!"

Cale watched her steadily, his handsome face impassive and his sensuous lips set in an unmoving line as he waited for her storm to ebb.

"I tried to help you," he said finally, when he was sure that she had finished. He took a step toward her, but then stopped, either because she backed away or because the lamp caught the hurt in her eye, lighting it up like a beacon. It wrenched strangely at his heart, and he continued in a gentler voice, "I tried every way I knew to get you to go back, but now, Jesse, you've turned a problem into a disaster." With a sigh, he crossed his strong buck-skin-clad arms over his chest and leaned back against the wall. Shaking his head, he hoped to gently impart to her the seriousness of the situation she had stubbornly got herself into. Looking away from her and out the window, he said, "You've brought forty-nine Texas Rangers to El Halcon's front door, Jesse, and he's far from pleased about it. On top of that, you've proven that you know

187

where his fortress is." His eyes shone like rings of gold reflecting the moonlight as he turned back to her. "By coming here, you've made it impossible for him to let you go."

Jessalyn swallowed the lump of fear that caught in her throat at his words and looked back at him with a defiant tilt that did little to hide the terrible pounding of her heart. With it booming like a steady drum in her ears, she took a step closer to him and then leaned forward into the full light of the lamp, her eyes meeting his.

"Then why don't you tell him to kill me and be done with it?" She shot the words like an arrow, and gave him a narrow glare that drove them straight on. Every ounce of Kendrik blood within her meant it. She'd rather die than live as the prisoner of the man who had killed her father, rather die than see him live another day on God's earth. And she'd have done almost anything to be free of Cale—forever.

With a cloud of anger paling the hard-cut features of his face, he clenched his fists at his side to keep the reins to his temper.

"You're lucky he hasn't, Jesse mine," he growled from between clenched teeth. "And he may decide to yet." With an agile move, he crossed the room and caught her wrist in his hand just as she raised it to strike him. "Right now," his voice was low, and his breath hard against the pink skin of her cheek, "he is too busy with forty-nine Texas Rangers pacing up and down the cliffs looking for a way in. But mind yourself, Jesse, your time will come."

Something in his statement caught in her mind.

She'd heard it once before, but this time it had struck an discordant note within her.

"Forty-nine?" she whispered, her gaze swinging downward and darting madly about the floor, as if trying to find a lost piece to a puzzle. "But there were fifty—fifty, not forty-nine." She looked back to Cale, her wide eyes soft as willow leaves as she searched his face desperately. There had to be some mistake.

"Not any more." Cale said it with pleasure—not that he relished killing a man, but because it seemed in some perverse way to prove what he had warned her of all along. Bringing the rangers here would force a slaughter, he'd told her that how many times—ten, twenty? The killing had started with only one man, but judging from their persistence, more would have to follow, until the ones that were left gave up. "It seems a young Ranger Smythe was so desperate to rescue his damsel in distress that he rode out alone to the cliffs." He recounted the details of the first blood to her, gathering strange satisfaction from the horror that caused her to shake her head in disbelief and pull away. "He found the entrance before we had time to conceal it, and we had to kill him." Tears rushed into the wide expanse of Jessalyn's eyes, and suddenly Cale felt himself struck by a wave of guilt so strong it knocked him silent. At that moment, he would have given anything to be able to take back his words. She needed to be told, but not like this—not with the insinuation that it was her fault the man was dead. *She* hadn't intended for it to happen.

"It's my fault," she whispered hoarsely before

turning away from him and burying her face in her hands. Tears seeped like liquid crystal through her fingers and streamed down the trembling backs of her hands. "What have I done? I never should have brought them here. I . . . It's my fault."

Dimly, she felt the warm circle of Cale's arms pull her close, and she pressed her palms against his chest in a pitiful effort to free herself. He was her enemy, a voice cried from the back of her mind—he was a partner to the man who had killed her father. But in the next moment, that voice was drowned away by a crushing need for the comfort he could offer and the trembling fingers that had sought to push him away now clung like a child's to the fringe of his buckskin shirt. Her soft, bitter sobs disturbed the dark, silent air, one after another shaking her small frame until it seemed as if she would shatter into a thousand pieces.

Lifting her into his arms finally, Cale kicked the chair aside and carried her to the bed. Laying her down there, he covered her gently and then stroked the silken strands of copper hair that fell like a blanket over her tightly closed eyes.

"Go to sleep, Jesse mine," he whispered, still stroking her shimmering hair as he sat on the edge of the bed. Looking down at her, he was surprised by how young and fragile she looked—like a tiny china doll with the moving eyes tipped shut. It was almost impossible to fathom the consequences of what she had done in leading the rangers to El Halcon's fortress. In the farthest stretch of his imagination he would never have thought that she could do it the day that he had first seen her at

Bent's Fort. In fact, he'd underestimated her every step of the way, perhaps because she was a woman, perhaps because she seemed so young.

He rested his hand on her shoulder as she stretched onto her back in sleep, her soft breasts peeking temptingly out where a button had come loose on her blouse. Feeling her heartbeat beneath his fingers, he moved his hand to touch the firm, white swell of her breasts. A tugging in his loins caused him to pull his hand away and lean his head back against the wall with a groan. There was another thing he'd underestimated with regard to Jesse—the strength of the hold she had on him. He realized it now, albeit reluctantly because it only made things more complicated, and he also realized that the sooner she could be let go the better. He couldn't keep her here forever, and the hatred that had been in her eyes when she looked at him had told him that she'd never stay of her own free will.

Still fiercely telling himself that she'd have to be sent away, he leaned down and kissed her parted lips lightly before standing up and walking quickly from the room. In the doorway, he stopped and looked at her again, trying to assess exactly what it was about her that tied strings to his heart. If he could figure it out, he thought to himself, he could erase those things from his mind, or find another woman who could mirror them. Without the obstacle of her accusing eyes, he considered every facet of her beauty, but no one seemed of singular importance—or else every one did. He was forced to conclude that there was something intangible about her that he found compelling, an odd combination of strength and weakness, of fire and ice. She was a world of paradoxes in one pretty shell, and that, in a word, was what had him by the scruff.

Shaking his head at himself, he stepped into the dark hallway and closed the door behind him, sliding the bolt into place before he walked away to find Sam.

The last tiny clink of the bolt rattled Jessalyn from her fitful sleep, and she rolled over onto her side, rubbing the hot, tearstained skin of her cheek against the pillow. Pulling the covers over her, she burrowed into them and curled her knees close to her. In her mind, she saw the face of young Ranger Smythe as he had looked the day he had offered to water her horses — young, sweet, and slightly embarrassed. It seemed impossible that he could be dead. He was probably no older than she, and certainly too young to have had his life taken away.

Her mind concocted a thousand alternative scenarios, but the irreversible fact was that none of them would change what had happened, nor could they change the fact that she was to blame. All that she could do was find some way to keep more from being killed. She set her mind to the problem with singular determination, and, after a time, the only possible answer came to her. Somehow, she would have to convince the Comancheros to allow her to go and send the rangers away. She would have to tell them that she had been mistaken about El Halcon, that he was not the one who had killed her father.

Even the thought of it left a bitter taste on her tongue, and she felt her heart again grow cold with hatred for a man whom she had never met. One day, she promised herself, one day she would see him pay the debt he owed her father. For today, though, she had to prevent any more blood from being spilled on her behalf.

Sitting up, she smoothed her disheveled clothing and ran the brush through her brassy hair until it cascaded down the curve of her shoulders like a sea of molten copper and gold. The dim light of morning filtering through the window told her that Sam would soon be bringing her breakfast, and this would give her the opportunity to convince him to help her with her plan.

When the bolt slid open, Jessalyn jumped to her feet with anticipation and stood fidgeting nervously as she waited for the heavy door to swing open. When it did, she saw to her disappointment that the bearer of the breakfast tray was not Sam. She did little to hide her feelings as a tall, muscular form appeared silhouetted in the doorway where she had expected to see Sam's smaller, leaner frame. Before her guest stepped into the dim mixture of lamplight and sunlight in the room, she knew who it was. There was something in his manner—a grace and easy confidence—that was unmistakable at any distance.

"Back so soon?" She bit the words out with a bitterness that let him know her softening toward him the night before had only been a temporary weakness. "I hoped that you and I had finished any business that might be between us last night," she added for good measure, and, at the moment, she meant it. She wasn't sure if she had ever hated anyone in her life more deeply than she hated him—except possibly El Halcon. Each time she looked at him, and this time was no exception, she felt wounded, ill-used, and betrayed all at once. Each time her eye caught on the beautiful, well-muscled curve of his body, each time her gaze met the burning golden flecks of his, her heart leapt into her throat and fell to her shoes at the same time.

An easy, melting smile curved the line of Cale's lips, raising the strong, tanned bones of his cheeks so that the smile touched his eyes.

"Sorry to disappoint you." He gave no indication that he had taken her words seriously. In fact, he seemed to be operating under the delusion that she was making some sort of elaborate joke. Setting the tray on the bed table, he lowered himself easily to the bed, and then waved a hand toward her breakfast. "A meal fit for a queen," he chided good-naturedly, his disposition obviously improved vastly over the previous night.

With an angry glare, Jessalyn crossed her arms in front of her and resolutely denied the beckoning in her stomach.

"Something has spoiled my appetite." She indicated to Cale with a snobbish nod in his direction. With an impatient glance toward the door, she added in a more civil tone, "Why didn't Sam come?"

Cale's brows drew together a bit at her question, and he felt a strange pang of irritation strike within him. It was the same sour note that he'd felt when Sam had done everything but beg to be the one to bring Jessalyn her breakfast. Now, having seen the attachment from both sides, he wondered what had gone on in his absence.

"Sam has other things to do," he replied flatly, though it wasn't the truth. In reality, Sam was probably curled under a rock somewhere, bawling like a baby who'd just lost his favorite toy. At the stricken look that paled Jessalyn's delicate features, he asked, "And why is it that you wanted to see Sam so badly, anyway? You going to try to talk the poor addle-brained babe into helping you escape?"

Jessalyn's eyes widened for an instant at his assessment of her original plan for Sam, and then she painted an impassive mask over her face, though she did not trust her voice to speak. Before she could collect herself, Cale saved her the trouble.

"It isn't likely." He gave her a sidelong glance, as if sizing up her reaction to the news. "El Halcon is Sam's brother. He isn't likely to betray his blood for comely looks and a few pretty smiles — not even ones as lovely as yours, my love." When she didn't speak, but only regarded him with blushing, wide-eyed indignation, he stood up and took a quick step forward, effectively pinning her against the wall. "This time, you seem to have got yourself into a problem that all of your sweet looks and innocent ways cannot buy you out of, Jesse mine. There is no one here who will betray Halcon to help you. They know it would mean their deaths and yours." He caught her small chin in his hand and held it tightly, his eyes bearing heavily into hers. "Remember that, Jesse. If you want to survive, you will mind that wicked tongue of yours, and keep those clever plans for escape to yourself."

Jessalyn returned his words with a glare that could have turned a charging grizzly into a pillar of salt. Apparently, she didn't want to survive, because her wicked tongue, as he had called it, was ready to spill out every vile insult she'd ever heard.

"I certainly don't need any more help from you," she said finally. Dear God, being this close to him was torture. She couldn't block out the images of the way that he had kissed her, had touched her. Half to remind herself of his true nature, she added, "You're a liar and a snake, Cale Cody, and a . . . ," she searched for another insult, "coward! If I live to be a hundred, I hope I never see you again. Unless it's to put a bullet where your heart should have been!"

Having had his fill of her temper, Cale silenced any further protests with his lips, holding her small face between the palms of his hands as she sought to pull her lips away. Softly, skillfully, he teased the angry stiffness from the sweet curve of her lips until they met his with a hunger that rivaled his own. Carefully, he traced the pout of her bottom lip with the tip of his tongue and then parted their quivering softness to taste the inner honey of her mouth. She shrunk back from him at first, but he coaxed her slowly into willingness, into surrendering to her own desire.

Vaguely, she heard the voice of protest rise within her and then drown like a crippled victim in the crashing tides of passion that swept over her. It bubbled to the surface again and again, making her feel repelled by the part of her that hungrily returned his kisses, that strained against the exquisite tracings of his fingers over her breast. Then, with every ounce of her that belonged truly to herself, she pushed her small fists into his chest, pummeling them against him wildly until, taken by surprise, he released her.

"Don't ever touch me again," she said in a voice that was eerily like the low growl of a cat. He jade eyes matched the otherworldly timbre of her voice as she stared him down, forcing her trembling limbs to support her. "I hate you for what you have done to my father . . . and to me. I'm not some school-girl you can charm into forgetting. I'll never forget the debt I owe you, Cale, so you'd best convince your friend to have me killed. If you let me go, I promise you, I'll come back and see you both dead."

Cale backed another step away, opened his mouth to speak, but then thought better of it and, turning on his heel, left the room. The high-pitched clink of the bolt in the lock shook Jessalyn to the bone as she stood frozen where he had left her. Pulling her trembling hands up, she looked disbelievingly down at their palms, her eyes tinged with madness. Through the tangle of thoughts in her mind, she realized, above all, one thing—she couldn't take back what she'd said, and by saying it she'd just sentenced herself to death.

Chapter Eleven

Jessalyn sat motionless on the small bed as one hour passed into the next. As each moment passed, she listened for the clink of the bolt in the door, both expecting and dreading the sound. She knew that it would have to come and that it would surely bring someone to take her to her execution. She was familiar enough with the legend of El Halcon to know that he killed his enemies without blinking, and she had sworn herself his enemy.

The silence around her stretched on mercilessly, broken only by the faint sounds of muffled Spanish and Comanche that floated in from the yard. Finally, near midday, the bolt slid noiselessly back and the door swung open. Jessalyn took a deep breath and straightened her shoulders before she looked toward the doorway. The captured air rushed from her lungs in a sigh of relief when she saw only Sam there, and she smiled tiredly up at him.

"I missed you at breakfast." She managed a weak attempt at humor. It was either tears or laughter, she knew, and she preferred to cling to the latter.

"So what have you brought me for lunch? I hope there is a file in it."

Sam's smile glistened white against his red skin as he leaned forward in passing by, waving the tray before her nose.

"Last meal for a condemned woman," he joked, and then immediately regretted his jest as he saw the color drain from her small face. Setting down the tray, he flipped the end of her nose playfully with an outstretched finger, and teased the sagging corner of her lips upward.

"No long faces, Jesse," he said gently, his raven eyes sparkling with a warmth that was sweet and childlike, hardly in tune with his surroundings or the life he led. "I was only kidding. We're not going to kill you—today anyway." He looked down to remove the wooden bowl that had been tipped upside down as a cover over her tray, and then glanced sideways at the young girl on the bed. "Whatever you said has my brother mighty stirred up, though. He doesn't trust anyone but me to come in here— afraid you might get away." His eyes twinkled with a combination of admiration and curiosity, and he asked, "So what did you say to Cale, anyway?"

"I said I'd kill him if I got the chance," Jessalyn replied bitterly. "And Halcon as well." She sat back against the wall, her lips pressed together in a pout that could have easily been borrowed from some terribly spoiled child, but her eyes were hard as ice. "And a few other things," she added, preferring not to elaborate on the string of insults she had dealt to Cale.

Sam nodded, still smiling, and handed her the

tray, which she took with surprising willingness.

"I thought it might have been something like that," he remarked nonchalantly. "Cale wouldn't tell me, but he rode out of here like he had a jackal nipping his ass." He covered his mouth with his hand in a childish gesture, and managed a look of guilt for his language. "Sorry," he added, and then sat down in the chair to wait for her to finish her meal. After a time, she looked up purposefully from her plate and cast him a thoughtful tilt of brows.

"There is something I need to ask you," she began, wanting to ask for his aid in her plan to turn the rangers away, but made cautious by Cale's earlier warning. When Sam returned her opener with a receptive, if vaguely suspicious, look, she continued.

"One of the Rangers has been killed." She could tell by the look on his face that he had already been aware of the fact, but his dark features showed no sign of regret. Hardening herself mentally against his coolness over another man's death, she continued, "It is my fault for bringing them here . . ." she drew in a slight breath, "and I want you to help me send them away before things get any worse."

Sam's regard remained steady and even, and his eyes never broke from hers as he spoke.

"What did you have in mind?" he asked, his dark gaze beneath a thick brush of coal-colored lashes possessed of a sweet expression that was out of keeping with his stony lack of emotion.

Mentally, Jessalyn gave a relieved cheer and racked one up for her side. At least he was still listening to her, and that was half of the battle. Now, if she could only convince him to trust her, to help. Still, Cale's warning about Sam's loyalties to El Halcon whispered in the back of her mind, warning her to be cautious. She couldn't make it seem as if she were asking him to betray his brother.

"I want you to take me down to the Ranger camp," she said in a rush, and noting the widening of Sam's eyes, she continued before he had time to protest, "I'll tell them that I was mistaken about El Halcon—that I'm here of my own free will."

"You think that is going to do any good?" Sam questioned incredulously. "One of their men is dead now. They're not going to just ride away because you tell them to." Hardly able to resist the desperation that lit in her fiery emerald eyes, he added in his own defense, "And besides, Halcon would never allow it."

Throwing the tray aside recklessly so that the half-filled plates slid off one side, crashed against the wall, and then spewed to the floor, she stood up and strode angrily to the other side of the room.

"I have to do something!" she insisted. With every ounce of human blood within her, she believed that. "Halcon will kill them all unless they give up. And as things stand now, they'll never give up. I have to make them leave!"

Throwing his hands up in exasperation, Sam stood up with a heavy sigh. Of all of the stupid things he'd allowed women to talk him into in the past, this had to be the stupidest. He was a fool for even letting her get started on it, and now he was going to make himself even a bigger idiot. He hoped his brother didn't find out about it, or they'd likely both be skinned alive and hung from the fence by their toenails.

"I surrender," he groaned miserably. "I'll take you to them, but you have to promise me that you won't try any tricks. It'll be my neck if Halcon doesn't find you exactly where he left you when he gets back from El Paso." He rolled his head back and looked wearily at the ceiling, planning how he was going to manage what he had just agreed to do. Thinking about the logistics of it, he moaned, "It might be my neck anyway." But Jessalyn wasn't listening. Her mind was already preoccupied with something else that he'd said.

"El Halcon is gone to El Paso?" she questioned, and Sam nodded in answer, confiding that his brother had ridden out that morning, but refusing to say why. Watching him from behind, Jessalyn didn't miss the straight set of the muscles that gleamed beneath the leather vest he wore as a shirt. It was obvious that he was hiding something, but she decided not to press the issue, and simply answered him with a casual "Oh," then went on to plot their course.

"We could leave tonight," she said, half to Sam and half to herself as she formulated a plan. "We could sneak into the ranger camp while it's still dark. I only need to talk to the lieutenant—the rest of them won't even need to know that we're there. We could be back here by morning." She neglected to add that they would be back by morning only if everything went exactly right, and if Brett Anderson didn't make any trouble for them, which he most

202

likely would. She'd just have to be very convincing, she told herself. Somehow, she'd have to make Brett believe that there was no longer any need for him to go after El Halcon. She'd have to impress upon him what the consequences of continuing would be, and hope that he was a reasonable man.

And that was the way the plan progressed between the brave young girl and her unwilling conspirator. When they were finished, they had plotted every moment of their mission down to the finest detail. There was only one thing wrong with the plan—it left no room for error or unexpected problems. But neither of them mentioned that, as if ignoring the possibility would somehow make it cease to exist. Still, both of them felt it, and by the time Sam left with the lunch tray, the hairs were crawling on the back of his neck. Watching the door close behind him, Jessalyn sat down on the bed again, rubbing her fingers in circles on her throbbing temples, and thinking about the night.

She paced the hours away numbly, moving between the bed and the window. Occasionally, she climbed onto the chair that she had placed beneath the window and looked out at the camp. It was fairly empty, as most of the men were either lying in wait for the ranger company or standing guard in the cliffs above the fort. Occasionally, she would see the glint of sunlight on a mirror as one of them signaled to another across the top of the stark canyon. Usually, the signal was followed by a rider going in or out without being picked off of his horse by a lookout's bullet.

Despite herself, Jessalyn couldn't help but marvel

at the organization and amazing strength of the fortress. With the narrow canyon entrance, and the high, sheer cliffs on either side that provided good aim on anyone below, it would have been virtually impossible for anyone to successfully attack. Crossing her arms on the windowsill and resting her chin on them, she surveyed the fortress with a calculating eye and wondered about the man who had built it and ruled it with an iron hand. She still had not met him, which was probably just as well, for it would be easier to kill a stranger.

If Halcon was indeed Sam's brother, then he would have to be a half-breed like Sam, she supposed. Somehow, that was much the way she had pictured him, only lacking Sam's sweet, boyish handsomeness. She saw Halcon with a scarred face hidden beneath a dark beard, and wicked, heartless eyes like those of a viper about to strike. Yes, that was The Hawk as she saw him, and she'd almost be disappointed to find him any less hideous or any more human.

Still, there was one thing that did not figure into her picture of the man, and that was the fact that she was still alive. He knew, quite obviously, that she would come back and kill him if he ever let her go—so he couldn't. In the face of this, she could not imagine that she had left him any choice but to have her executed. Why, then hadn't he done it? Perhaps he wanted to preside over the ceremony himself, she thought bitterly, and was only waiting for an opportune time. Or perhaps he knew that waiting in uncertainty was worse than knowing what would happen, and he was only prolonging her torture. Or perhaps he had something worse than immediate death planned for her. The thought made her shudder to the bone, and she banished it quickly. If that were the plan, she would beg Sam to give her a knife so that she could end her life with honor.

Jessalyn awoke to the sound of sloshing water and the clink of metal against metal. When she rolled her misty jade eyes open, she saw two men—the same ones who had brought the bathtub into her room the day before—carrying it away. She lay still, closing her eyes a bit and watching them through a brush of dark lashes, not wanting to attract their attention.

"El Halcon quiere este," one of them said to the other, indicating the tub with a nod.

"Yeah, well, if he wants his tub he ought to come and get it himself," complained the second man, who seemed, if it were possible, even bigger than the first. "I thought he was going to be in El Paso for a few days, anyway. Wish he was. Damn, he's been in one hell of a mood since yesterday."

"No luck for us, compañero," said the other as they squeezed the tub through the door. "He decide not to go on to El Paso after he meet with *los hombres.*"

When the door was safely closed, Jessalyn rolled over and groaned into her pillow. All of her cleverly laid plans had just been spoiled by two men and a bathtub. She had just barely managed to think of an alternate plan when Sam entered the room hurriedly. Standing inside the door, he looked self-consciously around, like he wasn't supposed to be there, and said, "Jesse, we have a problem."

In response, she nodded, "I know," she said, and with a wicked glint in her eye, added, "but I have another plan." She ignored the doubtful eye that Sam cast her. "Sam, can you get me a pen and paper?"

Sam lowered a brow and tilted his head warily, his long, silken hair falling slowly forward over his shoulder like a creeping serpent.

"What are you going to do with it?" he probed, determined that, this time, he wouldn't let her talk him into blindly following another plan. He still hated to think of the trouble her last one could have gotten them into had El Halcon decided to return a few hours later, by which time they would have already left for the ranger camp. It was a lucky thing for them that they had found out about Halcon's change of plans in time to abort their journey.

Reading the thoughts that brooded like grey clouds against his raven eyes, she gave him the most winsome smile she could manage and tried to look reassuring. She couldn't let him quit on her now, when so many lives hung in the balance, though she knew he cared little about that fact. Doubtless, he'd shot quite a few Texas Rangers in his trade already, and the ones that waited at the edge of the mountains would only be a few more on the list.

"I'm going to write down my message to them," she said, her green eyes glinting like gems in the uneven light of the dimming cell. "Then you can take it to their camp tonight."

The half-breed regarded her as if she'd lost her mind, putting his arms out in front of him as if to push something away and taking a step backward from her.

"Oh no." He shook his head resolutely. "You're not going to talk me into that. It'll never work, and besides, they would never believe that you really wrote the letter." He paused, then thought of another good reason not to go, and added, "Anyway, they aren't going to just let me walk into their camp. They'd shoot me before I got within a hundred yards of them." Thinking of the possibilities, he was more determined than ever not to be drawn into this new plan.

Bracing her hands on her slim hips, Jessalyn regarded him with the look of a hen determined not to give up her eggs.

"They wouldn't have to see you. Their camps wouldn't be secure from a bunch of Comanche infants. You could easily get in and out of there—anyone could." She scoffed critically at him like one schoolboy daring another to do some wicked deed. "And as for the letter, I have that planned already. I'll put things in there that only I would know, and that way there will be no question that it came from me." The insinuation that he was some sort of terrible coward for not helping her was more than evident in the tone of her voice, and Sam looked slightly embarrassed for himself as he spoke.

"Doesn't sound like much of a plan to me," he complained, looking very much like a bull reluctantly being led to slaughter. Throwing up his hands, he surrendered again to the power of female persuasion, and turned to leave the room, saying, "I'll go get a pen and paper." Without another look back he was gone, and Jessalyn stood alone in the silent room, wondering uncomfortably if she had done the right thing. She couldn't imagine that Sam would have any trouble delivering the message, but if anything did happen to him . . . She ran her trembling fingers through her hair, pulling it back from her face, and sighed deeply. There was no other choice, she told herself. Nothing would happen to Sam, and the rangers would leave Halcon country and finally be safe.

Still clinging to the willful tangle of her hair, she looked up at the adobe ceiling and wished she could see the sky. Surely God was up there still, presiding over the stars, hanging the moon in the right place—and watching over the men below it. Silently, she said a small prayer for their safety, and then turned away, wishing she could do more. Never in her life had she felt so helpless, never had she been able to do so little for those she cared for. It left her with a horrible suspended feeling, as if she were teetering on a thread a thousand feet above the earth. She had gone after that thread with a hacksaw and still had not been able to alter her uncertain future, yet a man whom she had never met could come along at any moment and choose life or death for her with the wink of an eye.

After a time, Sam returned with a pen and small palette of paper, which he complained was somewhat hard to procure about the fortress. Taking it, Jessalyn wrote the letter with care, addressing it to

Brett Anderson and carefully putting in references to several details from conversations that she and the lieutenant had shared. There could be no doubt on his part, she knew, that the letter had indeed been written by her. Still, she could only hope that he would believe the lies that she carefully penned onto the paper and that he would take the company away.

When she was finished, she gave the letter to Sam, who had been watching her and the door in turn since returning with the paper. Tucking it into the red Apache sash that wound around his tapered waist at the top of his pants, he smiled into her worried eyes.

"Don't worry." He reached out and took a stray strand of her coppery hair in his fingers, admiring it and then placing it behind her shoulder affectionately. "A Comanche infant could do it—remember?" His smile glistened white, and his eyes twinkled like the facets of an ebony gem as he took up the leftover paper and the pen and left the room. When he was gone, and the bolt had been slid safely back into place on the door, Jessalyn breathed a sigh of relief and sank down on the bed wearily. Before long, she had fallen into a troubled, but needed sleep that carried her back to the day that she had planted the stone roses in the garden.

Cale entered the small cell almost soundlessly, and left the door cracked to avoid clinking the bolt. The room was dark save for the small circle of light from the candle he carried, and he went silently to the bedside table and lit the lantern there. After a moment, it cast a soft glow into the room and bathed the sleeping figure on the bed in golden light. The vision held him silent for a moment as he looked down at Jessalyn, so sweet in sleep, her hair, strewn carelessly about the pillow, glittering in the lamplight like a sea of molten copper. Her dark lashes like the gentle fanning of a butterfly's wings fluttered almost imperceptibly against the flawless flush of her cheeks, hiding those beautiful, brilliant eyes that haunted his every moment.

He'd come to realize reluctantly, but quite clearly, in the last day that she had become an obsession for him. He wasn't going to be able to give her up—not even if he wanted to, which he didn't. Somehow, he was going to have to make her understand, to win her trust, and to find her love. There were so many layers of bitterness and hate within her now that it seemed an impossible task, but fate had given him no choice. He could not keep her caged forever and he could not let her go.

The call of a coyote floated through the window and shivered in the air of the small room, and her lashes fluttered open with a start. She looked at him first in a haze of confusion, and then quickly with a chill of hatred.

"What do you want?" she asked, her voice still soft with sleep, like the gentle whispers of a purring kitten. The sweet sound of it took away from the meaning of the words she'd shot at him, and she felt her back stiffen in irritation.

Standing above her, Cale remained impassive, undeceived by the unintentionally sweet tone of her voice. The black look in her bright eyes told him not to fool himself. She was going to react exactly as he had expected her to, and it was going to be a long battle to turn her around.

"To talk," he said simply, his own voice quiet and subdued, with none of the usual hints of laughter. It was one of the few times in his life he'd been completely serious about anything. For once, he couldn't see the humor in the situation.

Jessalyn shrugged, eyeing him wickedly, and tossed the blanket off herself, sitting up against the wall with her long legs curled to the side of her.

"There's nothing you can possibly say that would interest me," she said with exaggerated formality. "But I'm sure I won't be able to keep you from giving it a try." She looked daggers at his back when he turned and walked to the window to retrieve the chair, and then to his face when he brought it back and sat beside her bed.

Sitting in the chair, Cale braced his feet on the bedframe in front of him and brought his elbows to rest on his muscular thighs. Leaning forward, he caught the eyes of the girl before him, his whiskey-colored gaze warm and sparkling with a practiced charm. Even though he sat prepared for the abuse that would no doubt come his way, there was a slight vulnerability in his handsome, tanned face as he spoke.

"El Halcon didn't kill your father," he said honestly. He'd thought of several ways to approach the subject, but none seemed better than to begin at the heart of the matter. Seeing the disbelief and protest rising in her frosted eyes, he backed up his point. "I know what you think you saw, but it was just made to look as if El Halcon were responsible. I promise you, he didn't do it. He met with your father, and left . . . that is all."

She looked back at him with anger striking like summer lightning in the depths of her eyes, her mouth dropping open in shock. Another lie, she thought bitterly. Every word that comes out of his mouth is a lie! She knew what she had seen in the valley where her father had been murdered, and she hadn't mistaken the hand that had done the work.

"Next you'll be telling me that pigs fly and horses lay eggs," she retorted with a sarcastic smile. "I know what I saw, Cale. Don't make me out for a fool."

Patiently, the Comanchero returned her sarcasm with cool determination. It was now or never to convince her that they were both on the same side, and he was determined not to fail—if it took every ounce of discipline he had within him.

"You know what you think you saw," he said again, making the whole thing sound simple, as if nearly two months and a thousand miles across the desert were the insignificant result of some small misunderstanding. "But you were wrong. El Halcon didn't kill your father. They were . . . well, allies, of a sort—and friends."

"Don't tell me any more lies!" Jessalyn screeched, pressing her hands to her ears as her temper flew from her. With a quick, agile twist she stood up and raced across the bed to the floor, her hair billowing about her like wildfire. In a swirl of it she spun around and pointed an accusing finger in his direction. "I won't listen to you tell me any more lies!" Her voice echoed about the room like the cry of an avenging demon. "You think I don't know my own father. He wasn't a friend to El Halcon. How could they possibly have been allies? Allies in what? What business could they possibly have had?" She waited smugly for him to concoct a satisfactory answer to that.

"I can't tell you that," Cale returned, standing up. It seemed as if he would have a better chance looking at her from the same level. When she took a suspicious step backward, he wondered at the wisdom of the move, and stopped, continuing in a soothing tone, as if approaching a wild animal, "I'm not lying to you, Jesse. I haven't and I won't. I know who killed your father, and I would have gone after them if you hadn't insisted on starting out for Halcon country with fifty rangers. As it is, we'll have the men soon."

With a narrow eye, Jessalyn played along with his game, grabbing the reins to her runaway temper, and asking, "Who? Who are these men that killed my father in cold blood, and went to all the trouble to scalp him and leave Halcon's banner hanging there so that it would look like he did it? Tell me, since you seem to know so much more than I about my own father's death, what was their motive for that?"

Cale glanced up at the ceiling and then back down, planning his next words and bracing himself for a storm when he spoke them.

"I can't tell you," he replied after a short pause. And therein lay the problem. If he could tell her

213

everything about the men who had killed her father, and why they had done it, and why they had bothered to make it look like a Comanchero killing, he could have solved the problem between them. Unfortunately, he couldn't tell her. Too much hung in the balance. She was too young, too unpredictable, and too close to the rangers to be trusted with the truth.

"How convenient," she spat. "Couldn't you at least make something up . . . to ease my poor, feeble mind? I just can't seem to come to the right conclusions myself, and here I have led fifty men all the way across Texas for no reason." She tipped her chin downward, and fluttered her long lashes coyly at him. "Well, silly me. I can't imagine what possessed me to do such a foolish thing. I suppose it's all because I just need a man to take care of me. I . . ." Her words were silenced as Cale took a quick step forward and, catching her unprepared, covered her protesting lips with his.

Frantically, she pressed her palms against the hardness of his chest to free herself, but he only drew her more tightly against him, artfully softening her unwilling lips with his kiss. Slowly, with the skill of a diplomat, he broke away her defenses, parting her lips only to encounter a resolutely clenched row of even, white teeth. Smiling inwardly, he drew back a bit, tracing his tongue along the sweet pout of her flushed mouth.

"Such resistance," he muttered, looking thoughtfully into the fathomless depths of her eyes and smiling. He didn't think he had ever seen anything so beautiful as she was at that moment, staring up at him with wide, startled eyes, caught between flight and fury. Stroking his thumb along the crimson curve of her cheek, he found the trace of a tear there and wiped it away. Bending his head toward her, he brushed a kiss across the stain that it had left behind and whispered against her ear, "No more tears, Jesse. They don't become you. I want to see your smile."

His kind words surprised her, and brought a response opposite to their intent. Tears rushed like bitter rain into her spring green eyes, and she bent her head in shame to hide them. Even in the light of everything he had done to her, she still found her heart his prisoner.

"Please don't," she whispered, her voice quivering faintly into the air between them. "You've already proven that you can make a fool of me. Please don't do it again. I can't bear it."

Cale looked down at the silken coppery head beneath him, his whiskey-colored eyes thick with understanding and regret. He never failed to underestimate the depth of her pride or the magnitude of her strength. That was, perhaps, the one thing about her that drew him the most. Unfortunately, it was also the thing that forced her to push him away.

"I don't want to make a fool of you, my little sandstone rose," he said softly. "I ask only for you to match what you have already won from me."

"Which is?" she choked on the words, unable to believe she had spoken them, and refused to turn her face to him. In reply to her question, he murmured, "Surrender," as he tilted her chin up with his big hand and kissed her softly.

Sweeping her into his arms, he looked deeply into her eyes, the soft sherry-colored depths of his warm with kindness and sparked gold with desire. Lowering himself onto the bed, he cradled her in his lap, and sat with her in the dimming circle of lamplight where only a few moments before he had watched her sleeping. Looking down into her troubled face now, he felt a pang of regret for peace he had stolen from her. With a slight smile lifting the handsome lines of his face, he brushed aside the stray strands of copper that clung to her dampened cheeks, and then kissed her eyelids shut. Stroking her hair reassuringly, he tucked her silken head against his chest, and thought of all that had transpired between them since the day that he had seen her swimming in the spring pool and had grudgingly admitted that she was unusually beautiful.

"Lay down with the lion, little lamb," he whispered with a sigh. "Today is a good day for peace."

Chapter Twelve

The soft touch of Cale's breath against her ear as he bent to kiss its pink, velvet curve sent a wild shudder through Jessalyn's slender body, and she felt an all-too-familiar wave of desire surge like fire through every inch of her. With the last remains of rational thought in her mind, she hoped that today was, indeed, a good day for peace, for she had certainly lain down with the lion, and she knew she would be lost to him forever.

"Please don't lie to me," she pleaded breathlessly as she felt the feather-like caress of his outstretched fingers leave five tingling trails over the smooth cotton of her blouse. "I . . ." She parted her lips again to plead for mercy on her own behalf, but her breath flew from her in a gasp as his palm brushed the hardness of her nipple and his fingers moved to unfasten the buttons of her blouse. Unwillingly, she surrendered to the sweeping passion that heated her body like a fever and chilled her soul like ice. Arching desperately against him, she banished the voice that howled somewhere deep within her, ignoring it as it lashed her for her foolish weakness. *This* was the man who had used her and tossed her aside a dozen times at whim, it said. *This* was the man who had helped kill her father and then denied it. *This* was the man whom she had sworn to kill, but this was also the man she loved. She realized it with startling clarity now, the paralyzing mixture of hatred and love that bound her to him. Of the two, the worse was love. It tore her limb from limb, leaving her aching to the very depths of her soul. Aside from the pain of seeing her father cut down in the desert, it was the worst thing she had ever known.

A wild rush of ecstasy tingled just beneath her skin like the fluttering of a thousand butterfly wings as he parted the fabric that had hidden her from him, and the creamy curve of her breasts peeked timidly out. Surrendering to the power that he held over her, she ran her fingers into the tawny curls of his hair, surprised at the softness of it, and pulled his lips again to hers.

Slowly, deeply, he kissed her, his silent lips promising more than his words had ever allowed. Hungrily, she returned the promise with a vow of her own, yearning for the ecstasy of his touch, but also for the love that she thought she could feel, but that he had not promised.

With a touching tenderness, his lips parted again from her and trailed down the satin curve of her neck to the sweet hollow at its base. He nibbled hungrily there, as if tasting the honey of a flower, and lingered in the sweet scent of the spilled curls that danced over her shoulders. She moaned as he lay her back against the pillow, his tongue tracing a trail to her waiting breasts and then circling them with burning rings. She cried out as he reached the peak of one, taking it gently in his lips and nibbling.

"Cale," she whispered, desperate to be free and desperate to be loved in the same moment. "P . . . please . . ." But she couldn't finish.

"Please what, my little rose?" His voice was husky and his breath like a warm breeze against her skin. "Please don't, or please do?" He raised his head to gaze into her half-closed eyes. "Will you still be made of stone, little rose, or are you a woman after all?" He searched her troubled face for a moment, wondering himself at the answer, and then bent to kiss her again. His lips brushed hers softly at first, almost intangibly, and then slowly began again to coax her unwilling mouth into surrender.

With an ease that spoke of ownership, he moved his broad hand over the swell of her breasts and then traced the slim curve of her waist as she shivered helplessly beneath his touch. Suddenly, it seemed as if all of her life had been building to this one moment, as if all of the moments that had come before were merely a meaningless prelude, and as if there would be nothing after. It didn't matter, nothing mattered. All the world was this moment, the fire of his kiss, and the unbearable yearning for his touch — and for something more.

Her mind spinning at a fever pitch, she pressed desperately against his fingers as he moved beneath her skirt and caressed the lean curve of her thigh. Her skin burned with satisfaction where he had been and tingled with yearning where he had yet to travel. It was ecstasy and it was torture. She cried out wildly, her voice seeming far away, as he parted her legs and teased patiently around the warm, moist bud of her passion. His lips became hungry, urgent as he moved to kiss her again, possessing her lips confidently with his own.

Now, she was far beyond protesting as he lifted her to her feet and removed the last of her clothing, exposing her soft perfection to his view. Laying her back on the bed, he removed his own clothes and then bent to again taste the tender rise of her breasts. Slowly, his hands again traveled her velvet thighs. Parting them, he moved over her as she called his name and reached for him, desperate for something that she could not name. Behind her eyes, sparks of light fluttered like a myriad of butterfly wings and then shuddered through her body like lightning.

She gasped, and stiffened in shock as she felt his manhood press against her, but he kissed her softly, and then whispered soothing words against her ear.

"Hush, my rose," he whispered so softly that she barely heard him. "You've only just come alive. Don't turn to stone again." As gently as he could, he passed her maidenhead and moved into the warmth of her untried passage.

The fire that burned through her was like nothing she had ever known, and she moved wildly against him, seeking satisfaction, desperate for release, but she wanted more than that. She wanted his love — love as strong as that he had stolen from her.

Suddenly, her body exploded in an exquisite surge of heat, and she felt him spend his passion also. Wrapping her in his arms, he held her tightly as the tides ebbed around them, and, closing her eyes, she nestled into the hard curves of his chest, wishing again for his love. Stroking the soft curls of her hair, he sighed deeply, and wondered if he had done the right thing in surrendering to his desire.

A crash rang out in the hallway suddenly, and Cale would have thought it had come from inside his head except that it was accompanied by the frantic sound of familiar voices. Jumping out of the bed more abruptly than he probably should have, he reached for his pants and pulled them on hurriedly.

"El Halcon, El Halcon!" It was Oso's deep voice that boomed down the hallway. Reaching down, Cale pulled the cover over Jessalyn just before the door burst open and thundered against the wall where it shuddered to a stop.

"What is it?" Cale thundered, his eyes flashing like the edge of a blade. The air of authority that followed him across the room made even Oso seem small as he moved toward the other man.

The big Mexican glanced about nervously, looking like a man in fear for his life as he spoke.

"It ees your brother." He muttered the words, as if the slur would make them less damaging, and then finished reluctantly, "He has been shot."

The anger in Cale's eyes turned to disbelief and then to some unreadable emotion, and he stood frozen where the news had found him.

"Sam?" he questioned, his voice registering fear and shock. He almost couldn't make himself ask the next question. "How bad is it?"

"Bad." Oso fidgeted nervously, his eyes wavering from one side of the room to the other, but never to Cale. "Maria ees with heem now, but the rangers, they

221

shoot him up pretty good."

Cale looked up at the other man with an intensity that made even the stone walls shudder in anticipation of an explosion.

"Rangers?" His words held an unmistakable threat as they boomed through the suspended air of the cell, frightening even the shadows into hiding. "Are they still at the cliffs?" Oso nodded in response, and Cale continued, clenching his fists at his side to hold his rising temper, "What the hell was he doing there?"

Oso shifted his great bulk nervously from one side to the other, looking oddly like an overgrown schoolchild.

"I don' know." He didn't—and he didn't want to. The look in El Patron's eyes said unmistakably that someone was going to pay for this incident, and he hoped it wouldn't be he. Still, there was something he recalled about shooting the messenger for bearing bad news. "He was alone. He go to the ranger camp. It ees all I know." He threw his hands up in genuine innocence of the event. "I don' know not'ing more. He ees in hees room, Maria ees takeen out the bullets." Without another word, he turned and shuffled back through the doorway with surprising speed, grateful to be away from El Patron's wrath.

Jessalyn sat motionless on the bed, save for the unskilled efforts of her quivering fingers to replace the last button on her blouse. She had realized two things with startling clarity in the instants that had just ticked by. The first was that she was responsible for Sam's being shot, possibly even for his death. The second took a moment longer for her to face, and when she did, she felt as if her insides were being tied into knots and stretched tight. Cale wasn't a friend to El Halcon . . . he *was* El Halcon, the man who had killed her father, the man who had eluded her for a thousand miles across the desert, the man whom she had come here to kill. The cruelty, the sickening irony of it all caused her to stare blindly at him in the face of this revelation. When he stalked hurriedly out the door and disappeared, she stared unseeing at the dark portal that had swallowed him away.

It did not occur to her in the hours that passed that the door had been carelessly left open and that there was no guard to prevent her escape. She could not force herself to think of anything but the words that had passed between Cale and the other. The conversation replayed over and over in her mind, and each time she felt her soul grow colder. How could it all be true? She asked the question over and over to the walls' deaf ear. How could he be both the man she loved and the man she had sworn to kill? How could he be Sam's brother—dear, sweet Sam? That was her fault too. She should never have talked him into going to the ranger camp. It was her doing if he died, just as surely as if she had shot him herself. Oh dear Lord, she couldn't bear the thought of it. Sam, please, she pleaded silently, you have to be all right! She repeated it over and over again in her mind, as if she were by his side, coaxing him to hold tight to the slippery threads of life.

She didn't hear the heavy footsteps coming quickly down the hall, or waver her eyes from their downward focus as someone entered the room. Only when a hard fist closed over her arm and jerked her rudely from the bed did she recognize the presence of the intruder, and her eyes flew upward in shock. The face that met hers was painted so strongly with anger that she scarcely recognized it at first, and her mouth fell open in confusion as she stared wide-eyed at the man who only a short time ago had gazed on her in love.

"S . . . Sam," she stammered, fearing the worst from the hard lines that shaped Cale's face. "Is he . . . ?" She swallowed hard, unable to finish the question. She was afraid to know the answer.

"Perhaps you should come and see for yourself," Cale growled, his face pale, and his eyes narrow and dark with anger. Closing his fingers more tightly around her wrist, he pulled her through the doorway and down the dark hall outside. If the circumstances had been any different, she might have been elated at seeing the outside of her cell after so many days of captivity, but her gaze was fixed on the unmoving shoulders in front of her. She half walked, half ran to keep her arm from being pulled out of its socket as he dragged her down the length of the hall and started up the stairway at the end. Unable to see, she felt her feet tangle in her skirt on the way up, and she fell forward only to be jerked back to her feet by her arm. It never occurred to her to protest the abuse. She was too afraid to speak, or even to pull away.

Her small, bare feet were bruised and sore when they finally reached a doorway, and Cale threw her inside in front of him without a word. The room was thick with men clustered soberly around a bed in the center, where two women were bent over Sam's body. Jessalyn froze two steps inside the doorway where the force of Cale's shove subsided, her eyes darting wildly from one dark-skinned face to the next, and then down to Sam's motionless form.

"Oh, dear God, no," she whispered, still frozen near the doorway. She was afraid to breathe, to move, lest the force of it chase Sam's spirit from the room.

"Out!" She heard Cale's voice thunder from behind her as he planted a hand in the hollow of her back and shoved her forward. Without a glance at the strange girl or at their patron, the men filed out of the doorway, talking in low whispers and shaking their heads hopelessly. The two women near the bed finished bandaging two gaping chest wounds shortly afterward and departed with a pile of cloths that seemed stained with an ocean of blood.

Stepping to the side of the bed, Jessalyn stood numbly looking down at Sam, her hand absently moving to his pillow to stroke the silky strands of straight, raven hair. A tentative sigh of relief passed her lips as she felt the slight stirring of his breath on her arm. He was still alive. She clung to this realization—at least there was still some hope. Looking at the bloodstained bandages that covered two gaping holes in his chest, she sickened and paled to a ghostly shade of white.

"Oh Sam, I'm sorry," she whispered, now oblivious to everything but the terrible struggle for life taking place on the bed before her, and the crushing weight of blame due her for having caused it. How could she have been so foolish as to have sent him? she asked herself for the thousandth time. She should have known that the rangers would be ready to shoot anything that moved for an enemy. She should have known. Taking Sam's heavy, motionless hand in hers, she pressed it to her cheek, and whispered again, "I'm

225

sorry. You have been my only friend. I'm so sorry."

"Well, did you hear that, Sam? The lady is sorry." The cynical sound of Cale's voice from behind her snapped her head around, and she realized for the first time that he had been watching her. The anger in his eyes was more than evident when he looked at her, and when he took a step closer, she flinched away as if to avoid a blow.

"I ought to have you horsewhipped," he growled, making no effort to reassure her that he meant her no harm. In fact, the cold glare in his eyes said anything but. His tawny hair swirled about his tanned face in wild curls, as if he had nearly pulled it out with worry, and his movements were the quick and unplanned results of reflex. "Was it really worth Sam's life for you to escape from here, Jesse? Did you really believe that I would harm you, that you needed to use Sam's weakness for a pretty face to get away?" He spoke as if she were a foolish child who needed to be taught a lesson, and his tone raised the hairs on the back of her neck.

"What was I to think?" she protested, her high-pitched voice cutting through the air like a razor. "Tell me, Cale — or El Halcon — which is it that you prefer to call yourself?" She noted a slight glimmer of surprise in his face, and felt her courage grow at having the upper hand. "Tell me what I was to think. I was nearly raped. I have been locked away like an animal and led to believe that the great El Halcon is going to kill me as soon as he finds a spare moment to do it in." Her eyes lowered like a rifle taking aim, and they flashed a look of hatred that clashed in midair with the bolts of anger from his. Reckless with worry and grief, she pressed, "Tell me what I was to think!"

Cale's patience was at an end. For one thing, he realized that she was right about the unfairness of her treatment, and it only served to raise him to the final boiling point. Without another word, he turned on his heel and strode from the room, the hard line of his shoulders twitching with anger as he slammed the door behind him, leaving Jessalyn alone.

As the night wore on, Jessalyn sat silently by Sam's bed, her small hand clutched desperately to the deathly coldness of his. When his dark skin turned bluish from loss of blood, she screamed for help, and a dark-haired woman ran frantically in and checked Sam for signs of life. Next, she checked his wound, and then looked kindly down into the strange, pained green eyes of the girl who sat beside him.

"He will be all right." Maria placed a reassuring hand on the girl's shoulder, though she was hardly sure herself that Sam would last the night. "The bleeding has stopped," she added, taking some assurance from the fact that her poultice had worked. That, at least, was a small gift in what seemed a terribly cruel situation. Watching the girl turn her head away to look back at Sam, Maria wondered what was between them, but she did not ask. No one did. Everyone at the fort knew of the presence of the girl that El Halcon held as a prisoner, and they knew the rangers wanted her back. Maria had questioned everyone to learn something further, but she could not. Only El Patron and his brother knew the story behind the girl's presence here, and neither one of them would talk.

With a motherly hand, Maria stroked the girl's silken hair in sympathy, and whispered, "Pretty child," out loud, but to herself. In response, Jessalyn gave her another pained glance, thinking that the woman reminded her of her mamacita, and taking comfort in the thought. Without a word, she turned back to Sam, and the woman was gone.

The hours passed to days as the Comanchero struggled. Maria came several times each day to care for Sam's wounds and to bring food for Jessalyn. At first, Jessalyn tolerated her presence, and then finally began to welcome it, taking comfort in the older woman's companionship. They talked little, as Jessalyn could not force her mind to form words. Each time she tried, she would feel a rush of desperate tears rush to the forefront, and she would be forced to swallow them away in silence. Kindly Maria seemed to be bothered little by this, and she often talked for both of them, bringing news of the weather or of the goings-on about the fortress. She never did, however, speak of El Patron, for she anticipated that to be a sore subject. She knew that he had gone to see that the threat of the ranger company was removed once and for all, but she could see no benefit in telling that to the tortured girl who sat by Sam's bed.

Cale walked slowly through the remains of the ranger camp, unable to believe what he saw. He had expected to ride down on them out of the hills and slaughter them like a flock of sitting geese. He had not expected to come down out of the hills and suddenly find that they had turned tail and gone back where they'd come from. Had they anticipated his act of retribution for the life of his brother and run away? He could believe a lot of things of them, but he could not believe that. They might have been fools, but they definitely were not cowards. Why then, he puzzled, why . . .

From where he rode at its head, Brett Anderson twisted around in his saddle and looked back at the company. He didn't feel good about this, and he could tell from the looks on the faces of most of the men that they didn't either. None of them believed Jessalyn's letter any more than he did. Still, he had no choice but to obey the terms of it, as he was afraid that her life might have depended on her ability to convince him to take the company away. They were riding northeast now, back the way they had come, but it was only to convince the Comancheros — if they decided to follow — that the rangers had indeed given up. When they were far enough away, Brett intended to take a few of the best men and ride back, not to the cliff wall, but to El Paso. El Paso was the blackest hive of outlaws and human scum he'd ever had the displeasure to see . . . It was just the right place to find the kind of men he needed.

Sam opened his eyes slowly to a blur of spinning light and color, then closed them again. Several minutes passed before he gave it another try. Things were somewhat clearer, and without moving his pounding head, he looked around the room. His eyes stopped when he saw Jessalyn's ashen face above him, her green eyes staring to some unknown place outside the window and reflecting the color of the sky. He watched her silently for some time, as if watching a beautiful bird and not wanting to startle it to flight. Finally, he felt her hand move on his, and he gave her fingers a light squeeze. In response, she jumped slightly and jerked her eyes down to meet his in surprise.

"You're awake!" She said it as if she'd just beheld a miracle, and her wide emerald eyes began to sparkle in a pool of crystal tears.

Sam smiled the best he could in his weakness, and gave her hand another slight squeeze.

"I can't sleep forever." He couldn't resist the chance to make light of the situation. In reality, he knew how close he'd come — every muscle in his body was telling him about it. "Although, if I'd known I would have such a pretty nurse . . ." He started to laugh, but then quickly thought better of it.

Wiping the tears impatiently from her cheeks, Jessalyn fought away the urge to smile at his unconquerable good nature.

"We were so worried." She hoped to convey the seriousness of the situation. "It has been three days." Seeing a wicked look come into Sam's onyx eyes, she gave him a commanding frown. "Don't you even think of getting out of this bed, Sam Horn," she reprimanded him for the foolish thought that she had seen cross his mind. "You're going to be here for a good long time if I have to sit on your back and twist your ear to hold you down."

This time, Sam laughed despite the pain it caused, and then wished he hadn't when it set him to coughing and a curtain of black tightened about his vision.

"Yes ma'am," he whispered, closing his eyes as the room started to spin again. "But I don't think you'll have to twist my ear. I think it will be a good long while before I feel like moving anyway." He thought for a moment as the mists of sleep closed over his eyes, and then whispered through the fog, "Where's Cale?"

Jessalyn contemplated an answer for a moment too long, and when she opened her mouth to speak, the half-breed had already drifted away. It was just as well, she thought. She didn't know what she would have told him anyway. In truth, she didn't know where Cale was, and she didn't care. It did seem hard to believe that he would keep himself away when his brother had lingered so close to death. Then perhaps, his feelings for his brother were no more genuine than the ones that he had professed for her. Perhaps Cale was not a man capable of truly feeling anything for anyone, except hatred. It didn't matter now as far as she was concerned. In fact, it would be better if he did hate her, for she hated him. He was the man who had taken her father's life and then deceived her for months as she tried to hunt down her father's killers. She would never, she vowed, forget that fact again.

In the back of her mind, the memory of his touch, of the warm, honest glow in his eyes when he had looked at her, gnawed relentlessly like a rat trapped in a box. She loved him, and part of her knew it, but she would not let herself admit to this unholy transgression. That, in the end, would prove to be her undoing.

* * *

Sam was awake again and ravenously hungry when Maria came to bring the evening meal. Seeing him so obviously improved, she smiled broadly and did a little twirl around the room, causing the tin plates on the dinner tray to rattle in protest. Setting the tray down on the table beside the bed, she checked Sam's wounds gently, and then, giving them a nod of approval, stood back up.

"They look better," she remarked, knowing that the fact that the wounds looked clean on the outside did not mean that Sam would recover. There was still a good chance of infection from deep within, and she felt Sam's forehead for any sign of a fever, but found none. She gave a slight sigh of relief to herself and a silent prayer for his continued good fortune. If Sam could have heard her saying prayers to the white man's god over his body, he would have laughed her away for a fool. After all, what would their God want with a half-breed? Shrugging off her hand, he frowned, suspecting what she was up to.

"Stop fussing over me," he complained. "I'll survive." He gave her a wry, one-sided smile that spread to his now-bright eyes. "After all, I've only been shot. It's not the first time."

Maria frowned scornfully down at him with the look of a mother reprimanding a foolish child.

"It won' be the last either," she scolded, "if you do not stop tempting the Lord's hand, Sam Horn." With a last glance that was insistent, yet filled with fondness, she turned away from Sam, and said to Jessalyn before leaving, "Make sure that our foolish *vaquero* eats all of that broth." She nodded toward the tray. "And you eat all of your plate for a change also." She pressed a concerned palm to the pallid hollow of the girl's cheek, and added, "You look so thin." With a last glance from one young face to the other, she left the room without a worry that Sam would, indeed, be made to eat his broth as instructed. Maria could tell from the determined glint in Jessalyn's eye that Sam didn't have a chance. He was going to do what was good for him whether he liked it or not.

The door had not settled back into the frame when Jessalyn took up the bowl of thin broth and took a seat beside Sam. He protested each bite bitterly, complaining that the watery broth tasted strongly of Maria's potions and not a thing like beef. Still, he doggedly ate each spoonful as Jessalyn brought it to his lips with an authoritarian glint in her eye.

When Sam had finally finished, Jessalyn took her own plate and nibbled at the food there, feeling strangely self-conscious under his steady regard. After a time, he looked toward the doorway and then to her, and asked, "Where's Cale?" It was the same question he'd asked before falling asleep, but he couldn't remember the answer.

Jessalyn flinched visibly, either at the question or at the mention of Cale's name, Sam couldn't tell which, and sat with her eyes welded to the gray, speckled plate in her lap.

"I don't know," she answered honestly, hoping that he would not question her further. When he did, she bristled slightly, and raised a heated gaze to his eyes. "I don't know where he is. He left here angry several days ago and has not come back — no doubt because he does not want to see me. He knows I am responsible for what happened to you, and now he hates me more than before." She looked bitterly away toward the fading light of the window. "The feeling is certainly mutual."

Sam cocked a questioning eyebrow at her profile, wondering how much she had said sincerely and how much she had said to salvage her wounded pride.

"I know my brother well enough to know you're mistaken about that," he said, but if she heard him, she gave no sign except, perhaps, a slight hardening of her shoulders. Touching her hand where it lay over the bedcovers, he drew her troubled jade eyes to him, and added, "Perhaps you have mistaken anger at himself for anger at you."

Jessalyn shook her head with conviction. If Sam had seen his brother leave, he wouldn't have questioned the direction of his anger. It had been aimed full force at her for all to see.

"How is it that you call him your brother, Sam?" She changed the subject abruptly, looking at the half-breed with genuine interest. "You are so different from him."

Sam's raven eyes twinkled at her skillful maneuvering of the subject matter, and he gave her a slight smile to let her know that it had not gone unnoticed.

"Cale and I are half-brothers," he answered her question matter-of-factly. It was a question he'd been asked many times in the past, as he and his brother hardly looked alike. "We had the same father, but his mother was a white woman and mine a Comanche. My mother was the one who raised the two of us, though, and she is the only one he or I remember. She

234

often comes with her people to trade here."

Jessalyn frowned thoughtfully at his answer. It was hard to imagine Cale as the child of some loving mother. In fact, it was hard to imagine him having a mother at all. To her, it seemed as if he must have crawled to earth from some litter of hell hounds somewhere.

"Why do you call yourself Horn while he calls himself Cody, then?" she asked almost absently, still puzzling over the idea of Cale as the object of some doting Comanche mother.

Sam laughed at her question. The emphasis that white men put on their surnames had always surprised him. What good was a name if it was not unique, your own? How could it have magic if it had been used and reused by countless generations of people before you? Certainly, at some point, the magic would be worn out of the name.

"I think Sam Horn has a certain ring to it." He leaned his head back and closed his eyes slightly as if listening to sweet notes of music. Seeing her look back at him as if he'd lost his faculties, he added the truth. "Horn is part of my name-of-the-people, White Horn. I use it so that none will forget that I am one of the people."

Jessalyn nodded in understanding at his reply, feeling a bit embarrassed for having probed so far. She knew much of the Comanche way, and she knew that among them names were a very private and sacred thing, one not to be spoken of lightly. Her cheeks washing pink, she finished most of her meal in silence and then set the plate aside. She glanced momentarily at Sam, who sat watching her with steady onyx eyes that seemed to probe the secrets of her soul. Flushing a deeper shade of crimson, she hooded her eyes and looked out the window, hoping to shield her thoughts from him.

Chapter Thirteen

After a long silence had passed between them, Sam lay his head wearily back against the pillow, still watching Jessalyn through half-closed eyes.

"So why is it that you ask so many questions about my brother?" He asked the question as if he already knew the answer. "You seem to have a particular interest in him."

Like a cat with its hair rubbed the wrong way, Jessalyn straightened uncomfortably at his observations and gave him an evil, narrowed stare.

"He is the man I came here to find," she replied, her jade eyes turning to two cold stones set in a firebrand of hatred.

"To kill, you mean," Sam corrected with an easy tone that made it evident that he was hardly worried about the threat. It had been obvious to him for quite some time that young Jessalyn could no more have killed his brother than cut off her own right arm. Whether she knew it or not, she had fallen in love with Cale, which was unfortunate. A long line of women had been left behind in Cale's trail, and occasionally he'd even expressed regret about leaving some of them, but it had never stopped him from riding out. There wasn't much room in his life for a woman, not even one with Jessalyn's winsome qualities. Still, who knew, anything was possible, and Cale had certainly taken the whole problem with Jessalyn more seriously than was typical. Perhaps he was further in the net than anyone thought. Who could tell with Cale?

"Because he killed my father," Jessalyn's words broke him away from his thoughts, and he looked over at her with a strange new light of understanding in his eye, as if he'd just put the integral piece into a puzzle and had finally figured out what the picture was.

Jessalyn's delicate face was fierce with conviction as she defended her purpose further, "He had my father gunned down from a hilltop and then scalped and left for the buzzards. He deserves to die." She was more certain of it now than ever. Realizing that Sam suspected her motives for hating Cale had made her cling even more desperately to the wobbling convictions that had brought her after a faceless killer who went by the name of The Hawk.

Sam met her righteousness with a measured gaze that seemed to see right through her to the wall behind, and then asked, "Knowing Cale now, do you really believe that he would order that?" He interrogated her with a skill that would have been the envy of any New York barrister. "And if he had, do you really believe he would have left his calling card there for all to see?" Before she could formulate a protest, he added words that she had already heard once from Cale's own lips. "El Halcon did not kill your father, Jesse. They were friends and compadres. They had business together that day. We met with your father, and we left him. We had no idea there was an ambush set for him. If we had, we would have gone with him."

Jessalyn's green eyes widened with a mixture of disbelief and horror. She didn't want to believe his words, for, if true, they meant that she had led the rangers after El Halcon for no reason. Worse, it meant that a man had died for nothing.

"You were there?" she whispered, her breath trickling painfully into her lungs in short rasps and her mouth feeling dry and swollen. Her heart pounded viciously against her chest, and the blood thundered in her ears so loudly that she barely heard him reply and nod.

"You . . . you saw him leave my father alive?" she stammered, wildly looking for a thread to cling to. Again, her question was met with a nod, and she felt her strongest convictions crashing down around her. How could she believe what he said, yet how could she not? Would Sam lie to her? Had Cale told him to lie? She searched the serious lines of his dark face for any sign, but all she found was an unbending look of truth. Her gaze fell away from him, fluttering absently about the floor as she fought to reform her thoughts — and to rekindle her hatred. If Cale had not killed her father, then why had he allowed her to ride halfway across Texas on the trail of a mythical killer? Why had he ridden with the company, watching their every move only to alert his men, the very men that she had been tracking?

Another question stormed into her mind and hunted all of the others away. She wondered why she hadn't thought of it sooner.

"If El Halcon did not kill my father, then who did?" She asked the question even as the words first formed in her mind, and even though she still was not certain, she believed Cale's claim to innocence.

Sam shrugged the question away with a look that seemed strangely apprehensive.

"I don't know." It wasn't the truth, but he suspected that she couldn't be trusted with all of the facts—there was too much at stake. At the incredulous look that returned his question, he added, "You'll have to ask Cale."

Jessalyn's heart thumped in protest at the mention of his name, and she shuddered visibly at the thought of ever seeing him again.

"I'm sure he wouldn't tell me," she replied bitterly, her green eyes a pool of pain and betrayal. "We aren't exactly on speaking terms." She looked away from him toward the wall, as if it would by some magic advise her as to the solution to her predicament. "He hates me now more than ever." Her voice was no more than a whisper, and Sam wondered if she had meant the words for him or only for herself.

"Cale doesn't hate you, Jesse," he said, laying his head back against the pillow and closing his eyes. He felt incredibly tired all of the sudden, as if he could go to sleep for a month and never wake up. Feeling the blackness settle rapidly over him, he added, "I think maybe . . . he feels . . . the opposite," from beneath closed lids before he drifted farther away.

Watching him fall away, Jessalyn couldn't believe

what she had heard, or what she thought the words were intended to mean. Was Sam trying to tell her that Cale felt something for her? Certainly that was not the case. If it was, Cale had a strange way of treating women he cared for.

She pondered Sam's last statement for some time, watching him sleeping peacefully on the bed, seemingly unaware of the turmoil he had stirred within her. Finally she left his bedside and went to the small cot that Maria had fixed for her in the corner of the room. Laying down slowly, she drew her knees up close to her chest, and pulled the blanket over her head to shut out the questions that haunted the air around her.

The sound of voices awakened Jessalyn from a dream about the stone rose garden and her father. For a moment as she hovered between sleep and wakefulness, she thought the voices were born of the dream. Only when a dull twinge of pain from her stiff neck cut through her foggy thoughts did she recognize the voices as those of Sam . . . and Cale. She could not understand the words that they muttered, but the deep hum of Cale's voice was unmistakable, and it struck a familiar, unwanted chord within Jessalyn. Her face hidden from them, she cringed as she felt a string tighten within her — tighten to the breaking point — and she felt as if she'd be violently ill.

As she lay still on the bed, forcing herself to mimic the even breaths of sleep, her mind madly formulated plans to bolt away, to escape the fortress. If only there were some way that she could escape the room without their noticing, she thought. Mentally, she considered the layout of the room, and realized that there was no hope. Sam's bed was between her and the door, and even if she were able to crawl along the floor like an inchworm, she wouldn't stand a chance of getting out unnoticed. Her mind swam at the thought of having to face Cale again, particularly in the light of what Sam had told her. She was so confused now. She had been so weak before when he had lured her. How would she ever defend herself from him now that she knew he was not her father's killer, but her father's friend?

As the morning sun rose to stream cheerily through the window, the air in Jessalyn's blanket shelter grew unbearably hot, and finally she could stand it no longer. Reluctantly, she pushed the blanket aside, and rose unsteadily to her feet. She met Sam's eyes with a smile which faded immediately when her gaze wavered to Cale's. Forcing her small chin up, she deliberately recalled his abuse of her during their last encounter, and thus managed to remain cool as she walked past the bed and to the door. She had been prepared for Cale to stop her, and was surprised when he only gave her a casual glance.

"Where are you going?" he asked as easily as if they were on speaking terms. Still, the usual smile was absent from his face, and his eyes were dark with thought when they met hers.

Jessalyn returned his question with a stare the color of frost-tipped leaves, and brushed her fingers carelessly through the masses of coppery curls that danced about her face.

"To change," she replied steadily, and felt a note of

242

pride at her self-control. She was—she could tell by the expression on Sam's face—doing a perfect job of hiding the effect Cale's presence had on her. Sam gave her a knowing grin and a wink of approval for her efforts, and she returned it with a dazzling smile of her own before turning and disappearing through the doorway.

In the hall, she met Maria, who told her that her things had been moved and guided her to a large room further down the hall. Standing in the center of the room after Maria had left, Jessalyn sensed that she was no longer a prisoner. In fact, the large room seemed more as if it belonged in a fine San Francisco hotel rather than in a Comanchero fortress five hundred miles from civilization. Running a finger along the finely carved oak bed, Jessalyn looked disbelievingly around the room, noting the fine handmade furniture, the beautiful, intricately-woven Navaho blanket that covered the bed, and the wooden shutters that hung open beside the adobe-framed windows. Larger shutters with small, carved, rose patterns were closed over a doorway that opened to the shady porch outside.

Like a frisky foal finally let out of the stall in the springtime, Jessalyn trotted across the room to the outside door, and threw open the shutters. Leaning forward with the shutter handles still clutched in her hands, she swung back and forth with the doors, reveling in the smell and feel of the fresh, clean air. Filling her lungs with it, she smiled, her spring green eyes bright for the first time in weeks. Her cares forgotten in the ecstasy of the moment of freedom, she laughed, the sound of it hanging like music on the air.

Finally, she turned away with a bit of reluctance, and went to explore the room further. Her clothes had been carefully unpacked and hung in a wardrobe near the corner of the room. Beside the wardrobe was a dressing screen, and behind it Jessalyn found the bathtub that had briefly shared her cell with her. She smiled to find that it had been freshly prepared with a fragrant yucca bath, no doubt by Maria's hand. Within moments, she had shuttered the windows and slid the bolt into place on the door. Giving one last wary look around the pretty room, she slipped out of her clothes and into the warm water, closing her eyes in wonder as the warmth enveloped her slender body.

She lingered in the bath only long enough to scrub her skin clean and wash her hair, and then climbed quickly out and toweled herself. From the courtyard, she could now hear voices, some speaking in English, some in Spanish, some in Comanche, and some in an odd mix of all three. The memory of her first encounter with El Halcon's men made her shudder, and she went quickly to the wardrobe to find clothing for herself. To her surprise, all of her soiled clothing had been washed, dried, and hung neatly in the wardrobe with her other things. With silent thanks to Maria, she chose a blouse of soft sky blue cotton and a skirt to match and finished the outfit with her favorite knee-high Blackfoot moccasins.

She had finished dressing, opened the shutters, and was sitting on the windowsill absently brushing the damp curls of her coppery hair when she heard the hallway door creak open. It struck her as odd at first, for she had not opened the bolt. When Cale appeared in the doorway, her surprise faded, for she suspected that there was no place in his fortress to which he did not have access. Without standing up, she faced him, her cheeks flushed and her eyes bright as two diamonds.

"I see the bath has done you good," he remarked, standing in the doorway and leaning casually up against one side of the frame.

Jessalyn eyed him suspiciously, unsure of whether to regard his remark as an insult or a compliment. Finally, she chose to disregard it all together.

"Perhaps you mistake the reason for my bright spirits," she commented evilly, giving him a slight smile that bordered between sarcasm and devilry. Squinting out the window, she added, "I was just formulating an escape plan."

Cale darkened for a moment at her remark, wondering if she could possibly be so foolish. Though he was fairly certain she wasn't, he put forth a threat.

"I hope it is a foolproof one this time. If you're captured again, I'll be forced to leave you to the mercy of my men." He laughed cynically, and added, "And they have none."

Outwardly, Jessalyn appeared unabashed by his threat, but within herself, she shuddered at the thought and at the memory of her original capture. One thing was for sure—she wouldn't be trying to escape, nor was she certain that she had any reason to try. Perhaps Cale intended to release her now that she knew he had not been the one responsible for her father's death.

"You could let me go," she suggested, her jade

eyes hopeful and touchingly childlike. Somewhere deep inside, she wondered if she wanted to be released—and if she would be any less his prisoner were she a thousand miles away from him. Hooding her eyes to prevent the betrayal of her thoughts, she half-heartedly supported her point. "You have no reason to keep me here. Sam has explained to me that you were not responsible for my father's death."

Cale's eyes narrowed at her blind acceptance of his brother's word when he had told her the same thing only to have her violently disbelieve him.

"So if Sam has said it, it is true?" He placed the question before her like a double-edged sword.

"I believe him," she said, ignorant of the trap that had been laid.

He cocked his head thoughtfully at her answer and held her eyes with an intense golden gaze.

"Yet I told you the very same thing and you marked me for a liar," he observed dryly, looking at her with a hint of accusation in his whiskey-colored eyes. The prideful tilt of chin that returned his remark struck a strange chord within him, and the full line of his mouth quivered indecisively between a smile and a frown. Finally, he opted to see the humor in the situation, and grinned slightly, saying, "I guess I can't blame you."

Shaking his head and laughing to himself, he stepped into the room and closed the door behind him. The look on Jessalyn's pretty young face told him that their discussion—at least from her end—was likely to be a loud one. It wouldn't do for all of his men to hear him admitting his mistakes—and he had made a few with the pretty young firebrand who sat looking so vulnerable, framed like a picture in the window.

"I never meant to hurt you, Jesse," he said, coming to stand beside her in the warm square of midday sunshine from the window. "I was only trying to keep you from ruining a plan that your father and I spent months putting into action." He paused awkwardly, trying to find a way to explain to her that the things he had done had been for her own good, that he had not been trying to take advantage of her or toy with her feelings. "You don't know what you've gotten in the middle of here, Jesse." The hard glint in her jade eyes told him that he was failing to win her over. She only sat looking away from him, her young face a mirror of hurt and anger.

Gently, he reached out to cup her chin in his palm, and tilted her face up toward him. "I didn't mean to hurt you, Jesse. I only meant to keep you from getting killed — or from getting anyone else killed." As his eyes met hers, he felt himself flooded with a desire to wash the pain and anger from those emerald depths. At that moment, he would have given anything to have wiped the past several months and all of its torments from her life. He wanted with every bit of his soul to take away the shell of ice that she had frozen around herself and bring forth the innocent flower that he saw deep within her.

"I'll take care of you, Jesse," he whispered out loud, but to himself. He'd never said that to a woman before. In fact, he'd never even thought of saying it. Now, suddenly, it seemed as if there were nothing else to say. The fact that he had promised something of himself to her didn't even seem to matter, perhaps because she had already held that piece of him long ago. Still, the admission of it left him vulnerable—a position in which he rarely found himself—and he fell silent as he waited for her reaction.

Her eyes searching his face desperately, Jessalyn sat frozen where his words had found her. How could he be so cruel one moment and so tender the next? Was he offering her his help? his protection? his love? Her mind dashed back to the words that Sam had said the night before. Could it possibly be true that Cale felt something other than hatred for her? And what did she feel for him? The questions spun in her mind like specks in a dust devil, until finally, she pressed her fingers to her temples to shut them out.

"No more lies!" she exclaimed. She had the strange feeling that she had made that request before. Their lives seemed to cross through first one misunderstanding and then another, and she had the hopeless feeling that it would always be that way for them. Still, if there was ever to be any hope for them, there had to be truth now, the complete truth. "I need to know everything." Her eyes found his imploringly. "You have lied to me from the beginning—you say to protect me. Very well then, I accept that. But you can't protect me any longer, Cale. Please. You have to tell me the truth, all of it. What was your involvement with my father? If you didn't have him killed, who did? What is this plan you keep talking about?" There were a thousand more questions spinning in her mind, but she hushed them and let the three that she had asked suffice. They were the biggest stumbling blocks, she knew, and she held her breath while she waited for Cale to respond. This was it, the final moment of truth between them. If he could not trust her as a friend, then from here forth, he would be an enemy. The moments ticked by with painful sloth as Jessalyn watch him step away from her and turn his back. The hard line of his shoulders was unbending as he took a few steps toward the door and then stopped in mid-stride. His head was bowed in thought for a moment, and then he turned slowly back to her, his face still creased with thought.

"You want the truth," he said, clearly uncertain that what he was about to do was right. If only he could predict what her reaction would be. If only he knew whether the truth would bring her closer or drive her further away. With a deep sigh, he sat down on the edge of the small writing desk and crossed his arms over his broad chest. His gaze was intense as he met her wide, questioning eyes, and the hard lines on his brow deepened a bit, leaving him looking much older than his years. They had come to a moment of truth, he knew, and he had no choice but to stand helplessly by and wait for the outcome.

"The truth, my dear Jesse," he began matter-of-factly, "is that your father and I have both watched for years while the Texans stole the lands of the Co-manche, and killed their game, and slaughtered them by the thousands. Both of us knew what statehood for Texas would mean—thousands of immigrants, all hungry to grab a piece of land for themselves, all hungry to kill a few Indians and bounty a few scalps. Your father had a plan for getting Indian lands guaranteed in the Texas statehood agreement—but you know about that, of course. What your father didn't tell you was that he had a few silent partners in the plan. Last winter, he met with several of the Comanche and Kiowa chiefs at Sounds on the Wind's camp." He saw by the spark that lit in her eyes that she was beginning to piece together fragments of her father's behavior from the past several months. The eager look on her face told him that she had wondered at her father's secret meetings, but that she had never been able to find out the plan behind them. Now, she sat restrained by thin strings of control as she waited for him to solve the puzzle. He would have smiled at her impatience if the situation had not been so serious. As it was, he only returned her questioning gaze with a stare as cool and impassive as steel.

"His plan was for the Comanche and Kiowa to stir up trouble with the settlers at a few . . . opportune times to push the legislatures to be receptive to an Indian land settlement." He could see disbelief creeping into her wide jade eyes at the disclosure of her father's plan for bloody tactics to cinch the Indian settlement. Still, he had no choice but to finish telling her the truth—all of it. "The statehood was moving too slow for your father, and each month that it dragged on, the prospects for an Indian land boundary got worse. So your father came to me. His plan was for me to get the Apache and Comanche to cross into Mexico and raid there so that the Mexicans would follow them back across the Rio. He figured the sight of Mexican soldiers moving north into Texas territory would make the Texans scream a little more for statehood." Now the disbelief in her eyes had blazed into an angry wildfire, and her cheeks had gone red with rage, and so he finished the confession off quickly. "We were just about to put things into action when your father was gunned down."

Jessalyn sat staring blankly at him as her mind began to reel in protest of the picture that he had just painted of her father. She wanted desperately not to believe it, yet each detail that Cale had provided fit too neatly into the events of the past months. Her father had insisted on wintering in Sounds on the Wind's camp. He had slipped away often, leaving her behind, and had evaded her questions when he had returned. It all made sense to her now, and the naked fact that her father had not trusted her drove like a blade into her heart. Her eyes became a mirror of the torture in her soul when she spoke again.

"Why didn't my father tell me?" It was more a plea than a question. She desperately wanted there to be a reason for her father to have kept her out of his plan, a reason other than his thinking her unworthy of the task.

Cale felt a pang of sorrow for her at the forlorn tone of her voice, and he was drawn deeply into the sea of despair in her liquid green eyes.

"He wanted to protect you." His reply was quick and sharp, though he knew she wouldn't like the answer. It was the truth, and though he would have liked to have spared her, he knew she'd learn it sooner or later. Better that it came from him now than from one of his men later. Seeing tears tremble like dewdrops in the corners of her eyes, he crossed the room and sat beside her on the ledge. Taking her small, trembling hands in hers, he leaned down to catch her

251

eye.

"He was only doing what he thought was best, Jesse," he said softly, caressing her slender fingers against his palms as gently as if she were made of glass. "Your father wasn't some sort of god, Jess, he was just a man. Maybe he underestimated you—maybe he should have told you the truth—but he was only doing what he thought was best. He didn't want anything to happen to you." Cale tried to explain it the best way he could. After having watched Jessalyn Kendrik over the past two months, he was fairly certain that her father had not given her credit due—in fact, he himself had done the same. Her fragile beauty and youth had caused him to misjudge her abilities at every turn, and she had always proven stronger and more skilled than he had thought possible.

Raising her hands gently in his, he brought her fingers across her cheeks to wipe away the tears there and then brought them to his lips to kiss the drops away.

"Don't remember him badly, Jesse." His eyes were clouded with memory as he said the words. He could remember his grandfather telling him the same thing many years ago. Placing her hands back in her lap, he reached into his pocket and drew out the stone rose that she had dropped in the sand on a day that seemed a hundred years ago. Placing it in her palm, he folded her fingers around it and stood up. Bending over, he kissed the top of her coppery head lightly, and added, "Your father was a good man, Jess. He loved you very much." With that, he left her in the room by herself, but not alone. The air was

252

alive with Lane Kendrik's ghost, and Cale could almost see him standing beside the window stroking the willful curls on his daughter's bowed head. It was time that Jessalyn made peace with that ghost, Cale decided. If she didn't, it would haunt her forever, and that would be a far worse crime than any committed so far.

As he closed the door behind him, he heard her speaking in soft, low tones to the still air of the room, to the visitor who had come to finally say goodbye.

Jessalyn could not tell how much time had passed before she finally felt whole again. The sun was sinking behind the canyon wall and stroking the rocks with brilliant crimson paints outside the window when she again looked out. She had sat for hours, she dimly realized, talking to her father—telling him all of the things that she had stored within her since his death. She had sensed him so close to her then that many times she had felt as if she could reach out and touch him. Even the air in the room was filled with the sweet tobacco and leather scent of him, and his deep laugh seemed to echo in the warm winds of high canyon walls.

He was gone now forever, and she knew it, but somehow she felt that she could stand on her own. Perhaps that had been his purpose in lingering so near her after his death—to give her a few last lessons in life before he passed away. Whatever the reason, she now realized that what Cale had said was true. Her father had only tried to do what he thought best for her.

Looking down at the stone rose in her hand, she turned it over, running a finger along its delicately formed petals and smiling a bit. Cale must have retrieved it when she had dropped it by the Salt Lakes. She understood now why he had called her that, but she wasn't sure whether to see it as a compliment or not. The little sandstone rose was beautiful, but it was as cold as ice in her fingers.

She wondered if she had become like it, cold and without life, and if she would ever be the same as she had once been. She suspected that she would not. Even now that she had made peace with her father's death, all that she had once been had not returned. It was as if the light in her soul had dimmed a bit, as if there was still something missing that, if found, would make her whole.

Setting the rose down on the dressing table, she sat on the edge of the bed staring at it and absently brushing her hairbrush through her hair.

"What secrets do you have, desert rose?" she whispered to the silent rose on the table. "What makes you so cold when the air around you is warm?"

The rose didn't reply, but only sat twinkling up at her from the dressing table in the fading amber light. Finally, she took it in her hand again and laid back on the bed, clutching the bit of sandstone like a treasure against her heart.

"Stone roses don't grow." She heard her father's words of long-ago echo in her head, and again she recalled the day that he had knelt beside her in her stone rose garden. "They just stay the same always. They'll always be beautiful, and they'll never die—

but they'll never grow either."

So that was the secret, she realized. To really live was to risk yourself, and without risk, she would never truly find herself again.

Chapter Fourteen

Jessalyn awoke the next morning to the strange feeling that something was about to happen. Her heart was pounding in anticipation against her chest before she had opened her willow green eyes to the new day. Her lashes flew up suddenly, and she sat up in bed, her gaze darting about the room in expectation, but nothing had changed. Only when her mind had crept through the fog of sleep to catch up to her senses did she realize what had awakened her so suddenly. The air that crept through the cracks of the shuttered windows was literally alive with the sounds of excited voices and festive chatter. Words in several different languages mingled indiscriminantly as bits of conversations met her ear, and she thought instantly of the many rendezvous she and her father had attended in the past.

Shuddering with excitement, she jumped from the bed and danced a few steps toward the window before a cool bit of morning breeze slipped through the shutters and took her back. Looking down at herself, she realized that she wore only the thin cotton nightgown that Maria had left in the wardrobe for her. She smiled a bit at her own haste and went to the dressing closet. It had been so long since she had slept in anything other than her clothes that she had been ready to throw open the shutters and greet the new day in her nightgown.

As she reached to open the wardrobe, she noticed for the first time a soft buff-colored leather skirt and blouse hanging neatly over the top of the dressing screen. Curious, she took the garments down and held them out in front of her, admiring the fine Comanche beadwork that adorned the yoke of the top and the long fringe that swung gracefully from the yoke of the top and the bottom of the skirt. It was truly the finest work she had ever seen, she thought, running a finger delicately over the even stitchwork.

Holding the garment against her, she went to the mirror to further admire the look of it and smiled slightly at the reflection. A frown replaced the smile in the next moment and she lowered the garment a bit, wondering who had brought it and if it had been meant for her. If it had, she was hardly certain that she wanted to accept it. She paced back and forth across the room, considering the problem for a time, and then finally came back to stand before the mirror. This was what finally decided the issue. With a sudden flair of abandon, she danced to the dressing screen and tossed the garments on top.

Shuddering against the cool fall air, she pulled her nightgown over her head and stood with her slender form bared only for a few moments before she pulled on the skirt and top. To her surprise, they fit as if they had been created especially for her, the soft leather clinging alluringly to the gentle curves of her body. Smoothing the supple fabric over herself, she moved from behind the screen, reaching down to take her knee-high moccasins from the floor where she had left them the night before. Teetering on one foot and then the next, she slipped her moccasins on and drew the laces up tight.

When she had finished, she took the hairbrush from the dressing table and moved to the long, oval mirror. Standing in front of it, she brushed the long mass of her brassy hair forward over her shoulder and then tossed it back to dance in willful curls about her waist. All the while, she considered the new clothing in the mirror, admiring the beauty of the careful beadwork and wondering who had left her the dress. Most certainly, it had not been made by Maria; the work was obviously Comanche. Perhaps Maria had come by it somewhere else and left it for her, Jessalyn thought. Perhaps the dress was not meant for her at all — still, it had been left in her room . . .

A minute twinkle of light from the dressing table caught her eye, and she looked down to find the little sandstone rose where she had left it the night before. Thoughtfully, she cocked her head to one side and considered it, running a slender finger slowly along a glittering petal. In the soft morning light that filtered through the closed shutters, it was almost the same color that his eyes had been when he had given it to her, a deep, soft amber that seemed full of secrets, yet at the same time somehow comforting. She remembered the moment now in her mind, and a thousand scattered moments before that. She could see Cale now as if he were standing before her, each detail of the handsome face, the strong, square chin, the perfectly shaped nose, the sensuous, full lips . . . and his eyes.

She remembered the day that she had first seen him and how their eyes had met. She had felt then that he could look right through her—and he must have, for he had seemed to know her so well. He had played her like a song, as if he had understood the melody even before the words had been written. He had known at every turn how she would react, and how to steer her into the course that he had planned. It would have all worked very well, too, if she had not followed him to El Hueco that morning and seen him meeting with his men.

She wondered now what would have happened if she had not followed him that day, if she had never figured out his secret. Would he have talked her into giving up her search for El Halcon and then just rode away and out of her life? It certainly seemed that this had been his plan. Could he really have cared so little for her that he really only wanted to be rid of her, the way that you want to be rid of a pesky pup that keeps dogging your heels? The thought made her stomach flop upside down within her, and suddenly she felt ill. Surely it could not be so. She realized now that she loved him, at least in some bizarre physical way, and that she teetered dangerously on the edge of giving over her heart and soul to a man who had made her no promises. It was a horrible position to be in, something like standing in front of a firing squad and wondering at which moment the shot would come.

With a sigh, she set the brush down on the table and rolled her deep green eyes to the ceiling. What would come of this now? Would he release her? Would he force her to go? She could not bear the thought. Wrapping her arms around herself, she hugged tightly, as if against a sudden chill, and tried to banish such questions from her head. She could only wait and see. If she asked him, he would certainly think that she intended to force him into a marriage, and whatever happened, she'd not be a shotgun bride. Even if it meant that she would have to live without him forever, she would not be brushed away crying and begging like a smitten woman. Whatever happened, she'd have her pride.

The sound of the commotion outside again drew her attention, and she looked toward the door, wondering if it was locked, or if she was now free to move about the fort. Surely he knew that she would not be fool enough to try to escape. Briefly, she thought of the two men who had first captured her, and of the hundred more like them that were undoubtedly outside. She wondered how she would face them.

Gathering her courage with a deep breath, she opened the door and stepped into the empty hall. She moved down it slowly, surprised to find no one there, and with the vague feeling that she was guilty of some infraction of the rules. When she reached the outside door, she hesitated for a moment, then swung it open with sudden abandon. Her gaze collided immediately with a broad, buckskin-fringed chest, and she squinted upward into the sun to find Cale's eyes twinkling down at her.

"Going for a walk?" he asked good-naturedly. There was nothing in his voice or his face that seemed to indicate anger with her actions.

An uncertain tremor of flushed lips returned his smile, and she looked up at him with all of the confidence that she could manage.

"I . . . I heard voices outside," she explained. "I wanted to see what was happening."

Cale threw back his head and laughed at her, suddenly reminded of the saying about curiosity and the cat. Her eyes were green like a cat's . . .

"You save me a trip, my dear." He threw off the musings the uncanny color of her eyes had provided. "I was just coming to get you. We have a very important guest."

Strangely, a thousand horrible thoughts ran through Jessalyn's mind, and she searched his face for any sign of malice, but he seemed perfectly at ease. Seeing her wariness, he placed a reassuring hand on the small of her back and pulled her forward out of the doorway, saying, "After you, Jesse mine."

Walking a few paces behind her, Cale's eyes ran the length of her slender figure, and he smiled in admiration of the picture that she made in the new dress. He'd traded for it only that morning and had

261

left it in her room as she slept. He was pleased to see that she had worn it, and he wondered if she knew where it had come from. By the proud tilt of her chin and the independent glint in her eye, he guessed not.

Looking back at him, Jessalyn slowed her pace until he walked beside her, and she looked up at him through heavy black lashes.

"Just who is this . . . guest?" she asked, her voice still razor-edged with suspicion. She narrowed her eyes a bit and looked at him out of the corner when he returned her inquiry with a mischievous wink.

"Someone you know, I think," he replied obliquely, and when she scoffed in disgust at his evasion, he added, "You'll pleased to see him, I promise."

At that, the cloud of doubt in Jessalyn's green eyes turned to a full-fledged hurricane, but she shrugged her shoulders in an effort to seem unconcerned.

"We hardly run in the same circles," she said with exaggerated formality. "I can't imagine what friend we could have in common." She couldn't. Further, she couldn't imagine whom Cale would know that she would be glad to see. She quickened her pace unconsciously as curiosity tugged like a tiny gremlin at her moccasin strings. As they walked, she began to look around the camp, for the first time noticing the bustle of activity. Had she not been so accustomed to Indian camps and trading posts, she might have noticed sooner that the camp was alive with Apache men, women, and children, all scurrying anxiously about to do their trading. By the few words she caught, Jessalyn guessed that they had just arrived, and she wondered suddenly if the guest whom Cale spoke of had come with them.

"Is this guest with them?" she asked, nodding toward some of the newcomers. When Cale nodded in response, she smiled a bit triumphantly at having caught him in error. "Then you've made a mistake," she announced. "I hardly know any of the Apache. It's unlikely that your guest is a friend of mine."

"I am wounded by your words, daughter." The words in Apache, ground strangely against Jessalyn's ears, and she squinted up into the sun at the largest Indian she had ever seen. A smile bright against his dark face, the Apache added, "You should be more careful when you count your friends."

Unaccustomed to his language, Jessalyn stared blankly up at him, her dark brows lowered in concentration as she struggled to translate his words. Finally, she managed to grasp their meaning, and immediately after, she knew the identity of the speaker. To the best of her limited vocabulary, she formulated a reply in the language of the Mimbres Apaches.

"Mangus Coloradas," she remembered, and spoke, his name in Spanish as she had most often heard it. She wasn't certain how to translate it, anyway. She'd heard it said in Comanche as Red Sleeves, and in Kiowa as something like Roan Shirt, but she didn't know which was correct. She had only met the chief once before, and that had been

263

many years ago when she'd been little more than a child. She was fairly certain she hadn't called him by name then, and her father had always called him only "Mangus."

Leaning back a bit, the big chief smiled wider, the grin looking out of place against his stern features, and narrowed one eye at the green-eyed girl.

"You have forgotten me," he observed correctly, and then did his best to appear wounded, although, in truth, he was not surprised. He perhaps would not have recalled her either, had it not been for the fact that her father had been a trusted friend of his youth — and had she not had those eyes. He remembered the look of them as if he had seen her only yesterday, but now they were framed with the beauty of a woman rather than with the innocence of a child.

"It has been many years." Jessalyn flushed crimson at his blatant scrutiny and her obvious lack of adeptness at his language. It was a position in which she rarely found herself, since she spoke several languages fluently. Giving up, she added in Spanish, "It is good to see you again." Suddenly, she remembered him very well from the time that her father had taken her to the camp of Mangus's band, and she wondered how she could ever have forgotten him at all. Mangus Coloradas was not the sort of man one forgot. All of northern Mexico and most of the border country knew him as the devil incarnate, and almost everyone in southwestern Texas knew him as a peaceful, but uneasy, neighbor. Friends and enemies alike revered him as a fearless leader and a cunning man.

At her final surrender to a change in language, the fifty-year-old chief laughed like a youngster, his waist-length black hair spreading like a cape behind him.

"Your father has kept you too long with those stinking dog Comanches," he said, changing languages so smoothly it was as if there had been no change. With a wry glance at Cale to size up the effect of his only somewhat playful jibe at the Comanches, he added to Jessalyn, "You don't speak our language well."

Jessalyn returned his observation with a hint of a smile and a good-natured shrug of admission.

"Perhaps I will spend some time with the Mimbres and learn," she said wryly, and then caught a strange look from Cale out of the corner of her eye. Had he been angry at her suggestion that she might be around long enough to learn the language of his guests? She couldn't tell. As quickly as the change in his posture had come, it was gone beneath the cover of an easy mask.

"Welcome to *mi casa* again, my friend," Cale broke in, gesturing toward the large adobe that Jessalyn had only so recently left. He didn't like the turn the conversation was taking, and for a moment he questioned his wisdom in bringing Jessalyn to meet with Mangus. The last thing he needed was for a discussion of Jessalyn's treatment at his hands to get started. Mangus had been a good friend of Lane Kendrik, and he would undoubtedly see it as his duty to protect Jesse in her father's absence.

"Shall we go inside?" he urged, stepping out of the way and ushering Jessalyn toward the adobe with a wave. In a surprisingly accommodating fashion, she turned and started back down the path toward the house with the Apache chief towering over her from behind. Following the two of them, Cale rolled his whiskey-colored eyes hopefully to the wide blue sky and sighed. He hoped the good Lord was looking down on them in a fair humor that morning—after all, trying to do what he was about to do was basically asking for a miracle.

When they entered the cool, shadowy hallway, they found Sam slowly making his way down the corridor under the support of a crudely made crutch. Seeing them, he looked up and smiled in his usual boyish fashion, an open light of admiration in his eyes for the tall chief.

"I thought I recognized the fowl smell of Apache," he joked, his face serious but his eyes laughing. Waving his free hand in Mangus's direction, he widened his eyes and tossed his hair back with a shrug, attempting to look horrified. "Cale." He skillfully imitated the reproachful tone of an old biddy as he looked down his nose. "How could you have let this . . . this filthy Indian in here. Why, he'll dirty the carpets. He'll smell up the air. He'll perspire on the furniture. He'll . . ."

Having had enough, the old chief reached around Jessalyn to lightly cuff the young half-breed on the ear, and then drew his head back with Sam's long raven hair still caught between his fingers. Stretching it to its length but not pulling, he reached for his knife and said, smiling evilly, "I have always wanted a Comanche scalp. This one seems to have been eaten by the moths, but perhaps I could hang it from my horse's ass as a decoration."

At that, all three men broke into raucous gales of laughter, slapping each other good-naturedly on the back. A bit confused, Jessalyn stepped out of the way of the exchange and stood up against the wall. When they had finished, she remained there watching them doubtfully, her jade eyes narrowed with thought as she considered the relationship between the three men. Apparently, they knew each other well, which seemed strange to Jessalyn, as the Mimbres usually ranged quite a distance from the pass country. She was still puzzling the question when Cale ushered her on down the hall, falling into step beside her. Sam came slowly on behind them with Red Sleeves walking patiently by his side.

From beneath a thick veil of sooty lashes, Jessalyn stole a glance at Cale, who looked strangely thoughtful. She had never before seen his handsome face marked with such obvious concern, and she guessed that something very important was about to happen. Feeling her eyes before he looked down to discover them, Cale gave her a reassuring hint of a smile that seemed to melt away all of the lines of concern like magic.

"I want to see your father's plan through to the end." He spoke plainly, as Sam and Mangus had fallen far behind them. As they stepped into a room at the end of the hall, he turned to catch her eyes with an intensity that took her back in her tracks, and added, "I need your help."

Swallowing the lump that had jumped into her throat at the sheer power of his steely gaze, she took a step closer to him and spoke quietly so that the others would not hear.

"What must I do?" she asked, vaguely uncertain whether she was doing the right thing. Somehow, she felt like the fly wandering blindly into the spider's web. It occurred to her then that she knew very few of the details of the plan that had been hatched between her father and Cale, but it was already too late—the Comanchero was hurriedly briefing her on her duties in the scheme.

"We have to convince Mangus to take his warriors into Mexico and stir up enough trouble to get the government after him," he was saying, but Jessalyn only half heard him. There was a warning alarm ringing in her ears that almost drowned out the sound of his voice.

"Then he'll cross back over the border with the Mexicans on his tail," Cale was continuing, and Jessalyn had the vague feeling that she had missed something. Her eyes widened in shock as she realized what he had said, and calculated the implications.

"You're going to start a war with Mexico!" she observed rightly, but at the same time could not believe that it was true. Nor could she believe the icy, emotionless look in Cale's amber eyes. It was like looking into two stones polished as hard and cold as glass, and when he spoke, he talked as casually as if he were putting soup on to boil.

"The Tejanos need to be prodded toward a quick statehood," he said, his voice now down to a whisper as Mangus and Sam drew closer to the doorway. "Every day that goes by, they take more and more from the Indian. A war with Mexico will make them more anxious for the protection of the United States Army."

In anger, Jessalyn took a step back from him as if she'd been struck, her eyes flashing like uneven streaks of lightning.

"Hundreds of people will die!" she protested, straining to control the loudness of her voice, and now uncomfortably aware that Sam and Red Sleeves were nearly to the door. "I won't be part of it." She made her decision in a split second, and started toward the door. She couldn't believe that this had been her father's plan—to goad the Comanche and Apache into raiding and killing hundreds of settlers, to start yet another war with Mexico. She knew all too well the importance of the Indian boundaries being drawn in the state charter . . . yet at what price would justice be bought? She'd seen the brutality of Indian raids, and the treatment of captive slaves. Even if this had been part of her father's plan, she would not help to bring it about.

The vise-like grip of Cale's hand on her arm stopped her exit and spun her about roughly. Her eyes were as bright and cool as frosted grass as they met with the molten steel of his.

"You'll do as you're told, Jesse," he growled from between clenched teeth, the side of his jaw twitching in rage. Leaning close to her, he added, "You'll do as your father would have wanted, Jesse mine. Don't forget who is the prisoner here. You're at my disposal, Jesse, and if you want ever to leave you'll cooperate now." Roughly, he pulled her to the table that sat to one side of the room and pushed her into a chair. Landing with a thump, she stared up at him in open anger, her lips clenched so tightly that they had paled around the edges.

Looking down at her, Cale could see trouble brewing, and he wondered at the wisdom of having forced her to stay in the room. As a willing ally, she had the unique advantage of having a soft spot in Mangus's heart. Lane Kendrik had been a trusted friend of the Mimbres chief, and Cale had been counting on that trust to swing Red Sleeves over to his plan. Whether he like it or not, in the absence of her father, he needed Jesse. Unfortunately, she looked anything but cooperative as his brother and Mangus entered the room, and Cale placed a tight hand on her shoulder to keep her silent. One thing was for certain—he was looking down the road at what would be one of the longest hours of his life.

Jessalyn sat numbly in her chair as the three men standing over her head made their final plan. It was exactly as Cale had described to her. Mangus was to raid deep into Mexico, and then cross back over the border when the Mexican government mobilized men to hunt him down. It was bound to finally bring about the conflict over the ownership of the New Mexico territory that had been brewing for years, and to push Texas into statehood. It had another distinct advantage in that, with a Mexican war on their hands, the Texans and the United States would be anxious to pacify the Indians so as not to fight a two-front war. It was a brilliant plan, cleverly laid by the unlikely looking group of generals who now had risen to stand around the table.

It made Jessalyn sick to think that she had been part of it, and to know that her father had initiated it. The cost would be hundreds, thousands, of lives and a deepening of the hatred between the red and the white man. Looking from one face to the next above her, Jessalyn hated them all, and she hated herself for not being strong enough to stand against them and to refuse her father's wishes. She avoided looking at Mangus as he stood and, with a farewell to Sam and Cale, left the room. After him, Sam stood up and, looking first to Jessalyn and then to Cale, made a hasty retreat after the Apache.

Listening to their footsteps die away in the hall, Jessalyn stood up from her chair, tossing her hair like molten copper over her shoulder as she stood to her full height. In her shame, she could not meet the eyes of the Comanchero, but instead turned toward the door.

"You must certainly be the devil himself, El Halcon," she said bitterly, her voice quivering with the pressure of coming tears. Walking slowly out the door, she added, "And I have let you take my hand and lead me into hell. Even God couldn't forgive me now." As she left the room, her eyes were wet with tears and her mind was swimming with a kaleidoscope of horrid scenes of raids and massacres, marred skins red and white, but blood all the same color.

Watching her go, Cale understood her reaction, but at the same time wondered at it. Certainly she knew that they were doing what had to be done. Without firm land rights, the Indian had no chance, and he'd sooner see every white man in Texas dead than see the strong, gentle people who had raised him from a boy to a man vanished from the land that had once belonged to them. That was fair; that was right. He'd make Jesse see that somehow. If he couldn't, he knew she would never forgive him, and worse yet, would never forgive herself. With a slow sigh, he turned about on his heel and went to follow her.

He found her in her room, sitting quietly in the window ledge with her legs curled up under her skirt and her arms hugging them tightly to her. Her eyes were turned out the window toward the cloudless sky so that she did not see him when he entered. Tears ran like rivers of quicksilver against the smooth olive skin of her cheeks, and her lashes trembled against the deep green of her eyes like dark shadows against willow leaves. Cale stood for a moment in the doorway before he crossed the room and placed a comforting hand on her shoulder. As her crystal-rimmed eyes moved slowly up to him, he felt as if his heart had been torn out through his chest.

"Jesse," he whispered as if shushing a crying child. With the backs of his fingers, he wiped the tears from her cheeks and felt as if he had done the same thing a tragically short time before. In the back of his mind, he wondered if the two of them would ever find peace, or if the cruelty of his way of life would destroy her.

"It was the only way," he said, speaking of her part in the meeting with Mangus, but thinking of each time that he had maneuvered her as an unwilling pawn in his own plan.

"How can you be so cool about it?" she choked, struggling to keep control of her failing voice and looking up at him in disbelief. He spoke as if he were talking about pulling weeds from the garden rather than instigating the hand of one man against another. Still unable to believe that he fully realized the consequence of what he had begun, she added, "Don't you realize how many will die?" When he did not respond, she stood up and faced him with a hard glare through her tears. "Red men and white men, Cale, not just white. You're going to kill the very people you claim to love. How can you do that if you really care for them so much?"

With hard conviction that seemed to bounce her off like water off oiled leather, he met her confusion and anger steadily. In truth, he had long ago considered each of the protests that she now raised. In fact, he could recall weighing the cost of each of them with her father not so long ago.

"There is no other way." He repeated his earlier words, and, as before, he was certain of them. He never did anything until he had weighed the consequences and considered the alternatives, and this was no exception. "This statehood agreement is judgment day for the red man in this territory. If there is no hard and fast line drawn between the white man and the Indian now, the days of the Indian are numbered." Taking her chin in his hand lightly, he leaned down and delivered his next words with more force. "You know that, Jesse. You've been back east. You know how many people there are hungry for a piece of land, you know that they will keep coming as long as there is a piece they can steal from the red man." He could see a light of understanding begin to flicker through the clouds of confusion in her eyes, and he pressed on toward it. "The Kiowa would be the first to go, Jesse, those very Kiowa that you claim to love so much. Then the Comanche—your friends, Sam's blood." He could now see in her eyes a reflection of the clear picture that he, himself, saw of the future of the Indian if no settlement boundaries were established. Taking one last look into her soul, he added, "I'd rather see every white soul in Texas driven away or dead than stand back and let that day come. These are my people, my family and my friends. I owe them this much—and more."

Searching the handsome, determined set of his face, Jessalyn saw for the first time the torment of the two worlds that claimed him. His skin white and his upbringing red, his soul was somewhere in between, like a spirit trapped in purgatory. She recognized something of herself in that, and unconsciously she raised a hand to touch the chiseled curve of his cheek. She could find no words to express the strange understanding that had finally penetrated the wall she had built around herself, but stood staring into his eyes in mute understanding. Finally, he wrapped her in his strong arms and pulled her close to him.

"It's a hard road, Jesse, but we'll find our way." The words passed over her troubled mind like soft, faint clouds, and she wasn't sure whether she'd heard them from his lips or merely read them in his eyes.

Chapter Fifteen

Jessalyn sat astride Diablo's broad back as he pawed the ground nervously and reared slightly onto his hind legs beside Cale's buckskin. The buckskin snorted and backed his ears in irritation at the other horse's antics and then turned back to watch the approach of the bobbing mass of oncoming riders. Sitting in the saddle, the Comanchero looked as calm as his mount though the bulk of the Comanche nation rode slowly down the hillside toward him. The chiefs rode first, with brightly colored feathers dangling from their scalplocks and painted beads and quills hanging from the fringes of their buckskins. Behind them in a half-moon formation the warriors of the represented bands moved like a dark wall across the arid landscape. It was a sight that would have struck terror in the hearts of most white men, but the Comancheros only stood watching them impassively from the bottom of the bowl-shaped canyon.

The Comanche formation stopped fifty yards away from the waiting men, holding their small, nervous ponies at bay. A tall chief rode slowly from the front of the line and continued across the open ground toward the Comancheros, his dark eyes fixed on the tawny-haired leader who sat, still relaxed, astride his dun horse. The small metal cones that dangled from his horse's mane jingled against each other in the breeze, making a strange, eerie music in the thick silence. His name was Peta Nocona, Wanderer, and at twenty-five, he looked strangely young to be a leader of so many men—a fact of which he seemed flatly unaware as he stopped before the Comanchero and rested his hands comfortably across his horse's withers.

"So The Hawk has decided to fly north this autumn." He smiled a bit, and his dark eyes lit with a compelling sparkle. "It has been too long since we saw you last."

In response, Cale laughed. One thing about Nocona, he certainly had a talent for understatement. It had been more than ten years since they had seen each other, and both of them had been little more than boys then. Still, as Cale reached out to grab the other's hand above the forearm, the bond that lay between them was as strong as it had once been.

"You should come south more often, my friend," he replied, returning the Comanche's smile, and speaking in his language as easily as he spoke in English. "But I hear that you have been busy since I saw you last. You have a wife, and a band of your own. It is no wonder you do not have time for your friends anymore."

At that, the Comanche threw his head back and laughed heartily, and the tension in the air shattered like glass.

"It really has been too long," he observed, shaking his head, his smile broad and white against his dark skin. The smile faded suddenly when his eyes drifted away from Cale and settled on Jessalyn. With an unwavering regard, she returned his probing gaze, shifting unconsciously in her saddle. She had heard of Peta Nocona, but had never met him, though she knew his father, an old chief named Iron Shirt, rather well. When his appraisal of her deepened, she flushed crimson, and looked demurely away to Cale, who was watching her with much the same expression.

"Who is she?" the Comanche asked with more than mild curiosity in his voice. After a moment, he narrowed his raven eyes thoughtfully and added, "I know that horse . . ."

Unwilling to be spoken about as if she were not present, Jessalyn fought the urge to shrink into the grass underneath her horse's feet and crawl away. Raising her eyes to meet those of the chief, she said, in perfect Comanche, "This was the horse of Kerdik. I am his daughter, Jea-seh."

Recognition lit instantly in the eyes of the young chief, and his cool appraisal of her deepened with genuine warmth. "I heard of your father's death at the trading post of Hooked Nose. I share in your grief. Your father was a strong man and a trusted friend."

Jessalyn winced unwillingly at his mention of Bent's trading post, and inwardly felt a pang of remorse. She had once thought of the adobe-walled fort as her home, but now it seemed a million miles

278

away. She hardly felt like the same girl who had ridden out of there, and she wondered if she would ever go back.

"I am grateful for your kindness," she replied, her wide green eyes still trained on his. He regarded her with a bit of surprise at her boldness, leaning back slightly on his horse's back, and after a moment smiled at Cale.

"It appears that you have been busy yourself, my friend." He laughed heartily, his handsome face lighting with an easy smile that spoke silently of confidence and strength. "But no more of this," he added, nodding over his shoulder toward the crest of the hill behind him. "Come to the camp. We will eat, talk of younger days, and then of these new things."

Cale nodded his agreement, and the chief moved his horse around to fall into step beside the Comanchero. He cast another sidelong glance of ebony at Jessalyn, and instinctively she held her horse back a few paces. Watching the two men, she rode off to the side and slightly behind them, close enough to hear their conversation, but far enough back to avoid the Comanche's probing gaze. Their talk was of old times, of the exploits of boyhood and the freedom of youth. Listening to them—both of them leaders of many men—Jessalyn heard something behind their words that she had never noticed before. It was a solemn note of regret for independence lost and a carefully hidden desire to once again be free of the pressures of leadership. Watching the two men, Jessalyn knew that it was something they shared, something that they understood in each other, a common bond that held them together.

As they rode on further, Jessalyn looked back over her shoulder at the lines of warriors who now followed them. As was their custom, they had dressed in their finest and adorned their horses with beads and metal cones to come out and greet their visitors. It was a display of great respect for the guest — and it was obvious by the looks of awe on most of their faces that they indeed had great respect for El Halcon.

Again Jessalyn looked at Cale where he sat, tall and confident, next to the Comanche chief. She wondered how he had come to be what he was now, half white man and half Comanche, a devil to one people and almost a god to another. It seemed strange that she knew so little of him, yet had thrown herself into this bizarre plan of his. Only two weeks ago, she had violently refused to be a part of convincing Mangus to take the Mimbres Apaches into Mexico, and now here she was by Cale's side, trying to spur the Comanche nation to the warpath. She wasn't any more certain that it was right than she had been before, but he was, and suddenly this seemed enough for her. In her heart, she knew she would have followed him to hell and back if he'd bade her. This realization terrified her, for he had offered her so little of himself. In fact, she would have known virtually nothing if it hadn't been for Sam.

Thinking back to the hours she had spent with Sam in the week before they had left the fortress to meet with the Comanche, Jessalyn smiled. She wished that Sam were with them now, but his wound had not healed enough to allow him to travel, so he had stayed behind. While at the fortress, he had been her only link to the man inside the demigod who now rode before her. Through Sam's stories of their boyhood, she had come to know something of the elusive pirate who had stolen her heart. Now, with Sam gone, her link was broken again and she was left with a statue of stone whose only concern was for the progression of his sinister plan.

"The people can fight now or die later." Nocona's words caught her ear, and she recalled Cale having said much the same thing to her. "In the end, there'll be blood from one end of Texas to the other if there isn't a boundary drawn on the settlers," he had explained to her. "It's a question of a handful of lives lost now, or thousands lost later. There is no peaceful solution." He had paused then and, catching her with a hard stare that chilled her to the bone even in remembering, he had said, "You tell me which is better." She hadn't been able to answer—but that had been the point. There was no answer, at least none that didn't involve bloodshed, so here she was, by his side, helping to send the red man against the white.

She rode the rest of the way into the camp without looking at him again. Instead, she fixed her eyes on the ground in front of her stallion's hooves, and soberly tried to blot out the sensation of having many curious eyes follow her. Some of the faces she had recognized, but she avoided these also, feeling horribly conspicuous as she rode in front of the milling crowd. Bits of conversations drifted to her ears like puffs of down on the wind, and, despite herself, she listened to them. Many were about her father, and she soon found herself reminiscing with the men who rode around her, a silent partner in their conversations.

It was as she was intently listening to an old warrior tell the story of how her father had charmed the great bear that she realized a rider had fallen into step beside her. Her attention fell away from the conversation immediately, and, flushing prettily, she looked up at her unwanted companion. Her eyes met a warm, familiar face, and she drew back in wide-eyed surprise for a moment before her full lips rose into a smile.

"Sounds on the Wind." She said his name reverently, as a starving person might have spoken of his favorite dish, and then flushed deeper at her enthusiasm. Hooding her eyes away from him with a brush of sooty lashes, she added, "Why are you here?"

He smiled genuinely, and with an affectionate hand reached out to touch the strands of shimmering copper-gold hair that fell over her shoulders. Brushing the backs of his fingers across her soft cheek and along the line of her chin, he caught her eye.

"I might ask you the same thing," he said wryly, and then without warning became more serious, adding, "You do not belong here."

Jessalyn straightened in her saddle at his words like a cat bowing up for a fight, and met his eyes with an even regard. She wondered for a moment if his voice had really sounded like her father's or if she had only heard his words that way. Why, suddenly, did she feel as if Sounds on the Wind were the adult and she only a child, as if, were he to order her to go home, she would be forced to obey?

"It is my decision." She was surprised at how convincing the words sounded. "This was my father's work, and I intend to finish it," she added to further drive home the point that, if he had come to take her back to Bent's Fort, he was wasting his time.

The young chief drew back a bit at either the tone of her voice or the cool strength in her gemlike eyes, or perhaps at a combination of both things. This was neither the child that he had known before nor the lost fawn that he had last seen at Bent's Fort. Something had happened to her in these months that she had disappeared, and now she had a strength of her own that would have rivaled her father's. Watching her sit astride the magnificent Appaloosa stallion with her spring green eyes flashing bright and her hair dancing around her like flames in the wind, he realized that she had become a woman — and one to rival the strength of any man.

"I see," was all he could say, and his eyes traveled suspiciously to the back of the big Comanchero who rode ahead of them. He'd find out what The Hawk had done to his fawn, he vowed silently, and if there was reason, he'd see that man rue the day he'd hurt the little sun-hair. To Jessalyn, he said, "You will honor me by staying in my lodge. Sparrow Eyes will be happy to see you again. She has been worried about you ever since you left the trading post so with the roving-band-of-horse-soldiers." He could have added that his wife wasn't the only one who had been worried about Jesse, but he didn't. Enough had been said, and he could tell by the look on Jessalyn's face that she was relieved at his invitation. Perhaps he could convince her to leave the camp of the Comanche with him after all . . .

* * *

Jessalyn sat quietly beside Cale, her long legs curled neatly beside her as was proper among Comanche women. Her eyes dully observed the celebration that was in progress around the fire. It had been an evening of festivity, and all had joined in to toast the coming of the Comancheros and the gathering of several bands of Comanche who rarely saw one another. Encompassing the lodges of the Comanche and Kiowa, the winter encampment stretched for miles along the gentle valley of the Pecos river, and the air rang continually with the low, comforting sound of hundreds of different conversations.

As night drew in, the sounds changed to the quiet, sober tones of a give-away ritual, and finally to the low rhythm of chants and drums. It was a celebration of more than just the coming together for the winter. It was a celebration of a much-whispered plan to drive the white men back forever, and the coming of El Halcon could only mean that it was time for the plan to be put to action. A general feeling of anticipation hung in the air, and each of those gathered at the dance circle felt it in some different way, some seeing death in the future, others seeing life. All saw, finally, a ray of hope in the unlikely guise of the tawny-haired Comanchero chief. Surely, if anyone had the power to drive back the white-eyes, it was El Halcon, they thought. He was a man of strong magic, of wisdom, and of great love for the Comanche. They watched him with trust and admiration in their eyes, and showered him with gifts at the give-away. He returned their gifts tenfold, at least in their eyes, with gifts of metal pots, mirrors, and bright bolts of red and blue cloth.

As the excitement of the give-away began to die, many curious eyes turned to the beautiful white woman who sat by his side. Many knew her, and those who didn't had known her father. He had also been a good man, and a big friend of the Comanche—which was, they figured, why his own people had killed him. News among the Comanche often traveled as fast as if they were connected by telegraph, and all had by now heard of the brutal death of their white brother. It made them only more certain that the time had come for them to stand against the Tejano settlers.

Jessalyn's eyes drifted slowly around the circle of firelight as her mind again wandered over the past months, and then to the future. Her eyes settled on one familiar face and then the next, and she realized all too well that she had placed her hand in sending many of them to their deaths. It was a sickening cross to bear for one who only months ago would not even have been able to conceive of the idea of it, much less accept a part.

Tears glittered against the deep green of her eyes like dewdrops against new leaves, and she looked back into the flames, unable to watch the dancers or the spectators any longer. After a time, the pull of eyes forced her to look up again, and she met the dark, brooding gaze of Peta Nocona. He sat like an artist's rendering—a god framed by firelight—his unreadable gaze fixed on the strange, beautiful white woman across the fire. Beside him sat another white woman—his wife—who had once been Cynthia Parker, a Texan herself, but was now Keeps Warm with Us, a Comanche.

Looking at the other white woman, Jessalyn thought how alike the two of them were, caught in an undefined void between two worlds. But if Cynthia Parker felt the pull of the white world at all, it didn't show. In fact, had it not been for her blue eyes and light brown hair, she would have looked every bit a Comanche. Watching her, Jessalyn wished that *she* could forget the white world so well, wished that she could be completely on one side or the other, but she could not. She had known just enough of the world in which she had been born to be connected to it in some bizarre fashion. Looking away, and over the heads of the circle toward the smooth, velvet black sky, Jessalyn sought to push the cares from her mind, and the tears from her eyes. When she could not, she slid quietly back on her blanket, stood up, and silently left. If Cale noticed her departure at all, he gave no sign, and she pointedly did not look back as she slipped away.

Her mind drifted aimlessly as she moved through the maze of cone-shaped shadows that fell from the silent lodges in the bright moonlight. Strangely, she thought of a dog that she had adopted when she was young, perhaps ten or eleven. It had been a bad winter that year, and they had found the half-wolf dog sitting near the empty remains of a trapper's cabin, watching the door with big, sad eyes as if he expected it to open any minute. She and her father had camped there that night, and then had taken the dog with them in the morning, for it was obvious that no one had been in the cabin for some time. The dog had followed them all the way down out of the

Rockies, padding obediently behind the horses as if he'd always been there. When they got near to Bent's Fort, they had looked back and suddenly found him gone. Her father had said that he had taken back to the wild because he wasn't really the type to be somebody's pet, but they never really knew. She hadn't considered it since, whether the dog had really left them because he was too much of a free spirit . . . Strange that she should think of that now . . .

Unavoidably, her thoughts drifted to Cale, and she wandered blankly through the times that they had spent together, the times that he had seemed to love her, and the times that he had seemed to care little, if at all. They were equal balances on a scale that stubbornly refused to tilt either way. She wanted desperately to insist that he tell her the truth about his feelings. Yet, if she did insist, what would she be pushing toward—that he marry her? And did she truly want to marry him? Could she commit herself to the kind of life that he led, a life on the shadowed edges of the law? There were too many questions.

A chill wind dashed from behind one of the lodges like a crafty ice pixie and stole her thoughts away, dancing off with them into the night. Wrapping her arms tightly around her slender form, she shivered and considered going for a robe, but decided against it. Sparrow Eyes might be in the lodge, and would ask why she had left the dance. It would be best to avoid that. Sparrow Eyes had the most disturbing way of seeing right through her, and to have someone else know of her plight would only make it worse. Misery, in this case, didn't want company.

She had walked for a long time when she reached the outer rim of lodges, then stood looking out onto the uneven desert brushland. Not far away, she heard the horse herd moving restlessly around in the shelter of a shallow arroyo. They trembled the night air with low voices as she came closer, as if to tell her that she had disturbed their rest. She stopped before coming close enough to stir them further, and stood in the dappled moonshadow of a crooked tree that had somehow managed to get a foothold in the dry ground. Looking up at the deep night sky, she took a deep breath of the cool night air, and rolled her tired head from one side to the other to take the cramps from her neck. It had been a long day . . .

"Starlight, star bright . . ." she whispered with a little chuckle at herself. It was a game she had played often as a child, but she was too old to be wishing on stars now. Anyway, of the million stars that glittered like spilled diamonds against the blackness there was no way of knowing which had been the first that night. The sound of a footfall caught her ear like an unwelcome slap, and her hand went instantly to the knife that hung from the belt of her skirt.

"You won't need that." The voice was Cale's. "I'm unarmed."

Her eyes twinkled with more humor than she felt as she turned about.

"I'm not above throwing at an unarmed man." She returned, and then giggled again, intoxicated with the sweet smell of the fresh night air. As he came closer, she added, "So watch yourself," with another laugh, and met him with a wide, deep gaze that sparkled in the starlight.

"I always do," he replied, clasping his hands behind his neck and stretching his lean form backward with an efficient grace that would have brought a dancer to envy. From beneath the open, beaded leather vest he wore the tanned curves of muscle and sinew rippled with a life of their own, and he smiled to himself in awareness of her shyly admiring eye. "Long day," he observed with a sigh, and lowered his arms. It had been a long day, but that was hardly what was on his mind. What was on his mind was the incredible picture that she made in that dress, standing there like a goddess in the moonlight. It was the dress that he had given her, and it pleased him that she had chosen it to wear to the celebration. Like a man touching a nugget of gold, he reached out and ran the backs of his fingers slowly down the bare curve of her arm. Her tawny skin shivered like silk in the wind beneath his touch, and he smiled into her eyes.

"Cold?" he asked, his eyes glittering like two polished pieces of amber.

"N-no," she replied quickly, taken aback by the wildly stirring effect that his slight touch had on her. Now every muscle in her body tingled as if struck by lightning, and she felt swelteringly hot despite the now-frigid night air.

"You're shivering," he pointed out, his voice deep and warm. In his eyes there now glittered a hint of mischief against the whiskey-colored warmth.

Flustered, Jessalyn looked away, her cheeks flushing so deeply crimson as to be visible even in the moonlight.

"Y-yes." She tried to salvage some semblance of

her dignity, and retracted her first answer in her confusion. "I'm cold. I mean, it's cold out here." She felt annoyingly like a tongue-tied child, and he looked aggravatingly calm and maddeningly amused. Was he toying with her? She couldn't quite tell by the look in his eye, but that was nothing new — she never could. He blew hot and cold as he pleased, and she went from fever to chills at his whim. *It must be love,* she thought in that instant. *And what a miserable state of affairs.* She felt the warm caress of his hand against her hair as he brushed it back from her face and leaned down to catch her eyes.

"What are you thinking?" he asked, his smile now gone, and his perfectly formed face straight and serious. The softness in his eyes was unmistakable, and she felt herself being drawn unwillingly into their warmth when their gazes met. In defense, she stole her eyes away again, and fastened them on the ground.

"I wasn't thinking of anything just now," she replied in a deliberate monotone. It was one of the biggest lies she had ever told, but something inside her couldn't bear the thought of his knowing what had been on her mind.

"Then what were you thinking of before I interrupted you?" Cale skillfully pursued his evasive butterfly a bit further, and wondered if he'd ever understand the forces that drove her actions. She still trusted him so little. Even after nearly a month of working side by side to make her father's plan a reality, she kept him warily at arm's length. In some ways, he doubted whether it was wise to try and change that. He could still see no future for the two of them — not together, anyway. Dragging her closer would only make it harder to part, he knew, but he couldn't help it. Every time he looked into that angelic young face, those fragile willow green eyes, he wanted to wrap her so tightly in his arms that she'd never again be away from him. It was a torturous paradox, to say the least, and one that threatened to push away every other sane thought in his head.

"I wasn't thinking of anything before you interrupted me either," Jessalyn replied, and barely heard the whisper of her own voice over the raucous thumping of her heart. Dimly, she had the strange thought that she was surprised the dancers in the village could still hear the drumbeats over the thunder of her rebellious heart. The idea twitched the corners of her mouth into a smile, and she giggled despite herself. "I was wishing on a star," she replied grandly, and turned to face him with a dazzling smile. Suddenly, humor seemed as good a response as any. As she giggled again, she wondered if she was losing her mind completely.

Cale smiled back at her, himself drawn into the light of her unexplainable good humor. She looked like an angel when she smiled . . .

"And what were you wishing for, Jesse mine?" he asked in a grand and proper fashion that seemed to elevate the event.

Sparks of mischief danced like sugarplum fairies in her eyes, and she placed a hand to her mouth as if to hush him.

"I can't tell you," she whispered as if the night was filled with ears. "If I do, it won't come true." Throwing her hands out, she twirled away from him in a spinning cloud of buckskin fringe and fiery hair. The sweet music of her laughter floated onto the night like a warm breeze as she danced out into the full moonlight. An upstretched root upset her balance suddenly, and she spun to the sand with the grace of a ballerina. Reaching out to catch her, Cale fell also, and they lay side by side in the sand, laughing as if driven mad by the moon. Finally, he propped himself up on one elbow and gazed down into her sparkling eyes. That was all it took. He couldn't even remember what he'd been thinking the moment before about it being better to stay at arm's length. All he could think of as he bent to kiss her parted lips was how much he wanted her, needed her, and could not bear to let her go.

She returned his kiss fully, desperately, seeking in his lips some bit of reassurance that she could not find in his words. Every inch of her body, every ounce of flesh and bone wanted him to touch her, to love her. It was the most powerful thing that she had ever felt, and her heart pounded in fear of its strength. Her body seemed no longer to belong to herself. It was as if she had been taken prisoner, and she willingly surrendered to her captor.

Slowly, carefully, he coaxed her tender young lips to a fever pitch, and then moved to the soft curve of her cheek. His lips brushed the tender lobe of her ear, and she shuddered uncontrollably. Some sane corner of her mind braced her for the slice of taunting words, but none came. He only whispered her name softly, and continued the heated trail down the side of her neck, brushing the silken strands of hair aside with warm fingers. Where before their passion had been a form of battle, now it was evidence of surrender, and they clung to each other in mutual need. When she shuddered against the chill of the night air and frost-tipped ground, he swept her like a doll into his arms and effortlessly carried her back to the village. She snuggled against him like a happy kitten as he walked, her eyes tightly closed and her mind refusing audience to any protesting inner voices.

The camp was still alive with the sounds of the dance as he carried her through it, and no one noticed when he slipped through the doorway to the chief's guest lodge with the copper-haired girl in his arms. Once inside, he lay her on the soft skin pallet as carefully as if she were made of glass, and then went back to secure the door flap. He would let nothing and no one steal her away from him that night — not her Kiowa friend, not Peta Nocona, not land rights. Tonight, none of that existed. He'd shut it all out and had jealously barred the door. Turning away from the entrance, he knelt by the fire pit and threw a couple sticks of wood on the coals. He hardly noticed as they crackled and split into flame. His eyes were fixed on Jessalyn, who lay exactly as he had left her, so still that she could have been a statue.

Feeling his gaze, she opened her eyes drunkenly, and smiled up from the pallet, but did not move. She was afraid to move, afraid that if she did, it would break the spell move that had fallen over them. As he came to her, she closed her eyes again, and shivered in surprise and pleasure as he touched the bare curve of her thigh. Somewhere far away, the drums were beating . . .

Unwilling to be separated from her by the thin shield of buckskin any longer, Cale worked open the laces of her dress and pulled it from her. Desire flared in his loins at the sight of her silken curves now bared in the firelight before him, and he bent to kiss her hungrily before standing to remove his own clothes. When he returned to her, she arched pleadingly against his warmth, against his touch, and moaned his name in a voice thick with desire. In response, he moved his fingers lightly over the soft curve of her breasts, and then with his lips tasted their honey-sweet peaks. Teasing and nibbling, he drove her to a fever pitch as his hands moved away to caress the flat smoothness of her stomach.

"P . . . Please," she pleaded when she thought she would lose her mind to the wildfire within her. His fingers moved to part her thighs, and she moaned again, writhing against him in a blind search for satisfaction. The drums that had been far away grew louder, and she moved in time with them as his fingers explored the moist warmth of her womanhood and entered her gently. In shock, she gasped, and her eyes flew open to meet with his. Smiling, he kissed her forehead and then kissed her eyes closed again.

"Relax, my love," he whispered in a deep, throaty voice that reverberated through her. Conquering her lips again with heated kisses, he moved over her and she felt the gentle pressure of his manhood. The drums seemed to beat like thunder in her ears as he gripped her buttocks and worked carefully into her womanhood. With gentleness born of love, he moved fully into her, and hugged her to him as she cried out with a mixture of pain and ecstasy.

"It is like the first time again," he whispered. "But there will be no more pain." She barely heard him, for the drums were now so loud that they drowned out all else. She moved against him in time to their slow, sensuous rhythm, feeling a swelling and tightening within herself, as if she were a bud about to burst. The rhythm of the drums grew faster, faster, and she cried out in ecstasy only an instant before the thunder of the drums exploded in her ears. Then everything was silent.

Holding her close to him, Cale kissed and smoothed her hair, his soul swelling like it never had before. If someone had told him a year ago that a woman could have ever possessed him so completely, he would have called that person a liar. Now, he knew there wasn't a piece of him that was completely his anymore. The best part of it was that, as he lay holding her slight form securely in his arms, he didn't care a bit. He'd always thought that giving half of yourself away to someone else would make you only half a man, but now he could see it made you twice the man you'd been before.

Chapter Sixteen

Jessalyn awoke again in the silent hours before dawn. The rhythm of the drums and the chants of the singers had stopped at some unknown point during the night, and all had finally retired to their lodges. El Halcon's Comancheros had melted back into the desert to spend the night in their own camp, close to their favorite horses. Though they dealt with the Comanche and Kiowa often, few shared their patron's trust of the Indians' honor, and most preferred to catch their winks a safe distance away. It was a fact for which Jessalyn was infinitely grateful as she listened into the murky predawn air for signs of life and then breathed a grateful sigh at hearing none.

Feeling Cale's steady breath ruffle the downy hair on the back of her neck, she smiled a bit despite herself. A giggle tickled through her like giddy butterfly wings as she thought of what had happened between them, and then her body grew hot again with the memory. It had been like nothing she had ever even imagined before, their night together, and now she approached the morning after with more than a hint of regret that it was over.

Slowly she turned on her side and looked into his sleeping face. In her mind, she saw his eyes the way they had been the night before—warm and soft, and filled with need. How she wished that they would open now and look on her that way again—but somehow, she doubted it. She'd have lain dollars to dimes that when he awoke he'd be the same hard, independent man she had followed halfway across Texas. The thought of it tore through her like a freshly honed blade, and tears welled up in the emerald depths of her eyes. Without a sound, she sat up and pushed the heavy sleeping robe back from herself, shuddering at the chill in the dark air. A gasp rose in her throat as she felt the warmth of his arm sneak around her waist.

"Don't be in such a rush, my little rose." His voice came thick and throaty and his eyelids remained loosely closed. "Morning isn't here yet," he smiled sleepily, blindly trying to pull the cover back over her with his free hand.

Stubbornly, she resisted the downward pull of his arm, and again tried to slip from the bed, but found herself trapped in a strengthening hold.

"I want to leave before everyone wakes up," she insisted, whispering as if they were not alone in the large lodge. Impatiently, she pushed at his arm, and sighed in exasperation when he refused to loosen his hold. "Cale!" Her voice was louder than she had intended, and she looked around guiltily.

In response, he dragged one whiskey-colored eye open, and regarded her with annoyance.

"Even the sun won't be rising for hours yet, Jesse

mine," he replied, rising up a bit to tackle her gently back to the sleeping mat. Then, having found himself in good position, he leaned over her and silenced her protesting lips with a kiss. Despite his weariness, he felt a hunger flame suddenly within him, and he kissed her more deeply, amazed at the strength of his desire for her.

Weakly, she pressed her small fists against the hardness of his chest, struggling to remember her original purpose.

"It would be better if I left before everyone awoke," she whispered breathlessly as his lips trailed tantalizingly along the curve of her chin. "Cale, please . . ." Her voice trailed off as she felt herself beginning to spin helplessly into the wondrous abyss of his nearness. Just before she would have been hopelessly lost, he kissed her lightly on the end of the nose and propped himself onto one elbow, smiling down at her.

"As you wish, my love," he said reluctantly, his eyes still smoldering with the amber embers of the spark that had been struck within him. With a long, sweeping gaze, he took in the perfectly curved young form beside him. Groaning to himself, he rolled away from her and lay on his back with his eyes closed. Clasping his hands behind his head, he smiled mischievously beneath the curve of dark lashes.

"I suppose this is best," he conceded grudgingly, as Jessalyn scooted shyly from the bed and reached for the dress that had earlier been thrown so carelessly to the floor. She fumbled with the tangled buckskin clumsily, shivering against the cold of the lodge, and turning away to hide the embarrassment of her nakedness. If it had been possible for her to run from the lodge nude, she would have done it at that instant, but instead she doggedly tried to make sense of the disheveled garment.

Opening one eye, Cale laughed at the picture she made, and then, tossing the sleeping robe aside, stood up. Throwing a few sticks of wood onto the dying fire on the way, he crossed the lodge to where she cowered, his arms outstretched as if to help.

"Don't come over here!" she protested loudly, stumbling backward a few steps just before he would have touched her.

With the most insulted look he could manage, Cale cocked a quizical brow in her direction.

"I was only going to help you," he said indignantly, and took a step forward again. "Now stand still."

Wide-eyed, Jessalyn backed a step further away as her bottom lip dropped to her toes.

"Don't . . . don't!" Her eyes were uncontrollably drawn to the manly curves of his nude body. Y-you're naked!" she added in desperation as she found herself cornered against the back of the lodge. In the next instant, she was struck by the stupidity of her own statement, and feeling suddenly awkward and childish, she welded her eyes to the well-packed floor.

Throwing back his tawny curls, Cale exploded into a gale of laughter, which rang unashamed in the quiet night as if to wake the dead. His merriment continued as he snatched his buckskins from the floor and pulled them on. Several minutes passed before he could contain his convulsive laughter enough to speak, but when he had, he met with hard jade eyes that told him she didn't share his sense of humor.

"Don't look at me like that." He defended his view of the situation, trying to mask the hint of a smile that still tempted at the corners of his sensuous lips. "I wasn't laughing at you, Jesse."

Having struggled into her dress, Jessalyn felt more herself, and better able to defend her honor. Folding her hands over her breasts, she sneered back into his amused eyes.

"Oh, really?" She said it with the authority of judge, jury, and executioner, for she had appointed herself all three. "Well, then, what were you laughing at?" Without waiting for an answer, she took a step forward and stabbed at his broad chest with an accusing finger. "I'm sorry if I'm not so worldly as the women you're used to," she spat spitefully, staring up at him with eyes in which shone a mix of anger, hurt, and shame. "But I'm glad you find it so amusing. At least you haven't completely wasted your evening, then."

As quickly as his laughter had come, it vanished, and his eyes flashed as he reached out and snatched her accusing hand by the wrist.

"That's enough." Roughly, he pulled her to him and held her there, his hand crushing her small wrist in mute anger. Their gazes clashed then like two shards of flint, sending sparks into the air, and bending low, he seized her trembling lips. Their anger, rashly provoked, was quickly spent, and the kiss softened and warmed as he wrapped her protectively in his strong arms. After a long moment, he took a last taste of her lips and then held her close against him, resting his chin on top of her silky head. "No more of that, Jesse mine," he whispered softly, recalling each time he had seen that look of pain and shame in her eyes. Reaching down, he gently touched a finger to her chin and tipped her head toward him until he found the still-misted emerald depths of her eyes. For a moment, he stood silent, wondering if he'd ever seen anything quite so captivating as their particular color, or that special fragile quality they had, like a newly bloomed spring leaf struggling to survive against a late winter wind.

"I'm not your enemy, Jesse," he said honestly, his eyes glowing like the warm, comforting flames of a familiar hearth. Brushing a kiss across her flushed lips, he smiled slightly. "It is infinitely more pleasant to love than to hate, but my stone rose makes herself a very cool lover. What would I have to do to win that cold heart?"

Faced with a confusing bundle of choices, Jesse chose to hold silent. Could she dare admit that she did love him, that if only she could be certain of his feelings for her, she would gladly give herself up to him?

"You're asking for my trust," she finally pronounced instead of the admission of love that longed to spill from her lips. Clenching her nervous fists into tight balls against his chest, she added, "But you have done nothing to show me that it would be anything but misplaced." She saw anger blow into his eyes like a sudden storm at her words, and she flinched inwardly, but forced herself to hold her gaze steady. Now was their moment of truth, she knew, and whatever way the fates turned in the next few moments would determine the future for them. If he turned her away again, she was never coming back to him — or to any other man. Watching passion move like a silent wind behind his eyes, she held her breath, and hoped the fates were kind.

Cale would have had to have been blind not to have seen the moment of truth that stretched before them — and he wasn't blind. If she had pushed him to this point a month ago, he would have turned and walked away without a second of regret. If any other woman had put him to it, he definitely would have been gone in a heartbeat. But those were bygone days, unfortunately, and now he stood stock still, deafened by the silence between them, and trying to think of the right thing to say.

"Oh, Jesse, you're a cruel mistress," he sighed, and shook his head in resignation. He felt something like a whipped pup for the first time in his life, but, considering the circumstances, it really wasn't all that bad. Releasing her, he took a few steps away, ran his fingers roughly through the tawny curls of his hair, and then stood gripping them into a handful where they fell to his shoulders. Finally, he threw up his hands in surrender, and cut to the heart of the matter. "You've left me no choice but to say it. You've got me hooves, hames, and bridle, Jesse Kendrik. I love you."

His last words rang strangely in Jessalyn's ears, and she stood for a long moment, frozen in wide-eyed amazement. Dumbfounded, she searched his face and wondered if she had heard those words or only imagined them.

"I . . ." She paused, with no idea of what to say next, and a new flow of tears rushed into her eyes. Wringing her hands in front of her, she bowed her head, and stared into the fire. "God help me," she said quietly as her clouded eyes followed the trail of smoke upward through the lodge and out through the smoke hole. Watching the patch of star-spattered night sky, she added, "I love you, but I don't know if that's enough. Our lives are so different . . . there isn't any place . . ." She trailed off, watching the dim stars wink cheerily from millions of miles away and wondering how their lives could ever begin to blend together and form some sort of a future. He had his men, his life. He was a Comanchero, an outlaw, and she was a wanderer, an adventurer simply not cut out for a life of holing up in the mountains of the border country with a band of half-breeds and Spaniards. Oh, how she wished that they could ride away, right then, just the two of them, and never come back — but that was impossible.

In the face of the hopelessness of their future, she stood silently, watching her patch of sky and waiting for him to speak. Perhaps, she thought, at that moment he too was realizing that the world held no place for the two of them. When he did not speak, she looked back to find him still standing where he had been. There was something different about him from the moment before, but she couldn't single out one thing that had changed. It was more an overall change in his posture, as if the picture of him standing there had been painted with different colors while she had been looking away. He was once again

303

El Halcon, the man-god who ruled the desert, and his momentary weakness had vanished like a magician's scarf. Now, El Halcon returned her tentative regard with a hint of a smile that bespoke some hidden plan.

"One thing at a time, my love," he said softly, but definitely, as if to make certain his words were the last on the subject. Crossing the lodge in two easy strides, he reached to her and touched the willful strands of hair that fell like ribbons over her shoulder. In flawless Comanche, he said, "As the Grandfathers say, 'You must learn to be more like the Mountain and less like the Winds.'" It was the moral from a story that the old ones of the Comanche told often to the children to teach them the value of patience, and the meaning of it was not lost on Jessalyn. Despite herself, she smiled a bit at being reminded of the story that she had heard so many times as a child.

"More like the Mountain," she repeated in Comanche, unable to contain her smile, and then in English, she added, "If you say so, but this Mountain is leaving before the Winds around camp start telling stories about her." She chuckled at her own humor, her black mood erased by his obvious confidence in their prospects. As she stepped back from him, her giggle turned to laughter, and the sweet notes of it danced happily out into the night.

Watching her, the Comanchero couldn't help but laugh also, and he breathed a sigh of relief that she seemed content. Her questions about their future appeared forgotten, at least for the moment, and he was glad. They were hard questions, he knew, and he didn't have answers for them yet. Oddly, those answers would depend on Nocona, and the outcome of the next few days.

"If you insist," he agreed, albeit reluctantly, with her intention to leave. Given his choice, she would have remained at his side, but he could see the wisdom in her withdrawal. No place on earth was harbor to more wagging tongues than the Comanche camp, especially when the news concerned the beautiful young newcomer, who seemed to have attracted the attention of most of the men present.

With urgency fanned by the growing light that sneaked in around the closed door flap, Jessalyn pulled on and laced her moccasins, straightened her dress, and smoothed her unruly hair with her fingers. When she was finished, she stepped to the door, then stopped, standing uncertainly in the grey light. With a smile, Cale reached for her and took her in his arms, kissing her deeply, then stepped back to regard her seriously.

"In case I don't see you today," he said, knowing that there was, indeed, a good possibility that this would be the case. He anticipated spending most of the day in council with the Comanche and Kiowa leaders. "Don't be surprised if you see Chavez following you—I told him to."

Jessalyn's brows drew together almost the instant the words had left his mouth, and she frowned up at him.

"Why?" She quickly added, "I don't need anyone to take care of me, Cale. I've been living in Comanche camps since I could walk upright under a cow." When he seemed unmoved by her protests, she began

305

to issue them with more force. "For heaven sakes, Cale, I'm not a child!"

Crossing his powerful arms over his bare chest, he stood steadfastly and showed little sign of changing his position. In fact, he couldn't help but smile at her reaction—it was almost exactly what he had predicted. No doubt, she was going to give Chavez a tough day of it.

"Humor me," he said dryly. "There are a few too many interested male eyes following you around this camp. One of them might just decide to spirit you away while I'm not looking."

Jessalyn lowered a brow and gave him a doubting sidelong glance at the absurdity of his statement.

"Now that is ridiculous!" she scoffed at his words. "I know almost everyone in this camp—except, of course, your men, and I don't want them skulking around after me all day." Facing him with hard-eyed determination, she drew in a deep breath, and prepared herself for a long fight.

In the end, it was Jessalyn who walked proudly from the tent, victorious—or at least so she had thought. She had already bathed at the creek, gone back to Sounds on the Wind's lodge to dress, helped Sparrow Eyes make breakfast, and strolled about the camp to visit with old friends before she caught sight of Chavez not far away. The more she moved about camp, the more certain she was that he was indeed following her, and that Cale had set him to it.

The thought of the whole thing infuriated her, and at first she went in search of Cale to demand that he call off his man. When she could not find him, she set about plotting an escape from her unwanted companion. Finally, a plan came to her as she was going to check on Diablo, whom she had left on Cale's tether. Taking him from the tether, she led him casually across camp, stopping to talk to those that she recognized along the way. When she reached Sounds on the Wind's lodge, she tethered her stallion in back, giving him an ample serving of dried grass and grain as if to bed him down for the day. After that, she walked around to the front of the lodge and went casually inside, stopping to yawn and stretch by the doorway as if she were headed for a nap. Closing the door flap behind her, she waited only a hasty moment before she lay down beside the back wall of the lodge and rolled easily under the edge of the lodge cover. Taking Diablo from the tether, she led him quietly away, careful to keep the lodge between herself and Chavez until she was out of sight. Then she swung easily onto the stallion's bare back and rode away a free woman.

She let Diablo break into an easy lope for a time, enjoying the freedom of being, at last, alone with the sky and the wind. Taking a deep breath of the sweet, cool air, she looped the reins over her stallion's neck and stretched her arms into the air beside her as if to sprout wings. Gazing out to the farthest purple horizons, she could see nothing but small, rolling hills, deep, waving, golden grass, and occasional groves of scrub oak. They had left the desert behind in their journey to meet the Comanche, and, as always, the change of scenery had awakened the wandering spirit within her.

She passed nearly half of the day wandering aimlessly across the grassland, enjoying the freedom of being alone and the warmth of the false-spring day. Her stallion pranced and snorted happily, as alive with freedom as she, and she let him streak out across the low hills until he finally tired and settled to a calm walk. She thought little of where they were going, where they had been, or how far they had come. In fact, her thoughts were turned mostly inward as she contemplated the sea of changes that had swept her life away since the death of her father. Had it been only last spring? That seemed hard to believe. It seemed as though her time with her father had been a lifetime ago, and in a way, it had. That had been such a different life, that innocent, protected existence when all of her decisions had been made for her. Now her fate rested in her own hands, and she struggled to mold it into what she thought she wanted, only she wasn't certain exactly what that was now. One thing was for certain — she loved Cale Cody, and couldn't imagine what her life would be without him. On the other hand, she couldn't imagine what her life would be with him. It was a double-edged sword, and she turned it over and over in her mind, feeling it slice her soul in both directions.

So preoccupied was she with her thoughts that it never occurred to her to worry about the fact that she had left without carrying a weapon, save for the small knife that hung at her belt. Normally, her saddle would have been well equipped with her rifle and pistol, but she had left her saddle behind in her hasty escape from camp, and had not thought of the implications since. Only when she saw a rider top a small hill to her left did she reach for her nonexistent rifle, and realize her mistake. Her heart pounded against her chest as he rode closer on his lathered ebony mount, and she squinted into the sun to get a better view of him. It wasn't until he slid his horse to a halt a few feet from her that she recognized him and let out a relieved breath for the first time since he had disturbed her solitude.

"Wanderer," she addressed Peta Nocona, Wanderer, in flawless Comanche. Swallowing hard, she tried to calm her screaming nerves and to will the flush of color from her cheeks. "You . . . surprised me." She understated the effect of his sudden appearance. The fact was that she'd been far more than surprised—terrified would have been a better word, and even now, she felt horribly nervous. "I did not expect to see anyone else out here," she added, too embarrassed to keep silent and too shaken to think of anything better to say. In response, Wanderer only smiled and gave her a long, silent appraisal that she could feel from the pit of her stomach to the tips of her toenails.

"You looked like you might run away," he observed, as if enjoying her torment.

A spark rose in Jessalyn's jade eyes at his jab, and she hooded her eyes away to hide their irritation. Looking past him toward the horizon, she remarked, "I did not know who you were at first." She had defended herself clumsily, and now grew an ounce more irritated at the effect that his commanding presence was having on her. Straightening her shoulders, she looked him resolutely in the eye, and added, "I forgot my gun, or I probably would have

309

shot you first and wondered who you were later."

Awed by the beauty of the copper-haired girl, and impressed by her strength, Nocona threw back his waist-length raven hair and laughed.

"Well then, I am very lucky that you forgot your gun, because I do not doubt that you are a good shot." His midnight eyes sparkled like polished onyx for a moment more, and then his handsome face grew serious. "I have wanted to talk to you," he said abruptly, his features suddenly ominous.

Unconsciously, Jessalyn drew back at his sudden change of posture, her mind running ahead to grasp the possible import of his words. Why would he want to talk to her out here, alone? Suddenly, she wished she had never left camp in the first place. Nocona's narrowed eyes had the look of an eagle on the hunt, and she suddenly felt a great deal like the mouse. Warily, she held her gaze to his, and waited for him to continue.

"I knew your father well," he said slyly, pulling his eyes away and looking past her with a contemplative eye. His mission was elsewhere, but his thoughts were held by the fascination of two incredibly green eyes, like two drops of turquoise. "This plan of his, of Hawk's, do you think this is a wise thing?"

Jessalyn's dark brows drew together at the question, and she jerked back visibly in surprise. It seemed that Nocona was asking for her judgment over that of Cale. It was an inconceivable affront to his honor under Comanche tradition. One man never questioned the word of another, and certainly did not challenge it with that of a woman.

"My father felt it was the only way for the Indian

310

to keep the Tejanos from taking all of the land." She chose her words carefully, like a fox choosing its steps around the edge of a trap. What exactly did Nocona want from her? Did he sense that, in her heart, she could not come to terms with the thought of being the kindling behind a war?

At her words, the Comanche chief turned back to her and leaned close, catching her eye with such force that she felt as if she had been struck.

"But I want to know what you think," he repeated, gently, almost softly, as if trying to coax a rabbit from its burrow.

Her eyes darted nervously over the stern features of his face as she tried to formulate a reply. She had finally come to a moment of truth with her participation in Cale's scheme. Before, she had been asked only to give support by her presence. Now, she was being asked to send the Comanche to war by her own tongue, and she wasn't sure if she could do it. Within her, her loyalty to her father, her realization of the necessity of bloodshed for the survival of the Indian, and her own conscience raged like opposing thunderheads, until finally, she tore her eyes away.

"I do not know what is right." In the end, she held true to her own heart, and spoke with honesty of what she felt. "I agree that the only hope for the people is in the—" there was no word for it in Comanche, so she said it in English, "statehood agreement," and then in Comanche, "um—the agreement for Houston to be brothers with the Great White Father in Washington. If they do not agree now to draw a line that the settlers cannot cross, there will someday be no place for the people." She frowned, her small shoulders sagging in defeat, and added, "Perhaps the only way is war." All in all, that was the undeniable fact, and the more Jessalyn thought about it, the more she came to realize that Cale and her father had been right. Even though today there was enough land for both red and white men, in the future there would not be. That was the future that her father had seen and fought against, a time when the red man would live as a prisoner on the land that had once been his.

As if reading her thoughts, the Comanche swept a grave hand through the air, indicating the vastness of the open plains.

"The white man will never come to live on the staked plains," he said solemnly. "They want only the easy land. This is not easy land. There is little water, and the game is often scarce. We are safe here because we have nothing that they could want."

"They will come," Jessalyn said quietly, more to herself than to him. "When they have used all of the easy land, then they will want this land also." She said it with the certainty of one who had seen it happen in other places and knew it was true. She could remember so many places once unclaimed and open, where there now stood ranches—or towns. It sickened her each time she saw it, and she had witnessed in her father's eyes that he felt the same. All her life, he had told her stories of her grandfather's life in Kentucky when it had been wild and settled only by trappers and Indians—Indians who now either no longer existed, or had been pushed westward by the advance of settlers. "Someday, there won't be a wild place on this whole earth," he had said. "I hope I never live long enough to see that." In this respect the bullet that had spared him this by taking his life so unexpectedly had been kind.

For a time they sat in silence, watching the sun sink lower in the soft pink sky, Jessalyn's face pale with sorrow, and the Comanche's drawn with thought. He glanced at her occasionally as she sat looking out toward some invisible point on the horizon, and considered what she had said. In all that mattered, she had, in essence, mirrored the words of her father, for he had not taken the thought of war lightly either. Cale, on the other hand hated the settlers with the passion of a true Comanche. He and his men, Nocona knew, would provide the people with good guns, and would fight alongside them as brothers.

For himself, Nocona couldn't say exactly how he felt about the prospect of taking his men out to raid the white settlements. The thought of raiding had always stirred his blood when he had been a young warrior, but now, as a chief, there was much for him to think about: the safety of the camp, the coming birth of his first son, the prospect of burying the bones of lost men. All of this was balanced against the possibility of revenge against the whites, and that of keeping the Tejanos off of the lands of the people forever. There was so much to consider, yet he had so little time. It would not be long before the council would gather to discuss the plans to raid, and by then he must know where he would stand. Looking up at the sky, he prayed to his spirits for guidance.

Chapter Seventeen

Jessalyn sat in the shadow of the great council lodge beside Sparrow Eyes, helping the Kiowa women to piece together a lodge cover for a family that had been turned out by fire. It was an act of charity, so no one complained about the difficulty of sewing the cold, stiff skins. In fact, none of the women spoke at all. Instead, they sat with solemn faces listening to the snatches of conversation that drifted from within the council lodge. What happened inside, they knew, would determine the course that their lives would take when spring came.

Little Mountain of the Kiowa spoke in a voice that boomed like the wings of the great bird Thunder, and advocated war. With him stood Sounds on the Wind of the Kiowa, as well as Buffalo Piss, Old Owl, and Broken Kettle of the Comanche. Also with him stood El Halcon, the white spirit-man that the Comanche called brother.

Against war stood several old respected chiefs and war leaders, among them Iron Shirt, and Pahayuca, of the Comanche. Peta Nocona had not yet spoken, and this was what occupied Jessalyn's mind as she absently worked the stiff leather with her fingers. In her thoughts, she replayed each moment of her conversation with Nocona the day before. Had he given any indication then of whether he could advocate peace or war? She was certain not. In fact, he had cleverly drawn from her all that she knew of her father's plan, of his beliefs, of the statehood agreement, and even of her own thoughts—all without giving the slightest indication of his own thoughts. Now, she shivered inside at the thought that she might have driven him toward war—or toward peace.

The shadows grew longer and the air colder as she sat with the other women, each waiting, though none would admit it, for the same thing: for Peta Nocona to speak for peace or war. The discussion of the council moved slowly, though, and before Nocona's voice was heard, cold fingers and hungry children forced the women to leave their vigil and retreat to the warmth of their own lodges to prepare meals.

Jessalyn rose reluctantly with the others, dropping the lodge cover and bone lancing needle from her hands as if she had forgotten they were ever there. Peta Nocona had now slipped completely from her mind, driven away by a snatch of conversation overheard from the speech of El Halcon to the council.

"My men will fight beside their Comanche brothers," he had said, and now the words boomed louder and louder in Jessalyn's ears until she could hear nothing else. So confused had been her thoughts since the moment those words had touched her ears that she could not say whether she had heard them a few moments, or several hours, before. All she could hear was Cale's voice committing to go to war with the Comanche, and each time she remembered the words, they shot like a white-hot arrow through her stomach.

Perhaps she should have expected no less of him, but she had allowed herself to be fooled by her love for him. Her need to believe that there could be some sort of future for them had blinded her to the fact that this war was El Halcon's war, and he would fight in it just as he asked others to fight. Suddenly, she realized with sickening clarity the black future that lay ahead of them. The reality of it brought despair and anger to war within her. How could he have pretended to her that there was hope for their love when he knew he would be going to war in the spring! It was too cruel a joke even for him.

The thought of it turned over and over in her mind like a swirling dark cloud as she helped Sparrow Eyes to prepare the evening meal. When Sounds on the Wind entered the lodge, she didn't look up at him, but rose from the fire with a shrug of square-shouldered determination and moved without a word past him to the door. He made no move to stop her, but instead looked after her with a wrinkle of concern, and then turned to his wife.

"No good will come of that," he said, speaking of the ties between Jessalyn and the Comanchero. "The Hawk will devour our little butterfly and then take flight."

Sparrow Eyes nodded in solemn, but tentative, agreement. Having seen the two together, she wondered if it wasn't The Hawk who had been snared — whether he knew it or not. Still, she had heard his

316

bold words at the council, and she had seen the stricken look on Jessalyn's young face. On the other hand, spring was a long time away, and anything could happen by then.

By the time Jessalyn reached Nocona's guest lodge, her anger had fanned white-hot, and her eyes flashed like the blue-green coals in a bellows. Finding the lodge flap open, she hesitated only a moment before she slipped inside, blowing through the door in an angry hurricane of swirling coppery hair.

From where he knelt beside the fire, Cale looked up with a smile, but his grin quickly faded when he noticed her posture. With a guarded expression in his golden eyes, he stood up and looked down at her, his arms crossed over his powerful chest.

"I would say it's good to see you, my love," he said, still with a touch of good nature that struggled to make light of her foul mood. Looking down, he scratched the toe of his boot in the dirt and considered the fact that she seemed unamused by his attempt at humor. With a sigh, he added, "But I'm afraid you intend to make certain that it's not."

She stood silent for a moment, feeling her anger boil up within her and wondering where to begin.

"I heard what you said at the council." She regretted the words almost as soon as she had said them, and she looked away in shame. Eavesdropping on the council was, of course, dishonorable, and suddenly she felt as though she were the one who had done wrong. If Cale had thought of that, he showed no indication when she looked up again to meet his eyes.

"And what did you hear?" he asked matter-of-factly, making no move toward her. Instead, he stood coolly by and waited for her answer, though he was certain he knew what it would be.

Taking a deep breath, she gathered her courage and straightened, corseted by a cloak of fierce pride. Her eyes flashed like leaves tipped with frost as she took a step closer to the fire.

"You are going to war with them," she accused finally, certain of her words, and at the same time wishing fervently that he would deny it. Her hopes were dashed to her feet when he only stood his ground and nodded solemnly.

"Did you think differently?" he questioned, annoyed that she could have thought him so dishonorable as to ask others to fight when he would not. He felt the muscles tighten in the back of his neck when she braced her hands on her hips self-righteously. In the next instant, her courage faded like a mask of clouds and she looked sadly away.

"How could you have . . ." She trailed off helplessly, unable to find the words to express what he had taken from her the night that they had spent together, what she had given him. A tear trembled in the corner of her eye as she wrapped her slender arms around herself as if to keep out a chill. Finally, she finished lamely, "How could you have said you loved me? How could you have said you would stay with me, that we could be together?"

With a sigh, Cale crossed the lodge to her side and took her in his arms, stroking her tangled hair and soothing her like a child.

"I haven't lied to you, my love," he whispered against the sweet scent of her hair, and then kissed

318

the top of her head lightly. "This war is something I have to do, but it won't last forever. When this is done, we'll never be apart again." Gently, he lifted her chin and kissed her deeply before standing back to look deeply into her shimmering eyes. "Trust me, my little rose," he said softly, almost inaudibly, before kissing her again. "There will be plenty of time for us when this is done—a lifetime." With the backs of his fingers, he wiped the tears from her flushed cheeks, his sensuous lips curving into a reassuring smile. "I hope to never see these again," he added, managing to coax a trembling smile from her.

She couldn't have called herself anything but a fool at that moment, she knew, yet somehow she could not help but relent. If she'd been possessed of even an ounce of sense, she would have left him for good, but instead she found herself believing every word that he'd said, perhaps because she wanted so badly for them to be true. She could imagine many things for her future, but she could not imagine life without the man who had stolen her heart—it was like thinking of life without water.

In the next moment, she threw her worries away with wild abandon as his fingers trailed the gentle curve of her waist and his lips tasted the warm curve of her shoulder.

"You can't leave me," she whispered helplessly, her small fingers gripping the powerful curve of his shoulders as if to hold him to her forever. "You are all I have." Looking up at him through passion-clouded eyes, she met the fiery desire in his eyes, and fell silent for a moment in the face of its strength. "Please say you won't go," she said finally, and in the

319

back of her mind remembered a not-so-long-ago time when she had promised herself that she would never again tie her life to that of another person. In the wake of this thought came the memory of the desolation that had washed over her soul after the loss of her father, and she shivered noticeably.

"Don't be afraid, my love," Cale whispered, sweeping her from her feet and into his arms as if she weighed no more than a rag doll. "I won't be gone for long, and I promise to come back in one piece."

With a bitter sigh, she lay her head against the hard, tanned curves of his chest and resigned herself to the fact that there was no way she could keep him from leaving. Closing her eyes tightly, she fought to keep away her tears as he lay her gently on the pallet where they had shared their love. She didn't look up as she heard him close the door flap and then felt him fall beside her. Instead, she only closed her sea green eyes more tightly and tried to pretend that she was somewhere in the future, in a time when there was no war to be fought, when Texas had become a state and the Indians had been guaranteed their land, in a time when she and Cale could be left in peace. Somehow, she couldn't quite paint the picture in her mind, and that fact hung like a black omen over her heart. Something was going to go wrong, she could feel it, she knew it. Instead of the picture that she wanted to see, she saw instead her red brothers, the people that her father had loved so, lying dead on blood-soaked battlefields, left to rot like diseased cattle. She saw their children starved and beaten, with hollow faces that could no longer bring forth even tears. She saw proud people left with no pride at all.

Her mind was stolen away again by the artful stroke of Cale's fingers against the naked curve of her hips, and she moved against him desperately, like one who could see the world coming to an end and was desperate to spend the moments before they could slip away. Tears streamed uncontrolled down her cheeks as she cried out, half in passion and half in horror of the vision that had etched itself in her mind. And then, the vision was gone, its harsh colors forced away by the bright hues of passion as she felt his fingers enter her gently.

Her eyes flew open in surprise, but he kissed them shut, tasting the salty traces of the tears that still trembled against her thick lashes.

"I love you Jesse . . ." he whispered as he slowly teased the rhythm of her hips to a fever pitch. Parting her legs and moving over her, he kissed her flushed lips again, and added, "Above all else." In the last moment of sanity before passion swept him away also, he knew he meant it. He'd place nothing above her again — not even the fate of the Comanche nation.

Hungrily, he tasted the swollen peaks of her breasts, moving from one to the other until she arched against his chest and begged for release. Sitting back, he pulled her hips to him, easing his manhood into her waiting folds until she swallowed him fully. The rhythm of their love began slowly, and she moved against him with the grace of a dancer, reveling in her own passion, and in the realization of his. Finally, when she could wait for release no longer, she reached for him and pulled him to her, clinging to him to keep herself from being swept away by the crashing waves of passion that shuddered through her body. And then, in one white-hot instant, she found what she had hungered for, and she felt the warm evidence of his release within her.

In the aftermath of their love, the vision that had haunted her earlier returned, and, as he wrapped her securely in his arms, she clung to him and cried.

It was midnight before Jessalyn awoke again. Lying in the secure circle of the Comanchero's arms, she watched the low flames of the fire dance in the pit. She felt an odd sense of peace float over her — odd considering that her world was teetering precariously on the brink of war.

Slowly, she turned over to watch Cale while he slept. He stirred only slightly when she moved, his thick lashes quivering against the bronzed crest of his cheeks. He looked so peaceful there, so gentle. He might have been a simple farmer rather than the most feared and revered Comanchero in Texas. As she reached out to touch the tawny curls that looked almost blond against his dark skin, it was hard for her to imagine that he could have such power over so many people. How he had gotten that power, how he maintained it, she could not exactly pinpoint. He never threatened. He never forced a man to follow him. In fact, he rarely ever even raised his voice, yet others followed him as if he were some sort of god. He could put even the strongest men back in their places with little more than a glance, and often without their even noticing it. If leadership was an art, then El Halcon was most certainly a master crafts-man, and he had built a reputation for himself that stretched from Kansas to Mexico.

Pulling her hand back as he stirred again, Jessalyn was struck for the first time by the thought that she hardly knew him. In fact, she felt strangely as if she knew only the mask that he wore—the mask of El Halcon—nothing of the man inside. She was still considering that question and watching him intently as he opened his eyes. Their golden depths were so bright and clear as his gaze met hers that she won-dered if he had been asleep at all.

"What are you thinking about, Jesse?" he asked in a low, smooth tone that washed over her like warm water. After a moment, he added, "You look so . . . concerned." Dangerous might have been a better word, he thought to himself after he had said this. He'd seen that look before, and it usually forewarned a storm.

Rather than become angry, she only regarded him with a mixture of curiosity and pensiveness.

"I was thinking of how little I know you," she ad-mitted, deciding that it was a good time for honesty. There should be no more secrets between them, she thought. He had found his way so far into her soul that now she needed to be allowed at least a little way into his.

Shifting a bit, he braced himself up on one elbow and smiled slightly at her observation.

"I'd say that you know me better than most do," he said, only halfway kidding. Observing her frown of disappointment, he added, "But what is it that you would like to know?"

Jessalyn's mouth hung open a bit in surprise at his question, and she rolled over onto her stomach, tossing a bright spill of hair over her shoulder and looking into the fire.

"Where did you come from? What were you like as a child? How did you become El Halcon?" She turned away a bit more to hide a flush of embarrassment. In all her life, she had never before been one to probe another person with unwanted questions. Hedging for time, she went on, "And . . . and why does Nocona call you his brother? For that matter, how did you come to be among the Comanche at all?"

Cale laughed warmly at the barrage of queries, his eyes bright with mirth, and with love, though she could not see this from where she lay.

"Is that all?" he joked, as if the questions she had asked were a simple matter to answer. In truth, those were things about him almost no one knew, not even men who had been with him for years. In the past, Sam had been the only one who knew these things, and he preferred it that way. There were few men, or women, who could be trusted in his business, and he had learned young that it was best to confide in no one. Now, he carefully considered the questions Jesse had asked. Before answering, he drew a deep breath and sat up to add some more wood to the fire. When he was finished, he sat regarding her with dark whiskey eyes, thinking.

Still lying almost motionless on the pallet, Jessalyn waited for him to speak without looking up at him. Instead, she trained her eyes on the fire absently. It wasn't until he had begun his story that she realized she had been holding her breath in fear that he would refuse to answer.

"You asked how I came to be what I am." He sized up the question like a gambler assessing his opponent and wondered what she was going to think of the answer. "You also asked what kind of a child I was," he added, still speaking to the motionless back of her head as she lay on the mat. In truth, he was grateful not to have to aim his story directly into those clear, fragile, willow eyes.

"I was the same as most boys, I suppose," he went on, finally beginning his reply, and feeling rather strange at speaking of things that had happened so long ago. "My mother was English, pure blood, and my father mostly French—from New Orleans, which is where I was born. My mother died in childbirth when I was twelve. My father went west. He started up trading with the Comanche, then married a Comanche woman—Sam's mother. I grew up with the Comanche, and left when I was grown, or when I thought I was grown." He smiled a bit in the memory of his foolish youth. That was a tale in itself, but he chose to leave it out for now. Perhaps some other time . . . "I came home older and wiser, but my father was already dead. Sam was still pretty much a boy then, but full of fire and just reckless enough to get himself killed. He had an eye for the ladies, you see. Mostly other men's wives—an unhealthy interest, but he thought he knew enough to take care of himself." A small chuckle sparkled in his eyes and danced quietly into the air as he said that, and then he went on. "So finally after his mother didn't need him anymore, I started the trade business and took him with me. The rest of the men have come from different places. Most of them are wanted somewhere, of course, but they're a loyal bunch, and they profit well enough from the business." He paused for a moment to recount her questions. "You asked me about Nocona," he said then, and eyed the back of her head with a suspicious gleam, wondering what her particular interest in Nocona was. He was friends with most of the other chiefs also, many more important than Nocona, but she hadn't asked about them. "Nocona calls me his brother because we were compadres growing up, that is all," he said, but that was not the whole of it. In truth, there was a much stronger bond between the two, but it hardly mattered now. Anyway, he preferred to keep that private.

Slowly, Jessalyn turned over and then sat up to face him, holding the cover over her bare breasts. With a smile, Cale studied the picture that she made in the firelight. She was indeed beautiful — even down to the tears that glittered like dewdrops in the corners of her eyes.

"Now that I've told you what you wanted to know," he reached out to touch a stray curl that had fallen forward over her shoulder, then smiled into her eyes, "I think it is only proper that you return the favor. You say that I keep secrets, my sandstone rose, but you hardly volunteer information about yourself."

With a little shrug, Jessalyn brushed off the accusation that she was as elusive as he, and then looked away from him a bit, reaching up absently to comb her hair back from her face with trembling fingers.

"That's only because there isn't anything to tell," she defended herself. "You knew my father, so you know most of it. I spent my whole life with him, doing whatever he did—trapping, trading. Sometimes I stayed at Bent's Fort with Mamacita." She paused for a moment, and then looked up at him, but her eyes were far away. "I never knew my real mother. My father never spoke of her, and I never asked." In a soft whisper, she added, "I guess that seems strange," out loud, but to herself. Indeed, now it did seem strange that she knew so little of herself, and even stranger yet that she had never asked—or even wondered.

"And what were you like as a child?" Cale repeated her question back to her, stressing the word "you" until it had a slight ring of absurdity. Waving his hand into the air grandly, he added in the comically exaggerated voice of a poet, "Tell me, my dear, from what sort of seeds do stone roses grow?"

Unable to resist his charm, Jessalyn laughed merrily, and stood up, wrapping the colorful Navaho blanket around her and then throwing the tail back over her shoulder with a snobbish tilt of her chin.

"They grow from little pebbles, of course," she said, as if continuing the soliloquy that he had begun. "Little gray pebbles washed up from deep in the sea and planted on the night of the full moon in secret fairy gardens tended by bands of little pixies." With her fingers, she performed a puppet show in the air, demonstrating the dance of the pixies as she spoke, and then burst out laughing again at her own humor. When Cale began to laugh with her, she doubled over in mirth, wrapping her arms around her aching sides and falling to the pallet beside him. When she had finally caught her breath, she rolled over to look at him.

"Have any more silly questions?" she asked cheerfully, secretly proud of herself for having avoided his question. It wasn't that she had anything to hide, exactly—it was just that the question was such a strange one to answer.

"Not such a silly question," Cale replied, having again grown serious, and not having forgotten that she had sidestepped his original query. "On the contrary, one that you just asked me, as I recall."

Throwing her hands up in defeat, Jessalyn gave him a one-sided frown, as if to protest his spoiling of a good bit of humor.

"I was a normal little girl, I suppose," she answered with a slightly flip tone. Then, considering the past more soberly, she added, "Except that I was somewhat spoiled—or maybe not spoiled, but more like a little boy than a little girl, and homely with a capital *h*."

Cale raised a doubtful brow at her last statement, and tilted his head back to eye her quizzically.

"I don't know if I can believe you were ever homely," he said, appraising her from one end to the other as if she were a fine horse for sale.

"I was too," Jessalyn protested quickly, and then realizing what she was arguing for, flushed with embarrassment. "All legs and arms and about as graceful as a three-footed stork." She laughed at the picture, and then at how apt a description it was. Still giggling, she looked through the dark air behind

Cale into years gone past. "My father used to say that . . ." She paused, feeling a small aftershock from the grief that had shattered her spirit not so very long ago. Her frost-tipped eyes suddenly growing dark and removed with thought, she looked back to Cale with a hollow expression. "Did you know my father well, Cale?" she asked, almost absently, as if she contemplated a different question in her mind while she spoke the words. As she tipped her face slightly toward him, her gaze was glassy and fixed, like the lifeless regard of a china doll.

Cale's straight brows knit together at her sudden change in behavior, and he wondered again whether he would ever begin to understand the ever-changing creature that he had come to love. In some ways, it was like trying to understand the subtle currents in a pool of water — he could see the sources of some ripples, but others came from some upheaval within, and he could only wonder at their origin. So it was that he thought carefully before he answered her question.

"I knew him for quite a few years," he said finally, and she regarded him so strangely that he wondered at first if she had forgotten having asked the question. Then, interest sparked in her eyes and bade him to go on, so he did. "I would have said once that I knew him well. We'd spent a fair amount of time together, even fought together a time or two. On the other hand, I knew almost nothing of you, Jesse, and now I realize how much you meant to him. So, I suspect that I only knew about your father the things that he intended me to know." Silently, he marked a tally for Lane Kendrik, a clever man, and one who hadn't deserved to get shot in the back. Out loud, he simply said, "Your father wasn't a fool, and I imagine he didn't want you hanging around with his . . . less respectable business partners."

"He'd be turning over in his grave now if he could see," Jessalyn responded definitely, meaning no disrespect to the dead, but almost expecting the sky to open and thunderbolts to strike out at any moment. She had strayed so far from her father's memory now that it was hard for her to say anymore exactly how her father would have felt, or what he would have done had he still been alive.

Cale laughed warmly at her remark, and reached out to stroke the side of her cheek with the backs of his fingers.

"He probably would at that," he said, looking fondly into her beautiful young face, and marveling at the way that the firelight brought a glow to the pale olive curve of her cheeks.

Looking up at him and meeting his eyes without the cloud of daydream suddenly, she shrugged the thoughts away like an unwanted cloak, and reached up to catch his hand in hers. Looking down at the broad, tanned structure of his hand against her own paler ones, she marveled at the combination of strength and gentleness that they possessed. It was hard to believe now that she had once thought that those hands had been the ones that had ended her father's life. With an inward shudder, she considered what would have happened if she had been successful in her plot to kill El Halcon.

"What are you thinking of, Jesse?" Cale asked, noticing the changing tide of emotions that danced across her eyes.

"It doesn't matter," she said, forcing a bit of a smile to reassure him that nothing was wrong. "It's all in the past now." Leaning forward, she brushed a light kiss across his lips, and then sat back a bit to gaze into his eyes. "I love you," she said after a long stretch of silence. In response, he smiled, whispering, "And I you," before pulling her back onto the mat with him and kissing her with all of the deep love and longing that now lived within him.

When he propped himself onto one elbow to again look down at her, she was watching him with a curious, if slightly amused, expression. Lowering his brows and tilting his head to one side, he gave her a quizzical eye, to which she responded with a little giggle and a sheepish explanation.

"I was thinking of how well you fooled me," she replied to his silent question. "When I went after El Halcon, I was expecting a mestizo with a beard and a red armband with a golden hawk embroidered upon it"

This time, it was the Comanchero who laughed. With exaggerated flair, he shrugged, tossing his tawny curls back wistfully.

"Ah, that was in my younger, more flamboyant days," he remarked, his tanned face alight with mirth. "When Texas was a vast, open wasteland, I could afford to go around parading my identity, but after the rangers and the Old Law took shots at me a few times, I learned to be more conservative." Reaching up, he stroked his face sorrowfully. "I'm afraid that 'Hair Face' is only an affectionate moniker these days. I'm a clean-shaven fellow, and luckily

331

I'm recognized by very few that way."

Jessalyn nodded absently at his last words, but she had only halfway heard him. His mention of the "Old Law" had surprised her, and caught her attention for a moment. Her father had mentioned the Old Law Mob enough times in the past for her to know that being on the wrong side of the Old Law was deadly. Though the mob was poorly organized, its members were plentiful, and mostly influential in Texas. They had the backing of money and power, and when they wanted someone dead, they generally found a way to see that it happened. Cale hardly seemed concerned, and, in fact, had already moved the conversation on to another subject, but to Jessalyn, the mention of the Old Law spelled only one thing—death for the man she loved.

Chapter Eighteen

The days of the council meeting dragged into a week and finally into two, but no decision had been reached in the council lodge. Some spoke for peace and some for war, their arguments as opposed as the two branches of the sacred forked lodge pole that stood stoically above them. Each day, however, the tide leaned more toward war, and this angered those who stood resolutely for peace. Amongst the latter was old Iron Shirt, who finally withdrew from the council and took his small band home. His son, Peta Nocona, who still had not spoken for either side, watched the old man leave through dark, impassive eyes, giving no indication of which side of the argument would gain his support.

After several days of sitting near the council lodge to hear the goings-on within, the women tired of the endless rhetoric and resumed their normal activities. Having few chores to occupy her, Jessalyn had taken to riding away from camp each day to occupy the long afternoon hours. At first, she had made a habit of going to Cale's lodge to grab a few stolen hours with him when she returned, but she soon realized the displeasure this caused Sparrow Eyes, and forced herself to go to the Kiowas' lodge instead. As a guest in their household, she knew, any shame she brought on herself would also be visited on them. Cale protested her absence at first, but soon relented to her determination. It was a bitter win for her, as she suspected that his acquiescence was mainly an effort to avoid the cause of their problem—which was, of course, that they were not married.

That fact had plagued Jessalyn often, and the longer that Cale avoided the subject, the more she dwelt privately on it. Finally, a sort of vindictive wisdom caused her to refrain from his bed, even though each time their eyes met, she hungered for his touch. In the night as she lay alone on her pallet she conjured painful visions of beautiful Comanche women slipping under the edge of his lodge cover to share his bed. When her thoughts were merciful, she worried only over the prospect of his going to war or being killed by the Old Law Mob. When her thoughts were good, the women slipping under his lodge cover were ugly and built like market steers.

The question of marriage finally erupted into a full-scale war when, after having left Cale to sleep alone for two weeks, Jessalyn refused him again.

"I have had enough of this treatment!" he roared as he stood arms akimbo between her and the door. "I thought we had agreed to a truce! I want to know why you're treating me like I'm still the enemy."

Facing him down with the courage of a rainmaker, Jessalyn braced her hands on her hips and widened her eyes in false innocence.

"I don't know what you could mean," she chirped in a voice that was at once sticky-sweet and razor-sharp. Swinging her hips coyly from side to side, she did her best imitation of the young husband-hunters she'd once seen at an army dance at one of the forts. "Why," she added, batting her large eyes wistfully, "it isn't as if we were married." For the last statement, she had dropped the false tone and spoken with the firmness of a preacher calling down hellfire and brimstone on judgment day.

Throwing up his hands, Cale spun on his heel as if he couldn't believe what he'd just heard, took two steps away, and then turned back.

"Is that all!" he exclaimed, as his flailing hands landed in his hair and then closed over the curls as if to pull them from his skull. An odd change of emotion then tugged at the corners of his lips as he saw the humor of the situation, and he said again, with a touch of laughter, "Is that all? Good Lord, woman, why didn't you say something?"

Bemused at the apparent lightness with which he reacted to the subject, she stood silent for a moment. This was no small matter to her, and she wasn't about to let him treat it as such. Tossing her hair back, she threw up her fine chin and attempted to salvage some of her dignity.

"Why didn't you?" she spat back, and then would have liked to swallow the words as soon as she heard them. It sounded like something a five-year-old would have said. *Pretty clever, Jess, pretty clever,* she reprimanded herself angrily. *That ought to let him know you're someone to be reckoned with.*

Tossing back his head so far that his tawny curls fell

between his shoulder blades, Cale laughed so loud that the lodge poles seemed to rattle. It was only after a good dose of that laughter that he became serious again and turned back to her.

"Did you really think that I would take you to bed and then leave you?" Now, he looked deadly serious — or just deadly. Coming a few steps closer, he joined her in the bright circle of firelight, close enough to touch her, though he did not. "Did you really think that all I wanted was your body, Jesse mine?" he asked so softly that she had to lean closer to hear him, and, involuntarily, her eyes locked with the power of his. "You were my prisoner, remember." His voice seemed even lower and steadier than before, and it was almost as if she could read his thoughts and he wasn't speaking at all. "I could have taken your body any time — and don't think that I couldn't have made you willing. When I finally laid with you after all those months, I was asking for your heart."

Tears welled up in her eyes like summer raindrops as she realized what his words meant. Somewhere within, a part of her still harbored doubt toward him, this man, this legend, this devil to whom she had lost her soul, but she spoke from the part of her that trusted him completely.

"You have had it all along," she said honestly, her green eyes quivering like new leaves against a pool of tears. "But you never spoke of marriage. How was I to know?"

Reaching out, Cale smoothed the willful curls from her cheeks, considering her statement and wondering how a man could go from being so cold to being so smitten in only a matter of months.

"Good question," he said with a slight smile. "Well then, madam, tell me, can this wait until the council is over and we leave here, or should we go for a padre tonight?" For his humor, he won a slight smile that trembled uncertainly on her flushed lips. With a bit of abandon, he added, "That is, unless you want a Comanche wedding."

At that, she giggled through her leftover tears, and reached up to dry them from her stained cheeks.

"No, I'll wait," she said, "but I want this in writing." Rubbing her sore eyes, she added with a note of complaint, "I haven't cried this much in all my life. I think you're a bad influence on me, sir."

Grabbing her chin lightly, he shook it playfully back and forth, then leaned close to kiss her on the end of her small nose. "Well no more of those," he said. "As cold as it is tonight, you're likely to end up with icicles hanging off of your chin."

Giggling at the picture of herself as a Comanche bride with icicles hanging off of her chin, she slipped into his arms, looking up into the perfectly carved lines of his face.

"Well, you must have icicles hanging from your heart," she said cocking her head to one side and leaning back to see him better, "being so cruel to me. I don't know what you can do to make up for it." Her full lips formed a pout that she had perfected as a child. Neither man nor beast could refuse it. "You'll be lucky if I'll marry you at all now." She tipped her nose up coyly, silently wondering at the fact that only a moment before she had been bitterly angry with him. Once again, she realized that he had played first fiddle, but it didn't matter. Suddenly, she than happy to dance to the tune.

"Is that so," he countered wisely, his eyes sparkling with flecks of gold dust. "Well then, milady, I will just have to spirit you off to the church against your will and marry you anyway." He laughed—a bit ruefully, and added, "I'm sure I could get Sam to hold the shotgun. He's been after me to make an honest woman of you for quite a while."

Jessalyn's brows knit together questioningly—more at his tone than at his statement, although that struck her strangely also. Frowning at the odd look in his eyes, she pulled back against the iron circle of his arms and stood watching him. Was it regret over their marriage that she saw in his eyes, or was it only concern for his brother's condition?

"Oh has he?" she asked flatly, choosing to ignore the look that had flashed behind the mask he wore. Had she inquired about it, she was certain that he would not have answered her anyway. Effecting a dazzling smile to hide her thoughts, she arched her dark brows slightly. "Well, good for Sam. At least one of you has some decency." She made the remark so lightly as to almost overrule the note of truth in it, but Cale heard it anyway, and the shadows behind his eyes darkened even further.

"Don't let Sam fool you. He's just enjoying seeing his brother get caught in the net," he said with a lightness that belied the cold memory that shivered in his heart. That last conversation with Sam had hung like a weight around his neck ever since they had left the fortress. It pounded in his ears when he slept, and whispered to him in his waking hours each time he looked into Jessalyn's beautiful face. The truth was that Sam was in love with her — he'd admitted that straight out — and now, each moment of happiness that Cale found with the young beauty was, in a way, stolen from the purse of his brother. It was a hard situation, Cale realized now, and it would never have come to be if he had admitted to his own feelings for her sooner. Instead, he had allowed them to spend long hours together — Jessalyn trapped and alone, and Sam fulfilling the role of the protector. The most sickening part of it all was that he himself had been the enemy that had drawn them together, and he had been so resolute in his rejection of her that he had allowed Sam to foster a hope of having her for himself. With a sigh, he pushed the thoughts away again. There was no solution for them now, and, unfortunately, there would never be.

"Stay with me tonight," he whispered, capturing Jessalyn's uncertain jade eyes and then sweeping her from her feet and into his arms. With a mournful note that she did not understand, he added, "I need you here beside me, my sandstone rose."

With a sigh, she closed her eyes and breathed in the comforting scent of him. As he lay her gently on the pallet, she did not look at him. She could not bear the look of pain in his eyes, and she could not understand it. Most of all, she could not bear the thought that she might have caused it.

It did her no good to avoid his gaze, though, for the moment his lips met hers, she felt the same sadness that she had seen in his eyes. It was as if, suddenly, she was all that was left to him in the world, as if he needed her above all else, as if he meant to borrow strength from her because he could not find his own.

This time it felt altogether different as he slowly re-

339

moved her clothing and caressed the tender length of her, felt as if he needed as much from her as she needed from him. She wanted to carry him to the heights of ecstasy just as he carried her, to bring him freedom from the dark thoughts that troubled him.

Tentatively, she kissed the powerful curves of his bare chest, caressing the hard curves of muscle with her fingers, and then moving to unlace his buckskins. He watched her warmly as she sat up to pull off his ankle-mocs and then his buckskins. A smile touching the corners of his lips, he met her eyes, and made her blush slightly before he leaned back against the pallet to enjoy her explorations. As her small, soft fingers found the growing shaft of his manhood, all of his troubles left his mind, and he whispered some insane bit of poetry about the sweet scent of stone roses.

Finally, when he could wait no longer to touch her, he reached for her and drew her back to his lips, kissing her with all of the hunger that she had brewed within him. Savoring the sweetness of each inch of her, he tasted the velvet smoothness of her neck, the swollen ripeness of her breasts, the soft, trembling curve of her stomach.

Feeling her need rush like hot liquor through her veins, Jessalyn arched toward him, tossing her head from side to side and calling to him as he parted her smooth thighs and tasted the sweetness within. From far away, she thought she heard the drums again — that could mean war — but dimly she realized that it was only the pounding of her own heart. Before her eyes, colors danced to the sensuous rhythm that had begun to move her body, and as he moved over her and entered her, she saw them explode before her like a thousand shooting stars.

Cale sat exhausted in the council lodge, looking from one silent face to another, and then finally to the face of Nocona, who now was poised to speak. It was about time, Cale thought bitterly to himself. The protocol of the council had worn him thin over the past few weeks, and he'd just about reached his limit. It was hard for him to accustom himself to an environment where all spoke their minds, but none were in charge. It was anarchy as far as he could tell and so he never allowed it among his own men. He took their suggestions, but then he decided, and that was that, none questioned, and they all served whether they agreed or not. His thoughts froze as Nocona began his speech. It wouldn't be a long one, Cale knew Nocona was one to cut right to the heart when he finally decided to give his opinion.

Cale was right — it didn't take long, and Nocona spoke for war. That decided it for the most part, because even those chiefs who had spoken for peace now reluctantly swung toward war. It was better to fight as a wolf with the pack than to crawl away and hide like a pet dog, Old Owl said as the council finally reached agreement, and the other peace chiefs agreed with him.

Cale breathed a sigh of relief as the council began to discuss the details of the spring raids. He had been relatively certain all along that Nocona would speak for war in the end, but his friend's prolonged silence had still unnerved him. He'd not seen Nocona in some years, but in the past, Nocona would have been the first to take up the lance. The weight of responsibility had made him cautious, Cale surmised as he sat back and watched the young chief look steadily from one man to the next in the council ring. It was plain that, despite Nocona's youth, almost every man at the council respected him, and that was good. That respect would be useful in the spring when it came time to take the warriors into battle . . .

Cale's mind drifted unwillingly away from the sounds of the council, until he no longer heard what was said. Resting one elbow on his bent knee, and leaning back on the other one, he frowned into the smoke that rose from the fire pit, his eyes as intense as those of the hawk that had been his namesake. The handsome features of his face grew harder as he thought of the conversation that he'd had with Jessalyn the night before—and about the promises he had made. What would those promises mean now that war was a certainty? No matter how hard he tried, he couldn't picture Jessalyn waiting patiently at the fortress while he went away to fight. In fact, the picture that formed time and again in his mind was one of Jessalyn streaked with warpaint and brandishing a lance. He smiled a little at the thought, but it was too close to the truth to be very amusing. At least as her husband he'd have some control . . . maybe.

He tossed several strategies back and forth in his mind until the council finally disbanded with an agreement about the place and time to gather in the spring. Cale made note of the location with a frown, but said nothing. It would be a long ride for his men, and a long way to transport the rifles and ammunition he had promised to supply. Still, at the moment, he'd rather

342

have ridden a thousand miles than spend one more minute in council. As it was, he didn't stay around to talk, but walked quickly around the ceremonial circle and left as soon as was proper. Once outside, he paused to talk with Nocona for only a moment, then went quickly to his horse, intending to ride out to his men's camp and inform them of the council's outcome.

They'd be glad to hear it, he thought with a bit of a smile as he mounted his horse. The decision meant that they would be going home in a few days, and his men weren't the only ones who would be glad to see their own country again. He'd been looking forward to it himself. Still, he suspected that his men would be more grateful than he to be pulling out of the Comanche camp. Staying so long with the Comanche in their own territory had made his Comancheros as jumpy as flies on a hot tin griddle, and he had the feeling that if he didn't get them away soon, the Mexicans were going to start killing the half-breeds.

Spinning his mount about, Cale started toward the edge of the sprawling camp, but he hadn't even cleared the shadow of the council lodge when he spied a rider coming toward him from out of the dust that blew between the lodges. At first, Cale narrowed his eyes in disbelief at what he saw, but as the rider came closer, he urged his horse into a lope and met the other halfway.

"Well, where in the *h e* double *l* did you come from?" he asked as he extended his hand to join forearms with his halfbrother. Clasping his brother's arm and getting a wicked twinkle in his eye, Sam pulled sharply, almost unseating the larger man, and then Cale pulled back, almost unseating them both.

"Just happened by," Sam said simply, pulling his forearm free and checking it for bruises with a frown. "Damn, you've got a grip. You must be getting stronger, Cale." A wide smile lit every inch of his face. "Gomez tells me you've been sitting in council for a while. You Heap-Big-Chief yet, brother? I'd like to know because there was this girl I saw on the way in . . ."

Cale grimaced and squinted sideways at Sam. This was beginning to sound like a story he'd heard before — and it was also beginning to sound like the old Sam.

"Forget it. We won't be staying much longer," he said as they fell into pace in the direction of the Comanchero camp. "Not that I'm not glad to see you," he added as they rode away, "but what are you doing here?"

At the question Sam's face took on a sobriety that seemed almost foreign, and he sighed the same sigh that Cale had heard himself give a million times. At the sound of it, Cale leaned back a bit and cocked a brow at his half-brother. Something was definitely wrong, he decided. He'd never seen Sam so serious about anything that didn't involve a female.

"We have a little problem back at the fort," Sam began, still looking straight ahead gravely, as if he were playing a part that he had rehearsed many times.

"I could have guessed that," Cale remarked, still fairly untroubled, and halfway amused by Sam's unusual gravity.

Straightening back a bit, Sam prepared himself for a burst of temper, showing no signs of sharing Cale's good humor. He was fairly certain, in fact, that his brother's cheerful attitude was about to come to a screeching halt.

"Well, a few of Jessalyn's ranger friends came back after her." He met Cale's shocked expression with a straight face. Any minute now, the yelling was bound to start, and Sam understood now why he hadn't been able to convince any of the other men to bring the message. No one wanted to be thrown to the lions. In fact, he didn't like it much himself, but, bracing himself, he stepped into the ring, saying, "Right now they're spending a little time in our jail."

Cale's face grew tight with anger and his eyes began to burn like two bright coals as he considered the implications of Sam's news. Still, his voice was calm when he spoke.

"I assume you had no other choice," he said, but he might as well have saved the words. He knew that Sam wouldn't have shown the rangers the location of the fortress if there had been any other option. "How did they find their way in?"

"Ramon was with them," Sam explained, his own face becoming an angry mirror of his brother's.

"That bastard!" Cale exploded in a voice loud enough to chase away the stray clouds in the sky. "I should have killed him when I had the chance." His hands clenched tighter on his reins, and he imagined Ramon's neck there. He should never have let the man go when he knew the location of the fort. That was one mistake he wouldn't make again.

"You won't need to," Sam replied, smiling like a cat who had just caught a mouse. "We shot him and hung him out already — as an example."

345

Cale nodded and grinned evilly at the thought of Ramon's scrawny hide drying in the sun on the fort wall. It was the standard punishment for betrayal, and most men never thought about crossing him once they'd seen the sentence effected on another.

"What about the rangers?" he asked, matter-of-factly. "How many were there?"

"Only five," Sam replied. "That fancy lieutenant and four others." With a smile and a wink, he added, "We winged one of them, but other than that and a few complaints about the accommodations, they're fine."

The picture of Brett Anderson locked in one of his prison cells was more than even Cale's black mood could resist. Throwing back his head, he laughed, "I'll bet they have a few complaints." He pulled up his horse, and Sam drew his mount to a stop also. "Go on ahead and tell the men to pack up camp," Cale ordered, turning his horse back toward the village. In response, Sam nodded and started on toward the camp, as Cale added, "I'll wrap up things here and meet you shortly."

With that, they parted, Sam heading toward the Comanchero camp and Cale heading toward the village. On his way, Cale spurred his horse into an easy lope and reached the edge of the camp again in short order. When he found Jessalyn again, she was sitting alone outside of Sounds on the Wind's lodge carefully repairing a tear in one of her buckskin skirts. Her long legs were stretched comfortably out in front of her, clothed in neat, high black riding boots that looked freshly oiled.

As he came around from behind the lodge, Cale stopped for a moment to watch her, temporarily forgetting his hurry to leave the village. Her long copper hair fell forward over her shoulder so that he could not see her face, but he imagined a slight frown there as she concentrated on her work. As he stepped closer, she looked up with one eye, keeping the other bent on her work.

"The council finally broke up?" she asked with the same absent frown that he had imagined, and then bent closer over her work.

"Ummm," Cale replied, squatting down next to her and resting his elbows on his knees. As he leaned over to see her face, his brows drew together. "Why the angry face?" he asked, noticing her expression and wondering if somehow she had already heard Sam's news.

"I stuck myself," she complained, frowning, and then giggling at her own seriousness, she put down her work. "But I shall survive to sew another day," she joked, and when he didn't respond to her humor, she turned his own question back on him. "So why do you look so serious?" As she asked the question, a speck of fear came into her eyes, and she added, "Did things go badly at the council?"

"No. Things went well," Cale replied, catching her eyes and holding them before he spoke again. "We have to leave as soon as the men can pack up camp." His tone turned cool as he stood up—as if a sudden thought had closed him away from her. "Get your things together, Jesse, and saddle up. I'll explain it all to you later." With that, he strode away without waiting for her reaction, and she sat openmouthed watching him go.

"Well, yes sir," she muttered to herself with a grimace of disgust as she wrapped up her sewing things and

347

climbed to her feet. As she did, her hastily packed sewing equipment spilled onto the ground, and she reached down to scoop it up with growing anger. "Anything you say, sir. I'll just run along and pack up right away," she grumbled, now considering refusing to go with him all together. After all, he couldn't force her to go, and if she decided to stay with Sounds on the Wind and his Kiowa for a while before going back to the fortress, what could he do about it? An evil glint stole into her jade eyes as she considered the plan. How shocked he would be — how angry — and it would serve him right!

Then her fantasy burst like a bubble, and she realized that he'd only drag her away kicking and screaming. She could tell by the look in his eye that he wasn't in a mood to be crossed. Once again, she felt like a prisoner, and it seemed hard to believe that only the night before they had of spoken of marriage. Of course, it went without saying that now that little promise would be kicked to the wayside by this new crisis, whatever it was. And she wasn't sure she minded that too much at the moment. In fact, she wasn't sure that she ever wanted to get married to anyone, not if it meant having to take orders from someone her whole life, as if she were a child, or a dog.

Still, as she fumed on over the question of marriage, and orders, and obedience, she was busily packing her things in Sounds on the Wind's lodge. Only after she had finished that and saddled her horse did she manage to say goodbye to her hosts. They watched her with concern as she mounted and rode away beside the ghost-man, El Halcon, but they made no move to stop her. It was plain to see that young Jessalyn was a woman now, and that she would make her own choices. She was of strong blood, the Kiowa chief thought as she disappeared from view. This was good, for the path she had chosen for herself would be a difficult one.

Jessalyn fell slowly back into the group of Comancheros as they rode away from the creekbed that had been their camp. Her eyes were thoughtful and her ears were sharp as she watched Sam and Cale ahead. They rode closely together and spoke in low tones, but still she could hear them clearly. It wasn't long until she had heard the whole story, and then she wished she had never listened at all. She realized all too quickly that there was no solution to the stalemate that she had caused. It was like a deadly game of chess where the players on both sides belonged to her—no matter which move she made, someone she cared for would be hurt.

"You plead to me for their lives!" Cale exploded, spinning around to face Jessalyn, who sat still mounted a few paces from him. Around them, the empty desert had grown angry and red in the still evening light, as if to mirror the blaze in the eyes of the Comanchero who was its master. "You plead to me for their lives!" he repeated, reaching up to grab her arm and pull her from her mount, who shied away at his madness and trotted to where the buckskin stood tethered. "Have you lost your mind!" Cale exploded, shaking her as if she were a rag doll. "They trespassed on

my land uninvited, invaded my home, shot my men."
Jerking her to him, he pinned her against his chest and
stared down into her frightened eyes wildly. When he
spoke again, his voice was a low growl that chilled her
to the bone. "You tell me how I can afford to show
them mercy."

Jessalyn's head was throbbing so loudly from the
shaking he had given her that she could barely hear his
last words, and her arm had gone numb from the force
of his grip.

"How can you afford not to?" she asked in a voice
that sounded pitifully small in the desert vastness.
"Those men don't deserve to die." She could tell by the
look in his eye that she might as well have been pleading to a stone wall. "Don't you see?" she went on desperately. "I'm not just asking you for their lives. I'm
asking you for our future!" Her voice rose with desperation, and her jade eyes widened into two bright pools
caught between tears and hysterics. "How can we ever
have a future with five dead men lying between us a
night? If you kill them, you're tossing away our lives."

His anger burned higher at her words, and he
clenched his free hand tighter to keep from striking
her.

"Don't threaten me, Jesse," he growled, his voice
whipping her like a well-aimed lash. Reaching up, he
seized her chin in his strong fingers and bent low until
his eyes burned brightly into hers from only a few
inches away. "Don't threaten me, my love," he said,
and the threat in his own voice was unmistakable. "
will do as I see fit, and you will do as you are told."

Pressing her fists against the hard barrier of his
chest, she struggled to free herself from him.

"I won't stay and watch you kill those men!" she screamed finally, mindless of the fact that he had nearly lost the reins to his temper. Gathering the last reserves of her courage, she said again, "I won't." Still, as she spoke, every muscle in her small form trembled, and she felt as helpless as a leaf caught in a strong wind. Here, alone, captured in his arms, she realized with painful clarity that if he chose to keep her prisoner again, he could easily do it.

"You will do as you are told," he repeated with the certainty of God sending down a commandment, "or I will have them shot tomorrow — the minute that we set foot on my land."

Jessalyn could only stare back at him in mute anger. Every hard-set line in his face told her that he'd do it, and, with that, he had placed her in checkmate. By pleading for her friends, she would be condemning them to death, so now she could do nothing — nothing but hope that Cale would spare them out of love for her. What were the chances of that, she wondered? It was impossible to tell now. He was like a stranger to her again. In fact, he was exactly as she had once expected El Halcon to be, and this was the most horrifying realization of all. Could this be what he really was, a heartless killer who would buy and sell lives like some sort of god, but without a shred of mercy or an ounce of regret?

Chapter Nineteen

As she rode from the sunlight into the shadow of the high rock walls that hid the entrance to El Halcon's mountains, Jessalyn felt her blood turn to ice water in her veins. From somewhere in the rocks above them, a sentry gave a long, lilting call that tore the silent air like a new steel blade. In response, El Halcon's outrider echoed the call.

"Ay-iii-li-li-li-li-li!" It reverberated against the steep walls of the narrow entrance, and then exploded into the canyon beyond, bouncing off one uneven rock face and then another until it sounded as though a thousand lost souls had joined in the eerie song.

Each note struck Jessalyn like a hot arrow to the heart, and the skin prickled on the back of her neck as if a hundred tiny spiders were crawling over it. Gripping her reins tightly, she struggled to blot out the persistent echoes, but even when they had died away in the canyon air, still they pounded in her head. Desperately she wanted to turn back toward the entrance and run, but she knew she would have no chance of gaining freedom. As if Cale had suspected that she might bolt he had placed ten men behind her. Now, she rode help-lessly, swept along in the tide of men and horses as the Comancheros spurred their nervous mounts into a gal-lop.

With growing excitement, El Halcon's men again raised the welcome call, waving their sombreros and ponchos above their heads. In the rocks, the sentries stood up and waved their rifles, calling back to the riders.

The voices and the echoes mixed with the pounding of hooves against stone and the shrill whinnies of the horses until the entire valley rang with thunder. Like a vengeful winter storm, the riders exploded noisily into the deep basin that held the fort. At the gate, each slid to a halt to glance with disgust at the mutilated bodies of four men that hung upside-down from the canyon wall to one side of the fort.

Seeing them as she was forced into the mouth of the canyon, Jessalyn fought desperately to prevent her mount from being driven closer to the grisly scene. As she drew nearer, she felt her stomach retch at the sight of what had once been men, and she slid her mount to a halt. Gasping for breath, she looked away, and held Diablo steady as the rest of the Comancheros swarmed past her. Holding her hand over her mouth, she forced herself to look up at the bodies again. Were they from the ranger company? From where she stood, she couldn't tell, so badly decayed were the remains.

With a deep breath, she started to bring Diablo for-ward, but a strong grip caught her arm suddenly, and she gasped in fear. Turning quickly, she started to pull away, but then met with Cale's steady amber eyes and sat frozen.

"Those aren't your friends." He anticipated the question that held her heart suspended. Squinting up into the sun toward the corpses without a hint of emotion, he added, "Two of them used to be my men, but they betrayed me in leading your ranger friends here." He paused for a moment to look at the other bodies. "And it appears that we have also caught two of the men who killed your father. We've been tracking them for quite a while." At the wide-eyed disbelief that he received from Jessalyn, he added, "I believe you know the one on the end." He nodded toward the body. "Shot Evans, if I'm not mistaken," he said, and then turned his horse toward the fort. Glancing back, he caught her eye again. "You never really know who your friends are, do you, Jesse?"

Jessalyn didn't reply. She couldn't. She could only watch him go in disbelief and then look back to the horrible proof of his statement. She knew the dead man now, and suddenly a lot of things made sense — the way that Shot Evans had just happened by to help her discover her father's body, for instance, and the way that he had taken a sudden interest in her. But if he was her father's killer, there was still one piece of the puzzle that was missing: why? What possible reason could he have had for wanting to kill her father? It was true that he had never been a friend of her father's, but he had never been an enemy either. Why would he have wanted to see Lane Kendrik dead?

As the commotion around the fort died down, the buzzards crept back like descending shadows to the ripening feast on the canyon wall, and Jessalyn turned away, feeling her stomach rise into her throat. Slowly, she rode on through the fort gateway, staring straight ahead as she moved through the commotion of men and horses inside. She went past them like a sleepwalker, unsaddling her horse numbly and going to the room that had been hers before they had left. The things that she had left behind were there still, exactly as she had left them, and she touched them absently, drawing comfort from their familiarity. Slowly, she wandered from one object to the next—her dresses, her hairbrush, a beaded leather hair tie—looking at each but not seeing them. Then, a sparkle of crystal from the dressing table caught her eye, and she looked down to see the sandstone rose. Slowly, she took it into her hand and closed trembling fingers over it.

Clutching the rose against her chest, she sank slowly to the cool wood floor and leaned her head back against the side of the bed. Dark brows drew together over brooding jade eyes as she considered all that had transpired since they had left Comanche camp. It had only been a matter of days, but now it seemed like it had to have been longer since that wonderful night she had promised to marry a man whom she thought she finally knew. How that dream had come crashing down around her, and now its debris was ready to burst into flames. Somehow, she had to think of a way to stop the disaster that loomed larger and larger on the horizon. Somehow, she had to convince Cale to release the rangers. But how could he release them when they knew the location of his fortress?

Again she faced a double-edged sword, and no matter which way she leaned, the blade would cut just as deep. She couldn't bear to allow the rangers' deaths, yet at the same time, she knew that, if set free, they would only bring troops back to kill Cale and his men.

Pressing her hands to her ears, she struggled to blot out the horrible truth of it all as she lay weakly against the cool floor and closed her eyes. Sleep came to her finally like an angel of mercy, carrying her away to some calmer place as the last murky rays of sunlight left the room. As midnight struck, her body began to tremble with strange, terrible dreams. The harder she tried to run from them, the more they closed around her, until she could feel their icy fingers on every inch of her, tearing her soul from her in tiny pieces, pieces that had names . . .

She awoke to the sound of a bloodcurdling scream, and only after several moments did she realize that the voice had been her own, and that she was standing pressed into the corner of the room like a frightened animal. Leaning against the wall, she fought to catch her breath, gasping as her heart pounded wildly against her chest. A thin curtain of black swam before her eyes, and her head spun until she almost lost her bearings and fell to the floor again.

"Jesse?" The voice seemed so far away at first that she wasn't certain whether she'd heard or imagined it. "Jesse?" This time it was closer, and as the fog cleared from her eyes, she realized that there was a light in the doorway.

"Sam?" She squinted to see the bearer of the lamp. "Is that you?" She needn't have asked the question, because he had set the lamp down and found his way to her side almost before she had managed the words.

Standing beside her, Sam gently reached out to take one of her trembling hands. Rubbing it between his palms, he looked into her wide, confused eyes.

"Jesse, you're as cold as ice," he said, his dark brows

lowering with concern. "What happened here?" he asked, and then was almost sorry he had. If Cale had done something to hurt her . . . He left the thought unfinished. He wasn't sure what he'd do if it came down to a choice between Cale and Jesse.

When she didn't answer, he waved a hand in front of her glassy eyes, but she didn't respond. Finally, he took her by the shoulders and shook her until something snapped and she looked at him as if realizing for the first time that he was there.

"Jesse, what happened here?" he asked again, because now he had to know what had driven her so far out of her mind. It wasn't like her to act this way, he thought.

Jessalyn's eyes wandered away from his and darted about the room, as if she were searching her memory for an answer to his question.

"I don't know," she whispered slowly, still grasping for bits and pieces of the dream. "I was dreaming . . ."

Rolling his dark eyes back, Sam sighed deeply in relief, slight smile replacing the menacing frown that had been on his face.

"Is that all," he said, chuckling warmly under his breath as he put an arm around her and guided her toward the bed. "Well, if you would sleep in bed instead of hanging from the walls, you wouldn't have strange dreams," he chided, smoothing her long hair back as he laid her against the pillow. Pulling the covers over her with the gentleness of a mother tucking in a tired child, he sat down on the edge of the bed beside her, talking as he smoothed the blanket over her shoulders. "Don't do that again, all right?" he scolded, giving her a wink and a wide grin. "That beller you let out like to

357

brought me clean out of my pants. I thought Padre Gomez's devil had come to take me off to hell for my wicked ways." He grinned again at the opportunity to find humor at the expense of the white man's religion. It was a pastime he always enjoyed—especially when Padre Gomez was around. At the look he received from Jessalyn, he rolled his dark eyes. "Good Lord, woman, don't look at me that way," he said laughingly. "Your God has had more than a few jokes at my expense. I'm just paying him back."

"Sorry," Jessalyn muttered, her mind only halfway turned to the conversation. The other half was still replaying the scattered images from her dream. "Sam," she said, looking up at him with a sudden intensity that took him aback. "Cale said two of those men on the wall were the ones who killed my father . . ." She trailed off, for a moment wondering if she should be asking him the question at all. Perhaps Cale didn't want her to know, and she remembered all too well the last time that she had dragged Sam into the middle of a battle between her and Cale. It had almost cost him his life, and she didn't want to see him get caught in the crossfire again.

"It's true," Sam said matter-of-factly. "And they're the only two we're likely to get. The rest of them are too far out of reach."

Jessalyn's brows drew together in confusion, and, against her better judgment, she allowed herself to ask one more question.

"The rest of whom?"

"The Old Law," Sam answered as if he were surprised that she didn't know the truth, or hadn't guessed it. When she only regarded him blankly, he explained, "Shot Evans brought your father to that canyon for the bounty that the mob had put on him. The man we hung beside him is the one who shot your father from the rocks. The two of them planned to collect a pretty piece of change for the job." His young face had gone straight, and above his stark cheekbones his eyes now looked deadly as he gazed past her into the darkness. "I'm sure they figured they'd be right rich after they got the bounty for El Halcon too. That's why Cale tried so hard to talk you out of following our trail—at Bent's Fort, remember—but you insisted on trailing us, and Evans and his partner were one day behind you all the way." He shrugged off the look of shock and indignation that rose in her polished jade eyes as she realized how conveniently she had played the pawn. "I have to give Evans credit," he added, looking sideways at her with a hint of a rueful smile. "He knew you could track us down, and that all he had to do was wait for you to do it."

Jessalyn looked away from him in mute anger, and sat staring into the shadows of the room for several long moments as she pieced together the true circumstances of her father's death. He had been lured into a trap by Shot Evans and killed for the bounty placed on him by those who wanted to see his dreams of Indian land die. Then she had been cleverly maneuvered into tracking down those who were left to carry on his plan. What had seemed like unconnected events now fell into line as well-laid pieces of an incredibly good plan.

"What a fool I've been," she whispered more to herself than to him. "I should have known something was wrong . . . I did know . . . I felt it, but I didn't listen." Feeling her temper rise until she thought she would explode, she threw back the covers and sat up. "I've been so stupid!"

Sitting back, Sam regarded her calmly, like a man watching a storm brew on the horizon from the safety of a warm house.

"There's no point in going over that now, Jesse." His voice was low and soothing as he spoke, and he reached out to take her clenched fists in his hands. Shaking his head, he smoothed her small, knotted fingers into the palms of his hands, and then looked up into her eyes. "You got fooled by a good trick, but it's over now. You have to just tally it up to experience and forget it." When she opened her mouth to reply, he caught her eye and shook his head. "Ssshhh," he whispered. "It's over."

Jessalyn started again to protest, but then stopped when he only silenced her again. She wanted to tell him that it wasn't over, that there were still five lives hanging in the balance because of her stupidity, but she couldn't. Instead, she only held tighter to his strong hands, and sat staring into his eyes as he started to sing quietly a song in the language of his mother's people. It was a story that often put young Comanche children to bed, and eventually, Jessalyn surrendered to its sweet rhythm and settled back into the bed, still holding his hands in hers as she closed her eyes.

From the shadows of the doorway, Cale stood watching them like an intruder in the garden, and his eyes burned with envy. Sam knew a part of her that he himself had never touched. Sam was her friend; she trusted him. Never had that trust been more obvious than now, in this private moment, as she lay clutching Sam's hands in hers. She had let down the proud armor that usually guarded the deepest part of her and allowed him inside. That was the thing that burned the most. He'd felt it dimly ever since she had nursed Sam back to health, each time he'd caught the two of them by surprise only to hear their laughter die and see the shields descend back over Jessalyn's clear eyes. Now, the look that had passed between the two of them cut like a knife, and he turned away to put an end to the pain.

His eyes were solemn and dark as shadows as he walked silently back down the hall. There was no doubt in his mind that he had Jessalyn's love and that he loved her, but there was a wall of mistrust between them that kept them always, in some way, apart. It was the result of the life he had chosen for himself, he knew, and now it seemed that he had come to a choice between preserving what he had or keeping Jessalyn. But if he let the rangers walk away knowing the location of his fort, as she wanted, it would mean taking his men on the run, and he owed them more than that.

His strides carried him down the hallway and out into the cold night air as he tossed the thoughts back and forth in his mind. In the courtyard, he stopped and leaned against the adobe wall of the main house, gazing up at the mountains that peaked over the walls of his canyon. Their crests glistened white with snow in the moonlight, and for the first time, he realized that winter was halfway over. It seemed like such a short time before that he and Jessalyn had watched the summer storms brew over the mountains, and now they were covered three feet thick in snow.

He sighed deeply and pushed off of the wall, continuing his walk toward the stables. There, he lit the lantern, and stood for a while watching the Palouse horse that was Jessalyn's mount. He'd had a horse a lot like that himself once, he remembered with a hint of a smile, but the damned animal had broken away from the corral one day, and they had never found him again. Likely, he found a way down out of the mountains to freedom, Cale thought, and as soon as the thought crossed his mind, he froze. Likely, he found his way out . . .

"That's it!" he exclaimed so loudly that every horse in the stable cocked an ear toward him. Slapping the Appaloosa enthusiastically on the rump, he grabbed his own saddle from the saddle tree and went to where his buckskin stood dozing.

"Wake up, Smoke," he said, leading the reluctant stallion from his stall and throwing on his saddle and pad. "You and I have a little work to do."

Jessalyn crept hurriedly down the hall on silent moccasined feet, her eyes darting about warily. She didn't doubt that she wasn't supposed to be going to the rangers' prison cell, but she also didn't care. Her only regret was that she couldn't find the key to open the cell and set them free. She'd searched everywhere she could think of that morning when she had learned that Cale had mysteriously ridden out on some errand during the night, but she couldn't find the key. She could only guess that one of Cale's men had it, and that thought dashed her hopes of letting them go.

Before she reached the cell, she realized that her plan had been foolish, for Cale had stationed a guard outside the door. She should have expected that, she thought, as there had always been a guard on her when she was his prisoner. Doubtless, five Texas Rangers were considered much more dangerous than one woman.

She straightened haughtily as she approached the guard. Luckily, he wasn't one of the men who had gone with them to the Comanche camp, and thus he wouldn't know of the trouble between her and Cale.

"I've come to see them," she said with an air of authority and a hard glint in her jade eyes that dared him to defy her. In response, the big mestizo unlocked the bolt and stood back from the door, drawing his pistol from his side holster.

"Tell me when you are ready to come out," he said in a voice particularly devoid of emotion. "And have them all stand at the back wall when you open the door, or else I'll shoot 'em!" His thin face cracked into a bloodthirsty smile that told her he'd do it, and she slipped through the door without giving him another look.

Inside, the cell was so dark that at first she couldn't see, and she stood against the door for a moment until her vision adjusted.

"Jesse?" It was Brett's voice, but she could only see his outline coming to her from the far wall. "My God, it is you? I thought you were dead."

Her vision cleared just in time for her to meet his deep blue eyes with a reassuring smile.

"No, I'm well enough, as you can see," she replied, a bit surprised that she felt a twinge of resentment at his statement, either because it implied that she couldn't take care of herself or because it assumed that Cale would have hurt her. To turn the conversation away from herself, she quickly asked, "Are you all right?"

In reply, Brett shrugged, and then nodded toward one of his men who lay on the cot nearby.

"Gardner was shot," he said, an obvious vein of anger running through his words. "He's recovering though. At least they were decent enough to doctor him before they locked us up in here. Our main problem now is how we're going to get out of here before Halcon gets around to having us hung."

Jessalyn flinched a bit at his statement, and Brett paused, eyeing her thoughtfully. With a storm building behind his deep blue eyes, he took a step closer to her and then asked, "Has that bastard done anything . . ." He paused, trying to think of a tactful way to say it. Finding none, he asked simply, "Has he hurt you, Jesse?" and then gritted his teeth waiting for the answer.

Nervously, Jessalyn took a step backward and then turned away from him, wringing her hands in front of her. He was treading dangerously close to things that she could not tell him of. She had no idea how much he knew of her and El Halcon, but the very nature of his question seemed to indicate that he knew little. That was good, for the less he knew, the less danger he presented.

"As I said in my letter to you, Lieutenant, I have stayed here of my own free will. I was wrong in assuming that El Halcon killed my father. In fact, he was my father's friend, and he has proven that by bringing to justice the men who killed him." From the corner of her eye, she saw him move a step closer and reach toward her, but she turned around quickly and moved away from him. "I wish you would have left things alone. As it is, you present a problem for him, but I am trying to convince him to let you go."

"You might as well save your breath," Brett countered squarely. "When we leave here, we're taking you with us."

If the statement hadn't been so horrifying, Jessalyn would have laughed at it. It was absurd for Brett to think that he was in a position to save even himself, much less her, and she cursed his arrogance in refusing the help that she offered.

"I have no intention of leaving," she said, her eyes leveling at him like two cool bits of stone. Somehow, she had to make him realize that trying to take her with him would be the same as signing a death warrant for himself and his men. "But I do intend to do my best to see all of you out of here safely. Please just accept my help and go quietly if I can arrange it."

Standing calmly, like a man firmly anchored on a solid base of principle, Brett shook his head and met her determination with an equal will.

"We won't leave you behind for him." He was more certain than ever now that her plan was to sell herself to El Halcon as ransom for their freedom, and he'd rather see all of them dead than walk away on those terms.

"You must!" Now Jessalyn had begun to loose the reins to her temper, and she struggled to regain her good sense before she said something she would later regret. When the ranger stood obviously unmoved by her outburst, she took a step closer to him and met his stone gaze with one of green fire. In a voice steady, and low enough for only him to hear, she said, "He is my husband." When the lieutenant took a step back in shock, she added with a hint of satisfaction, "Now you see why I can't leave. I want you to go if I can arrange it, and not to come back. By coming after him, you'll only be hurting me."

Brett stood for a long time watching her, wondering if what she had said was true, or if she was still only trying to protect him and his men.

"You married that dirty Mexican?" he muttered in disbelief, turning away from her and pacing the length of the small room.

She only smiled at his question. Inadvertently, he had told her many things, chief among them being that he had no idea of El Halcon's true identity, for Cale was hardly Mexican. Evidently, Brett was operating on the same legends and assumptions that had brought her to those mountains searching for a bearded mestizo with a hawk armband.

"You shouldn't judge a man you don't know," she said, now feeling confident of her advantage over him. "I believe in him. He fights for the same things that my father fought for."

"You mean that nonsense about Kiowa-Comanche land grants?" Anderson asked as he stood turned away from her, his hands clasped neatly behind his back. "That is a farce, Jesse, a lost cause. Your father might have had a chance if he could have gone to Washington as he'd planned, but it's too late now for anything short of an act of God." The tone of his voice as he spoke conveyed plainly that he was not in sympathy with the cause to which she had devoted herself, and when she protested against his statement, he drove the last nail in the coffin without an ounce of regret. "Don't be foolish, Jesse," he said, still without looking at her. "President Polk has unofficially promised the settlers Texas, every square inch of it, for homesteading, and Congress is behind him. Indians don't vote. Settlers vote, and that is what counts, after all. The statehood agreement is signed, sealed, and all but delivered. Nothing is going to change it now."

Jessalyn's triumphant smile had faded, and now she stood watching his stiff posture in disbelief as her heart fell to her shoes. Could it really be true? Had everything they had been fighting for been a lie? She wanted desperately to believe that Brett was only telling her these things to save himself, but somehow she knew better. He was, above all, an honorable man, and he'd never have invented such a thing—besides, he had no reason to. So it must be true, she thought miserably. It must be true.

"But surely they intend at least to honor the Republic's current treaties with the Indians?" she said, clinging to the last bit of hope she could find in what looked like a very dim future. Some land, even the land that was currently promised to the Indians by the Republic, was better than nothing at all. Even before she had finished the question, the lieutenant had begun shaking his head slowly back and forth.

"No, they do not. They've made some flimsy promises about sending troops to keep the peace, but it will never last," he answered, this time with a bit of regret in his own words—not because he was sympathetic to the cause of the redskins, but because he knew how many good men would be lost in fighting them. To him, it seemed worth letting the Indians have their land in order to save the lives of hundreds of men—but then, he wasn't a politician, and to him it didn't matter

367

that Indians didn't vote. It didn't matter either that they weren't Christian, or that they didn't farm or improve the land. The fact was that they could fight like devils, and they would when the settlers started taking over their lands. That was the only thing that mattered to him.

Slowly, deliberately, he turned back to face Jessalyn where she stood frozen in horror, like a china doll that had been dropped to the floor and had shattered into a thousand pieces.

"If you and your . . . husband have any more tricks up your sleeve, you had better use them now," he said, his shoulders sagging with the look of a man who had seen enough things go wrong in the world, "or it looks like it's going to be a long, bloody summer." His attention turned suddenly to the wounded man who had just awakened on the bed, and he sighed deeply as he reached for the alcohol and bandages that he'd been given as medical supplies. "Go back to your husband, Jesse," he said quietly over his shoulder as he leaned over the man. "There is nothing more you can do here. If you find a way for us to leave, then we will go on your terms. If you still want to stay, then that will be your choice, but don't sell yourself for our freedom. It isn't worth the price."

Without turning away from him, Jessalyn took several steps backward toward the door, and then called for the guard. The door creaked open, and she stepped numbly into the bright light of the hallway, almost running into the guard where he stood. Feeling as though she were wrapped in cotton, she stepped back from him and then walked slowly away down the hall. The daylight around her seemed dimmer, and the sounds of the fort seemed far away as she went to her room and closed the door behind her.

It was as though her mind were suddenly somewhere far away, and she couldn't force herself to bring it back to deal with Brett's words. She saw him again and again, repeating the words that he had said only moments before, but now it was as if he were speaking in another language, as if she could not understand him at all. His words had come in that strange language once before—only then they had been telling her that her father was dead. Now, they were telling her that his dream was gone too. So now there was nothing, and she realized for the first time that it was a merciful thing for a man to die while his dreams were still alive. Perhaps, if her father had lived, he could have changed the outcome, but, if not, then she was glad he would not be there to see the land that he loved drowned in a ocean of blood, and the people that he had fought for cut down like dogs.

For herself, she didn't want to be there to see what Texas would become either, and perhaps that was her own weakness. Perhaps she should have been strong enough to want to stay and fight, but instead she only wanted to take what was left of her spirit over the mountains to some place that still belonged only to God.

Chapter Twenty

Jessalyn sat high on one of the cliffs above the fort, her soft willow eyes looking into the distance as she spoke.

"How much longer do you think he'll be gone?" she asked, dimly realizing that she had asked the same question at least a hundred times over the past five days. Beside her, Sam gave a noncommittal shrug and rolled a rag onto a piece of bent wire to clean the barrel of his gun.

"Don't know," he muttered, his patience with that question having worn paper thin. Frowning, he threaded the rod into the barrel and plunged it back and forth, at the same time anticipating her next question. "And I don't know where he went, either — no one does. But I'm sure he had a good reason." Pulling the cleaning rod free, he held the gun up to the light and looked down the barrel, tossing his silken hair back with an efficient shrug. "Cale's like the breeze, Jesse." With his free hand, he made three grand circles in the air, as if to indicate the swirling of invisible currents. It seemed appropriate for Cale; who knew what drove the man? "He does his own thing, and he hurries for no man." Cocking his head sideways, he considered his own bit of philosophic wisdom and smiled broadly in appreciation. "Hmmm . . . I like that." He unwound his long buckskin-clad legs and stood up, sweeping a deep bow before her, and saying, "Sam Horn, philosopher and poet extraordinaire, handsome hombre and feared bandito, loved by many, but known to few . . ." Propping his foot on a small boulder, he leaned forward and threw out his chest in a majestic pose, holding the dismantled gun stiffly at his side. "What do you think?" he asked, holding his breath so as to keep his chest muscles in full bloom.

From where she sat, Jessalyn shook her head, and cracked a reluctant half-smile at his humor. Somehow, he always managed to coax her into laughter when she had intended to be serious.

"I think you've been sipping too much of that peyote," she complained dryly, and then bowed her head to hide a giggle at the disgruntled frown that he cast in her direction. "It looks to me like you've slipped off into the spirit world."

With a sudden expression of pain, Sam clasped his hands together over his heart and swept to one knee before her.

"Ah, you wound me, lady, for it is only your beauty that has made me intoxicated—those eyes, that nose, those ears, that little smudge of dirt on your chin." Throwing his head back, he pressed the back of his hand to it. "It's too much, I tell you—too much."

"Oh, Sam, stop that," she said, looking up at him from beneath lowered brows. "You're making me sick to my stomach."

"Ah, but you've quit asking me about Cale," he pointed out, sinking back down to a comfortable position, and resuming his cleaning chore. "That has to be worth . . ." Looking up, he paused, and squinted into the distance, muttering, "Well, I'll be damned."

For a moment, Jessalyn eyed him with confusion, and then she followed his gaze. Her heart stopped in her chest when she saw what had caught his attention, and she stood up to gain a better view.

"That's him," she said, more because she wanted it to be true than because she knew that it was, for the rider that they were both watching was too far away to identify.

"Most likely," Sam concluded with less enthusiasm than Jessalyn. In fact, he hadn't been looking forward to Cale's return at all. The fort had been in a welcome state of calm since Cale had left, and now his return meant that everything that had been brewing was going to come to a boil.

"So you've been talking to my . . . uninvited guests, I see," Cale surmised, looking solemnly up at Jessalyn from where he sat at the other end of the heavy wooden dining table. "I suppose now you're going to ask me to let them go again?"

Jessalyn's fingers fell open numbly, and her fork dropped to the table with a clang as she sat staring at him in disbelief.

"Didn't you hear what I said?" she asked, her eyes wide with indignation at his cool response to the news that she had been waiting for days to tell him. Surely, he could not have mistaken her words, and surely he knew

372

what the news of the statehood agreement meant. How could he sit there acting as if she had only brought some trivial matter to his attention?

Cale's handsome face showed no response to her question, and he leaned casually back in his chair, taking a long drink of wine before he spoke.

"I heard you," he said matter-of-factly. "But I knew about the agreement already. I heard about it yesterday in El Paso." A slight flicker of sadness turned his eyes away from her, like candle flames ruffled by an unseen wind, and he said quietly, "It's bad news."

Jessalyn's angry posture softened at the change in him, and she suddenly understood the reason he had been so cool and withdrawn since he had ridden in earlier—be already knew about the statehood, and he knew what it meant. He knew that the things they had worked so hard to attain had been snatched from their grasp, and his heart ached just as did hers.

With a sigh, Cale picked up his wineglass and gazed darkly into the thick, crimson liquid, but it wasn't wine that he saw—it was blood.

"I suppose, you want to know what I intend to do about it," he said, swirling the wine slowly, and watching the colors reflect off of the glass. "That seems to be the question foremost in everyone's mind." His eyes cut to her so suddenly that she jumped back in her chair out of reflex. "Tell me, Jesse . . ." he raised his tawny brows slightly as he asked the question, "what would you do?"

"Quit," she shot back without taking a moment to consider the question. In fact, she had spent a great deal of time pondering the question in the days that he had been away, and she could think of no other way out. Even as she spoke the words, though, she knew that he would never heed them. The tone of his voice as he spoke again made it more than evident that he considered her answer cowardly.

"And what would you do if your skin was red . . . say, Comanche red? What would you do?"

"Fight," she replied honestly, but reluctantly. The mere contrast of the two answers marked her as a traitor to the people she had sworn to defend, the people she claimed to love, and she sickened inside at having said them. Worse than her betrayal was the look of disappointment in Cale's whiskey-colored eyes. For the first time, he was looking at her with pity, as if she were some poor unworthy thing that couldn't measure up to the challenges of his world.

"Come now, Jesse, I thought you had more spark than that," he baited her deliberately. "You would quit on this before it's finished?"

Anger flashed like white lightning across the green sea of her eyes, and she raised her chin defiantly, determined not to be shamed by him.

"It is finished," she said in a low voice that trembled in the air between them like the devil's mist on a cool morning. Then, leaning back, she changed her tactic, withdrawing from his game of cat and mouse. "But tell me anyway what you plan to do. That is really the issue, since you are the one in charge here. After all, this is your country. You're almost a god here. You can make anything happen — or so the Indians say. What miracle have you planned to save the day, Cale?" The bitterness in her voice bit the empty air as she spoke, but she did not try to moderate it. More than anything, she needed a whipping post on which to vent her despair, and with his accusations Cale had offered himself up.

Despite the thick shell that he had molded around himself, Cale winced at her angry words. He regretted now having ever brought her into the plan at all, for it had brought her nothing but heartbreak. She was so innocent — she had believed that they would succeed, while he had known that the odds were bad, especially after Lane Kendrik's death. Now, his pain at the death of their dream was deafening, and he could only imagine the depth of hers. Setting down his glass, he gripped the sides of the table and stood up, leaning toward her.

"No, my love, I'm afraid I can't make just anything happen here. I can't make the future become what we had hoped for, and I can't make Texas what it was before. The fact is, it's doomed. Eventually there'll be settlers on every square inch of it, and we both know what that means." The quicksilver that sparkled in the corner of her beautiful eyes and then trailed down her satin cheek told him that she understood the vision he painted. "It's a bad world when people kill and steal from each other only because their skins are different, and I'm coming to find that I can't change it. What I can do is try to get my friends the best weapons available, so they will at least have an even chance. If they surrender, they might as well be dead, but if they can fight hard enough, long enough, they might just get a little piece of land to live on. It's not what we wanted, but it's something," he paused and sighed deeply, pushing back from the table and taking a few steps away. Reaching up, he ran his hand through the unkempt tawny curls of his hair, and then looked out the window at the amber and crimson of the descending sun. "I've arranged for messengers to tell Nocona about the statehood agreement, and to arrange a drop for new guns in the spring." Turning back, he took a few steps toward her and smiled slightly. "And it seems you've goaded me into showing mercy for your friends. They should be on their way out of the mountains about now — safe, and all in one piece, though I may live to regret it."

Shock registered on Jessalyn's delicate face, and she felt her heart skip a beat in her chest.

"But, Cale," she began, and then paused, torn between the man she loved and sparing the lives of the rangers. "They'll bring back an army."

At that, Cale smiled wisely, and gave a slow, knowing look in her direction.

"I think not," he told her, crossing his arms over his chest. "You see, my men will dynamite that passage as soon as they've sent the rangers out. No one will be coming through it again." At the confusion in her face, he grinned despite his former foul mood, and explained, "That's what I have been doing for the past week — looking for another passage we could use to get in and out of the mountains. You see, I remembered this Palouse stud I lost once, and how he found his way out of the mountains somehow. I knew there had to be another passage, and I went looking. It's a little further around, but it'll do."

Jessalyn sat like a statue in her chair, daring not even to breathe lest it should break the spell that had softened him. Within her, she felt her heart swell with gratitude for his change of heart, and with hope for their future. Perhaps now they would have some chance for a life — if only they could go away somewhere together, and leave El Halcon behind on the plains of Texas where he belonged.

* * *

Jessalyn lay quietly against the warmth of Cale's strong chest, her eyes deep and warm, like two hidden pools of water in some enchanted forest. Her skin tingled still with the memory of their lovemaking, but her mind was not at peace. Finally, she rolled her eyes upward toward Cale's face to see if he was also awake, and finding the same thoughtful look in his eye, she spoke.

"Cale, do you think it is best for the Indians to fight?" The question had plagued her ever since he had told her at the dinner table that he felt the Indians had to fight or die. "Brett says that things aren't as bad for the Indians as we had thought. He says that the U.S. plans to set up garrisons to keep the settlers from moving on to Indian country even though there is no official guarantee in the statehood agreement. It's not what we hoped for, but it is something." She felt his chest rise and fall with a deep sigh, and she knew before he spoke that he intended to contradict her statement.

"It'll never happen," he said with a steady certainty in his voice. "The fact is that the Texans want to see every last red soul exterminated, and the citizens of the United States will be more than willing to turn their heads to the distasteful business in order to get the land." He kissed the top of her head lightly and smoothed her silken hair, as if to reassure himself that she was still with him. "It'll happen. It's just a matter of time — unless the Indians can defend themselves. Texas is in for some hard times. This annexation isn't going to be the great union that people think it will — it'll be a marriage made in hell, and who knows what will be left to rise up out of the ashes."

"A marriage made in hell," the words echoed in Jessalyn's ears, and she shuddered uncontrollably, clinging more tightly to him. But it wasn't the union of Texas she was thinking about — it was her own. Would hers be a marriage made in hell also? How would they ever find peace in the oblivion that he predicted, and that probably would come to be?

"Sssshhhh," he whispered from above her, wrapping his arms protectively around her small frame. "Did I upset you?"

"No. I was thinking about the rangers." She spoke the lie before she'd even had time to realize what she'd said. Afterward, she wondered why she had said it at all. Perhaps, she decided, she'd been thinking about them in the back of her mind, and that was why she'd said it. For a moment, she wondered if Cale would be angry, but he only chuckled sardonically.

"Don't worry about them. They're probably having a good meal and a hot bath in El Paso now," he said, and then laughed again, as if the whole matter were now a mildly amusing joke. "Now that I think about it, your lieutenant friend should thank me. He's a real ranger now — not just a cavalry man pretending to be one. There's a damned sight of difference between the two."

Astonished at the obvious admiration in his voice, she propped herself up and looked at him, her dark brows drawn together over narrowed eyes.

"You're a fine one to say that," she complained, still unable to believe what she had heard. "You being one of their biggest targets."

Still smiling a bit, Cale met her disbelief with the vise look of an elder schooling a child.

"There is no shame in honoring a worthy opponent.

Haven't you ever heard the Comanche say that?" Laying his head back against the wall, he gazed up at the ceiling, his amber eyes far away in thought. "Anyway, there isn't so much difference between the rangers and us, except that the law is on their side — but the right is on ours. So it comes down to which is better to serve, the law or right. You can't really blame a man for fighting for what he believes in."

Looking up at him, Jessalyn smiled and reached up to touch his face, her hand trembling. If she could have captured those words, she would have worn them like pearls around her neck, for they were proof that he had changed from what he was. The man that she had formerly known could never have looked at the world from another's point of view . . . and been so merciful.

Turning his eyes to her, Cale took her hand in his, kissed the backs of her fingers lightly, and then closed his fingers over them. A smile teased at the corner of his gold-flecked eyes as he lowered her captured hand to his chest and then kissed her forehead.

"Think I'm getting soft, ey," he surmised from her expression, and then smiled. "Just don't let it get around. I'd have a hard time making a living as a ruthless bandito if everyone knew."

Jessalyn's face fell suddenly, and she sat up, her eyes filled with desperation.

"Cale, please, let's go away," she blurted out the words that had hung like a weight over her heart, but her heart only sank further at the hard look that came over his face. Somehow, she had to convince him that there could be no life for them here. "We'll never find peace here. You have to know that. I'm begging you — let's just go away — up north, maybe, just the two of us." Bowing her head, she looked away from him, unable to bear the cold steel of his eyes. He was going to refuse her. "I love you, Cale, but I can't be El Halcon's wife." Her voice was almost inaudible as she spoke the last words.

Pulling her to him, Cale tipped her chin up to his with the ends of his fingers and silenced her protests with a kiss.

"Sssshhh," he whispered to still her. "Not tonight." Leaning down, he took her lips again, gently at first, and then with rising passion until their bodies burned with fire where they touched. She doubled her fists against his chest at first, to push him away, to demand that he answer her, but finally, she surrendered to the consuming fire that he had ignited in her. There was no use in fighting him, she knew; he would only use her own body against her . . . Besides . . .

Her thoughts exploded like a soap bubble as his fingers wound their way sensuously down the trembling line of her body, and she began to explore the hard curves of his chest in return. His skin was warm beneath her fingers, and she marveled at the strength and grace of the play of muscles beneath her touch, like skilled dancers moving to a soft, primal rhythm. Her own body joined unconsciously in the dance as he slowly teased the flushed peaks of her breasts, tasting their sweetness and whispering her name in soft, songlike tones. Nibbling at the tender crests, he felt her body shudder as if with a chill, and he moved to kiss her lips again.

"I will never let you go, my rose," he said softly, his voice covering her like a warm blanket. Kissing her more deeply, he slid his hand over the hard-muscled urve of her leg and then parted her slim thighs to taunt he bud of her womanhood. "Never," he whispered gain as she swayed against his touch, her soft lips arted with the breath of passion. Holding back his wn desires, he again tasted the sweetness of her reasts, his fingers slowly kindling the flame in her womanhood. Her slow rhythm increased to a fever's itch under his skillful teasing, and she cried out with nreleased desire. Finally, she reached for him, and he noved over her, testing the warm nest that waited for im alone.

She returned his kiss hungrily, moving her hips gainst him as she felt his manhood press against her, ertain that she could not wait another moment for re-ase. Exquisite shivers ran up and down her spine as he ntered her slowly, she sought to pull him more deeply nside her. The moments crystalized around her — as if ach were timeless in itself — and then passed through er like ghosts. She longed to hold on to them, to pack hem away in the corners of her soul and keep them for-ver.

Their desires raged, like opposing storms, drawing hem closer and closer together until they were one. hen, in one brilliant instant, their passions culmi-ated, and their souls were separated again.

"It's a hard choice, Cale," Sam said earnestly, and hen cracked a smile, his dark eyes alight with boyish nischief. "But if it were me, I'd take the girl."

Shaking his head, Cale scoffed good-naturedly at his rother's kidding, but the slight smile didn't extend to is eyes.

"Well that goes without saying." Reaching over, he gave Sam a half-hearted shove, knocking him partway out of his saddle. His smile fading, Cale continued, "But it doesn't exactly solve the problem." He squinted up at the steep slope ahead of them and then loosened the buckskin's reins to give him a better shot at the slippery rock slope. Falling in behind him, Sam let his own reins out and took a deeper seat in his saddle.

"Seriously, Cale." The tone of his voice had changed from its former mirth, and Cale glanced back over his shoulder quizzically, again amazed that the word was even in Sam's vocabulary. This time it was Sam who showed no sign of amusement as he returned the other's glance squarely, defending himself, "Yes, I do know what that word means — if that's what you're wondering," and then continuing with his statement, "You won't be letting anyone down if you decide to go." Inside, he wasn't exactly sure of that, but he said it as if he'd read it from stone. In every man's life there came a time to move on, and perhaps this was Cale's.

As they topped the hill, Sam stopped his horse beside his brother's and their eyes caught like the links of a steel chain.

"It's like climbing this hill," Sam said, squinting away into the distance, the noble lines of his face showing the wisdom of his Comanche grandfathers. "You can either continue down the other side, or you can go back down the way you came. On the one hand, you know what this trail has to offer, but on the other hand there may be something wonderful ahead on the other trail."

"Damned redskin logic," Cale complained, more because he knew Sam was right than because Sam's logic offended him. Without a word, he spurred his horse

own the other side of the mountain, stopping at the
ottom to wait for Sam.

"You realize that the brunt of my leaving will fall on
ou," he asked before Sam had even cleared the slope.
Of course, I'll be back now and again, but it'll be your
how to run."

Shaking his head, Sam extended his arm to his
rother with a hint of a smile.

"It'll be our show," he corrected Cale's statement.
Always."

With a solemn nod, Cale gripped Sam's arm below
ne elbow and smiled.

"I guess you're right." He couldn't help feeling as if
e were already saying goodbye, even though he knew
nat those farewells would have to wait — at least until
pring came and the guns were delivered. Still, he felt
ne strange loss of a leader surrendering his command
> one who had once been an apprentice, and he hoped
is apprentice was ready. Looking at his brother now,
e was pretty sure that Sam had learned his lessons.

Releasing Cale's arm, Sam tossed his hair back and
aised his square chin with a wink.

"Besides, I make a better bandito than you. I have the
oloring for it. They're already calling me El Coyote,"
e laughed, his smile bright against his dark skin, and
Cale laughed with him.

"El Coyote," Cale repeated, cocking his head
noughtfully as if to taste the metal of the words. "I like
ne sound of it."

Jessalyn sat astride Diablo's broad back, looking
own over the Continental Divide and breathing in the

fresh, sweet air. It was spring in the high meadows, and the air was alive with the scent of new blooms. Turning back, she watched Cale's mount climb the slope behind her, and smiled. He had been her husband now for almost four months, yet each time she turned around, she felt almost surprised to see him here, and her heart leapt against her chest. It was almost as if she were dreaming, and expected at any moment to awake.

It had been his idea to go over the Rockies. They'd been camped at the foot of the great giants after delivering the rifles to the Comanche. He'd just looked up at them one day, and said, "Jesse, what do you say we go over those mountains — just to see what's on the other side?" So they'd said goodbye and away they'd gone with only two pack horses and the necessities, which was exactly what she was accustomed to. It was just the two of them now — and the ghost of El Halcon, who was always with them.

She often saw him stop atop a rise and look back toward Texas, but he never stopped for long. When he saw her watching, he would only smile, kiss her fears away, and turn his horse west again. Now, as he crossed the ridge beside her and continued down the high-meadow slope, he didn't even stop to look back toward the country that had once been his own. Watching him, Jessalyn felt her heart swell again, and she smiled to herself. Her father had been wrong — stone roses could grow, after all.